# DARK
# RISING

**St. Martin's Paperbacks Titles
by Greig Beck**

*Beneath the Dark Ice*

*Dark Rising*

# DARK
# RISING

Greig Beck

St. Martin's Paperbacks

First published 2010 in Macmillan by Pan Macmillan Australia Pty Limited

This is a work of fiction. All of the characters, organizations, and events portrayed in this novel are either products of the author's imagination or are used fictitiously.

DARK RISING

For information address St. Martin's Press, 175 Fifth Avenue, New York, NY 10010.

ISBN: 978-0-312-59980-5

Printed in the United States of America

Pan Macmillan Australia edition published in 2010
St. Martin's Paperbacks edition / August 2011

St. Martin's Paperbacks are published by St. Martin's Press, 175 Fifth Avenue, New York, NY 10010.

10  9  8  7  6  5  4  3  2  1

*For Alexander, my best Ideas Man. And for Barbara—*
*whatever did you do to end up stuck with me?*

# Acknowledgements

I want to thank Cate Paterson for her support both locally and internationally, Joel Naoum for his professionalism, patience and determination to draw the best from my work, and Nicola O'Shea for the black art of copyediting. And finally, to scientists everywhere, whose discoveries are the fuel for fiction writers all over the world.

Red winds, the disfiguration of faces, and people being swallowed into the ground. The moon is buried in darkness and the world is folded.

Signs of the Yawm al-Qiyamah, the Day of Judgment, Mohammed ibn Ismail al-Bukhari (810–870)

# One

Beneath the ruins of Persepolis, modern Iran

"Are you ready to witness history being written, my friend?" Mahmud Shihab appeared from the back of the canvas tent like a ghost. "*Salem Agha-ye*, Hakim," he said softly and kissed the military man on each cheek before grasping his upper arms and looking earnestly into his face. "History being written in this, the very cradle of Persian antiquity—it is fitting, yes?"

"*Salem mamnoon*, Shihab. Yes, *inshallah*, God willing." The soldier nodded and parted his dry lips in a yellow smile, showing rows of teeth stained by decades of smoking the pungent local Marlleak cigarettes.

Mahmud Shihab led Hakim to the back of the tent, where a modern metal door was embedded incongruously in the ancient stone wall. He entered a code into the recessed keypad and the heavy door swung inwards soundlessly. As Shihab escorted the military man down a dimly lit corridor carved into the interior of the ancient Persepolis ruins, a proud smile curved his lips at the thought of the design and engineering feat he had mastered beneath this once great city of the kings. Above them, its mighty stone skeleton still dominated the landscape and had survived twenty-five centuries of rain and rock-cracking heat—a powerful symbol of a time when Persia had commanded the world.

And now Shihab had been chosen to oversee a project so important that its success would shape Iran's place in the world for the next century, or perhaps even forever. The operation was codenamed Zirzamin Jamshid, The Basement of the Kings. Shihab liked the name—Jamshid was a mythical king who, legend had it, had buried his amassed treasures throughout his mighty empire. The president had chosen the name himself, and had told Shihab that there was no more valuable treasure than the capability to produce nuclear weaponry beneath the scorching earth of the Iranian desert. Shihab recalled that first meeting with the great man, his intense countenance and his softly spoken command. "Bring me success and you will bathe in riches in this life and the next." He had been too nervous to reply and had only nodded and bowed.

Hakim sneezed, interrupting Shihab's thoughts. Beneath the ruins, the temperature was pleasantly cool, but the atmosphere was dry and filled with fine powdery dust that sparkled in the cones of light thrown down from the low-wattage ceiling lamps.

Shihab smiled. "Ah, Hakim, it is impossible to keep the dust out at this level. But just think—those very particles could be all that remains of a former king or prince of Persia."

Hakim blew his nose—Persian king or not—on a dirty brown handkerchief. He had just pushed it back into his pocket when they came to a steel miner's cage floored with thick rubberised matting. They entered the cage and Shihab pushed the single smooth lever to the downward position. The cage dropped silently into the darkness. Shihab smiled with pride, counting the passing layers of toughened concrete and lead shielding. The facility was all his own design, built to give off as small an energy signature as was possible. He knew full well the capabilities of the US spy satellites—high-resolution digital images were only one of their talents. These days they could sniff out heat, power and radiation signatures to fifty feet below the surface. So the Iranians needed to be careful, needed to go deeper.

After many minutes, the cage slowed with a hiss and stopped at a darkened corridor and a fortified steel door, considerably stronger than the one they had come through at the surface. Shihab entered another code and hidden rollers pulled the large metal slab out of the way. He closed his eyes briefly as a blast of negative air pressure rushed past him, only opening them when he perceived strong light on his eyelids. Before them was a chamber of almost surgical whiteness.

Shihab and Hakim knew what was expected, having performed this ritual many times. They both sat on the benches provided and removed their shoes. From a recessed cupboard they drew out particle-free garments, donned lightweight polymer all-over suits, pulled rubber-soled shoes over their feet, and used a small towel lightly moistened with demineralised water to wipe their faces, neck and hands.

When Hakim had finished, Shihab clipped a small radiation badge to the soldier's breast pocket. "They're the latest—each one contains a small sheet of radiation-sensitive aluminium oxide. When it's exposed to radiation, the tag shines with a visible blue glow. We all have to wear them now. Let's hope they don't shine for us today, yes?"

The two men moved to the facility's final access stage: a glass booth with another metal door beyond. The entry requirements here were far more stringent—as well as keying in a numeric code, Shihab had to lick his thumb and place it over a small mesh circle on the entry pad. Fingerprints and DNA were obtained, scanned and verified before the curved glass door slid back. Anyone trying to access the facility without proper authorisation would find himself locked in the chamber as it rapidly filled with lethal tabun gas. Clear and odourless, the gas immediately shut down the human nervous system, and then just as quickly dissipated, allowing safe removal of any bodies.

Red lights turned green and the metal door hissed open. Shihab entered first, then stood aside, allowing his companion to see the progress achieved since his last visit to the Jamshid I facility.

They were in a round, gleaming laboratory, 500 feet from one end to the other with a ceiling height of at least another

100 feet. The walls were covered in banks of computers and monitors, all online and glowing gold or green. The entire area was a sea of electronic chattering and blinking lights, save for one large window overseeing the chamber.

Shihab gestured towards the centre of the circular laboratory. "This is it, my friend, the sphere. This day will mark the first steps in the rise of the new Persian caliphate, *Allahu Akbar.*"

"*Allahu Akbar,*" Hakim repeated automatically.

Shihab watched Hakim's face as he stared at the giant silver orb that looked like the planet Saturn. It was fifty feet around and circled by a waist-thick polished cylinder.

"It is magnificent, Mahmud, you are to be praised," Hakim said as he slowly moved his eyes over the strange device, and then around the chamber.

Dozens of Iranian, German and North Korean scientists buzzed around the banks of computer monitors and the sphere itself, preparing for the first live test of the device. One of the Germans, a tall, bespectacled man with a blond toothbrush moustache, gave Hakim the thumbs up. Rudolf Hoeckler was being paid a Persian fortune to bring the laser-enrichment technology models to working status. Shihab knew that Hakim disapproved of mountains of Iranian money being paid to anyone from the West, but it was difficult not to like the tall German. Hoeckler was in a constant good humour and had made amusing attempts to learn Farsi.

"Blue hair eels in the morning, Herr Hakim," Hoeckler said now with a grin, obviously pleased with himself for mastering yet another phrase in their language.

Shihab chuckled and took Hakim by the arm to lead him towards a small set of steel steps. "We're just about ready," he said. "Let's go up to the observation room and have some tea. We have been requested to call the president the moment we have the results."

Shihab handed Hakim a small, gold-rimmed glass of the steaming local tea. He knew that after the dry of the desert, the soldier's mouth would be watering in anticipation. "You know, my friend, a successful production run today will be good for both of us, *inshallah*."

Shihab hoped the test run's success would not benefit the soldier *too* much. He liked Hakim's quiet presence and his stay-out-of-the-way approach to managing the security of the site. A big promotion would mean reassignment, and the facility may end up with a more intrusive guard. Shihab would take one Hakim over a hundred of those psychopathic Revolutionary Guard any day.

He put down his cup and wiped his hands down his sides; it was nearly time. On the computer screen nearby, a single line of ten glowing circles were all green except for one—and then this too changed to green, indicating a positive *all systems go* sequence. Shihab started the image recording of the laboratory floor and commenced the data transfer program to distribute the information back to their sister facility. The second site was a few months behind Jamshid I, so if anything went catastrophically wrong with this test they would learn from those mistakes. *Please, oh merciful Allah, don't let there be any mistakes*, Shihab prayed.

He keyed in a few commands and the overhead lights in the laboratory dimmed. The technicians and scientists pulled protective visors over their eyes and the observation window darkened to deflect any laser scattering. Shihab pressed the microphone switch down and his voice echoed over the floor of the chamber. "Is everyone ready?"

He scanned the floor for any dissent, and licked dry, nervous lips. Hoeckler turned and smiled. Shihab felt a bead of perspiration run down beside his left ear. He drew in a deep breath, feeling his heart thump sickeningly in his chest.

*"Allahu Akbar,"* he whispered as he entered the final codes and made a single stroke on the keyboard.

An infernal shriek tore through the laboratory and permeated the thickened glass as if it were paper. In the centre of the laboratory, where the sphere had stood, there was now a blackness darker than night. At its core was a pinprick of nothingness that hurt Shihab's eyes. He felt as if he were caught in a thick mucus that trapped his limbs. Time slowed, or perhaps stretched, and a cold darkness spread out into the laboratory. It was the only thing moving; everyone else seemed frozen in time too. As Shihab watched, he realised to his horror that the growing mass of darkness was absorbing everything in its path. He watched helplessly as the bodies of his colleagues elongated and then began to tear as they were pulled towards that dark curtain of space.

His eyes briefly met those of Herr Hoeckler for a second—or perhaps it was for an eternity—before the large man was engulfed, his body stretched into a plume of flesh-coloured streamers.

*We all died when I pressed that final key*, he thought, *and now we are in hell.*

From the corner of his frozen vision, Mahmud Shihab saw his friend, Hakim, become a long white streak as he was dragged mercilessly into the void. And then his sanity left him as he saw his own tongue and the lining of his throat distend from his body and rush towards hellish oblivion.

# TWO

Offutt Air Force Base, Nebraska—US Military Space
Command

"What the fu—" Corporal Marcs scooted his office chair
across the floor of his horseshoe-shaped booth to replay what
he had just seen on one of his screens. "Holy shit. Major,
you gotta see this! VELA just picked up a whale of a radiation spike from the Middle East."

Offutt Air Force Base was one of the most strategically
placed and defensible military bases in the world, home to
the Strategic Air Command, the 55th Wing and also the primary hub of the United States military network-centric space
command. Its role was to manage the constellation of military hardware orbiting the planet and oversee the billions of
bits of information received from their flock of extremely
attentive high-orbit birds. Normally the command centre was
a place of professional calm. Today all hell was about to break
loose.

"What the hell are they doing?" Marcs went on. "This is
strong gamma—just gamma—where's the rest of the radiation package? Is this a detonation?"

Major Gerry Harris was instantly at the corporal's shoulder. A brilliant military specialist, Harris had been heading
up the space command centre for the past eighteen months.
His background in physics and information technology gave
him the perfect credentials needed to understand and manage the complex information received by the satellites and

translated by the sophisticated computer applications. But
these signatures defied logic; they refused to make sense even
to his analytical mind. The advanced VELA satellites used
radiofrequency sensors to detect electromagnetic pulse prints
and could measure the strength of high-intensity ionising radiation even from high orbit. If there was a higher than natu-
rally occurring radiation signature across the X-ray, alpha or
beta particle, neutron or gamma-ray spectrum, a VELA would
see and taste it. But these pulses? Their sudden appearance
and strength made them seem almost non-terrestrial.

"Can't be a detonation," Harris said. "These guys shouldn't
even have fission capability yet. And if it's some sort of subsurface nuclear test, why aren't there any seismic signatures—and
why are we seeing this single particle in such concentrations?"

Harris paced for a moment, then started yelling commands
across the floor to his technicians. "I need all our birds with
digital, thermal and ground-penetrating imaging capabilities
looking at these coordinates now!"

Then he reached for the phone on Corporal Marcs' desk.
"Get me General Chilton," he said. "ASAP."

Frank and Lorraine Beckett had been driving in stony silence for the past hour. They had left the Interstate at the
Limon hub after sharing soggy, coffee-flavoured peanut
butter sandwiches and disintegrating donuts—apparently
Lorraine had left the top loose on the goddamn thermos, yet
again.

Both in their mid-fifties and comfortably stout after years
of double-portion dinners and chocolate candy in front of
the TV, the Becketts were making a once-in-a-lifetime road
trip, from their home in Knoxville weaving all the way to
Santa Barbara on the West Coast. It was a joint gift to each
other to celebrate their twenty-fifth wedding anniversary,
but what had seemed like a magical and exciting idea when
they planned it was turning out to be days on end of feature-
less highways, frightening-looking hitchhikers and roadside
motels with orange and brown décor that should have been
put out of its misery in the mid-seventies. To really ice the

cake, Lorraine's stomach was acting up again and Frank was threatening that if she let loose one more fart in the car he was going to leave her at the next bus stop.

*Praise the Lord,* he thought. Just one more hour on Highway 24 and they'd be in Colorado Springs—which meant warm showers, a nap before dinner and maybe even some plain, home-style food that would help slay the dragon making war in the pit of that damn woman's stomach.

The flat purple-grey highway cut through the dry and scrubby landscape like a new zipper down an old canvas sheet. Frank was starting to get his good mood back, and was about to break the silence by telling his wife a bad joke when the car died. Everything just stopped at once. Frank coasted the car to a halt, frantically pushing buttons and stamping on pedals.

"Did you see that, Frank?" Lorraine said, pointing through the front windscreen. "The sky seemed to shimmer slightly, like we were driving through a curtain of oil." She touched her fingers to her face and they came away slick and bright red. "Frank, I'm bleeding."

Frank noticed that his nose was streaming blood too. "Outta the freakin' car!" he said. He didn't want them soiling the beautiful leather seats with bloodstains. There would be a nasty amount to fork out on the insurance if there was even minor interior damage.

The dry prairie air assaulted their senses and made them grimace after the Suburban's air conditioning. Lorraine staggered and her face looked slick and waxy with shock.

As Frank went round to swing the car hood open, he spotted something lying on the road ahead. "What the hell's that? That weren't there before."

"Is it a deer?" burbled Lorraine through a handful of blood-stained tissues.

The clouds were moving rapidly across the flat land all around, and as they slowly approached the mass, a long shaft of yellow sunshine illuminated the lump on the road. It looked meaty and slightly moist. Frank had to will himself to take a step forward; his animal instincts were screaming at him to get the hell out of there.

Lorraine held Frank's arm and remained slightly behind his left shoulder as they neared the strange organic mess. "Oh my god, Frank, what is that?" she whispered.

Slight tics and squeaks emanated from the lump, and as they got closer they realised that the sounds were caused by the mass thawing in the sun—a sparkling coat of frost dripped, twinkling onto the road surface. Frank knitted his brows; the thing seemed to be sprouting up from the hard black tarmac. Not pushing up through it exactly, just . . . stuck.

"This can't be real," he said. "It's some kind of sick joke."

Half of the mass looked like a man wearing a white laboratory coat, but the other half was stretched out like elongated taffy. It looked like plastic that had been heated and then frozen solid again. The face was wet-raw, like the skin under a blister, and where the eyes should have been were just hollow, ragged sockets. The mouth was intact, and above it a blond toothbrush moustache twinkled with ice crystals. But what really made Frank's stomach lurch was the pink organic matter that protruded between the bared teeth like a veined, deflated bag. It had to be the guy's lungs—pulled or blown out.

Lorraine staggered to the side of the road and vomited. "Frank, I'm bleeding inside!" she screamed. The mess of digested bread and donuts was streaked with blood.

Frank went to her, blinking rapidly to clear his stinging eyes. But it wasn't tears running down his cheeks, it was blood. When Lorraine saw him, she started to cry.

Frank sat down heavily next to his wife. "I don't feel well, Lainey."

He looked over at the creature again and noticed something he hadn't seen when he was standing above it. On the pocket of the lab coat was a small badge that was pulsing with a soft blue light.

# Three

Major Jack "Hammer" Hammerson shouldered open the heavy panelled door of his office and headed straight for a hulking oak desk near the back wall. The impressive piece had once stood in front of the enormous set of double windows that dominated the room, but old warrior habits die hard and the Hammer never liked to have his back to a door or window. The desk, like most things the Hammer bumped up against, had to give way.

Major Hammerson was one of the hard men of the military. His face could never be called friendly; its deep clefts and creases hinted at too much outdoor living and quite a bit of blunt force trauma. You didn't need to read the major's background files to know he could incapacitate an enemy in less than seven seconds. Hammerson headed up the elite Hotzone All-Forces Warfare Commandos—HAWCs, for short. His uniform, except for rank, was insignia free. His only identification was a plastic card with a barcode and the lightning bolts and fisted gauntlet of the US Strategic Command.

Major Hammerson and his special unit had been reassigned to USSTRATCOM eighteen months ago, and it seemed a good fit. The United States Strategic Command was one of the ten unified combatant commands of the United States Department of Defense. They controlled the nuclear weapons assets of the US military and were a globally focused command charged with the missions of Space Operations, Integrated Missile Defence, Combating Weapons of Mass Destruction, and Other Special Operations. The "Other Special Operations" was where Hammer and his HAWCs came in.

Normally a blunt and brusque man, today the major was in a great mood. In just over three weeks, and for the first time in five years, he would be fly fishing in the land of the midnight sun. He was taking two weeks off to camp out in a little place he knew up high on the Kenai River bend in Alaska, where the tides from Cook Inlet washed in the biggest king salmon found anywhere in the world. Biting cold air that made the breath fog, and water so clear you could see the pebbles on the bottom at near any depth. Hammerson sighed and rubbed his large hands together. Just a few curious grizzlies for company and the odd bald eagle watching suspiciously from overhead. He knew that a record ninety-seven pounder had been caught in those parts, and he reckoned there was a hundred pounder with his name on it.

The Hammer was practising long, slow casting motions across his desk when the phone rang. He hit the receive button on the console and barked a curt "Hammerson" while still jerking on an imaginary rod. When he heard the deep voice on the line, he sat forward immediately and picked up the handset.

"Sir."

He listened with the intensity he always gave the highest-level mission briefings. His face was like stone, the only movement his eyes narrowing slightly.

"I agree, that size pulse could signify weaponability," he said. "Yes, something a little more surgically precise would be best. We can be ready in twenty-four hours, sir."

There was a click as the connection was severed. Hammerson held the phone in the air for a second before replacing it softly in its cradle. Time to reactivate the Arcadian.

# Four

Captain Alex Hunter lay uncovered on a hospital cot in a
room of steel, chrome and blinding white floor and wall tiles.
His arms and legs were restrained by Kevlar cuffs attached
by medium-gauge, pencil-thick wire cable to a special metal
railing running around the outside of the cot frame. The room
bristled with camera lenses, microphones and speakers.

Medical officer Lieutenant Alan Marshal stood behind
the heat-tempered observation glass and looked at Hunter's
resting form. Although the soldier seemed to be sleeping
peacefully, a storm was brewing behind his tranquil countenance. The tangle of two hundred and fifty-six electrodes
and wires attached to his head showed that he was suffering
both a migraine and an epileptic seizure simultaneously. Yet
there was no external sign at all. Marshal shook his head.
Alex Hunter was both medical miracle and mystery. Hunter
was the US Army's first super-enhanced warrior—part of
a special military project codenamed Arcadian. The army
wanted to know how this soldier could be so quick, so strong
and heal so quickly. Alex Hunter was the project's only success; all attempts to surgically or chemically reproduce his
abilities had been an abject failure.

Marshal looked through the records he held in his hand.
Several years ago on a clandestine military mission in northern Chechnya, Captain Hunter had been wounded by a single

bullet to the head—he'd been as good as dead. His commanding officer, Major Jack Hammerson, had brought Hunter's comatose body back home. There were two options: watch the young man wither away to a shrunken grey wraith as he lay trapped within his own body; or try something different . . . something experimental. And so Alex Hunter was entered in the Arcadian program. Two weeks later, Hunter opened his eyes, sat up, smiled and said he felt fine. He was more than fine; he was a new type of human being.

Marshal pulled an X-ray of Alex's skull from the file, holding it up to the light so he could see the small dark mass at its centre. The projectile was still there, but instead of causing a mass of surrounding damage as expected, it—perhaps in combination with the treatment—had triggered a range of physical and mental changes that had astounded the scientists. There was evidence of significant rerouting of blood to Hunter's midbrain, the area largely responsible for selecting, mapping and cataloguing information. It was also the primary powerhouse of endocrine functions, which controlled responses to pain, and the release of adrenalin and natural steroids. The flush of extra blood into this relatively unresearched area of the brain triggered massive electrical activity, waking new or long dormant abilities. The young man's agility, speed, strength and mental acuity had increased off the scale—all beneficial side effects that hadn't been fully expected.

But as the changes to the soldier continued, it became clear that some were not so beneficial. And some worried the scientists immensely. A foot constantly jammed on an accelerator usually resulted in the engine overheating—or exploding. In Hunter's case, his acceleration meant he sometimes experienced bouts of rage that were barely controllable; furies that boiled within him, barely chained by his will. It wasn't yet fully understood whether the rage fuelled his enormous strength and speed, or if it was the complete opposite: his strength and other abilities, when they reached their peak, ignited the rages.

"Marshal, take a look at this and tell me what you think."

The sound of his superior colleague's voice made Marshal jump. He turned and took the hard copy sheets Captain Robert Graham was holding out. The captain pointed to a row of long chemical names and numbers.

"High proteolipid and phospholipid count across the entire cranial sphere . . . hmm, not sure, never seen anything like it," Marshal said. "Could it be cross-contamination of the data?"

Graham shook his head. "Nope, I've checked several times and the count keeps coming back the same. I've never seen anything like it either, but I've got a theory. Crazy as it sounds, it looks like the myelin sheathing in his brain is undergoing some sort of restarted mylination process."

"Impossible!" blurted Marshal.

The myelin sheathing in the brain stopped wrapping itself around the brain's axons and neurons by the age of twenty. No one knew why it stopped then—most scientists theorised that the brain figured it could think fast enough by that age—but the one thing they did know was that it didn't restart.

Graham folded his arms and looked at his younger colleague with raised eyebrows. "Well, from this data I'd say he's undergoing remylination. It could be what's turbo-charging his ability to think and make decisions. The treatment certainly wasn't meant to do this, and I can't believe it's the result of a significant penetration trauma."

Marshal couldn't help sounding excited as his mind worked through the implications of the physical changes. "Remylination. Now that would be something—this guy walking around with a potential cure for MS and Alzheimer's locked within him." He flipped another page on the printout and looked back at Graham. "Hey, do you think it could it also be responsible for his psychogenic disorder?"

Hunter's improved mental abilities, amplified senses and staggering physical improvements were bordering on miraculous, but both scientists knew the man was paying a high price for them.

Marshal went to the electronics console to check on

Hunter's current readings. "I still don't get it," he said over his shoulder. "These don't even look like human brain waves anymore. There's an encephalogical thunderstorm going on in there. His body should be responding with a massively elevated heart rate, increased oxygen consumption, or at least rapid eye movement signalling disturbance. But his blood pressure is still one twenty over seventy, full resting normality for a man his size. We've had this guy in four times and we know even less now than when he left the first time." He looked at the senior officer. "Do you think we should halt treatment until we know more?"

Graham came and stood beside him, running his eyes over the chaotic lines displayed on the screen. He shook his head. "No, we continue. But I agree we need to know more. These EEGs are too imprecise. We really need to use MRI, but the magnetic field could cause the bullet to shift and bingo—we got one brain-dead HAWC. And I, for one, would want to be well out of the country when the Hammer took that call."

Alex could hear the girl's voice. She was alone in the dark and was calling his name—frightened, so frightened—she needed his help. The ancient tunnel was desolate, black and icy cold, but his extraordinary senses allowed him to perceive the danger all around him.

It was Aimee. She screamed his name again, so terrified and alone. The walls of the tunnel were collapsing, suitcase-sized granite blocks were falling in on him. Alex used his enormous strength to lift and throw the blocks out of his way—but the more he threw, the more rained down on him.

He screamed his pain and anger into the dark.

"Holy shit."

The EEG alarm screamed as the machine's four reading pens crazily mapped Alex's alpha, beta, theta and delta waves onto the printout. His encephalogical storm was turning into a full-blown hurricane. Lieutenant Marshal tried to make sense of the wild oscillations and spatial disturbances, but even to his trained eye, the pages were now almost black with impossible scribbling.

Marshal moved back to the observation window in time to see Alex's body convulse upwards. The soldier made a fist with his right hand and slowly tried to bring his arm up. His muscles bulged and sinews stretched—and a fatiguing metallic sound echoed through the observation room's speakers. The iron railing on the cot started to bend.

Aimee screamed again. He wasn't going to make it in time. More stones were falling in on him and the leviathan was rapidly approaching from below. Alex had to do something—now. He pounded the rock with his bare hands, smashing the ancient boulders in an effort to break a path through to Aimee.

The creature had him now. It had hold of his arms and was trying to drag him down to its lair. He had to break free; he had to try harder. Anger and fury pulsed through him—he would tear it apart, he would destroy it.

The two scientists stood immobile at the toughened glass of the observation window. Lieutenant Alan Marshal knew he had his secondary physical manifestations to accompany the psychocranial quake taking place in Hunter's mind. No longer the face of calm, Hunter's visage was a mask of pure rage. His eyes were still closed but his lips were pulled back to reveal gritted teeth that gleamed whitely against his flushed and perspiring face. Veins bulged in his neck and shoulders as he struggled with the monster in his mind. He tried to bring his right arm up—and the specially strengthened steel bar on the cot groaned and bent another inch.

Marshal stared in awe at this display of raw strength. He had witnessed many things in his years of medical military service—feats of outstanding bravery, bursts of impossible energy or Herculean effort under pressure—but no one should be able to bend high-gauge military steel like this soldier was doing.

"That ain't gonna hold," Graham said. "We need to wake him. Give him 20ccs of dextroamphetamine."

As he spoke, the steel railing gave way with a metal snapping sound usually only heard in heavy industry accidents. Alex's arm broke free and whipped back and forth across his chest. His clenched fist connected with a solid steel cabinet alongside the cot and sank six inches into the metal.

"Lieutenant, get in there," Graham ordered.

Marshall had a look of incredulity on his face. "You want me to go in there with just a syringe? Are you shitting me? I'm not going in there with anything less than an elephant gun."

"For Chrissake, I need you to buy me some time," Graham snapped. "I don't know how, Lieutenant—sing to him if you have to—just get in there. That's an order."

Captain Robert Graham picked up the phone and, without taking his eyes off the carnage behind the glass, spoke just four words.

"Get me Hammerson, now."

# Five

Zachariah Shomron's hands shook so much he nearly spilled his cup of hot chocolate on the new oxide crystal radiation unit—OCRU for short—that the department had just acquired. It was a delicate and beautiful machine—a blend of sci-fi aesthetics and high-tech pragmatics. Gleaming silver-steel casing and glass domes held rosettes of gadolinium silicate-oxide crystals—the best option for detecting gamma rays and high-energy X-rays. The OCRU displayed the invisible heavy particles as light pulses within the vacuum domes—the more brilliant the glow, the greater the strength of the radiation and its proximity. The visual display was accompanied by a computer application that translated the light pulses into radiation sievert strength, and also calculated distance and direction. *Ohhh yeeessss*, Zachariah mouthed as he ran his long fingers over the glass domes. This was a work of art with a scientific purpose. And it was his paper on geo-astrophysical gamma ray bursts that had swayed the university budgeting committee to pass the funding for the purchase of the expensive Swiss precision device.

Zachariah began the software load into the OCRU, watching the lines of code scroll up the screen. Gamma rays had a well-deserved deadly reputation, but their power and prevalence throughout the universe meant that the first to harness their cosmic muscle would have access to an energy source that was infinite in quantity and strength. Perhaps he could be the first to design some sort of stellar mining project—now that would be really cool.

Zachariah, or Zach to his friends, was what was affectionately known as a university "drop-in." He was a brilliant young man who, with doctorates in gravitational astrophysics, particle physics and pure mathematics, and a specialisation in black holes and cosmic dark matter, could have had his choice of any number of advisory or teaching positions at Tel Aviv University or any other place of higher learning around the world. Problem was, Zach didn't want to do anything in the real world. How could he? There was so much more to learn and never enough time. As soon as he finished one degree, he enrolled in another, and another; he had been the same since his first senior class at the age of thirteen—always moving forward and expanding his encyclopaedic knowledge of the cosmos and its strange forces.

After his parents were killed in a bomb attack, school had become his shelter and books his friends. They were always there for him, faithful and factual, and had nothing to do with war. Not like his parents, who had both been victims of this war that seemed without end. His father had died when he wrestled to the ground a man who carried a live grenade. His mother had died shielding her young son from the full force of the blast. When Uncle Mosh and Aunt Dodah had taken Zach in, they had worried about his withdrawal into a world of reading. But it soon became clear that it was just his way of dealing with his personal tragedy.

Tall and skinny, with long bony hands on the end of even longer bony arms, Zachariah was a man in perpetual motion. He always had something to do and rushed about, knuckles cracking, feet tapping, hands flying over computer keyboards or drawing things in the air for others. A pair of wire-rimmed spectacles completed the image of the stereotypical uber-nerd.

Zach slurped the last drops of his chocolate, threw his mug onto the bench and switched the device on. With the OCRU, he would soon be able to detect anything from a normal daily pulse of gamma right up to a mega blast. The Earth had encountered mega-range blasts before. A prehistoric far-galaxy short burst of gamma rays had once been suggested as a possible reason for the mass extinction of the dinosaurs. Luckily, those types of events happened about once every 500 million years. Even luckier for Earth was that no gamma bursts had ever occurred in its galaxy. *And just as well*, Zach thought; a single ten-second burst from a source just 6000 light years away would strip the planet of its atmosphere and burn all life from the surface.

The computer screens flared to life, showing graphs and charts with unexpected intensities, and the crystals glowed strongly, bathing Zach and his laboratory in blue light. *This can't be right*, he thought.

He typed in a few commands, muttered a brief, "Impossible," turned the device off and gave it thirty seconds. When he powered it back up, the result was the same. "Impossible," he said again and picked up the phone to call his current professor, Dafyyd Burstein.

"*Shalom*, Dafyyd, you're not going to believe this—I've just picked up a terrestrial nanosecond gamma-ray burst. And that's not all. I believe the pulse came from the Middle East . . . from the central Iranian desert."

General Meir Shavit was the head of Metsada, the Special Operations Division of Mossad. Short and grizzle-haired, he had served his country for over fifty years in both military theatres and dedicated intelligence services. He could even boast an apprenticeship under the fearsome Ariel Sharon in the infamous Unit 101—Israel's very first Special Forces command.

From its headquarters in Tel Aviv, Mossad oversaw a staff of around 2000 personnel. It was one of the most structured and professional intelligence services in the world, and also one of the deadliest. It consisted of eight different specialised departments—one of which was General Shavit's Metsada, responsible for assassinations, paramilitary operations, sabotage and psychological warfare. If the army was the spear and shield of Israel, then Metsada was its secret dagger dipped in poison.

General Shavit's assistant opened the door and showed in the young woman who had been seated in the large comfortable waiting room outside the general's office.

"*Boker tov*, Captain Senesh," Shavit greeted her.

"*Shalom*, General."

Adira Senesh stood stock-still at attention until the assistant departed and the door closed, then her face broke into a wide grin and she moved quickly to embrace the general, who was slowly getting to his feet.

"You look well, Addy."

"I feel better for seeing you, Uncle."

Adira was Shavit's favourite niece. Her name meant "mighty" in ancient Hebrew, and it suited her. She was related to the famous Chana Senesh, who was sent by the Kibbutz Sdot Yam to save Jews in the Nazi-occupied countries and was betrayed to the Nazi regime. Severely tortured, she never informed on her friends and was sentenced to death by firing squad in 1944. Her bravery was exemplified by her refusal to be blindfolded so she could look the soldiers in the eye as they pulled their triggers. The general knew that the brave Senesh blood also flowed strongly through the veins of his handsome niece.

Adira was above average height and had to bend slightly to kiss the general's cheek. With a smooth olive complexion and dark eyes like pools of oil, she could have passed for any normal young woman who liked to spend her time perusing the shopping arcades of downtown Tel Aviv. However, when shaking her hand one felt the calluses and raw strength of a soldier trained in unarmed and armed combat. Adira Senesh was a captain in the Metsada and acknowledged as one of the best trained operatives in the field. She was responsible for single-handedly entering a Hamas terrorist tunnel network and rescuing a captured twenty-two-year-old border guard. No terrorists had survived.

Her courage and skills were never questioned, but it was

her mind that set her apart from the other Metsada professionals. She was a Middle East specialist, and had spent many years studying the present and past cultures, politics and military capabilities of Iran, Syria and Lebanon. She could speak and read Farsi, as well as many ancient Persian dialects. She made General Meir Shavit proud as an Israeli and an old soldier, but even more so as her uncle.

"Come sit down with me, Addy, I need to speak with you."

The general waved her to a hard leather couch and poured each of them a small cup of strong black coffee from a silver urn. Then he sat opposite her and took a sip of his coffee. "We have problems with our friends in the east. Yesterday, our Iranian monitoring department picked up an enormous radiation signal emanating from about thirty miles northeast of Shiraz—probably at or under the Persepolis ruins."

Adira lowered her cup. "What type of radiation? What strength?"

"Mainly gamma and some minor X-ray. The gamma sievert intensity was off the scale, and though it only flared for less than a second, it was at least blast strength."

Adira sat forward and put down her small china cup. The general watched her face carefully. He knew that current intelligence predicted the Iranians were not expected to have any real capability for nuclear fission for many years. The thought of them conducting tests with a potential working model was sickening for any Israeli. The Iranian president was a fanatic who believed he spoke with the authority of God. Many times he had called for Israel to be burned from the pages of history; most recently just days after he had boasted of Iran achieving nuclear fuel purification capability, when he had claimed that the "Zionist regime" would soon be eliminated. The only thing that held the madman back was the knowledge of Israel's military might. Though Iran was many times larger than Israel, it didn't yet have the military technology, or the muscle and steel, to go head to head.

The general was not alone in his view that if the Iranians gained weapons of mass destruction, the usual deterrent of MAD would not apply. The Mutually Assured Destruction principle only worked when a nation actually feared destruction; it was meaningless to a leader who believed that vaporising his people in a fiery conflict with Israel would make martyrs of them all. It was common knowledge that the new president of Iran, Mahmoud Moshaddam, was a deeply religious man who frequently quoted from Qur'anic scripture in his speeches.

"Captain Senesh," the general continued, his use of her rank indicating the importance of what he was about to say, "I do not believe we can afford to take a wait-and-see position on this. I will be mobilising our network in Iran to gather information. If the Iranians have detonation capability, we would be taking a huge risk by sending in a strike—just a single Iranian nuclear blast over Israel would mean millions dead, and perhaps lead to another world war. We will take that risk if we have to, but first we must try other options."

Adira held his gaze, a question in her dark eyes.

The general breathed out slowly and a look of pain crossed his face. "We need to go in, Captain, but not alone this time. We need our muscular friends from across the water. The Americans are bound to go in, and when they do, we will be with them." General Meir Shavit paused and looked deep into his niece's eyes. "Addy, Iran cannot have this terrible power, now or ever. You must bring it down around them; leave nothing standing, leave no one to remember anything."

Adira nodded once, her face like stone.

"There is one more thing." The general handed Adira a sealed folder. The red cross on the front signified its secrecy. "The Americans have developed a new form of warfare, like nothing we have ever seen before. Our best agents have been able to obtain little more than a codename: *Arcadian*. We hope to have more information soon, but for now . . ." He shrugged as he indicated the slimness of the file. "They will probably use this weapon on the mission, Addy. Seek it out, and bring it or the seeds of its creation back to us. It may be Israel's only hope in the coming storm."

# Six

Major Jack Hammerson stared at the computer in front of him but without seeing what was displayed on the screen; instead, his focus was turned inwards, contemplating the call he had just received from an old friend. General Meir Shavit had confirmed what Hammerson already knew about the Iranian gamma pulse, its strength and location, and that none of it was good.

It had been one of America's fears for decades: a nuclear-armed regime that hated the West. Everyone in the military had expected it to be the North Koreans—a nightmare, sure, but they were manageable, they were for sale. But Iran—*shit!* After twenty years, there was still no hint that they wanted to play ball. This was the start of an arms race across the Middle East that would lead to unsecured warheads being mislaid, sold or stolen, then potentially turning up in some terrorist's arsenal. If some idiot with a hundred bags of ammonium nitrate could blow the shit out of an Oklahoma office block, kill 168 people and cause nearly three-quarters of a billion dollars worth of damage, then the thought of a nuke hidden in the back of a pick-up didn't bear thinking about. For Israel, it was even worse—they literally had the devil on their doorstep.

Hammerson gripped one of his large hands in the other and cracked his knuckles. The Israeli general had assumed the US was going in and had offered it access to Mossad's Middle Eastern covert networks, scientific resources, plus a ground base for landing and take-off. Shavit had been most insistent that the US team meet at the Israeli base before travelling on to Iran. "Acclimatisation" he had called it. "Bullshit" Hammerson called it. The general was up to something. He'd also promised two Israeli experts—one a specialist in the field of geophysical and astrophysical sciences; the other an authority on language and logistics. Hammerson guessed at least one of them would be a Mossad torpedo.

If the Iranians had nuclear technology, then the balance of power would shift and Israel would be tempted to strike before an Iranian delivery system could be perfected. It was no secret that the Israelis had been equipping their fighters with long-range fuel tanks and performing practice runs over the Mediterranean for the past five years. Of course Iran would retaliate, other countries would take the opportunity to take a bite out of Israel while it was occupied, Israel in turn would up the ante, and pretty soon the whole goddamn continent would be on fire. Forget about oil from the Middle East for the next few decades. The only winner there would be Russia, who still had billions of barrels of its own black gold held in reserve.

Hammerson knew an Israeli attack would be a waste of time as the Iranians tended to bury their secret bases so deep that even the best ground-penetrating bunker-busters would only sever the supply tunnels. In a month they'd just dig 'em back out. Best way to deal with it was to send in a small team to infiltrate and destroy the capability from within. Shavit had agreed; most likely that was what he'd wanted all along.

Hammerson picked up a small bayonet-shaped letter opener from his desk and turned it over in his fingers. He smiled grimly. *Okay, I'll roll the dice and see what that old fox Shavit is up to.*

The phone on his desk rang again.

A sickly faced Lieutenant Marshal and two enormous military orderlies stood with their backs up against the tiled wall of the hospital room. On the floor at their feet were three broken syringes, their contents never administered. One of the orderlies had a swelling black eye and his arm hung at an unnatural angle from a dislocated shoulder.

On the bed, Alex Hunter's body seemed at war with itself. His teeth were bared and both arms, broken free from the restraints, hammered at everything around him. The heavy metal cabinets either side of the cot were heavily dented, the one on his left showing a deep split in the quarter-inch steel.

Captain Graham, his eyes fixed on the carnage within the room, was speaking frantically into the phone. "He's having an episode—he's tearing us apart."

"Put me through," Hammerson said.

Graham hurriedly pressed the communication button and the major's stern voice boomed through the speaker in Alex's room.

"Arcadian!"

The EEG flattened and Alex quietened. A few seconds later, he opened his eyes.

"Captain Hunter, report," Hammerson ordered.

Alex blinked for a few seconds before responding. "Fort Bragg Medical Centre—assisting science personnel with further physiological and psychological testing." He looked around him and saw the wreckage and the paralysed orderlies, still too shocked to move. He exhaled and said with a hint of resignation in his voice, "Seems I had another dream while I was under, sir."

Alex looked at Lieutenant Marshal. "Did I hurt anyone?"

"Everyone's okay, Captain Hunter," Major Hammerson responded, before any of the medical staff could speak.

Alex rubbed his face hard and dragged in a long juddering breath. "My dream—it was Aimee again," he said softly to Hammerson. "Have you heard from her? Is she okay?"

Hammerson wasn't surprised by the question. The dreams had been the same for months now. "Saw her just the other day," he said. "She's fine and getting on with her life."

"Good. Okay, that's good, I guess."

Hammerson's voice became stern again. "Captain Hunter, I've got some new team members for you. I'd like you to come up and take a look. Be here by 0800 tomorrow."

"O-eight hundred, confirmed, sir."

Alex stood and stretched, rubbed his face and pushed both hands through his perspiration-slicked hair. As he headed towards the door, the injured orderlies backed up a step. He stopped in front of the man with the bulging black eye. "It's Carl, isn't it? I'm real sorry, Carl, it was an accident."

The orderly flinched, but gave a crooked smile. "No problem, man. Just glad you're on our side."

Hammerson's voice blared into the small room. "Good man, Carl—take some extra R&R on USSTRATCOM. Just remember, you got injured in the gym."

Alex apologised again, then turned and pushed through the laboratory's soundproof doors.

Captain Graham switched the intercom back to his phone, making the conversation private. "Jack, there's something else. It's Alex's brain . . . it's . . . different now. We can only hypothesise based on the EEG and echo pulse readings, but we believe there's been an increase in neocortical matter. His brain isn't any larger—we think the additional mass is accommodated through new brain folding, possibly on both sides of his interhemispheric fissures. But without an MRI we don't know what that extra folding means. I'd love to get in there and have a look."

Graham's eyes went to the small electric bone saw in the cabinet of surgical equipment.

"You think it's the goddamn treatment causing it?" Hammerson asked with an edge to his voice.

"Maybe, maybe not. Maybe a combination of the treatment and his original injury. You ever hear of Phineas Gage, Jack? . . . Not surprised; he was a railway worker back in the 1800s. Had a metal spike punched into his head. He survived, but it changed him from a happy young man to one who became violent and eventually feared by the entire town. There are all sorts of conflicting stories about the feats of strength he supposedly performed after the accident. When he finally died and they opened him up, they found a brain that was very different from anyone else's. Thing is, Jack, they believed his brain had continued to change long after the spike was removed. Of course, it might not be the same for Captain Hunter—the extra brain folding could be some form of physical response to the original trauma; or maybe the treatment initiated something else in there, something that's ongoing. Well, you can see that I'm guessing—could be a hundred things. Bottom line is, we don't know what the extra matter is for, or, more importantly, what it'll eventually do to your man."

"Could it kill him?" Hammerson asked.

"Not sure, but I doubt it in the short term." Graham anticipated Hammerson's next question. "Jack, we thought about halting the treatments, but we think that may either kill him or send his system into an irreversible vegetative state. At this stage, all we can do is watch and learn. He's unique, Jack, and very valuable. When can we have him back?"

"In a month or two, Graham. Just give him back in one piece."

Graham was silent for a moment, then spoke with a lowered voice. "Don't forget our agreement, Jack. He's yours until he's killed or incapacitated. Then *we* own him." The scientist's eyes went again to the bone saw.

# Seven

"But there was no thermal energy release—there was nothing on the seismographic sensors, not a single tremor. I know it was subsurface, and I bet they had concrete and lead shielding, but that gamma flash must have gone straight through it—a controlled nuclear test blast should have been better contained. The radiation signature reads like something non-terrestrial."

Zachariah Shomron was arguing furiously with his professor; or rather, with himself, using his professor as an audience.

Professor Dafyyd Burstein clasped his pudgy hands together above a stomach that was straining over a thin belt and raised his eyebrows in a look that he reserved for his best students, those who raised brilliant questions and probably already knew the answers. "Are you saying a stellar mass somehow fell to earth in the Iranian desert, Zachariah?"

"Yes, no, of course not . . . maybe. It's just that the pulse had all the characteristics of a cosmic gamma burst, but it's impossible that it originated from Earth. Though it only flashed for microseconds, it gave off thousands of sieverts. A nuclear blast only delivers about 300 sieverts per hour downwind, but it also throws out neutrons, alpha and beta particles and X-rays. The only thing that saved Iran from being incinerated was the flash's micro duration . . . and then, it just turned off. It's impossible! This is so weird—it's getting into dark matter territory."

"*Yoish!*" exclaimed Burstein. "Okay, okay, we can discuss all this later. I came up to tell you that there's a large and serious-looking government type waiting to talk to you in the foyer. Have you been late paying your bills again, Zachariah?"

Burstein took Zachariah by one of his bony elbows and led him towards the door, nodding as the younger man kept up a stream of near impenetrable musings on obscure gamma-wave effects.

Zach stopped mid-sentence when he saw the man in the foyer. He was the most perfectly square human being Zach had ever seen, all hard edges that looked machine-cut, starting from his flat-top crew cut and broad shoulders, and continuing down to column-thick legs stuffed into charcoal suit pants. The man took a step forward and Zach automatically took one back.

"*Boker tov*, Zachariah Shomron."

Zach saw the man quickly check a photograph he held in his hand as if to validate he had the right person.

"*Shalom*," Zachariah said and tentatively held out his hand for the other man to shake.

Instead, the man pressed a letter into Zach's hand. It had a distinctive stamp on the front—a blue, seven-candled menorah, the seal of Mossad. There was also an inscription in Hebrew: "Where there is no guidance the people fall, but with an abundance of counsellors there is victory." *Good advice about "good advice"*, Zach thought.

The man spoke as if reading from a script: "Zachariah Shomron, you are aware that national military service is mandatory for all Jewish men and women. You have the thanks of the State of Israel for completing your assigned service. Though you elected to resume a normal working life, you remain an inactive reservist until you are forty years of age. At the discretion of the State of Israel, in the event of war or extreme national risk you may be reactivated." He paused and stared into Zach's eyes. "That risk now exists and you have been reactivated. Sir, your instructions are all in the letter."

Zach looked quickly at the envelope and furrowed his brow. "What? I've been reactivated? No, I can't fight—"

The man cut him off. "Your assistant will meet you at

the airport. *Elokim Yerachem Eretz Yisrael.*" He saluted and turned to leave.

"Er, yes," Zach replied, confused by why the man should salute him. "God bless Israel . . . Wait, wait—I have an assistant?"

"It's all in the letter, sir."

Zach stood with his mouth open, watching the man disappear down the corridor. *Why now?* he thought, then, *oh God, no*, as he remembered the short article he'd written years ago for the university newspaper complaining about the restrictions Israel placed on Palestinian scientists. He'd known at the time it was going too far, but hadn't expected anyone important to read a university publication. Seems he'd be wrong. *Mossad*, he thought, and pushed his glasses back up his nose. *And an assistant . . .*

Major Hammerson pushed his chair back and walked towards the large windows. He stood at ease with his hands clasped behind his back and watched Captain Alex Hunter walk across the clipped grass of the parade grounds. Hammerson had just spent an hour with his HAWC team leader, primarily bringing him up to speed on the new Middle Eastern project. His brief to Alex was simple: negate Iran's ability to organise and deliver a nuclear weapon of mass destruction. He had explained to Alex about the size of the gamma pulse and its unnatural characteristics. It meant the Iranians had either developed an enormous nuclear capability, or something else just as lethal. Either way, America had to act.

After the briefing, Alex had asked again about his test results; he always did after one of his medical visits. Hammerson hated having to be evasive or deceive him, but he had his orders. Regardless, he didn't think Alex was ready to hear all the information on his condition just yet. And Hammerson was damn sure he wasn't ready to give it.

Alex Hunter was probably the closest thing Hammerson had to a son. Truth was, he was proud of him. In effect, Hammerson had been responsible for his very creation, bringing him back to the US after the accident and handing him over to the medical men. Afterwards, Hammerson had taken the young man under his wing and moulded him into the soldier he was now. And shielded him, sometimes from his own military command.

Unfortunately for Alex, his lethal skills combined with his amazing new capabilities meant he had become something more than just another elite soldier. *A subject that exceeded expectations*, the scientists had said. There were some who didn't want just one Alex Hunter in the elite forces; they wanted 10,000 of them.

While Alex succeeded in missions that others couldn't even contemplate, he was a high-value asset. But the first time he failed, the first time he stayed down or didn't regain consciousness, then he would be wheeled into one of the military's covert science labs and probably never return. Hammerson wondered how many months or years Alex had until that happened.

"Sometimes I can feel myself changing—and it doesn't feel good, Jack," Alex had said during the briefing. All Hammerson could offer was some slick response about such change being fairly normal, just the legacy of a serious trauma. Truth was, it looked to be the price of Alex's life.

Hammerson sucked in a deep breath and exhaled through his nose. *It was always my decision, son. I can't yet know if it was the right one.* All Hammerson did know was that he would do everything in his power to keep Alex out of the labs.

# Eight

Alex felt good today; a slight headache behind his eyes, but that was normal following one of his visits to the medical unit. He was looking forward to being back out in the field—he found it difficult to sleep well unless his body was being subjected to the physical demands and stress of a dangerous and complex mission. To compensate he had been spending half his days either in the gymnasium or on the track carrying hundred-pound weight discs in a backpack. Without the energy burn, his mind wouldn't shut down properly and night-times were the worst. He was slowly learning to control his body while he was awake, but at night, in the dark, he couldn't govern which doors in his mind were opened or the emotions that were unleashed. Night-time was the danger time, when he sometimes destroyed his room in his sleep.

It was the night rages that had finished off his relationship with Aimee, sending her fleeing from their room in fear for her safety; that and his dangerous assignments all around the world. Alex and Aimee had travelled to the depths of the Antarctic together, seen wonders hidden for a thousand millennia, lost friends, colleagues and good soldiers, and barely survived being pursued by an ancient monster beneath the ice. Afterwards, they had tried real hard to make it work, but in the end Aimee had left him.

Alex remembered all too well the night, a year or so ago, when he and Aimee had gone for a pre-dinner drink at a little bar in Milwaukee. A football team on a stag night had been in the bar too, and when Alex returned from the rest-room he had seen Aimee slap the face of one large brute as he tried to squeeze her breast. Fifteen minutes later, Aimee had called Major Hammerson requesting urgent assistance— for the footballers. A lot of big men had got badly hurt that night, some permanently. It had cost the military a lot in hush money, and the guilt still hung over Alex's head like a dark thundercloud.

The problem was that Alex had enjoyed the destruction— once he started, he couldn't stop. He'd wanted to hurt those guys; more, he'd wanted to kill them. And the release had felt good.

He still thought of Aimee, her dark hair and fair skin, the quick temper that made her blue eyes go hard as ice chips, then soften and darken to a deep ocean blue when she kissed him. He wondered whether she was fully recovered from the Antarctic expedition and her own nightmares. He also wondered whether she still thought about him, whether she was really over their time together. He didn't blame her for leaving. It was the best thing she could have done for both of them. He couldn't contemplate what he would have inflicted on himself if he had ever hurt her.

He remembered her face after the fight in the bar—the look of horror and disbelief on those beautiful features. She was terrified—not of the men who had assaulted her, but of him. "Jack Hammerson's Frankenstein monster" she had called him in a moment of anguish and confusion. She had tried to laugh about it later, but from then on, deep in her eyes, he'd seen tension and wariness.

She was right: he was a monster. A monster created by an accident on a battlefield on the other side of the planet. She had begged him to seek medical opinions from specialists outside of the military, but he couldn't even do that for her. Hammerson had said no. Aimee had exploded when Alex tried to explain. She didn't believe his reasons and wouldn't listen to him after that.

Alex trusted Jack Hammerson; the major had looked out for him, always got him home safe, and Alex owed him his life a hundred times over. He would die for the Hammer, and he would also kill for him. He just wished he hadn't had to lose Aimee.

Alex walked slowly towards the small group of men Hammerson had put together for this mission. The HAWC recruitment pool was drawn from the ranks of the Green Berets, the Navy SEALS, Special Forces Alpha, and Hammerson's old stomping ground, the Rangers. Hammerson's job was to select the best of the best—soldiers with outstanding skills in various forms of physical or technological combat techniques. Each man or woman in this unit was a controlled killer; a force of nature unleashed by the Hammer as and when necessary. Now it was Alex's job to test them for final preparation and mission readiness.

Alex looked analytically at each of the four men. Two he'd worked with before and two were "potentials." The new men both looked to be in their thirties—battle-hardened professionals. Alex needed to get inside their heads—give them some scenarios and ask how they would resolve them; talk to them about their successes and how they'd achieved that success; about their failures and what would they do differently next time.

Alex enjoyed testing the recruits. They nearly all believed they were made of iron, world-beaters, and in their own units they probably were. But in the HAWCs they were among peers; they joined a small team of men and women as good as or better than they were. Sometimes it took a little while for them to adjust, sometimes they needed a "push," and the part Alex liked best was when someone pushed back.

He looked at the four faces watching him; all had an even expression except for a mean-looking guy with red hair who was barely concealing his irritation. *My money's on you for the push-back*, Alex thought.

He acknowledged the two men he knew first; each nodded once in return—Second Lieutenant Hex Winter and First Lieutenant Samuel Reid. Both had been HAWCs for a while now. Hex Winter, at just thirty, was the youngest HAWC

Alex had vetted and had also come from Alpha. Hex stood about six feet four inches and only weighed in at around 190 pounds—he looked a bit like a scarecrow with a coat hanger stuck down the back of his shirt. His nose had been broken several times, his hair was white-blond, and his eyes were the pale grey of a North Atlantic storm swell—the name "Winter" was appropriate indeed. When Alex had first met Hex, the thing that caught his eye was the multiple knives the lieutenant carried on one hip—unusual in an age of guns. Alex had been able to identify the standard US long-bladed Ka-Bar—his own pick due to the blade's low chromium steel mixture, which kept a razor edge in combat. In the field you could dry shave with it. Or open a man's throat from ear to ear before he even knew he'd been touched. But the other two were less familiar. One was a German Kampfmesser 2000, the standard knife of the elite Bundeswehr and the strike forces of the German Army. It was a beautiful weapon, a laser-cut seven-inch stainless steel alloy tanto blade with a distinctive forty-five-degree chisel-shaped end—balanced and deadly. The third was a new version Kampfmesser, the KM3000, with a spear-point blade instead of the 2000's tanto point—not as tough, but better balance and weight for throwing.

Alex had asked for a demonstration of it in action, pointing to a crossing of beams in the waist-high fence running around the edge of the oval, more than fifty feet from where they stood. Without hesitation, Hex Winter had spun the knife in a backhanded motion at the fence. Alex's enhanced vision had seen that the knife was going to find its mark, dead centre, before the blade had even travelled half its distance.

The young man came with a few other "tools of the trade" as well, including an upgraded M24 long-gun variant sniper rifle with his own modifications—longer receiver, detachable sight on a raised rail with maximum sound suppression. It also took a more powerful .338 Lapua magnum cartridge—accurate to 5000 feet with enormous penetration power. A beautiful and deadly precision weapon. When Alex had asked Hex about his accuracy, he'd replied that he could split Alex's thumb at a mile. After the knife demonstration, Alex had believed him.

First Lieutenant Sam Reid, older than the others by a few years, was an electronics expert who exuded confidence and was as laidback as they came. Hammerson had personally selected Reid for HAWC training—he was a Ranger, 75th Regiment. Sam—"Uncle" to his friends—was the best man on the planet for military strategy and red zone logistics, and had an IQ of 160 that put him into Mensa territory—brains as well as brawn. After Alex's accident, his problem-solving abilities and mental acuity had become vastly superior to most men, but First Lieutenant Sam Reid was in a league of his own.

Then Alex turned to the two new men. "I'm Captain Alex Hunter," he told them, and asked for their rank and military history.

The man on the left of the line stepped forward first. He was the shortest of the group, standing at around five feet seven inches in his boots, but what he lacked in height he more than made up for in breadth—he had a barrel chest and arms like a bear. Alex also noticed his hands were extraordinarily rough and calloused.

"Second Lieutenant Rocky Lagudi," the man said, and saluted.

Alex grabbed the man's hand, turned it over and looked at it. *Deadly*, he thought. "Black belt?" he asked.

"Yes, sir. Shotokan Karate 8th dan Master. Also Zen Doh Kai, 7th dan."

All Special Forces personnel were proficient in lethal and non-lethal hand-to-hand combat methods, but Zen Doh Kai was a deadly martial art that used lethal hard-edge striking. Alex had witnessed some full-contact bouts and it had been like watching bare-knuckle cage fighting for masochists.

Lieutenant Lagudi tried to turn his hand back over, but Alex held it—a subtle but effective test of will and strength. Rocky tried again, exerting all his strength this time, but his hand might as well have been trapped in a steel vice for all the give he got from Alex's single-handed grip. Alex could easily have pulverised the stocky lieutenant's fingers and all his metacarpal bones, but released instead. *Okay*, he thought, *perhaps you'll be the one today.*

"Carry on, Lieutenant," he said, and listened to Lagudi's overview of the various combat assignments he'd taken part in and his background in the Green Berets. Seemed Lagudi was the battering ram, the first man over the top. *Good*, thought Alex, *a brave heart in that huge chest. I can use him.*

Second Lieutenant Francis O'Riordan looked as Irish as they came, with his close-cropped startlingly orange hair and his pale skin. When he opened his mouth though, his accent was pure Bronx, every statement ending with a stab that made it sound like a question or a challenge. "Irish" O'Riordan was from Special Forces Alpha, specialised in chemical engineering, and was proficient in explosive device construction, placement and disposal. The rumour was he could create a bomb from the contents of the average refrigerator.

Alex had read the man's report. His previous Alpha team had been the best squad going—until they got blown to pieces. Irish had come home on a stretcher; the rest of his unit were spread over a hundred feet of steaming jungle. In the debrief, Irish had stated that Captain Dianne Chambers had ignored advice from her team and run them into hell—a claymore web: one way in, no way out. Follow-up psych sessions detailed a simmering anger against female authority, but also said O'Riordan was fit for duty. To date, he had continued to excel. Alex could see a mote of hostility in the man's eyes now. *Anger is okay; controlling it is the key*, he thought. *Time for a little push.*

"Where do you call home, Lieutenant O'Riordan? Riverdale, Throggs Neck?" he asked.

Alex knew a little about the Bronx as he had spent some time at Fort Hamilton in New York. Though the Bronx was one of the most populous areas in the United States, and some of those areas were the toughest in the country, parts of it were fast becoming gentrified and Riverdale and Throggs Neck were two suburbs that were now more movie star than "gangsta" turf. Alex heard a slight snigger from the other men at the question.

O'Riordan's eyes slid to Alex and narrowed for a second before he went back to staring straight ahead. "Nah, sir. Born and raised in South Bronx just down from Fordham. Born and bred there, but it ain't my home now; ain't never goin' back."

It was a tough area—primarily Hispanic, African-American and Italian. A kid with red hair would stand out like crap on a snow cake—Irish would have had to do a lot of fighting growing up.

Alex stared directly into the man's face as he said, "Put too much cream in your coffee, did they? Had some bad sushi at your last poetry reading, Lieutenant?"

O'Riordan's jaw muscles worked and his eyes burned as they stared into Alex's face. Alex could tell that it was only his army discipline keeping him in check. After a few more seconds he straightened. "Nothin' to go back to. Some asshole bein' transported to Rikers broke outta custody and tried to drag my dad outta his car at a stop light. Well, my dad, he was one of the last of the red Irish rhinos, he wouldn't give in for nothin'. Even though that car was a pile of crap, he weren't givin' it up to some asshole car thief. Got a face full of lead for his trouble, and Ma took two in the gut. Nothin' there for me anymore; army's home now . . . sir."

Alex looked hard into the man's face for a few seconds more, nodded once and turned away. *Hmm, a lot of anger there that's going to need to be channeled,* he thought. He'd read O'Riordan's psych report again just to ensure this guy wasn't going to explode under pressure. Still, he figured they were good to go for the induction. There was just one more thing.

"All right, you new soldiers, this is the Hotzone All-Forces Warfare Commandos and we are the best on this planet. The pay's no better, there are no fast cars, no cheer squads—in fact, as far as Mr. Joe Citizen is concerned, we don't even exist. Our casualty rate is higher than any other Special Forces unit in the United States, and if you're ever captured—well, like I said, we don't exist. But what I can guarantee you is access to the best weaponry, intelligence and training the army has to offer. And if you like a challenge—well, you'll find yourself being challenged like at no other time in your life. As a HAWC, you don't just save lives, you save countries."

Alex paused and looked at the two new men. Rocky Lagudi's face was serious, but Irish O'Riordan seemed to be barely holding a smirk in check.

Alex spoke directly to the redheaded man. "This is your opportunity to speak your mind—to ask me questions, ask your fellow HAWCs questions. There may not be a better time, or any other time. Things happen fast in this outfit."

He waited for a few seconds, and when both men maintained their silence he continued. "Most of the year you'll be in training. You will learn new skills, use new weapons and technologies, and you will be tested time and time again in drill missions across various terrains and hostile environments. Just because you're in the HAWCs doesn't mean you have a right to stay in the HAWCs."

Alex saw Sam Reid give a half-smile. He and Hex had been through the tests and knew what they entailed.

"And then there are the live operations," Alex went on. "Arduous, dangerous projects that no one else wants and no one else could succeed at. Projects that are given to us because we are the deadliest, most feared unit on the entire planet." He smiled grimly. "Gentlemen, listen up. We are about to take on just such a project."

# Nine

Ahmad Al Janaddi tried hard to keep the nervousness from his voice. It was the first time he had been called to appear personally before the president and his future could very well hang on his performance. It didn't help that the men in charge of the Iranian military, the Islamic Revolutionary Guard and the intelligence and security services were also present, along with the leader of the Islamic Guardian Council, a group of elders charged with ensuring that all the Republic's decisions adhered to the path of Islam.

Al Janaddi was the newly promoted leading scientist at the Jamshid II site, and it was his task to inform the group about the recent "anomaly" at the Jamshid I site at Persepolis. He drew in a short breath and looked briefly at the faces staring back at him. President Moshaddam appeared to be listening patiently, but may just as easily have been bored by all the technical details.

The only face that was truly engaged was that of Parvid Davoodi, the vice-president. The complete opposite of the president, Davoodi was well educated and an economist by training—and his liberal perspective, based on his studies of modern economic theory and the free market, often brought him into conflict with his more hard-line colleagues and his president. Unlike Moshaddam, Davoodi was for open dialogue with the West. He'd spent some of his early life in America and held a PhD in Economics from Iowa State University; like a lot of moderate Iranians, he didn't see the West as evil, just different.

Al Janaddi continued with his report. "All the Persepolis material that was transferred to our Jamshid II complex has been reviewed many times and we believe we have an understanding of what caused the destruction of the primary site. In essence, the modifications to the laser-enrichment sphere made by the German scientist Hoeckler had an unexpected side effect. Due to his radical design and choice of laser, the high-speed molecule collisions were a lot faster and contained a lot more energy. In effect, his design did more than just split the atoms from their molecules; he actually caused them to crash into each other at the speed of light. Hoeckler's sphere became a miniature particle collider." Al Janaddi paused, but no one except for Davoodi seemed interested. He tried again. "We believe we created a miniature black hole within the sphere."

Davoodi sat forward. "You think that was the source of the gamma rays, not just a fissionable accident?" he asked.

Al Janaddi knew the vice-president had an amateur interest in astronomy. "Yes, *Agha-ye*, Vice-President, we believe the data is undeniable here. If it were a leakage there would be continuing radiation in the mega-sievert range. But there was no heat, no explosion—just a form of . . . implosion. The gamma anomaly held its form for point-zero-two nanoseconds before evaporating and collapsing back into itself, taking with it everything within a 500 foot radius. Allah be praised that this was so, as it drew its own gamma radiation flash back in. There is barely any residual radiation left; the facility's structural design contained most of the deadly particle emissions and the implosion digested the rest."

The scientist chose his words carefully. Though the Jamshid I site at Persepolis had been under the governance of his former colleague Mahmud Shihab, it was still quite possible that he could be arrested for being associated with the destruction of the property of the Islamic Republic of Iran, which carried an immediate death sentence. He felt the dead eyes of Mohammed Bhakazarri, Chief Commander of the Islamic Revolutionary Guard, slide across him. He swallowed and continued.

"Let me show you the data feeds of the last few minutes prior to the anomaly in the facility." Al Janaddi opened a large flat laptop computer and called up the movie display software, selected the appropriate time slice and pressed play. "What you are seeing now is the laboratory floor—the uranium-enrichment sphere is the globe in the centre of the room."

The screen showed many scientists and engineers in the lab. As the lights dimmed, they pulled visors down over their eyes and turned to face the sphere. The sphere seemed to glow as the room darkened around it, and then, for just a few seconds, the room filled with white streaks before everything went black. A dreadful howling sound made even the viewers widen their eyes and grip their chair rails. Al Janaddi slowed the footage to a frame-by-frame perspective. Even so, the speed of events was rapid and it was difficult to understand what they were actually seeing. All of the personnel in the lab seemed to blur and warp, stretching towards the sphere as if they were made of elastic. The slowed-down howl sounded almost musical now, like a large brass horn.

Al Janaddi halted the display and enlarged a small section, showing the faces of the scientists in detail. Most showed expressions of surprise, but among them there were also fear and agony. Then they were gone.

"Gamma radiation within the facility spiked at eight thousand sieverts," Al Janaddi explained quietly. "That's almost incineration wavelength. Further away from the sphere, the concrete and lead panelling shielded the pulse shock wave somewhat, but we know it travelled beyond the facility. But there is no significant radiation at the site now; in fact, nothing much above normal. It was there, and now it's gone."

Davoodi spoke again, slowly. "Are there any survivors? Have the bodies been retrieved and blessed?"

"There are no survivors, but . . ." Al Janaddi licked his lips as he gathered his thoughts. "We believe we have recovered the remains of Mahmud Shihab, the lead scientist of the facility. But at this point we're not one hundred per cent sure if—"

The president unfolded his arms and narrowed his eyes at the scientist. "Tell us what you have, Professor. Everything—quickly." Though the tone was even, Al Janaddi could feel the underlying warning to be absolutely candid.

"Yes, my President. Please appreciate there is much we still do not fully comprehend, and we need many more tests for final confirmation, but a body . . . er, a partial body, was shipped to us this morning. We believe it is Dr. Shihab, but identification was possible only from the security tag found on a pocket and a partial thumbprint from the left hand."

Al Janaddi sensed Parvid Davoodi watching him closely. "Severe burning?" the vice-president asked.

Al Janaddi's lips moved as if testing his words before he spoke them aloud. He shook his head and looked down at the ground before continuing. "Yes, there was gamma insult to the physiology, and some of the personnel recovering the body suffered quite severe secondary radiation poisoning, but that was not what confused us."

The scientist drew in a deep shuddering breath and opened another file on the laptop—a single colour photograph that filled the screen. Though he had seen it before, he winced at the image. The top half of the body was almost unrecognisable as human. The head and face were the worst—they seemed to have stretched and widened. An eye a foot long stared out of the image, while the mouth—held open by the swollen, distended tongue—seemed to be screaming from the very pit of hell.

Even the veteran soldiers, who had seen all manner of mutilations on the battlefield, sat with mouths open in either disgust or shock. After a few moments, most of the group looked away, all except Mahmoud Moshaddam. The president's gaze burned into the scientist; Al Janaddi felt as if it penetrated to his very core.

"What else?" Moshaddam said softly. "There is something more—I can feel it. I will not ask you a third time, Professor. Tell us everything."

The scientist wrung his hands and nodded. "The Persepolis anomaly occurred just forty hours ago and over 400 miles from where we are now. However, when the body was recovered it was severely decomposed, as if Dr. Shihab had been dead for many months. Somehow, between his disappearance under four days ago and reappearance, his body has undergone nearly half a year's decomposition. We believe that when he disappeared, he didn't just go *somewhere* else—he went some *when* else."

Mohammed Bhakazarri was shaking his head. "Professor, are you aware how many billions of rials that site cost the Islamic Republic of Iran? Are you aware of the camouflage and misinformation that we needed to facilitate to mask it? And for what? What have we got for our billions and all that work other than a deformed, dead scientist?"

Al Janaddi had expected this from the military. They resented the fact that scientific personnel were in charge of the Jamshid projects. But his defensive strategy wasn't aimed at the military; it was for the benefit of the president. It was common knowledge that Mahmoud Moshaddam was a deeply religious man who saw the hand of Allah in every event that occurred. This knowledge had shaped Al Janaddi's argument.

"Yes, I am aware of the cost, Chief Commander Bhakazarri—both in terms of the loss of personnel and rials. But I think we may have expended our money very wisely. This may be the greatest gift Allah, may his name be praised, has bestowed on our great land for a thousand years."

The president's brow knitted and he sat forward. Silence hung in the room and all eyes were now firmly on the scientist.

"Black holes are the deadliest and most powerful entities in our universe," Al Janaddi continued. "And Iran just created one in a laboratory. The Europeans and the Americans are still theorising about the ability to achieve this with their giant particle accelerators. They know that creating and securing a black hole would deliver an energy source unparalleled on this planet. Gamma-ray bursts from outside our galaxy have enormous power that could supply the entire world's energy needs for a billion, billion years. Rather than bury the Jamshid project, we must try and reproduce the work that was done at Persepolis and see if we can harness these mighty entities and their almost limitless power."

Davoodi raised an eyebrow and half-smiled at the scientist. "I am not an expert, but I understand, Professor, that a single gamma burst can release more energy in ten seconds than our sun will emit in ten billion years. How do you propose to contain this monstrous force once created? Also, what would stop these unstable entities from escaping your facility and devouring Jamshid II, Iran, or the entire planet for that matter? We just lost Jamshid I in the blink of an eye, and probably alerted the West that we are working with fissionable material. The next *accident* could be the last for everyone in Iran."

The vice-president leaned forward and steepled his fingers. "I suggest we shut down all testing until we have a better understanding of the risks of trying to tamper with these monstrous freak occurrences."

Al Janaddi closed his eyes for a moment and sighed, opening his arms as if in resignation. "Perhaps you are right. There is much we don't know at this point, Vice-President Davoodi. But maybe that is why we must undertake further study to understand and perhaps harness this power. If we don't, the West will."

There was complete silence. All eyes turned to the president. He seemed deep in prayer: his eyes were closed, his hands were clasped and he was murmuring softly to himself. At last he opened his eyes and spoke.

"It is clear to me that this is Allah's gift to the Iranian people. He has shown us the path forward and it would be blasphemy to ignore his message. No more will our enemies be able to threaten embargoes on our petroleum or the destruction of our oil fields. When we have an energy source that does not need to be sucked from the ground, that we can pluck from the very stars themselves, that has been given to us by Allah, blessed be his name, then we can lead the entire Muslim world to a new age of superiority. We will be able to stop our oil production and watch the West return to chaos when the source of the black blood that their machines gorge themselves upon is suddenly turned off."

Then the president's brow furrowed as if he had just had an unpleasant thought. He reached out to Chief Commander Bhakazarri and took hold of his upper arm. "They will come—either the pigs of Zion or the Americans. If enough of the radiation escaped, they will have seen it."

Bhakazarri made a fist and brought it slowly down on the table in a subconscious act of crushing his enemies. "You are right. Either by air or by stealth, they will come. We must be ready"

"And what of Persepolis—what remains of the facility?" The president turned from Bhakazarri back to the scientist, his eyes narrowing in contemplation.

"Nothing, my President. Nothing except the tunnels leading to the complex. There was no heat, no noise and no ground tremors—the facility was either totally absorbed . . . or sent somewhere else."

The president nodded slowly. "Truly a gift—Allah and all the prophets be praised." He turned to Bhakazarri, his eyes now alight with the fire of excitement. "We must be ready— with words and a plan, and some steel as well, my friend. We will tell the bureaucrats at the United Nations that we wish to discuss closing down the Natanz facilities, with their assistance, in return for their lifting of all sanctions. They already know about the Natanz operation, and that will keep them satisfied. It will also be enough to keep the Americans in check, at least diplomatically."

He spoke to Al Janaddi again. "Professor, you are authorised to bring the Jamshid II facility up to full production capability immediately. You are personally responsible for the success of this project."

The president closed his eyes and leaned his head back, as though listening to some distant voice. "We need to keep the unbelievers away from Jamshid II at all costs. They may know about the Persepolis site, but there is nothing there for them now. Perhaps we should have a reception waiting for them nevertheless. To draw them out, sap their strength."

Bhakazarri gave a flat smile. "I will ready the Takavaran immediately, my President, and cast a net around Persepolis. I will also ensure that our professor and Jamshid II are doubly safe. Around them I will place a noose."

Al Janaddi suppressed a groan. The Takavaran were the most brutal fighting force in the entire Middle East. All fanatics, they likened themselves to the Persian Immortals and their death squads had a habit of crushing enemies and locals alike. Their chain of command included Bhakazarri and God—in that order. The Jamshid II facility at Arak was about to undergo a very unpleasant experience.

The president had asked Mostafa Hossein, the leader of the Islamic Guardian Council, to remain behind when the others left. He motioned for the old cleric to be seated next to him and took him by the hand.

"I heard it," he said. "I heard Israfil's horn. The hour has come." The president began to quote from the Qur'an: "At a time unknown to man, but preordained, when people least expect it, Allah will give permission for the *Qiyamah*, the Day of Judgment, to begin. The archangel Israfil will sound a horn sending out a blast of truth. The Earth, Moon and Sun will be joined together and swallowed by darkness." Tears ran freely down his face, but his eyes were shining and rapturous. "The scientist Shihab was returned to us a disgusting beast. I believe he stood at the crossroad of Jannah and Jahannam, of heaven and hell, and was judged by Allah to be sinful. He was sent back to us in that foul, deformed shell as punishment.

"The angels themselves have revealed to me that soon the Hidden One, the Mahdi, will reveal himself. Allah has led us to discover this great power so we may prepare the world for the arrival of the Enlightened One." The president recited again: "The ground will move and the skies will blacken. All men and women will be made to cross over the black abyss, whence the flames of Jahannam will leap up. The believers will cross safely to Jannah; the others will be cast down as beasts. Afterwards, the Mahdi, the Hidden One, will lead the truly faithful to a land that is returned to the empire of Allah and cleansed of all idols, non-believers and sinners."

The leader of the Islamic Guardian Council was a deeply religious man, but he was wary of the way the young president drew on an unfounded personal spiritual authority. He knew the president believed that the teachings of the Prophet signalled a resurgent Islamic caliphate and the coming apocalypse. His fiery rhetoric when it came to the might of Iran or his dealings with the West were both exciting and intimidating, but it seemed everyone but the president himself knew Iran could never survive a head-to-head conflict with the West, especially with the American forces. Iran's weapon was the threat of withholding oil production, not firepower. Now Mostafa Hossein was concerned that Moshaddam was positioning himself to draw on an ancient prophecy to proclaim himself as some kind of prophet, perhaps even a descendant of the greatest prophet of all. Moshaddam was obsessed with the Mahdi, or Hidden Imam, a direct descendant of the prophet Mohammed, whose return would herald the Islamic Day of Judgment and the end of the world.

The president closed his eyes and gave a small backhanded wave, signifying the meeting was at an end. "I can hear the horn still," he whispered. "Israfil speaks to me even now, my friend. He tells me: ready yourself for the return of the prophet."

Mostafa Hossein leaned over to kiss both of the president's cheeks then moved to the door. He needed to talk to the Supreme Leader.

# Ten

"Why not drop us into Iraq? That's secure now." Alex was looking at the map of the Middle East that Hammerson had spread out on his desk.

The Hammer shook his head. "Secure, maybe. Sealed and silent, not a chance. We put you down anywhere in Iraq and Tehran will know about it within the hour. Same goes for Kuwait, Saudi and Bahrain. There's no backup, and time is your enemy—you'll need all the head start you can get. Has to be Israel, then you cross over to the target zone."

Alex raised an eyebrow at his superior officer. "Cross Syrian airspace, over Iraq and then drop into Iran—that's a lot of unfriendly eyes. Choppers are too slow, and that also rules out trekking in from the Gulf . . . Hmm, HALO?"

Hammerson smiled, pushed his chair back and brought his large hands together behind his head. "Oh, yeah. I'm thinking I'm going to throw you all out the back of a B2 Spirit at 35,000 feet and see what happens."

"Night drop?" Alex asked.

Hammerson nodded. "High and dark. Twice the fun."

Alex grinned. If a human being truly wanted to experience speed, forget about travelling in the cockpit of a jet or racing car. Just do a High Altitude Low Opening jump. All HAWCs had to perform HALOs as part of their special training; however, 35,000 feet was the absolute maximum without wearing a full pressurised suit. The air temperature was well below freezing at that height and frostbite, hypothermia and glass-eye were a possibility. Usually, though, you weren't there long

enough for any of those to occur; the real danger came from
the low air pressure that could cause pulmonary or even cere-
bral oedema—swelling of the lungs or brain. The latter led to
blackouts or hallucinations—you simply forgot why you needed
to open your chute. Terminal velocity was around 200 miles
per hour for a freefall, but with the low air pressure you
could reach double that velocity. Hit the ground at those
speeds and they'd be collecting you with a mop and bucket.

"The new suits you'll be using with the visors down will
give you adequate environmental protection and we can rig
in disposable oxygen," Hammerson said. "Drop will take
around three minutes, two minutes of which are going to be
pretty unpleasant, doubly so for our Israeli contingent." Hammerson pulled a more detailed map and photographs out from
the pile on his desk.

"Israelis? New suits?" Alex knitted his brows.

"Some regional collaboration—we'll get to that. Infiltration will be approximately one mile south of the Persepolis
ruins. Extraction point to be determined by you. We'll have
a surface-skimming gunship ready; by then we won't care if
anyone hears or sees us."

Alex studied the map of Iran and the photographs of the
Marv Dasht basin spread out before him—nearly 650,000
square miles of dry desert, mountains and age-old hostility.
"Surveillance?" he asked. Getting captured in Iran as a spy
wouldn't make for a very pleasant few days—torture and execution would ruin a good holiday every time.

"Nothing electronic, but you can bet there'll be a few
lenses pointed skyward. The B2 will be well above that for
your drop, and your suits won't show up on the way down. On
the ground . . . maybe."

Alex nodded. "We can deal with anything on the ground."
He paused for a moment then said, "We don't need help.
They'll just slow us down."

"This time you might. The complex technology and hostile
environment means we'll need specialists—in astrophysics,
languages and logistics."

Alex shook his head. "I've got Sam Reid, he knows plenty

about nuclear fission and the technology. And you're telling me you want me take a language specialist? I don't expect to be doing much talking."

"I know, I know, and one or both of them will probably be a Mossad Torpedo. But we need to work with the Israelis on this—the last thing we want is them making a strike on Iran. Consider it a small price for being able to use their bases and resources. Besides, we think the situation may be more complex than just some sort of test burst. The Israelis have more eyes and ears in Iran than we'll ever have. My gut feeling is you may need them. There'll be a further briefing on the ground in Israel."

"Two of them, five of us. If they fall behind, they stay behind."

"Okay, then. Best case: seven in, seven out. But it'll be your call on how you execute your mission objectives. Now, let's see what we've got to cover your back, soldier."

Hammerson moved the maps aside and turned his computer sideways so they could both see the screen. He was already logged on to the USSTRATCOM intranet, the internal secure website for the strategic command's senior officers. The first page he opened was for research and development, where he selected "defensive weaponry," then "arid environment body armour."

Alex whistled. The screen showed what looked like a sand-coloured robot. The new dry-zone combat suit combined a total-cover uniform with a synthetic material base and armour plates covering the chest area, back and shoulders. Over the neck, stomach, knees and elbows it was armadillo-segmented for maximum mobility. The facial area was open, but a high-tech helmet covered the head and travelled down the side of the face to halfway along the chin. A visor could be pulled out and down from the brow brim.

"Got to be lightweight," Alex said. "Is the plating a polymer structure?"

"Nope, not even close. Benefit of being in the HAWCs—we get all the experimental stuff from the labs. What you see there is the result of millions of dollars of research and a lot of free education from Operation Desert Shield. In a dry environment it'll be your new best friend; this suit material is thermally created using the latest in para-aramid synthetic fibres. I say thermally because there's no stitching, it's actually grown then fused together. Strength-to-weight ratio is about five to one—we use this stuff in warplanes now. Its basic design is to keep out heat, sand and dust but retain moisture. It won't stop a bullet, but it will stop a knife thrust, unless someone like you is doing the thrusting. What will stop a bullet is the plating—what you thought was a polymer structure is actually a zirconium dioxide ceramic. This stuff ranks an 8.5 on the Mohs scale of hardness. Steel is only about a six. It's light, won't melt, is non-conductive and non-magnetic. Helmet is the same material and has all your communication equipment built-in."

"Wow, can it fly?"

Hammerson laughed. "Soon. That'll be in the next gen." He sat quietly for a moment watching Alex before reaching for a folder and speaking again. "There is one more thing; the exoskeleton and para-aramids will need to be upgraded for radiation shielding. The material will be compressed to simulate the dense atomic structure of lead, with only minimal extra weight, and without the heavy metal toxicity."

Alex nodded slowly. "Hmm, you think the Iranians are still leaking radiation?"

Hammerson gave a shrug. He opened the folder and lifted out a photograph. He looked stonily at the image for a few seconds before he slid it across to Alex.

A disfigured body was displayed with half its torso flattened and stretched over ten additional feet. It was spread out on a canvas sheet and displayed like the rotting carcass of a washed up deep-sea animal. Pieces of white material and road tar were still embedded within its mass.

Alex shook his head and frowned as he slid the photograph back. "Radiation does that?"

Hammerson shrugged and looked down at the image. "We have no idea what does that. Or how that . . . man, came to be on American soil. What we *do* know is that he was a German national by the name of Rudolf Hoeckler. He was one of the leading theoretical particle physicists in the world. We've since learned through our intelligence networks that he passed into Iranian territory eighteen months ago, and our agents have told us they believe he is still there. It was our firm belief that Hoeckler was assisting them in their uranium enrichment program. We don't know how he got to Colorado Springs, but he still wore his Iranian ID tags and lab coat."

He sat back. "Autopsy report said he was frozen to 2.7 degrees kelvin, and been in a vacuum—to quote the report, 'predominant symptoms of someone who had been in a non-terrestrial atmosphere.'" Hammerson raised his eyebrows, then grinned humourlessly. "That's not all. The corpse was heavily irradiated and caused some secondary contamination before it was sealed in a lead casket. You see now why we're including some heavy particle protection inbuilt into the suits."

After a moment, Alex nodded. "Yes, understood."

"Let's move on." He turned the screen back around to face himself and keyed in a few more commands. "As usual, I'll let you choose your own small weaponry, but there is something new I'd suggest you consider. Say hello to the KBELT—Klystron Beam Emitted Light Technology."

Alex could see the major's eyes moving admiringly over the images; he knew that sometimes his superior officer missed the fieldwork. He turned the screen back to Alex again.

*Welcome to the twenty-first century,* thought Alex. The shoulder-mounted rifle was all black, but a list of palettes below told him he could have it in a camouflage colour to match his terrain. No stock, held like a sawn-off pump action, with a square casing over the trigger. The barrel started to smooth and round until it ended in a moulded bulb effect at the muzzle. *Hmm, too small for a hardened projectile*, Alex thought. *Must be another compressed gas round device.*

Hammerson was staring at the screen almost lovingly as he began describing the weaponry. "The latest weaponised emitted-light technology. Miniaturised power pack collects electrons and packs them into the klystron tube here, which acts like a linear beam vacuum. Will deliver a one million joule energy pulse that will travel at close to the speed of light to your target—no jamming, no recoil, no deviation and the speed means little chance of evasion. Two settings—high and low energy pulse. High energy will cut a pencil-sized hole through anything; low energy will give you the same result as 100 pounds of TNT—all delivered in a single, focused, explosive punch."

"Limitations?"

"Not many, but some things to consider. This generation of laser device requires an enormous amount of energy—that's why it contains its own generator. Next version will have a replaceable battery and be small enough for pistol form, but it won't be ready for this project. What it means for you is that after twenty shots it'll need to recharge for about two minutes. Second consideration—it only spits a pulse, no beam. The lab boys found that the laser streaming tended to bloom over distance, which reduced its intensity. The pulse is effective and keeps the power-packet delivery intact."

"Nice, I'll take six, and one for the farm." Alex was leaning forward and smiling in anticipation.

Hammerson chuckled. "You can have one—the trade-off is you give the lab a field report on your return. It'll be ready in a few hours, after we camouflage-coat it. One more thing—we're giving you some spiders. Take a look."

Hammerson called up a video that showed a scientist placing on the ground a small steel box, roughly the size of a packet of cigarettes, with a circular black disc on one side. The camera refocused for a few seconds on an empty car about fifty feet in the distance, then returned to the box. The box stood up on eight spindly segmented legs and scuttled towards the car, covering the distance that separated them in a matter of seconds. It clambered onto one of the car's wheels, a small red light flashed once and it detonated. After the rain of debris and smoke had cleared, nothing remained but a crater in the ground.

Hammerson cocked an eyebrow at Alex in a "get a kick

outta that?" look. "We've come a long way from the static claymore," he said. "Tomorrow's mines are a combination of robotics and computerisation. Forget the technical name for these—we just call them spiders, you can see why. Easy to use, low failure rate, high-yield blasts. They can be set to detonate on physical contact or on a timer. Hell, you can program these things to set up their own ambush. Your combat suits come with two, pre-coded with a built-in signature catalogue so they can tell us from the bad guys."

Alex could tell Hammerson loved this stuff. Both men had the greatest respect for the military research and development branch. The new materials and weaponry those guys brought to the field gave them an edge, and sometimes that was all it took.

"Questions?" Hammerson waited a second and then went on. "Okay, dust off in six hours. Gather your team. Go in fast and come out smiling, soldier. Good luck."

"Thanks, Jack."

They both stood and Alex shook Hammerson's hand. Already the excitement was boiling within him. Alex never worried for himself; he figured he was already on his second chance anyway. Every mission was simply an opportunity to push himself a little harder, to test himself just a little more. To flex muscles and senses that seemed to evolve every day. But for some of the other men on the team, it meant a death sentence.

Alex had lost good soldiers before, and he'd lose them again—that's what they'd all signed up for. All he could do was ensure they were field ready; the rest was up to them. As for the Israelis, if they wanted to tag along, fine. He just hoped they were either very tough or very smart.

# Eleven

Zach sighed as he saw the size of the crowd in the departure lounge and gave up any thought of finding a seat. He felt shabby and moth-eaten among the herds of affluent and well-fed Israelis and returning Americans. *Funny*, he thought, he only ever noticed his own clothing when he went out in public.

He hoisted his backpack into a more comfortable position, and took a few more steps around the lounge. He felt weighed down—every one of his pockets bulged with sweets, eye drops, nose spray, and myriad other medications he needed to survive a long flight. There were even wads of American money his aunt had pushed in quickly as he left—she was sure it was some sort of "reward" holiday he was going on.

In one of his hands he held a curling copy of Clarke's *2001: A Space Odyssey*—his much loved travel read. In the other he tried to control all his *other* travel documents . . . unsuccessfully. They all dropped to the carpet in a sliding rush, and as he bent to retrieve them, his water bottle flew from his backpack and bounced off the back of his head to roll slowly across the floor. *Aiiysh*, he whispered.

He put his hand out for the bottle just as a small hiking boot trapped it, and held it. He looked up slowly. A tall young woman stood looking at him with her hands on her hips and one eyebrow raised. "Dr. Shomron?"

Zach looked back down at his water, decided to ignore it and stood up. She was tall; not as tall as he, but tall for a woman. And fit—he could see the muscles in her neck, and her upper body looked athletic beneath a camel-coloured shirt. She had a military bearing.

She still hadn't moved, or blinked, but continued looking at him as though he had broken a law and she was about to arrest him.

Suddenly he remembered the contents of the letter he'd been given. *My assistant, of course—Adira something.* He stuck out his hand. "Yes, yes, that's me. Zachariah Shomron. But please call me Zach." He tried to smile, but still felt a little nervous and awkward.

He'd had assistants before—usually awe-struck or intense young students—but this woman looked like no assistant he had ever encountered. She grasped his hand firmly, sandwiching his knuckles between strong, callused fingers.

"Dr. Shomron, I am Adira Senesh, and we need to get a few things clarified. Please follow me." She still hadn't smiled; she dropped his hand and led him through the airport.

"Uhh, we only have twenty minutes until departure," Zach said while making a show of looking at the large faced watch on his skinny wrist.

She didn't turn around. "They'll wait for us."

*He's more of a boy than I expected. Achhh, I hate babysitting jobs*, Adira thought as she looked up into a lens beside a door with no markings and no handle. In a moment it buzzed open and she led the young man in, nodding to a seated, severe old woman who glanced up briefly, and then motioned to one of three doors.

Inside there were two chairs and a table—that was it. Adira pointed at one of the chairs and the young man sat down with eyes wide behind his spectacles. She looked at him again. *He's nervous—good.* She could hear his feet tapping, and his fingers steepled, flexed and danced on the table in front of them.

"You are Dr. Zachariah Ben Shomron." She paused for a moment and leaned forward. "You are twenty-four years old, have doctorates in gravitational astrophysics, particle physics, quantum and pure mathematics. You have written numerous papers on black holes, strange particles and cosmic dark matter. You are currently a tenured professor at Tel Aviv University . . ." Adira recited by heart another few minutes of detail about his life, some of it not on public record, which left the young man in no doubt about her command and influence. She knew when people heard the minutiae of their life being revealed by someone they didn't know it usually created a sense of exposure, anxiety and helplessness, which made them open and receptive to authority.

The professor cleared his throat and asked quietly. "You're not really my assistant, are you?"

Adira smiled without humour and sat forward even further. "To anyone who asks . . . yes I am, and I'm also a Middle Eastern linguistics specialist." Her smile evaporated. "But really, Professor, *you* will be assisting me. My underlying role is to ensure that Israel's interests are protected and defended. I am about to describe our primary objectives to you, Dr. Shomron, and you will not say anything to anyone, or go anywhere, or do anything, without first checking with me."

Adira stared into the young man's face for several seconds before speaking evenly. "Be without any doubt, on this mission, you report to me."

Zachariah looked pale. "This is a mission?"

# Twelve

Ancient Arak—Middle Iranian Province of Markazi

Ahmad Al Janaddi exhaled the sweet-smelling smoke of his cigarette into the stinging dry morning air. He stood at the entrance to a camouflaged tunnel cut into the side of the mountain from where he could look out over the ancient city of Arak. Arak was an old city even at the time of Mohammed, built upon the ruins of an even earlier town called Daskerah, which in turn had been built on the settlement of Dolf Abad. The ruins of Dolf Abad were still accessible via the many ancient caves in the region; caves the excavation teams had since made good use of. The tunnel mouth Al Janaddi stood in had been carved to look like one of the hundreds of natural openings throughout the mountainous region.

One hundred and eighty miles south of Tehran and nearly 300 miles north-west of Persepolis, this region had always been considered military high ground. Rising over 5000 feet above sea level, it marked the beginning of where the dry desert turned to the bitterly cold and mountainous Markazi Province.

The ancient land was riddled with caves. Some, like the holy Shah Zand Cave, contained writing and symbols from the very first Persians. Some were even older than that—Al Janaddi had seen the carved script of the pre-Persian Elamics and Zoroastrians decorating the deeper cavern walls, as well as some inscriptions from languages older than recorded history. Legend had it they were the utterances of the very angels themselves. To this day, no scholar had been able to decipher them. Al Janaddi had stood before those words and wondered whether the men who wrote them thought they too could change the world.

The scientist's footsteps echoed in the silent corridor as he returned to the main laboratory. The Jamshid II facility under Arak had been designed differently to the complex once hidden beneath the ruins at Persepolis. The magnificent silver sphere was still there, for blasting uranium hexafluoride gas molecules to a speed-of-light escape velocity, but the separated Uranium 235, once the objective of the enrichment process, was now a discarded waste product. The purpose of the new Jamshid facility was to explore and refine the molecule collisions themselves.

The main chamber had been stripped of all electronic monitoring and recording equipment; it was bare save for the gleaming silver sphere at its centre. All the equipment and personnel had been moved to a specially designed secondary command centre 500 feet from the sphere chamber. As there would be no residual radiation remaining after each test run, the technicians would be able to re-enter quickly and replace any lost equipment in a matter of days. The facility's personnel should be safe this time. Only unfeeling electronic eyes and ears provided the sensory feedback. Lead-lined panelling and concrete reinforcing surrounded the room, causing a striking echo effect when even the simplest of tasks was performed there. The new equipment was more advanced—a benefit of the president's increased budget for the project, which he was now calling a "divine event." The in-lab cameras were equipped with high-speed drives and extremely sensitive media to record images at 10,000 frames per second, and sound could be analysed over the super and subsonic wavelengths. Al Janaddi was expecting there would be more data to study this time around.

He looked over to where a technician was painting a white line all the way around the sphere and shivered as he recalled his recent conversation with President Moshaddam.

"I need you to install seating for, say, a dozen martyrs in front of your beautiful sphere," the president had ordered.

"Er, you mean in the observation room, my President?"

"No, I do not. I mean in the sphere room. Close to the device itself."

Al Janaddi was glad the conversation was taking place over the phone so Moshaddam could not see his face. He closed his eyes for a moment as he remembered the body of Professor Shihab. He knew what proximity to the sphere could do to human tissue. He also knew what the testing of live subjects would do to any hope of international recognition for his work. He prayed that he wouldn't be ordered to sit in one of those seats himself.

"As you wish, my President," he'd replied. What else could he have said?

Now Al Janaddi wondered again about the men and women who would be chosen to behold the opening of the "Gateway to Allah" as the president was now calling it. Those souls were about to be transported somewhere, be it heaven or hell. The image of the misshapen corpse of Dr. Shihab leapt into his mind, and with it the taste of bile in the back of his throat.

# Thirteen

Hatzerim Air Base, Southern Israel

The B2 Spirit came to a halt on the shimmering runway, lowering slightly on its wheel arches to rest like a giant dark bird of prey. The radar-repellent coating ensured there was little reflection from the sun, and darkened windows and a sleek shape gave it a swift and futuristic appearance. The modified Spirit, with a wingspan of 170 feet, dwarfed the smaller Israeli F161 fighters that crowded the edges of the runway.

The B2 normally carried a terrifying armoury; depending on its role in battle, it could pack up to eighty 500-pound conventional weapons or half a dozen nuclear-tipped city-busters. Today, its cargo was only marginally less lethal—five elite soldiers jumped from the darkened interior and walked across the tarmac. With their insignia-free uniforms and hats pulled down over dark glasses, it was plain the men weren't there for sightseeing.

An Israeli soldier standing outside what looked like a squat pillbox saluted the HAWCs without looking at them and opened the heavy glass door. Once inside, Alex was slightly surprised to see that the small building was heavily fortified and loaded with surveillance lenses. It was otherwise bare save for a metal door leading to an elevator. The soldier pressed the elevator button and turned on his heel, the tempered glass door clicking shut behind him.

With a hiss the elevator door slid open. Alex stepped in first, followed by Sam and Hex. Rocky and Irish brought up the rear, but both stepped forward at the same time and for a brief second both pairs of broad shoulders became wedged in the opening.

"Finished?" Alex said to the two men.

Rocky stood aside and made a waving gesture with his arm. Irish stepped in, mumbling under his breath.

"I feel safer with you two here," Sam said, and winked at Rocky who grinned. Irish ignored them.

The elevator dropped rapidly, and when the doors hissed open they revealed a white corridor and two more soldiers standing behind a desk. One nodded at the HAWCs; the other just gave Alex a flat stare.

Sam elbowed Alex in the ribs, gesturing upwards with his chin. "Blast shield," he said softly.

Alex looked up and saw embedded in the ceiling behind the Israelis an inch-thick line of steel. The Israelis could seal in or out anything they wanted to. *Such is life in the Middle East*, he thought.

The nodder spoke. "Captain Hunter?"

"Yes," Alex said. He didn't salute or move to shake the man's hand.

"There are rooms set up for you and your men. You alone are to attend a briefing in one hour."

"Two of us will be attending," Alex said. "First Lieutenant Reid will be joining me." He motioned to the hulking HAWC standing just behind him.

The nodder turned his head slightly and said something softly in Hebrew to the man next to him. The man grunted in response and the nodder spoke to Alex again, a small downturned smile on his face. "I'm sorry, there are specific instructions—"

*"Bachur, ani yode'a ivrit ein be'ayot."* Sam cut the man off with a single, softly spoken sentence in perfect Hebrew.

The nodder's cheeks reddened and he said, "Please follow me, sir."

Alex looked at Sam and raised his eyebrows.

"Just called him a kid," Sam said, "and told him I understand Hebrew."

Alex nodded. "Good. We're not here to make friends."

Outside their rooms, the man stopped and turned again to the HAWCs. "Captain Hunter, I will be back to collect you in one hour."

"Us; you'll be collecting *us* in one hour," Alex replied.

Exactly fifty-nine minutes later, there was a knock on the door of Alex's room. The nodder was back.

Alex felt pretty good after a shower and half an hour's rest, and as he and Sam followed the young Israeli down the corridor he could feel all his senses opening to the building around him. In one hand he held a sealed folder; the other he placed against the wall a number of times as they walked—he could feel the vibrations of a lot of machinery and people through the mortar and reinforcing. *Pretty sizeable base hidden below the desert*, he thought.

They reached a double set of white doors and the nodder knocked once and turned the handle. He stood back and gave his familiar nod before disappearing back down the corridor.

Alex pushed the door open and stepped into the large room, followed by Sam. It held two desks, one with several closed folders on its surface, the other with a plate of sandwiches. Two people stood there waiting, both silent.

Alex looked first at the man—he was tall, all angles and elbows, and wore a pair of nerdy wire spectacles. He was young and clearly nervous; his fingers danced in constant motion on the end of scarecrow-thin arms. Alex looked away before the kid passed out from the tension.

The other Israeli was a young woman—also tall, moderately attractive, no make-up. She didn't need it—strength and health radiated from her clear eyes and olive cheeks. She didn't seem nervous at all and scrutinised the Americans with a confident gaze.

She walked towards the HAWCs with her hand outstretched. "Good afternoon. I am Adira Senesh, and this is my colleague, Dr. Zachariah Shomron. We will be assisting you on your project."

Alex shook her hand and almost smiled; her palm was strong and callused with the grip of a weapon carrier. Their eyes locked—no movement, no flinching or blinking; each seemed to recognise the potential lethality in the other. Adira nodded and released his hand, turning to Sam to shake his hand as well.

When Alex took Zachariah Shomron's hand, the young man could not look him in the eye. His nerves became even more noticeable through various tics and twitches. The two Israelis could not have been more different, Alex thought. He remembered the Hammer saying that one would be a Mossad torpedo. No prizes for guessing which one.

Alex looked around the small room. "The general's not joining us?"

"No," the woman said. "We are authorised to speak on his and Israel's behalf." She waited a second, presumably to see if Alex was going to have a problem with that, then led the two HAWCs to sit down. Sam immediately attacked the plate of sandwiches.

"Events are moving quickly, Captain Hunter," the woman said, "and may be more complex and serious than we thought."

She turned to her nervous colleague and said something rapidly in Hebrew. Zach looked anxious; he was obviously receiving some sort of instruction. Alex could tell Sam was listening to her words; he caught the lieutenant's eye and gave an almost imperceptible shake of his head. The big HAWC got it: *listen, but don't let on that you understand.*

Zachariah Shomron gulped a few times, cleared his throat and then began to brief the HAWCs on the scientific details of the mission. He spoke for two hours, his confidence building as he got onto familiar territory. He described the strength of the gamma pulse and its potential emanation point, and flagged the unusual lack of any fallout plus the puzzling sudden disappearance of any latent emissions. He also told them that Israeli intelligence services had reported that the Iranians had recovered a heavily irradiated body many miles from the initial site, believed to belong to one of the scientists involved in the test.

"In my opinion, the signatures of the radiation pulse do not fit any geophysical creation—natural or man-made," he told the HAWCs. "They do, however, have the characteristics of a gravitational entity called a black hole. I believe that either by default or design, the Iranians created a gravity event—something like a miniature black hole—in their laboratory. It probably absorbed the entire facility and then evaporated before it fell to the centre of the planet under its own weight."

Sam had been listening with his mouth hanging open. He shook his head slightly now and leaned forward. "Dr. Shomron, on a recent project, I had the pleasure of working with the scientists in Geneva as they prepared to test-fire their massive particle collider. The scientists explained to me the principles behind high-energy collisions and the theoretical creation of strange new particles, possibly even mini black holes, but the technologies required are, in a word, massive. The facility in Geneva is just over sixteen miles long, clad in reinforced concrete and steel, and took over twenty years to build out in the open. The Iranians couldn't duplicate that on the surface, let alone underground. They just don't have the technological expertise."

Zach pointed at Sam's chest as though awarding him a medal for asking the right questions. "You're absolutely right, Lieutenant. But that assumption is based on standard high-energy collision technology using rotational speed over distance as the medium for particle impact. There are other ways to create the necessary speed without the distance— you just need to find a stable acceleration trigger. I believe that somehow, some way, the Iranians found that trigger."

He pushed his spectacles back up his nose, one foot tapping restively on the carpet, as if it were trying to talk the rest of his body into getting up and taking a walk.

Adira spoke to Alex. "The pressing importance is described by two critical pieces of information." She held up a finger: "One, we now know that Natanz, although a working enrichment facility, was just a front. That facility must have cost them billions of rials, but they were willing to sacrifice it to the United Nations to hide what they were doing at Persepolis, the site of the powerful gamma pulse. We believe that the Persepolis facility is now destroyed or has suffered a serious setback. And two," she held up a second finger, "we believe they have another site, which they have rushed into full production. Whatever they did at Persepolis, they liked it and are now trying to reproduce it."

Alex noticed her fingers had now clenched into a fist. "But reproduce what," he said. "A black hole? Why? What can they possibly do with it? My understanding is that these things weigh thousands of tons and disappear almost as soon as they are created—how does one contain or use something like that? What could they gain from creating this type of entity?" Alex had his own theories, but needed to get the Israelis to cut to the chase.

This time Zachariah cut Adira off. "You're right, Captain, a black hole just a little bigger than this room would weigh as much as our planet. But in just ten seconds it could output more gamma radiation than the sun could in 10 billion years. You don't need to create a large black hole—and you wouldn't want to, as even a small one could interact with regular matter and start a chain reaction that would continue to devour the planetary substance until Earth was destroyed. But that energy source, that magnificent energy source—just imagine if it could be harnessed. It would render all other energies and fuels obsolete. Future wars will be fought over fuel, or lack of it. This power could be a primary reason for making war redundant!"

Zachariah Shomron was almost bouncing in his seat with excitement. Adira placed her hand on his forearm and squeezed—perhaps to settle the young man down, Alex thought, or cut him off before he said something she didn't want him to.

"You asked what the Iranians could do with this type of thing, Captain Hunter?" Adira said. "Well, how about a type of particle-beam weapon directing a 10,000-sievert burst of gamma radiation? They could destroy anything with that beam—the only thing that would stop it would be ten feet of solid lead or the curve of the earth. Everything else it touched would either disintegrate or be carbonised." Adira's eyes burned as she spoke; not with Zachariah Shomron's scientific curiosity, but with anger.

"You seem well informed for a linguistics expert, Ms. Senesh," Alex said, keeping his gaze flat as his eyes met hers.

Before Adira could respond, Zachariah bounced to his feet. "And what about space travel, time travel or even inter-dimensional travel? Black holes aren't just universal garbage compactors—we still don't know what really happens when you enter the singularity. Does matter contacting with dark matter cancel you out? Are you simply absorbed, crushed, or do you go somewhere else . . . or some *when* else—a different time, a different universe perhaps? All we know is that once something passes through a black hole, it exits our universe. In fact, in 1921 Kal—"

Sam held up one hand. "Dr. Shomron, if you're going to talk in detail about Kaluza-Klein or superstring theory, you're going to lose us. Can you break it down a little further?"

The young Israeli steepled his fingers, enjoyment showing at the corners of his mouth. "I was, sorry. Okay, um . . . in the most basic terms, a black hole is defined by an inner and outer perimeter. The outer rim of the black hole, really its definition, is called the event horizon; past this point there is no return . . . of anything. Black holes really aren't black, they have no colour—the blackness is actually the *absence* of colour. The absence of anything really—colour, light, heat, everything. Once past the event horizon, you enter the actual entity, the singularity."

Alex opened his folder and retrieved a small pile of eight by ten glossy photographs. He held the first one up to the Israelis—it showed the biological mess that had once been the German scientist Hoeckler. Adira didn't flinch, but Zachariah paled.

Alex tapped the gruesome image. "How does this fit in? This is, or was, a German national by the name of Rudolf Hoeckler. We know he was working with the Iranians on a secret uranium-enrichment program, but it seems he got himself caught up in some type of accident. His body was recovered just outside of Colorado Springs—we don't know how he got there, and we suspect Germany and Iran don't know how he got there either—or, for that matter, that he got there at all."

"I . . . I knew Professor Hoeckler," Zachariah stuttered. "He was a brilliant physicist, and had some groundbreaking ideas on the laser enhancement of particles in the fissionable materials purification processes. In fact, the laser techniques he used . . . hey, that's it! There's your acceleration trigger—Hoeckler must have had a breakthrough. Or thought he did. This is amazing."

Zachariah went through the photographs, nodding as though confirming what he suspected. "He was irradiated, right?"

"At least 500 sieverts," Alex said. "Made a lot of people sick before he was sealed into a lead crate."

"Amazing. I've never seen this sort of physical distortion before—in fact, no one has—but I've read theories on it. Have you ever heard of 'spaghettification?' " Zachariah didn't wait for an answer. "It's where the atomic structure of mass is stretched by enormous gravitational tidal forces—like what's theoretically supposed to happen when you're falling into a black hole. Your physical fibre becomes elongated as your somatic structure comes under the influence of the most powerful gravitational force in our universe."

"Very interesting, Dr. Shomron," said Alex as he put the images back in their folder. "That could theoretically explain his condition, but how the hell did he get onto American soil?"

Zachariah's brow creased as though he was trying to tease apart a tangled physics equation. "I don't know for sure, but if I had to guess I'd say that he was washed back . . ." He paused and tapped his lips with his fingers. "The universe doesn't like an imbalance—if he exited to another universe, then, through basic universal elasticity, he should have been washed back into our universe. But if he weren't, then something else had to be washed in in his place to restore the balance. I guess it was lucky he even appeared back on Earth.

You know, there's a theory that postulates other dimensions and universes as strings and—"

Adira raised her voice over her colleague's. "You asked what the Iranians would do with this type of technology, Captain. If it were a rational regime we were dealing with, I might be able to answer that question, but it isn't rational. Mahmoud Moshaddam reads the Qur'an as if it's a script for his own life; he truly believes that if mankind is cleansed from the planet the pious believers will rise again to form a true Islamic caliphate worldwide. Every time he makes a speech, he includes some reference to the apocalypse. Captain Hunter, we must not underestimate Moshaddam's ability to create some sort of man-made extinction event just to see his vision come true."

Alex noticed that Adira's hand had made a fist again and her eyes bored into his as she spoke. "We need to find that second site as soon as possible; we can't afford to wait and see what they plan to do with this technology. We have agents working day and night in Iran to find this information for us. Make no mistake, Captain, this technology is beyond dangerous. It needs to be eradicated immediately."

# Fourteen

It was late afternoon by the time the briefing and strategy session was finished, and Alex had talked through the HAWCs' approach plan. Afterwards, back in his room, Alex put a call through to Hammerson and updated him on the new Israeli theories.

Hammerson called back fifteen minutes later: the mission profile had changed. If the energy pulse was the result of new technology, Alex was to upload or secure that technology and await further orders. Priority was now information retrieval; destruction had become the secondary option.

Hammerson said he was sending Sam an "exa-box" from a local US technology outpost. Alex had heard of them: small flat boxes the size of a cigarette pack with multiple ports for being plugged into any computer. The small boxes had the ability to store one exabyte of information—that was a "1" with eighteen zeros after·it. Alex had been told the device could easily store all the words from every human language that had ever existed—and be slipped into your back pocket. Today, information was power, and an exa-box was the latest way to steal and transport it.

Alex lay on his bunk and stared at the ceiling. *Secure the technology, and get it back home . . . hmm.* How were seven foreign agents going to secure a heavily guarded laboratory in the middle of a foreign country while he tried to back up an exabyte of data? He closed his eyes and thought through some scenarios. None looked easy or made a lot of sense, but there was one that stuck in his mind: where he and his team were unsuccessful. If their mission failed, Israel would send in a squadron of F-161 Sufa Falcons armed with laser-guided AGM-45 Shrike missiles and some big AGM-130s with thermobaric warheads for deep ground penetration. Or worse—a single mega-kiloton missile to vaporise everything for miles. The fallout would be off the radioactive spectrum. A lot was at stake here.

Alex was also worried about taking Dr. Shomron along. He wasn't concerned for the woman—if she was Mossad—either Kidon or Metsada—she could take care of herself. But the young scientist, even with the HAWCs there, would be significantly exposed. That said, Alex knew Shomron would be needed on the ground. He may be the only one who could actually identify what it was they were looking for. *But does he know what he's getting himself into?*

Alex shifted on the cot, trying to get comfortable. His mind was racing and his headache had returned. *Damnit, can't babysit them all,* he thought. *And if the scientist volunteered, it was his own head after all.* Still Alex couldn't shake the feeling that he didn't have all the facts. *Something's missing, but what?* All the puzzle pieces weren't being laid out. *Too late now,* he thought, *we're committed.*

He tossed and turned for another fifteen minutes, then surrendered to his body's agitation. *Gotta burn some energy,* he thought as he got to his feet.

Adira found the American HAWC captain wandering along the corridor, trying various doors. At first she'd assumed he was spying, but the T-shirt and towel around his neck and the embarrassed look on his face convinced her he was genuinely looking for somewhere to exercise. She knew herself what the body was like before a mission.

She looked him up and down and grinned. "No gymnasium or running track, and don't ask about a soda machine either. To use one of your own American phrases, you're not in Kansas anymore, Captain. And don't even consider jogging up and down the corridor or you'll be shot."

She laughed and let him off the hook. "I can offer you a

coffee, and we can talk through more details of the plan. If you want, you can even do some push-ups on my floor."

Alex laughed too and gave a slight bow of the head. "Lead on."

She took him to a room more spartan than his own. She kicked a seat around for him to sit on and flicked the button on the electric kettle, which boiled furiously. "Instant, no sugar, no milk, and no cookies. The water also tastes like metal." She turned to look at him with raised eyebrows.

"Just the way I like it," Alex responded with mock enthusiasm.

Adira handed him the steaming metallic-smelling brew, then sipped her own in silence. She could feel the tall American looking at her, assessing her. For the first time in many years she felt awkward, self-conscious. *Achhh, stop it*, she thought. She knew there was something on his mind; something he wanted to ask. She waited.

Alex looked at her over his cup. "Ms. Senesh, why do I feel you're simply looking for a lift and some US armour plating, and once we locate the target you'll go on a killing spree that ends up making the mission more kamikaze than Special Ops?"

If not for her training, Adira may have spluttered coffee over herself. She hadn't expected an American to be so direct, or to try and flush away her cover so quickly. Now she wondered if she'd ever had any cover with this agent. Best to "play ball," as the Americans called it.

"Captain Hunter, my orders are to assist Dr. Shomron in the detection of the facility and, if necessary, to aid you in the destruction of any threatening technology. That is all." She kept her gaze steady as Alex's eyes drilled into hers.

He shook his head slowly. "I'm not sure you're worth the risk, Ms. Senesh. Dr. Shomron will be a physical liability, but I can manage that. What I would find distracting is you making a mess while we're trying to do our jobs."

Adira felt a flush of anger colour her cheeks but she responded as evenly as she could. "Captain Hunter, Israelis have never been a liability on any mission, *ever*. With us you

will succeed, this I promise. You should be aware that if you
were unsuccessful in your assignment, then our government
would mount its own mission. It would, unfortunately, be a
little more heavy-handed than what you are planning. The
Iranians will retaliate, of course, and also shut off their oil
supply lines. And, while they're at it, activate hundreds of
terrorist sleeper cells internationally. It will get very expensive and very bloody for all of us. My orders are to assist
you, and I give my word that I will follow your commands at
all times."

Adira was breathing heavily when she finished. No one
had ever dared infer she was either a risk or a liability for
any mission.

Alex looked into her face for several seconds; she didn't
flinch.

"Ms. Senesh," he said, "our priority is to understand what
we are dealing with before there is any 'destruction of threatening technology.' We don't even know yet what it is we
would be trying to destroy. This threat has come from out
of nowhere, and if it's anything like Dr. Shomron has described, then frankly I would prefer to be dealing with a
nuclear bomb. Destruction is the fast and easy option, and if
we could go back in time and stop yet another way mankind
has worked out to annihilate itself then I'd be the first to do
it. But we can't. The genie is out of its bottle—it's already
here." Alex put his cup down and brought his hands together
in front of him. "You and Dr. Shomron will be assisting us
in intelligence gathering—we need to better understand the
threat. Both our countries may have to face it again somewhere, sometime. This may be our only chance to know the
devil, so to speak." Alex looked hard again into her eyes and
opened his hands. "Can you do that for us, Ms. Senesh?"

Adira held his gaze, trying to see if he really believed
what he had just said. She knew that the only reason Israel
still existed today was because it had greater firepower than
its neighbours, all of whom would love to see it obliterated..
She looked from his eyes to the rest of his face; she could

see strength and honour in his features. *A noble man*, she thought, *and perhaps a little naive.*

Adira smiled and lifted her near empty cup in a salute. "Of course, Captain Hunter. If we can get close to the technology, the blueprints, or even the scientists who designed it, we can help you understand it."

She liked the tall HAWC, but she had her orders. Leave nothing standing, and find the key to the new American weapon, Arcadian. She hoped Captain Hunter wasn't going to be a problem.

Back out in the corridor, Alex assessed the Israeli woman again. He knew she was a professional, and didn't doubt she could mask her emotions and hold her composure, probably even under torture. Still, he could tell she hadn't been telling him the whole truth.

"Metsada or Kidon?" he asked her.

The question elicited no surprise, not even a blink. "Metsada: level five. And you, Captain, how long in the HAWCs? I heard about your work in the Antarctic."

Alex smiled but didn't reply. He should have known that the Mossad information network would be just as active in America as it was everywhere else in the world. He was relieved she was Metsada. The Kidon were assassins, just brawny torpedoes. The Metsada matched their lethality, but added in the key element that differentiated a good agent from a special agent—intelligence.

"I need to check in with headquarters and grab your kits," Alex told her. "Bring Dr. Shomron with you over to our billet— Lieutenant Reid will introduce you to the guys." He gave a small salute and peeled off at a branch in the corridor, then he stopped. "One more thing: try not to kill anyone, will you?"

It was Adira's turn to smile.

# Fifteen

Rocky Lagudi took a step forward. To Adira, he looked like a man who hadn't had the opportunity to talk to a woman in a very long time. Though inches shorter than she was, he straightened his back and bounced on his toes to try and look her in the eye. Sam Reid and Hex Winter nodded and said polite "hellos," while Francis O'Riordan simply slow-blinked at her and Zachariah.

Adira stuck to her cover story with the three HAWCs. She knew that she would have to break from it during the mission, but not until the time was right. She had worked with Americans before—they were competitive. Best if these men focused on the mission objective and not a Special Forces rival. She suspected that they'd find out about her soon enough—after all, Alex Hunter now knew the truth.

Adira shifted the attention to Zachariah, encouraging him to talk about the gamma pulse, its dangers, its possible origination point, and also what they suspected was being engineered from within Iran. She guided him in his delivery, skilfully ensuring he gave the men just enough information to inform them as necessary, but changed his course when she thought he was straying into an area she wasn't prepared for them to go just yet.

All the men asked good questions, with Sam Reid again displaying a knowledge of particle physics that clearly astonished Zachariah. At times it seemed to Adira that Zach and Sam were speaking a language that was inaccessible to the rest of the room.

The red-headed HAWC, the one they called Irish, tilted his chair back, resting his shoulders and head against the drab green plasterboard wall behind him. "But why do you two need to be with us?" he asked when Zach had finished. "No offence, miss, but we can be briefed right here, right now. Or we can get voice comm updates while we're in the field. He's a smart kid and you look fit, but you're just gonna be baggage when the hot rain starts comin' down."

The temptation to kick the man's chair from under him was nearly overwhelming. Adira reined in her irritation and explained as patiently as she could that they had significant knowledge of the language and local customs, and would be making use of an embedded Israeli network that would be vital in getting them in and out safely.

But Irish wasn't finished. "We don't need you guys there for that. Just give us your logistics and we'll take over. Besides, we've got our own networks in place. Bottom line, missy, you science types ain't cut out for this type of field work."

Missy? Adira felt a spot of anger start to burn deep in her stomach. She exhaled slowly through her nose—she needed the HAWCs onside. Her tone was a little more authoritative this time. "Your own networks? Lieutenant, your *networks* are paid informants who despise you. They would gladly sell you all for another handful of American dollars. You will need us, and the Israeli spy infrastructure, to complete your mission safely, and we are going to be there. We are tougher than you think, *Second* Lieutenant O'Riordan. Besides, I believe it is your superior's call, and that's already been made. I'm sorry."

"Israelis are gonna make us safe and we need 'em?" Irish scoffed. "Lady, I don't think so. You guys've been draggin' us into fistfights for twenty years, and, frankly, we're the only thing stoppin' you being burned off the map. You reckon you're tough? How hard can it be to use a tank against kids in rags throwin' rocks? No wonder them Palestinian mooks hate you. I'd say you need us more'n we need you."

Adira narrowed her eyes and was about to respond when

Zach stepped forward with a face as red as fire and a voice only slightly cracking with nerves.

"You have the ignorance to question our worth or our spirit? We Israelis die every day for what we believe in. Our country was created in 1948 and since then we have produced more scientific papers than any other nation; we have more museums, have planted more trees, and have the highest living standard in the entire Middle East. And we do all of this without ever knowing a day free from war or terror. Israel has never retreated or lost a war—can you say that? No, I didn't think so."

Adira looked briefly at Zach with surprise and admiration. *He's braver than he looks*, she thought.

O'Riordan's clenched hands came down hard in front of him and he started to rock his chair forward. Adira's hand shot out like a striking snake. There was a *thunk*, and a blackened sliver of metal stuck out of the plasterboard less than a match-width from O'Riordan's temple.

"Kids in rags?" Adira spat. "*Jiffa!* Your stupidity is matched only by your lack of knowledge about our conflict. We live under a rain of hundreds of rockets per week. Our women and children are torn apart by ball-bearing explosions, and when they lie on the road, broken and in misery, the terrorists hand out sweetmeats while dancing and ululating in their streets. The average Palestinian wants peace with us, but there is a cancerous core that wants eternal conflict. We simply cut out that cancer; like surgeons."

Before O'Riordan could do something stupid, Hex Winter stepped forward and pulled the thin blade from the wall. "Twin-edged, night-blackened blade, vase-shaped handle, foiled grip. Looks like a Fairbairn–Sykes stiletto, but it's shorter and got no pommel."

Adira could tell he was trying to diffuse the situation. She smiled a thank you, though she kept one eye on O'Riordan as she half-turned to the tall, fair-haired HAWC. "It's our own design—an Israeli wasp throwing spike. You throw it like a spear; it's not designed to swing in the air, hence no pommel to balance the weight. My brother taught me to throw it."

Hex hefted the knife, spun it around in his fingers expertly and laid it over the back of his forearm for her to take. "You'll have to show me your throwing technique and concealment one day," he said. "Or maybe your brother will." He winked at her.

Sam Reid stepped forward to take the knife before Adira could. He held it up close to his face. "Israeli wasp knife, you say? Seen these before, but it wasn't in some backyard family knife-throwing competition. It was during a mission in the Indian Ocean, just south of Oman—me and a few Ranger buddies were tasked with intercepting a North Korean ship suspected of carrying yellowcake for delivery to Iraq. By the time we got there it was a ghost ship. No survivors, no bodies and no cargo. Plenty of rads on the Geiger counters though—something hot *had* been there. Saw a few of these knives stuck in the side of some boxes below deck. We found out later that we'd just missed Operation Goldenbird—one of the Mossad's little meet-and-greet parties. Very clean job."

Adira took the blade but didn't respond. Outside of Metsada, missions were never acknowledged. Nevertheless, she sensed the mood in the small room shift from one of tension to professional interest and respect.

Except for the redheaded O'Riordan, of course. He just mumbled, "What's a *jiffa*?"

Sam spoke again, ignoring Irish's question. "We don't have to be friends, but there *will be* military respect. And that's an order." He looked from Irish to Rocky and then across to Adira and Zach.

Adira just nodded. Zachariah shifted uncomfortably and said, "Can we start again?"

"What's a *Jiffa*?" O'Riordan still wasn't smiling.

WOMACK Army Medical Centre, Neuropsychological Unit—Fort Bragg

It was just after midnight. The door to the lab opened and shut with little more than the sound of a breath. A figure dressed in army fatigues moved in the dark to the recessed filing cabinets with a sure-footedness that came from prior knowledge of the room's interior.

All the cabinets were locked; not by something as simple as a flat key tumbler, but with the latest algorithm-based electronic security. Each drawer was in effect a stand-alone safe, protected by a quarter-inch of toughened steel and a ten-digit keypad.

The figure crouched beside one of the drawers and pulled back the plastic glove on his left hand. Written on his wrist were eight numbers, which he entered into the keypad. A small red light turned green and the drawer popped open half an inch. The figure counted the folders within, stopped at a designated number and withdrew the file. He shone a pencil torch for a second on the title: *Arcadian*. It was the one.

# Sixteen

Mostafa Hossein, the leader of the Islamic Guardian Council, watched President Moshaddam climb the podium in the UN Assembly hall. It was the first time an Iranian president had delivered an address to the world's leaders and their representatives and he received a standing ovation as he stood at the lectern and looked out over his audience. To date, the president's rhetoric had swung between brilliantly pragmatic to frighteningly apocalyptic, and Hossein knew that his appearance at the Assembly had been eagerly anticipated—by some for the entertainment value alone.

Hossein nodded to several of the Middle Eastern representatives as he took his seat. Though Iran was in diplomatic conflict with many of the Western nations, Moshaddam had his international supporters and could count on them to deliver enthusiastic applause for any barb he may wish to sling at the West today.

The president had been embarrassingly excited in the car, almost feverish. He was like a small boy who was only just managing to keep some great secret behind his lips, Hossein thought. He was calm now though—smoothing his slightly crumpled brown jacket, before drawing from his pocket a wad of notes which he spread on the lectern. He shuffled them, looked up and smiled, then went back to silent reading and more shuffling. The silence in the room thickened, until it was almost a living thing filling the room with expectation and suspense.

Moshaddam raised his arms, held forth both his open hands, closed his eyes and finally began to speak.

"Distinguished heads of state, distinguished representatives, excellencies, ladies and gentlemen, praise be to Allah the merciful, the father of us all, the all-knowing and almighty God, for blessing me with this chance to speak to you here today, representing the great but humble nation of Iran before you, the international community.

"The Almighty did not create humanity to make war on each other. He did not create humanity to lie, steal or cheat each other. Nor did he create humanity so it could batter, burn and bomb each other. Some nations are rich beyond belief, but they want more; they have nuclear arms, but don't want others to have them; they profess to follow God, but allow their own people to degrade each other with unspeakable acts." The president lowered his hands, opened his eyes and sought out the unblinking stare of Harvey Benton, the United States' UN representative. Moshaddam smiled slightly.

His voice rose in volume and emotion as he continued. "How can any nation profess to love its fellow men while it allows its own people to murder each other in numbers the size of a small nation?

"Distinguished people, I ask you, can you drink oil? Will money soothe the father of the child who has been crushed beneath a building that was destroyed by a bomb? Can you be happy amassing ever more wealth while there are nations that endure ever more poverty, suffering and misery?"

There was total silence in the great hall. Moshaddam smiled condescendingly at Benton and leaned towards him slightly, as if daring him to challenge his words.

"Who has more authority? The man who rules with the sword, or the man who leads with love and infinite wisdom? I tell you, the people of Iran choose love and wisdom. Today, most honoured dignitaries, when you sit down to your cake and sweetmeats, remember those who do not have even a single piece of bread due to the evil sanctions imposed by this gathering of nations. I have met many good and great leaders from around the globe who are living in fear, who are being strangled and bullied by a few permanent members of this very council. How can . . . no, *why* can a few nations, through the power of their wealth, their bombs and armies, decide to occupy and harvest the riches of other nations while we all sit idly by?"

Hossein saw Benton catch the eye of the ambassador for Britain, who shook his head and rolled his eyes. Many other Western nation representatives wore expressions of disbelief or disdain. Hossein wasn't surprised. He stole a quick glance at the Israeli representative. The man's expression was stony, but his face was blood red. However, the Middle East nations, a few from South America and even some from Europe were nodding enthusiastically. *And so the geopolitical lines become drawn again*, thought Hossein as he stroked his long grey beard.

The president lifted his hands in an almost beseeching manner—theatrics not lost on Benton or the other Westerners. "I say on behalf of all people of the Middle East: please leave our lands, we do not need you. Leave our people, they do not want you. Leave our faith, or you will answer to Allah and be judged most harshly."

He fell silent for some minutes, and a murmur began to ripple around the Assembly. At last, the president put his open palms on top of one another over his heart. "There are over 6 billion people in our world," he said, "and they are all equal before Allah. Do you think he would let some be free and others be subjugated? All are God's creatures and worthy of respect. May the Almighty bless the heroic struggles of those valiant warriors of any faith who fight aggression, oppression, invasion and subjugation. For those who defend their faith, they shall talk to God before all others."

Moshaddam closed his eyes and spoke softly, as if in prayer. "Oh almighty God, all men and women are your creatures, and we beseech you to reveal the Hidden One, the Twelfth Imam, the Last Prophet, to guide us. Show us the Perfect Human who has been long promised, and let us be among his followers who strive for his cause. Make us worthy for the return of the Prophet."

The president's eyes remained closed as he raised his finger and wagged it at the gathered delegates as if they were misbehaving schoolchildren. Hossein wondered if he was going too far.

"The Last Prophet will return, the Hidden One, the Mahdi, and make himself known to the world of humanity. His return will be the most significant event since the coming of Mohammed, and will have dire consequences for the infidels and the apostates. His return will herald the Final Judgment and the end of history. He shall return at the head of the Forces of Righteousness to do battle with the hordes of evil in one final, apocalyptic war. When evil has been defeated once and for all, the Mahdi will rule the world for a thousand, thousand years and bring about perfect spirituality among all peoples."

Moshaddam opened his eyes, looked up at the spotlight high above him and smiled. He covered his heart with his hands once again, bowed and gathered his notes.

Every representative from the Middle East was on his feet, stamping and applauding. The rest remained seated, with expressions of rancour or confusion on their faces. Not since Yasser Arafat brought a gun into the Assembly had there been such an obvious division amongst the gathered nations.

Hossein saw Harvey Benton head quickly for the door, his phone in his hand.

Hossein sat in the black Mercedes and watched as the Iranian president was rushed towards the waiting car. Two massive, black-suited bodyguards pushed photographers and journalists roughly out of the way to clear his path. A huge grin split Moshaddam's face and his eyes shone with excitement. He climbed into the car and pulled Hossein in close to him so he could be heard over the flash of cameras and the shouts of the demonstrators held back from the vehicle.

"My friend, they were like flies in honey. I believe Allah put them all under a spell as I spoke—and I know why. I felt the Divine light again. Did you see the halo appear around my head when I mentioned the Mahdi?"

Hossein smiled but his eyes remained flat and impassive. The president was a deeply religious man, more so than any other president they had ever had, and like all good Muslims he lived his life solely by the teaching of the Qur'an. His fervour went far beyond that, however, and he was prone to seeing portents and prophecies in the most ordinary of things. It was said the president could see the names of the prophets in the curve of a hummingbird's tongue.

Hossein closed his eyes and sank back into the plush leather seat. He would talk to the Supreme Leader on his return. It was one thing to poke a finger in the eye of the United States; it was quite another to stand before them and talk of war.

# Seventeen

Marv Dasht Basin, Southern Iran

The lighting inside the B2 Spirit turned a deep red and the
double doors of the undercarriage slowly opened with a
barely perceptible whine. The stealth craft slowed in its dash
across the foreign airspace and a bone-chilling cold washed
in as the speed corona caught up with the sleek dark shape.

At 35,000 feet, nothing below was visible to the team
clinging to the thin platform at the edge of the bomb doors.
All they were aware of was an empty blackness and the scream
of high-altitude wind being shredded by thousands of pounds
of supersonic aircraft.

All eyes were on Alex.

*Go.* Alex heard the command in his earpiece and nodded
at the team. Without a second thought, he dived into the
square of rushing blackness. The others followed.

Six human missiles streaked towards the earth, arms
held tight by their sides and feet only slightly splayed to create an aerodynamic lightning-bolt shape. They cut through
the thin air at nearly 400 miles an hour. The scream of the
wind at this velocity would have shattered their eardrums if
not for the helmets and lowered visors. Alex couldn't contain the elation he felt and almost whooped with delight.
Even so, he knew this wasn't the highest jump that had ever
been achieved. In 1960, an American Air Force captain by
the name of Kittinger had descended from over 100,000 feet
wearing a special pressurised suit. He'd reached a speed of

700 miles per hour, and nearly lost a hand due to the failure of his pressurised suit glove. The hand had swelled to the size of a football by the time he finally made landfall.

The sun was coming up over the horizon, and at this altitude Alex could see the curve of the globe falling away around his team. There was little cloud below them and the green and brown of the Marv Dasht Basin at the foot of the Kouh-e Rahmat, the Mountain of Mercy, was visible. Soon he made out a small patchwork of sand-coloured structures at the foot of the mountain—the ancient ruins of Persepolis. They appeared to grow directly out of a massive spur of stone, hewn by giants from the surrounding natural rock. The lights of Shiraz, some thirty miles to the southwest, twinkled among the predawn shadows.

Technically, the HAWC team could communicate with each other via the microphones built into their helmets, but the roar of air rushing past at high speed meant that conversations were limited to single-word commands or acknowledgements. It didn't really matter; the HAWCs only needed to be briefed once—they knew what they had to do.

At 20,000 feet, and a word from Alex, the team split into two groups. Alex had given Hex the lead over the Red team—Irish, Rocky and Adira; while he would lead the Blue team in, comprising Sam and Zach. Normally Sam would have been the Red team leader, but Alex wanted him to cover the young Israeli scientist as well as provide him with logistical support. They would only separate for a few miles, but if one of the teams was spotted—or, worse, engaged—the other team would provide covering support or complete the mission solo.

Sam had drawn the short straw and had jumped with Zach strapped to his chest. Not such a bad deal for Sam really, as the young scientist absorbed most of the blasting wind. At those descent speeds and without hardened stomach muscles, Zach would be cramping for days.

Alex watched out of the corner of his eye as the Red team became dots in the distance. He didn't dare turn his head too much; even the slightest shift while in freefall at maximum speed could cause a broad looping turn or change of direction. He thought of Adira's courage and the blind commitment she and her countrymen displayed. As expected, the Israelis' network had come through before the Americans' and Adira had organised for a few members of the local Mossad cell to meet them. Alex was in awe of these agents who often lived for years among another country's people, knowing that being found out would mean extreme torture and violent death. Even on mission completion, their successes could never be acknowledged publicly as retribution had been known to follow many years later. These networks were tough, dedicated and highly professional.

Thinking of the spy networks brought to mind his last conversation with the Hammer and the news of the break-in at the Fort Bragg medical facility. "It could have been Mossad," his superior had said. Alex knew his file was kept in the underground vault called "deep secure," but exactly what the file contained even he didn't know. Hammerson had informed him that the intruder had obtained an administration shell—Alex wasn't identified by name, and there were no photographs. But the supposedly secure facility had been compromised, and now someone knew enough about him to target him. And if it was Mossad then that information might find its way to Adira Senesh.

Alex didn't have time to worry about that now. Ground was coming up fast—it was nearly showtime. A chute was usually deployed anywhere between 5000 and 2000 feet. In a HALO jump, the covert low opening meant that no canopy plume would be deployed until below 1000 feet—you hit hard, but you were visible and therefore vulnerable for less time. With the extra weight, Sam would feel it the most—unless, of course, he used Zach as a cushion. Alex smiled; he knew exactly what Sam would do.

*Impact.* Alex heard the grunts over his comm unit. At the velocity they were travelling, the chute gave an average-sized body a lot of jolt when it was slowed by eight-tenths of its drop speed in a few dozen feet. However, that was nothing compared to the impact on landing. At twenty-five feet per second, even with the best bent-knee drop and roll, there were a lot of sore bones the next day. Alex counted off the grunts. *Good*, he thought, *all down.*

Sam unhooked a groggy Zach from his harness and half-dragged him to cover, while Alex quickly buried all the parachutes in the soft sand. An outcrop of rocks gave them some protection so they could communicate with the Red team who was now several miles to their direct north. *All down, no broken bones. Good start*, thought Alex.

He looked over at Zach who had his visor up and was throwing up onto the sand.

The Red team were burying their chutes when two blips of light flickered at them from out of the semi-darkness. The HAWCs flattened to the ground and drew their weapons, but Adira held up her hand and responded with a triple flicker from her own torch. Two men dressed in the robes and head shawls of desert tribesmen walked towards the group. One kept his eyes on the large Americans while the other spoke in hurried Hebrew to Adira. It was obvious to the watching HAWCs that she carried some rank by the way they treated her with military deference.

"They called her 'Seren.' I think that means captain. Hey, she outranks us," Lagudi said, straining to overhear.

"Not in our fucking army," Irish said.

Adira seemed to be asking numerous questions, and the men gestured in turn towards the north and the surrounding countryside. With a final few words, the men saluted Adira, nodded to the HAWCs and tracked back out into the dry and abrasive landscape.

Adira pulled her sidearms from her backpack—two Israeli-designed Baraks. Hex raised his eyebrows, recognising the pistols and approving. Alex had offered her a handgun, but Hex could see why she had declined. The Baraks were blunt and businesslike, with double-action trigger, polymer square frame and rounded barrel; fast, durable and accurate weapons that gave the power punch of a magnum without the weight.

Adira strapped both holsters on so the gun barrels pointed down towards her groin, creating a "V" shape at her front that gave her rapid access and no side flaring. She slapped both pistols and practised her draw—fast. She looked very comfortable with the weapons.

"Marry me," said Lagudi with open admiration.

Adira ignored him, walked quickly back to the HAWCs and gestured out into the surrounding country. "There is a lot of activity in the area—we were right to think we were expected. There are numerous small teams of Takavaran—Iranian Special Forces—very tough and highly trained. We need to avoid them at all costs."

O'Riordan rolled his eyes and shook his head as if to dismiss the threat. Adira spoke directly to him. "We must not engage with these Iranian forces or we—"

"Ah, for Chrissake, lady, I'm sure they give you Jewish guys a run for your money, but if you haven't noticed yet, we ain't you. They said the same fuckin' thing about them *elite* Iraqi forces, and our *standard* ground troops bent 'em back in a day."

Adira stepped forward, her flat hand coming up towards Irish's sneering face. "You are a stupid man," she said.

Irish, probably wary of the last time her hand had come up, blocked her as if it was a strike, then punched his other hand hard into her chest.

Adira went down, but not onto her back as Irish was probably expecting. She corkscrewed her body on the way to the ground, giving momentum to her legs, which swung around and knocked Irish off his feet. The second he hit the ground, she was kneeling on his chest, a finger and thumb pressed to each side of his windpipe. "Stupid men die here," she hissed into his ear.

Hex tapped her on top of her helmet. "Let him up."

O'Riordan bounced to his feet, his face as red as his hair. He went to step back into Adira but Hex grabbed him by the collar. "Don't make me report this to the captain."

Irish wrenched himself free from Hex and swung around to face the darkened desert. He pulled his gun free and shot three quick, silent rounds into the night, then reholstered his gun before turning back to the group.

"You okay?" Hex said.

Irish nodded and looked away as if slightly bored. Adira shrugged and went on with her information.

"There are small squads around the ruins, and also some four-man teams spotted in other regions. My men will gather more information and report back to us."

Hex looked again at Irish, "We can deal with the Iranians if need be, but we can't afford to get pinned down in a firefight. They've got the home-team advantage and a lot of backup."

"I agree; they can afford to stand and fight. We can't," Adira said with a flat stare at O'Riordan.

Hex could swear she gave him the hint of a smile.

He called in the information about their position and the Mossad intelligence about the Takavaran, then ordered his team to join up with the Blue team, now less than a mile to the south of the ruins. Adira volunteered to bring up the rear. *She obviously isn't ready to let the big redheaded HAWC get behind her just yet*, Hex thought with a grin.

# Eighteen

Alex, Sam and Adira lay hidden among a tumble of rocks surrounding the ancient Persepolis ruins and scanned the dry plain before them.

Even at this distance, Alex marvelled at the size of the ancient edifices—nearly a mile in length and half that again in depth. Adira had told him it had taken over 150 years to build the palaces that had once been the centre of both the Persian nation and the entire known world. Its construction had taken six generations, and in its day it would have been the Taj Mahal, Buckingham Palace and the White House all rolled into one.

Alex blinked some grit from his eyes and studied the magnificent structures—even after 2500 years the towering walls, with stairways now leading to empty sky, inspired awe. Massive ornate columns like giant petrified trees and colossal faceless lions still stood guard over the Iranian desert. He squinted—carved into one mighty wall was a massive raised relief of a snarling beast bringing down a bull. The face was dark and polished perhaps by the oils of a thousand hands that had touched its visage for luck.

Alex exhaled slowly, and looked beyond the ruins at the immense plain surrounded by mauve cliffs with sharp, broken edges. He found it hard to believe it had once been a fertile valley—now all that remained was dust, scrubby bushes and a scorching breeze that reddened the eyes.

"No cover except for those pine plantings a couple of hundred feet out," said Sam. "Not gonna be easy if someone's looking out for us. Looks like a few tourists still hanging around as well."

Sam was right about the cover—the dry Marv Dasht plain provided few opportunities for concealment. Thousands of years before, the rulers had commanded the plain be levelled and planted with lush gardens, with ponds for visiting desert caravans. That beauty and abundance had been destroyed by thousands of years of searing summer heat and freezing winter nights, and now only wind-blasted walls and broken columns stood in the dusty basin.

"Not tourists—Takavaran," Adira said, nodding towards some men near the ruins. A small group dressed in casual clothing were lounging near a broken-down car, which another group was wandering around taking photographs. "Our networks told us that Persepolis has been closed to the public since the accident. My bet is that the entrance is under that canopy—probably via a tunnel dug beneath the foundations of the Apadana. It's the most solid standing structure in the ruins—used to be King Darius's reception hall."

Alex took one last look around the desert basin floor. "I agree. Okay, we go tonight. First prize: we enter with minimal noise and heat and leave without a trace. Second prize: full engagement with lethal prejudice, and we still leave without a trace."

Sam nodded. "Go in fast and come out smiling."

The trio agreed on a route up to the Apadana structure, then slithered backwards from their concealment point to rejoin the team and finalise the plan.

"Are we safe, *me'at achi*?" Adira asked Zachariah, who was reading some numbers from a small silver device he held in his hands. He smiled at her use of the term "little brother." Adira wasn't much older than he but obviously regarded herself as being years beyond him in maturity. Sure, she was bossy, but he couldn't help liking her. She was like a cross between a protective older sister and a strict hall monitor.

"Of course, *ima*," he replied.

The Hebrew term for "mother" made her laugh as she held her hand over the little box to shield the screen from the sunlight so she could read the numbers.

He liked her laugh as well, but he was still wary of her. She was iron hard in her beliefs. *Perhaps she has to be to do the work she does*, he thought.

Zach hadn't had any contact with the military once his compulsory service period had ended, and certainly no connection with Mossad. He remembered the words spoken by the general who had awarded his father a posthumous Medal of Valor. "Without sacrifice, there is no freedom. Without freedom, there is no life. God bless those who give their all for us." Zach hadn't understood it at the time. All he'd understood was that this small, shiny piece of metal was meant to be a trade for his father's death, and his mother's too.

The bomber had been trying to get into a wedding party apparently; his father had probably saved dozens of lives. But all Zach had felt at the time was anger—with the bomber, and also with his parents. Then, gradually, he became proud of them, awed by their courage, their readiness to die to save others.

*Adira would be like that*, he thought as he looked up at her.

Zach thought he probably loved Israel as much as she did; he just didn't have the same ingrained hatred and anger she had. Even after losing his parents to the bomb blast, he had quickly moved from that initial anger to a sense of sorrow for the desperation that drove some men and women to the ultimate act of murder—or sacrifice, depending on your perspective or geographical location.

He blinked as he realised he was still staring at Adira, and turned back to look at the small screen in his hands.

A large shadow fell across him. "What've you got there?" Sam Reid asked.

"High-sensitivity field Geiger," Zach replied. "Fully miniaturised, stainless-steel housing, halogen filled with mica end-window. Measures alpha, beta, gamma and X-radiation in the macro and micro range—and right now it's telling us . . . yep, just as I knew it would—the atmosphere is benign. It's in the nanosievert range, just above daily normal. That's good, I suppose, but strange considering we read a macro burst of gamma from here only a few days ago."

Zach held out the device so Sam could see the small screen for himself. Sam took it and rubbed it with his thumb, then turned it over, feeling the weight.

"Nice. You'll have to tell me where I can get one of these."

Zach cleared his throat and took the box back, breaking into a toothy smile. "Nowhere, I'm afraid, I built it myself." His face became serious again. "You know, if I hadn't witnessed that immense radiation spike myself, I may never have believed it ever occurred. It confirms what we've been thinking—this is more like a gravitational burst from dark matter. Terrestrial radiation just doesn't act like this. I've got to find out what happened in there."

Zach strode up to Alex brandishing the small Geiger counter. Alex took it from him, looked at the screen, pressed a few buttons, shrugged and handed it back.

Zach scowled and wiped the small screen on his sleeve. "Captain Hunter, I really need to get in there at ground zero to ascertain the effects of the—"

"I agree, Dr. Shomron," Alex cut in. We'll need your expertise. You'll be accompanying Ms. Senesh, Lieutenant Reid and myself. We go in after dark. Will there be anything else?"

"Ah, no . . . Okay, that's great . . . I think."

Zach suddenly realised that he'd gotten what he wanted, but that meant entering a hostile guarded perimeter and possibly being shot on sight. He suddenly wished he were back in his lab drinking his Aunt Dodah's hot chocolate to calm his nerves.

The day crawled past with agonising slowness; the team had nothing to do but rest through the late afternoon heat.

Alex took the opportunity to show Hex how to use the KBELT laser. "Remember, if you need to use it, narrow-beam shots only. I don't want broad pulses lighting up the valley floor—there may be high-altitude surveillance."

Hex's hands flexed in the air, willing it out of Alex's grip so he could hold it. Alex handed it over. "Twenty shots and then it'll need to recharge."

"I won't need anything like twenty," Hex said, and headed over to a low rock to sit down and practise sighting along the bulb-like barrel.

The setting sun threw long sharp shadows across the vast, ancient ruins, and Alex watched as its last rays crawled across the stone, briefly illuminating the crevices and recesses of the decaying buildings. With the disappearance of the sun, the air temperature dropped rapidly. The heat would continue to be radiated up from the sand and rock, but in another few hours they could expect it to be close to zero.

Sam brushed sand from his pants as he got to one knee. "We've picked up twelve men in proximity, operating in two squads of six. I agree with Ms. Senesh that they're Iranian Special Forces. Their randomness is too practised—they're too good at looking ordinary. I expect they'll have night vision and possibly even heat-enhancement scopes. Our suits will mask the body-warmth signatures, and we can follow the old tree line until we're just half a mile out. Also, there's the remains of a perimeter structure—little more than a shallow ditch—that we can belly-crawl along. We'll have to move as a single line, head to boot to head, so we don't present a human shape or register too much movement for any potential motion scanners. Going to take a bit longer, but it'll be quieter."

"They're Takavaran—we should kill them all immediately," Adira said.

Zach looked at her with a mix of horror and disbelief on his face.

Alex shook his head. "No—we don't know for sure yet who they are, or how many are in the ruins. We go with Sam's plan. Once inside, Dr. Shomron will collect the necessary information to allow us to ascertain exactly what the Iranians have been up to. We should be inside for no more than sixty minutes."

"Question. The plan is to ghost in and out. What happens if the Iranians wanna make some noise?" Irish spoke directly to Sam, but Alex responded.

"Full engagement, maximum lethality. We can't afford to have the whole Iranian Army tracking us. If they detect us and attempt to wage war, they must be quickly neutralised. No messages can get out."

The team nodded.

"Hex, you organise and deploy the perimeter defences," Alex ordered. "We'll commence the operation at 1100 hours. Any more questions?"

There were none.

Alex looked around the group. Adira seemed quietly indifferent; Zachariah sat with round eyes, twitching and pale; and the HAWCs were smiling grimly or resolute. All was as he expected.

# Nineteen

Chief Commander Bhakazarri of the Islamic Revolutionary Guard pushed another *ghotaab* cake into his mouth. The fried pastry dipped in honey made his fingers sticky, so he sucked them noisily even though his nails were dark with dirt. Without looking up from his paperwork, he extended his hand to find another glistening, nut-filled treat. He could relax now as his deployment selections were complete. He was confident his commandos could handle anything they encountered.

His IRG was a separate entity from the regular Iranian Army. Feared for their brutality and fanaticism, the Islamic Revolutionary Guard were initially created by the Ayatollah to maintain internal security. However, the IRG had grown well beyond this role and branched out into assassination, torture and the training of jihad fighters.

Like many military forces around the world, the IRG had their elite unit—the Takavaran. Bhakazarri oversaw the selection and training of the men in his Takavaran units; they reported to him and him alone.

The Takavaran commandos were the equivalent of the US Special Forces, and none were more feared in the Middle East than the Takavaran Zolfaghar—the wolves. They believed they carried the souls of the ancient Persian Immortals within them and were better trained, better equipped and more fanatical than any other Middle Eastern unit. Bhakazarri knew even the Metsada would avoid them if they could; the best outcome the Israeli agents could hope for when encountering one of these brutal fanatics face to face was mutual destruction.

It was too late to defend the Jamshid I facility at Persepolis—it had already been erased by the accident. Bhakazarri had spread two dozen men loosely in and around the ruin's perimeter in the Marv Dasht desert, more as a trap than a defensive force. It was Jamshid II at Arak that needed to be protected. Here he had deployed his best men in two mission profiles. The first was a contingent of fifty stationed in the facility itself. If an enemy infiltration team actually managed to find and enter the hidden laboratory, they would be cut down before the first security door was breached. The second mission deployment was another sixty Takavaran dressed in the robes and shawls of desert traders and spread in ten four-man units throughout the countryside. Their humble tents would conceal ground radar, nightscope equipment and all the necessary firepower required to obliterate any foreigner that set foot on Iranian soil.

Bhakazarri had ordered at least one of the infiltrators to be brought to him alive, especially if they turned out to be Americans. The humiliation of the Great Satan would be extreme if Iran could parade captured US spies to the international media.

He pushed another cake into his mouth and snorted. Although he had given the order, Bhakazarri wasn't counting on any living Captives being brought to him. His Takavaran rarely left anything behind but body parts. *Ah, well*, he thought, *you send in wolves and someone gets savaged*. It didn't matter; the Americans would still pay to get the bodies back, no matter what their condition.

Alex and Sam were checking their weapons when Adira and Zach joined them. As standard equipment, the HAWCs used the Heckler & Koch USP45CT pistol, or CT for short. Smooth and matt black, it was a powerful sidearm made of a moulded polymer with recoil reduction and a "hostile environment" nitride finish giving maximum corrosion resistance.

"H&K," said Adira. "Big and slow, I remember. Hope your targets stay at walking pace for you tonight."

Sam chuckled.

Alex clicked the firing mechanism into place and sighted along the barrel. He liked the feel in his hand. "Not anymore," he told Adira. "This CT has a variant trigger—pull and discharge in a single smooth split-second motion. Maybe not the fastest handgun, but certainly faster than a standard Israeli Barak." He smiled at her.

"What makes you think these are standard, Captain? Besides, sometimes speed is determined by what's *behind* the gun. When this is over, we'll have to see who is faster, yes?"

Sam stifled another laugh as he finished screwing on his sound suppressor and twirled the elongated gun in his hand. Most silencers suppressed sound through muffling; the upgraded CT used frequency shifting—it didn't so much muffle the sound as shift it beyond the range of human hearing. Sam slid the weapon into its holster, which was strapped down into a special pocket in his suit.

Alex looked at his watch: 10:45 P.M. "Get 'em together, Uncle."

Hex came in first. He crouched down, holding the Klystron laser across his thighs. With his grey eyes, white-blond cropped hair and futuristic weaponry, he looked like a warrior from a time still to come. Alex could tell he was itching to fire the laser and pitied Hex's first target—he wouldn't miss.

Rocky and Irish came in next.

Alex spoke directly to Hex. "We can't allow ourselves to be trapped in those ruins. If the Iranians attempt to enter the facility in force, move into ambush positions, or engage. You are unilaterally authorised to remove any and all perimeter threats."

Hex simply nodded.

Alex took the lead on the insertion team. He was the only member of the four-person unit who was without nightscope equipment—his own enhanced vision gave him all the light amplification he needed.

The evening was clear but moonless, making the basin floor appear impenetrable in the darkness. The air temperature was cold, just a few degrees above zero, but still dry enough to suck the moisture from their eyes and mouths. The slow going would have a dual benefit: besides drawing less attention to them, it minimised exhaustion and therefore caused fewer exhalations—which would show on any watching thermal scopes as orange mist plumes.

It was just after midnight when they reached the tent covering the entrance to the tunnels. Sam and Zach moved forward to the steel door, Sam holding a small steel device he intended to use to bypass the digital security and Zach with his radiation meter. Out on the desert floor, Alex could see the slight movement of two of the Takavaran teams. One team was near an old truck, half the men asleep underneath it. The other team was closer to the ruins, the men lying with their backs against the stone, obviously drawing on the warmth stored there during the day.

"It's already open," Sam whispered. He coiled some wires around the small device and jammed it back into its sleeve. He drew his gun and crouched beside the door.

Adira pushed the metal panel slightly and went down on one knee on the opposite side to Sam. As the door swung inwards, they both pointed their weapons into the black tunnel beyond.

Zach held up the Geiger counter to check the radiation levels. "All clear," he said, and resheathed the device and fell in behind Adira.

Alex put his hand flat against the stone wall. Suddenly he felt a stab of pain in the back of his head. It turned to agony as the pressure built and shifted in his skull, as if there were tectonic plates in there grinding against each other, adjusting to make room for something. *Not now*, he thought. *Not more change, not now.* He closed his eyes for an instant and inhaled deeply. A rippling sensation passed through his head and down his spine and the pressure unwound slightly.

His hand tingled against the stone and he realised he could sense vibration—some kind of life presence inside the ancient structure. It was a swirling, chaotic storm of emotions—the lingering remnants of human pain and suffering. The living had been rapidly extinguished here, but he couldn't tell if it was by violent death or by some other force.

The pain behind his eyes subsided and he removed his fingers from the stone, curling his hand briefly into a fist as if it had been burnt. He turned to the group, pointed at himself with one finger, at Sam with two, then Adira with three and at Zach, four. Then he pushed open the steel door and silently disappeared into the darkness, his small team following in the order he'd indicated.

# Twenty

Ahmad Al Janaddi looked with a critical eye through the four-inch-thick lead-plated glass window at the Jamshid II facility's main testing floor. Images from every section of the room were displayed on multiple screens, the recordings taken in a continuous loop. Sophisticated computer programs allowed him to pass much of the control of the experiment over to the electronic equipment, and the high-speed drives would capture images of the event down to the micro-millisecond. Further data on atmospheric density, thermal, infrared and other spectrum wavelengths would also be collected. Nothing would be missed this time.

The reinforced concrete chamber with its lead-lined panelling was both awe-inspiring and intimidating. The sleek and gleaming silver globe sat at its centre, surrounded by walls studded and spiked by hundreds of different sensors and lenses that would observe the creation of a perforation into the very matter of the universe. It could have been a small spaceship that had landed and was preparing to disgorge creatures from another planet.

A thick white line circled the floor around the unearthly shimmering sphere. This was where the president's "volunteers" would stand during the event—the "opening of Allah's Gateway" as he liked to call it. Al Janaddi remembered the screams of anguish that had shrieked from the speakers the last time the sphere had been activated. *These men and women may as well be stepping into a furnace*, he thought. He just hoped the waist-high black steel cylinders covered in lenses and sensitive recording equipment that also stood on the line would be able to withstand whatever occurred; at least then they would obtain a basic understanding of how, when and where the subjects went. The sooner they knew that, the less likely the president would demand more people "volunteered."

With the current design, the experiment could be repeated as many times as they wished. But it took time: the concrete had to dry, the lead panelling had to be moulded into place and the sphere repositioned. The president was growing more impatient by the day, and it was not uncommon for Al Jannaddi to receive calls in the morning and the evening to discuss progress.

He looked up as the volunteers were led in—eight villagers, a few local clerics, and a young couple, a man and a woman, who looked out of place amongst the elderly group. This small gathering was the "lucky" pious—men and women who had begged to be given the opportunity to stand before their God.

Al Janaddi studied the youthful couple for a moment. They both wore the uniform of the young conservative: he, a cheaply cut blue suit with stiff white shirt and no tie; and the girl, a black manteau—the heavy overcoat that buttoned from the collar to below the knee. Her only personal touch— whether as a small sign of individuality or rebellion—was her scarf, which was royal blue with small golden tulips and intricate crimson scrolling reminiscent of Persian calligraphy. It framed her beautiful face with its perfect milk and honey complexion.

The couple turned to each other, their hands clasped in prayer, just the tips of their small fingers touching. *What are they doing here?* Al Janaddi thought as he watched the attending technicians prepare them for the event.

The head-to-toe, fully lead-impregnated protective suits, each weighing around 100 pounds, were finished with regular sunglasses. The president had suggested that each martyr should have an automated homing beacon with global satellite positioning implanted under the skin, which would act like a mini black box device. As he had said to Al Janaddi:

"As long as we get one of the boxes back, then the surrounding flesh doesn't matter."

Once the volunteers were in place, one of the clerics led them in prayer. The haunting sound stretched and bounced around the enormous chamber and it was hard not to feel touched by the melodious chanting. The cleric explained that some of them would be martyred, that they would stand before God to be judged and, if they were pure, would be exalted and given eternal sanctuary in Jannah for themselves and all their relatives.

The young couple looked at each other and their hands met. She took hold of his fingertips and smiled shyly. Al Janaddi looked down at his slightly scuffed shoes and wondered what it was like to have such an unwavering faith. Perhaps if these poor, brave, foolish souls knew they had little chance of surviving, they may have prayed for something very different.

He gave the order for all the technicians to exit the chamber, then, over the speaker, bade the volunteers to go with God. He noticed a puddle of urine at the feet of one of the older villagers and felt a pang of sympathy for the ragged little carpet weaver—perhaps not all of them expected to find heaven after all. *Allah keep you all safe*, he thought.

He turned to his command centre, where every scientist and technician was hunched over the banks of monitoring equipment. He raised his voice slightly: "Green light in sixty seconds." He was greeted by an array of thumbs ups and a few *Allahu Akbars*.

"Countdown in ten seconds," he said. His heart sped up in anticipation and he continued the count: "Five . . . four . . . three . . . two . . . one . . .'He switched on the homing beacons and initiated the particle acceleration lasers. The lights dimmed.

They were all returning now. Al Janaddi thought it like a conjuror's trick—one minute the international grid screen showed all twelve of the beacons clustered around the sphere in the Arak facility, then in the next moment they disappeared.

Then, almost magically, they began to reappear on the grid, scattered all over the globe—some high in mountains or below the ground, some deep beneath the oceans. Al Janaddi counted: *Five . . . eight . . . eleven . . . one short.*

Many of the beacons faded quickly, perhaps crushed by deep-sea pressure or melted by volcanic flow beneath a mountain range. But a few continued to deliver their electronic signal loud and clear. Now Al Janaddi needed to retrieve those bodies before anyone else.

He reached for the phone and spoke quickly to Commander Bhakazarri, who would mobilise the recovery forces, retrieval teams for the bodies still in the Middle East and using agents or local sympathisers when the "packages" were in less accessible countries.

While Al Janaddi was providing the exact longitude and latitude locations of the homing beacons, his eyes widened. One of the beacons was on the move—slowly, but definitely shifting from where it had first arrived.

One of the test subjects had returned alive.

# Twenty-one

The darkness was thick and absolute; and the smell of fresh-cut rock was sharp in the dry atmosphere. Normal human night vision was poor in near total darkness, but the changes to Alex's brain had increased the level of rhodopsin in the rods of his eyes, giving him vision more like that of a hunting animal or nocturnal bird of prey. But even his amplified vision picked up little more than shapes and angles in a tunnel devoid of even the faintest starlight.

Luckily, Alex had more than night vision to rely on. His rewired brain was able to receive temperature differentials that delivered thermal images—and, recently, other senses had been opening to him as well. He was able to perceive an impression of living things—literally, to sense the proximity of another life force. The ability was growing, and he knew it wouldn't be long before those impressions turned to shapes, then to an exact mental picture. It was these new senses he relied on as he led his team forward in the blackness of the Persepolis catacombs.

A slight whistling came from Zach's nostrils as they moved silently down the tunnel and Alex was tempted to turn around and pinch the scientist's nose.

After a few seconds, they came to a pool of absolute blackness in the gloom—the empty elevator shaft down to the main facility. Alex looked back over his shoulder and could just make out a line of single bulbs strung along the ceiling. *No juice left here*, he thought. He stared down into the dark pit—he couldn't detect any form of electronic hum or power at all. *Good, no juice down there either.* Presumably that meant the electronic locks had disengaged to ensure personnel weren't trapped inside by generator failures.

The shaft was deep and the cage was at the bottom. Whoever had last entered had never left. *Persepolis is hanging onto its ghosts*, he thought.

He put one leg over the edge of the pit, and Sam and Adira lined up behind him.

"Should I stay here?" Zach whispered. The sound of his voice in the tomb-like silence was a jarring intrusion.

Alex looked at Zach and held his finger to his lips. Then he pointed at Zach's chest, then down into the pit—Zach was going.

Zach's teeth chattered. The nightscope he wore made everything around him a ghostly green, and the absolute silence meant that all he heard in his helmet was his own breathing and an intermittent dry swallowing.

When the American captain pointed at him and then down into the pit, he felt his stomach roll. The sensitive nightscope failed to pick up even the faintest fragment of light down there. For all he could tell, that hole descended all the way to the centre of the Earth.

Captain Hunter looked back at him and placed his fingers to his lips again. *It's his eyes*, he thought, *they look strange; they shine unnaturally, like a wolf.*

*They're all so calm. I should never have said I needed to come with them*, he thought, as Captain Hunter disappeared into the hole. Zach willed his legs to move, but instead they threatened to collapse. Adira grabbed him by the arm and led him to the edge of the pit. For once she looked taller than he did. *I'm crouching, why am I crouching?* he thought, and dry-swallowed once more.

It took them twenty minutes—a half-mile climb down the side railings, then a small drop into the open cage of the elevator. Alex noticed Zach was breathing heavily; he knew the kid would suffer even more on the way back up.

The blackness was all-consuming at this level. The night-vision goggles only delivered faint green outlines. Unless they could switch to white light soon, much of the investigation from here would be done by feeling around with their hands.

Alex's enhanced abilities told him they were standing in a corridor facing a fortified steel door that was slightly ajar a few inches. A black tunnel stretched both to the left and right, into the unknown depths of the Persepolis ruins. Alex put two fingers into the gap at the door and rolled the heavy steel back with ease. He was thankful it was open—judging by its density and thickness, they didn't have enough ordnance to break through if it had been sealed shut.

He felt the emptiness as soon as he stepped through the doorway. Where once had stood an enormous laboratory with walls of computers and electronic monitoring equipment, now there was nothing but scoured ground leading to a large circular pit that smelled of cut rock, ozone and something repellent.

"What happened here? Go to torchlight," Alex ordered. He pressed a stud inside his helmet rim, and a coin-sized disc covered his left eye. It was one of nature's little secrets, discovered by English pirates hundreds of years before and adopted by the US military. It took up to thirty minutes to recover full night vision after being exposed to light, but night blindness affected the eyes independently. Covering one eye ensured it remained night-ready when the lights went back out.

In the light of their helmet torches, the Blue team could appreciate the magnitude of the devastation. The ground where they stood looked to have been rubbed raw then somehow liquefied. Strangely coloured streaks and swellings ran across the floor like the gristle and arteries of some great beast's innards.

Zach's helmet torch beam swung rapidly back and forth across the strange mosaic under his feet. "What happened?" he replied to Alex. "Not exactly sure, but I can tell you what *I* think happened. These marks are the effects of an enormous gravitational tide. I believe a black hole existed here—perhaps for only a millionth of a second—and it swallowed the entire facility. Whatever was here before—men, machinery, rock—has simply ceased to exist in our universe."

The team backed up and formed a circle, their combined torchlight brightly illuminating the strange mélange under their feet.

"What's that in there?" Sam knelt down and removed a glove so he could feel the texture of the surface. "Wood, metal, plastic . . . is that a pencil, part of a chair? It's all fused together—like it's been melted and then solidified. But not by heat." He ran his hand over the small lumps and depressions. "Dr. Shomron, is this is an example of your spaghettification?" he asked without looking up.

Zach was staring at the ground as if in a trance and it took him a moment to register his name and the question. "Yes. Yes, this is theoretically what happens when the molecular structure of physical matter is stretched within an enormous gravitational tidal surge—an attractive force so impossibly strong it bends and elongates time and space. Anything this close to it gets turned to taffy as it's drawn in and consumed. My guess is that the gamma rays irradiated this entire site and bleached it of every living organism, right down to the virus level. Everything that was here is either gone, dead, or ended up like this."

Alex nodded. "Other than validating what we suspected, there's nothing here for us. Go to dark, let's go."

He was about to switch off his torch, when something on the ground caught his eye. Embedded in the confused mess, deformed but still recognisable, was a human tooth. *Gone, dead . . . or ended up like this.*

Alex switched off his torch and headed for the steel door. Sam, Adira and Zach followed. The discs slid back off their left eyes, and all except Alex went back to nightscopes.

At the door, Alex had the urge to turn—he could sense something in the blackness around him. Perhaps there were such things as ghosts, he thought, trapped in some kind of tormented limbo by the trauma that had occurred here. He shook his head to clear it of the morbid idea.

Tavira, Portugal

The smell of diesel fuel and dried fish wafted across the deck as the three de Macieira brothers prepared to pull in the nets. It would take all three of them. The new green cord-nylon was much lighter than the older rope twine, but the men's years added weight to the drag; every pull took longer, was heavier, and hurt a little more.

The hatch was off the fish freezer and chill air spread from the dark interior, even though Paulo rarely bothered to load much ice these days. The men pulled fish from the mesh of the nets and threw them into the hold. Rarely did anything go back unless they were really *merda pescado*, shit fish.

Carlos, the eldest brother, smiled to himself; he could feel good weight in the final net and couldn't resist peeking over the side. The water was jade green and almost milky— the high algae content in the cold Atlantic Ocean robbed it of any transparency below ten feet. The net came up slowly and now all three men felt the weight. Paulo, the youngest at sixty-one, joked that perhaps they had finally found the ocean's plug and would need to walk home if they pulled it free.

They could see the mass in the net now, large, about ten feet long, and a light colour; it was not struggling so it must have already drowned in the mesh on its way to the surface. The water here was deep—around 150 feet—and they had heard of fishermen catching strange fish and crabs that had been whipped up from the seabed to mid-water by strong deep-ocean currents. The thing flopped onto the deck; at first glance it looked like a body, although perhaps not a human body.

Paulo gasped, let go of the net and clutched the small pewter crucifix around his neck with both hands. Santo muttered,

"*O meu Deus,*" and crossed himself. Even Carlos, the oldest and most practical of the brothers, felt a wave of fear ripple through him.

"*Sereia; mermaid!*" he said. A girl brought up from the depths—it could be nothing else. Her beautiful face was the colour of honey and milk, though her skin looked hardened, like stone or ice. Her dark eyes were open and unclouded; strange for a body brought up from such deep water. The brothers could feel the cold coming off her—perhaps the freezing Atlantic depths had preserved her for a while. But even the cold would not have protected her eyes and angelic face from the normal ravages of the fish and crabs.

Carlos looked around at the horizon—no boats large or small anywhere. He looked back down at the girl. Maybe she hadn't fallen overboard and into the depths; maybe she had fallen "up" to them. His eyes traced her perfect face, her small rounded breasts and tiny waist . . . but from there things got crazy. From the hips down, her body stretched and elongated into a twisted rope-like mass; to Carlos, it looked like a long flowing tail—a mermaid's tail. A scarf was tangled in her long hair—it was royal blue with small golden tulips and crimson Arabic-looking writing.

Santo leaned over the girl to pull back some of the fish netting—as he did, blood ran thickly from his nose.

# Twenty-two

Ahmad Al Janaddi was standing at the door of the containment cell when the president's call was transferred through to him. He listened for a few minutes and gathered his strength; there were tears flowing down his cheeks. Looking back into the cell he felt the gorge rise in his throat once more. He turned quickly away as the thing started to howl again.

"Yes, my President, we have recovered most of the bodies and also the special subject I mentioned. Yes, the lead lining of the suit seemed to give the man some physical protection and he still lives . . . in a manner."

The scientist compressed his lips and turned again to look through the cell window. It was true the creature lived, but it would never be a man again. When they tried to cut away the heavy lead-impregnated suit, they discovered that suit and man had somehow combined. The black hole had created a soup of flesh and lead, reformed it and delivered it back to them. Now the creature was contained in a large tub; spread out, its body covered nearly twenty feet, with tendrils and flaps of flesh splaying in all directions. It was able to move around and raise itself up. Al Janaddi knew this because a small square mirror on the wall above the tub had been smashed into sparkling splinters. He guessed the creature did not want to see its own image. He could not blame it.

He swallowed and moved his gaze up to its face. One eye was a milky white; the other, though still clear and brown, was over three feet long. Sickeningly, it still managed to fix on the scientist whenever he entered the room. That single eye held a plea—perhaps for a quick death and release from the permanent hell it was now trapped in.

The president was hungry for information about what the man had experienced. Where had he gone, what had he seen? Had he been judged and allowed to cross the bridge to Jannah, or did he fall to Jahannam?

Al Janaddi squeezed his eyes shut for a moment. "I think he was judged unworthy, my President; maybe even more so than Professor Shihab." The voice on the phone grew louder.

"It will take us some time to prepare another event," Al Janaddi replied. "Even if we . . . Here? Yes, of course, my President; we would be delighted for you to observe our work first-hand."

Al Janaddi sucked in a juddering breath as he listened. *Please don't ask me to take the phone in to . . . him*, he thought.

He answered the final question as best he could. "I'm afraid we may never know what he saw, my President; all he does is scream."

Something thumped wetly against the door. Al Janaddi turned to see that horrific face pressed up against the window. The screaming stopped for a moment and the giant lolling tongue writhed as if the creature were trying to speak.

Ahmad Al Janaddi wiped more tears from his eyes. "Allah forgive me," he cried, and sprinted away down the corridor.

Out in the Iranian desert, something lay motionless on the ground, disorientated. One minute it had been feeding with the others of its kind on the massive carcass of a plant-eater at the edge of a brackish swamp, warm blue sunlight bathing its back; the next it was here. It remained immobile as its senses slowly returned. The gravity was lighter here, giving its body more strength, but the air was thinner and drier. Though its exoskeleton contained a wax-like lubricant, the dry atmosphere was irritating and it needed liquids to survive—to feed on.

It raised its eyes on their cartilaginous stalks and surveyed the area. It had no idea what predators might stalk
this strange barren land with its intense golden sun. Fan-like
mouthparts extruded from between its bony mandibles and
sampled the air, tasting the aromas. It could detect water,
vegetation, salts and minerals, and strange fluids in creatures it had never known or sensed before.

It called—a subsonic sound that frightened a falcon overhead and woke a band of shivering bats sleeping in a cave
miles to its south. To the rest of the animal kingdom, the
sound was not perceptible, especially to any modern biped's
ears.

The creature compressed its gristly carapace plates against
the heat—it needed to be away from the burning yellow sun.
Articular membranes and muscle fibres pulled its chitinous
exoskeleton segments together and it burrowed its pointed,
armoured body a few feet below the surface of the sand. The
going would be slower than above the ground, but it would
retain more body fluid by staying out of the heat.

In the distance, the city of Arak was waking. Its inhabit-
ants had no idea that the universe had delivered a little piece
of hell to their doorstep.

# Twenty-three

Alex sensed something else in that dark tunnel, something more tangible than the tortured souls he'd imagined trapped there. There were people approaching—he could feel the vibrations of their footsteps.

He held up a flattened hand. The team stopped and crouched left and right behind the steel door. Alex silently pulled the door closed, leaving just a small gap.

He put his hand against the cold steel so he could read the vibrations from the other side. Three large men approaching—*must be part of a Takavaran squad*, he thought.

He looked at Sam and held up three fingers. Sam stared hard until he could make out the gesture in the dark and then nodded. Alex quickly glanced over his shoulder—there was no cover, nothing to provide some form of concealment or a defensive position. They had their backs to a pit that may have fallen to the very base of the Kouh-e Rahmat mountain.

They waited in silence until they saw torchlight shining through the slit of the doorframe. Now, the entire team could hear the sound of the men's low conversation.

Adira moved close to Alex and whispered into his ear. "They're coming in."

Alex nodded and gave her and Sam a closed fist signal, followed by a chopping motion left and right. Both were expecting the command and immediately pressed themselves to the wall either side of the door. Adira grabbed Zach and pushed him down behind her. She drew one of her unsilenced Baraks but Alex waved it away, pointing at his ear.

She shrugged, reholstered it and drew out one of her slim black blades instead. She adopted a fighting pose and waited.

The colossal steel door rolled back slowly and two men entered the black room, facing the pit and fanning to each side of the doorway. They were large and moved fluidly for their size. A third man stood in the doorway and shone a strong torch directly into Alex's face. In a smooth motion, Alex grabbed the front of the man's black fatigues and flung him out over the pit. The first his comrades knew of his fate was when his torch, still in his hands, flew over their heads. Their shouts as they entered the battle obscured the sound of the body hitting the bottom of the black abyss.

Two soundless bullets from Sam took one of the men in the eye and the chest. He fell dead before he could fire the gun he had drawn.

Adira threw one of her slim blades at the third man, but he avoided the killing strike, rolling sideways and taking it in the flesh of his shoulder. He was up quickly with a gun in his hand, swinging it smoothly around to aim at Adira. She delivered a vicious front snap-kick that should have knocked the gun from his grip, but the Takavaran were no ordinary soldiers; they were strong, well trained and very familiar with close-quarter combat. Instead of loosening his gun, all the kick did was cause it to misfire into the pit. The sound of the unsilenced discharge in the enclosed shell of the laboratory was excruciating, the echoes bouncing around like a giant's stone drum being madly beaten.

The Takavaran regained his balance and threw out his arm, hitting Adira on the side of her head with an open-handed strike as he brought his gun back around to aim directly at her chest.

"*Harah*," Adira cursed in Hebrew. She drew both her Barak pistols and fired four shots into the large Takavaran before he could loose another round. The force of the bullets pushed him backwards and he too disappeared over the rim into the black void.

Adira turned to Alex and shrugged. He shook his head and put his fingers in his ears.

"Party's over," he said. "Double-time it!"

Zach was still flattened on the ground. Sam pulled him to his feet as Alex leapt through the open steel door and began herding them all to the elevator shaft.

"Sam, Ms. Senesh, you two first," Alex said loudly. There was no need for silence anymore, and their ears were still ringing from the gunfire.

He looked at Zach and knew the slightly built young man was never going to make the rapid ascent straight up for half a mile. He told him to wait where he was and disappeared back through the steel door. In a moment he reappeared with a length of black material torn from the uniform of the Takavaran Sam had shot. He bound Zach's hands together with it, then looped them over his own head.

"This is just for insurance," he said. "I'll climb you out, but you still have to hang on."

Alex could feel the young man's arms shaking with nerves against his shoulders. He sucked in a deep breath and reached for the first rung.

Zach thought about protesting. Even though he was tall and thin, he still weighed about 150 pounds and he doubted Alex could carry him all the way to the top. He looked up the dim shaft and could just make out Sam and Adira about seventy feet up, climbing quickly. As Alex began his climb, Zach felt as if he were flying. In no time they had caught up with Sam and Adira, and Zach glanced quickly at their glowing green faces as he flew past. Adira's was astonished, while Sam was smiling.

Near the rim of the shaft, Alex stopped and tilted his head as if listening. All Zach could hear was the faint sounds of Adira and Sam climbing to join them. Then Alex spoke into his helmet comm: "Move it; we got company."

The captain raced up the remaining fifty feet in a few seconds and threw Zach off his shoulders like a large bag of linen. The scientist lay gasping as if he had made the climb himself; his nerves shortening his breath. He untied the black fabric around his wrists and looked across to Alex to thank

him. The HAWC had thrown himself flat on the ground at
the shaft rim and was sighting down into the darkness with
his gun.

Zach rolled over and looked down into the pit. Sam and
Adira were almost invisible, even with his light-enhancing
equipment. He looked at Alex again and saw total calm. The
HAWC's eyes shone strangely as they stared unwaveringly
down into depths of the elevator shaft.

Zach held his breath.

Alex watched Adira and Sam slowly ascend towards him.
They still had another sixty-odd feet to go and he could tell
they were tiring. He couldn't climb down and carry them
both—that would make them a bigger target. The best he
could do was try to give them some cover.

Another Takavaran squad had arrived in the ruined lab.
There was no telling how many of them had been waiting
down there in the depths. One of them shone a torch up the
shaft of the elevator. There wasn't time for Alex to aim and
fire before the man pulled his head back. Next came an arm
and a pistol, and bullets buzzing rapidly up the shaft like a
swarm of angry bees.

Alex fired as best he could, but even with his keen eyesight the target was too dark and small over the distance.

Adira was falling behind, and had let go with one of her
arms to draw a Barak and shoot down into the darkness below her. Alex guessed the shots were intended to act more as
a deterrent to buy them some time, rather than with any
hope of actually taking down any of the Takavaran.

Sam was first over the edge. He was breathing heavily
and his arms must have burned from the strain, but he lay
down beside Alex and took aim into the shaft. Alex doubted
Sam could see anything, but knew his second-in-command
would fire a supporting volley if he did.

Alex waited for the pistol arm to reappear. In a few more
seconds he saw movement, but this time it wasn't a gun that
was aimed at them, but the head of a sleek rocket-propelled
grenade. Time had just run out.

* * *

Adira could see the rim of the shaft and the outline of Alex's head still high above her. She was a strong woman, but after the long climb her arms wobbled with fatigue. The gunfire had given her a burst of adrenalin, but this too had been eaten up by the strain of the ascent. *Stand and fight*, a small voice said inside her head, but she knew that holding on one-handed like last time would be impossible now, and probably just result in a dropped weapon. And that was not going to happen to a captain in the Metsada.

Each new rung was agony, and the small shapes at the top of the shaft seemed just as far away as when she'd last looked up. *Stand and fight*, the voice said again. Just as her hand left the rung to reach down for her weapon, she saw a large figure leap headfirst into the shaft. Unbelievably, he caught the wall rails twenty feet down, right below her. She felt a strong arm wrap around her waist, pull her off the wall and sling her over his shoulder. Alex Hunter's voice said in her ear, "Cover us."

Adira felt a brief moment of unreality wash over her, then, with her front half hanging down into the shaft, she pulled both of her guns free and rained bullets down into the pit. As Alex was hauling her over the edge, she saw the flare of the initiation charge on the rocket-grenade booster. The flare pushed the grenade out of the launcher before the sustainer motor ignited to propel the small rocket at its target at nearly 600 feet per second. Adira yelled one of the most feared words in any battle: "Incoming!"

Sam turned and grabbed Zach, dragging him along suitcase-style. Alex didn't bother putting Adira down; he just ran after Sam with her held across his chest. They had only covered about forty feet before their world turned orange and they were thrown forward by a molten percussion blow that flung ancient stone fragments at them at near-bullet velocity. Adira heard the storm of rock fragments whack into Alex's back before he flew forward to land on top of her.

They were saved by the small rocket grenade hitting the granite roof of the tunnel; although dense, the material absorbed some of the initial fragmentation. The few feet of distance they'd covered and their armoured suits had stopped anything penetrating their bodies, but Adira knew they would be bruised and sore for days. They were lucky; it had been a simple fragmentation device. If it had of been one of the newer thermobaric explosives, it would have cooked everything in the tunnel—suits or no suits.

Adira and the others looked back into the boiling smoke. The stone tunnel would have collapsed over the elevator shaft, and the Takavaran would have known that when they fired the RPG.

"Hmm, committed," said Alex as he got to his feet.

Adira nodded and looked up at him as she struggled to one knee. He wasn't fatigued or hurt, and he hadn't needed special equipment in the dark. She remembered the general's order to seek out the Americans' special weapon—the Arcadian. *Could this be him?*

Alex put out his hand to her. She ignored it and got to her feet, dusting herself down as she said, "Next time, I carry you."

On the slight broken rise above the basin, Hex heard the muffled explosion and saw the tent covering the entrance to the ruins billow as the shock wave travelled out of the underground complex. He also saw the two teams of Takavaran outside fly to their feet, draw their weapons and close in on the doorway. Their movements were not panicked, but fluid and professional.

Hex spoke quietly into his comm unit. "Wolf packs closing."

From within the ruins, Alex responded. "Engage."

# Twenty-four

On a sunny afternoon on the other side of the world, Major Jack Hammerson sipped his coffee and watched a live feed of the Persepolis site from a recalibrated orbiting satellite over the Middle East.

It was just after midnight in Iran, and from a height of about 1000 feet the light-enhanced Persepolis ruins were a dark greenish-blue, the angular shapes of the Apadana, Throne Room and Treasury only vaguely visible. He zoomed in on the image to just a few hundred feet above the age-old buildings.

As he took another sip, he saw the human-shaped specks of light closing in on one of the ancient structures, then smiled as a dot of white flashed out from the surrounding hill line to touch on a glowing point at the ruin's perimeter. It repeated again, touching on another area, and then again. There were quick muzzle flashes from near the ruins—and the white dot raced out to touch the muzzle flashes, which immediately stopped. The pattern repeated six more times before it ceased.

"Hmm, looks like the KBELT works just fine," the Hammer said out loud.

His phone rang and he lifted the receiver to his ear while taking another sip of the steaming coffee. His eyes never left the screen as he spoke. "We're on the ground . . . insertion successful. Yes, sir."

He listened, then his computer beeped as a packet of new information was received. He read it quickly. "Understood,

sir. Supplementary energy pulse information acquired—
redeployment to new target is ASAP."

His caller spoke again and Hammerson's eyes narrowed
slightly. "Don't worry, sir. We'll have the technology soon . . .
or no one will."

Hidden among the rocks, Hex looked along the smooth end
of the KBELT and lined up another of the Takavaran as he
ran towards the entrance to the Jamshid I facility. He pressed
the trigger and a million-joule energy pulse of super-
compressed emitted light leapt from the muzzle to touch the
man on the forehead. He dropped immediately. By the time
the light was visible, its trail had already disappeared, which,
combined with the soundless discharge, meant the Takavaran were at a loss to pinpoint its origination point.

Lagudi slammed into the rocks just down from Hex and
Irish and held his pistol up close to his chest. Hex motioned
one-handed to both men to hold fire—he knew his weapon
would be the most efficient, and silent, in the dark desert.

Irish had Hex's sniper rifle and he aimed at one of the last
two black-clad men. Over the distance and in the near total
darkness, it was a shot that even Hex would have struggled
to pull off. Irish fired and missed, fired and missed. The
noise of the gun and its muzzle flashes gave the Takavaran
the origination point and they fired in a continuous volley up
at the HAWC, forcing Irish to hunker down behind the
rocks. Then they began to advance, taking turns to shoot
while the other scurried twenty feet closer to Irish's position.

Hex cursed under his breath: they were good. He aimed
the KBELT at the nearest Takavaran and pressed the button
trigger. The Iranian fell forward into the dry sand, close
enough to his comrade that the smoking, red-black burn
hole in his temple was probably visible. The last man leapt
to take shelter behind a large flat-faced boulder. As he dived,
he pulled a small radio from under his robes and began to
dial in a signal. Time had run out for the HAWCs—their
position was about to be compromised.

Hex broke cover and stood. He moved the KBELT's

calibration down to the broader range low-energy pulse and pressed the button twice. The effect was startling: two golf ball-sized spheres of lightning flew towards the flat-faced rock. The first smashed the boulder into smoking shards of debris; the second did the same to the concealed Takavaran. Stone and flesh rained down to the dark sand for many seconds afterwards. Hex raised his eyebrows. *Satisfying result*, he thought.

The last echoes of the explosion bounced off the mountain, rolled across the desert basin and then out to the wide, cold plains. Silence once again fell over the ancient Persepolis ruins.

Hex looked up at the sky. *Please let there be only friendly birds watching*, he thought. Then he stared coldly at O'Riordan, his wintry eyes the only sign of his annoyance with the new HAWC.

O'Riordan's face was redder than usual. He glared at Hex for a few seconds before shouting, "I could've hit him if I had a light sabre as well, Mr. Luke fuckin' Skywalker."

Hex studied the man for a further few seconds, then turned away and pressed his comm stud.

Alex paused at the outer door of the Jamshid I facility as he heard the message from Hex: "Twelve down. Clear."

"Roger that," said Alex. "Come on down, bring Irish and Rocky. Over."

Alex waved his small team out of the ruins. The tent over the entrance was gone—blown away by the force of the blast. There were bodies lying around the perimeter; in the dark he could see their thermal images fading as they rapidly cooled in the icy night air. He spotted a small round burn hole above the right eye of one of the Takavaran. As expected, Hex hadn't missed.

Alex pressed his comm stud again. "Good shooting, Lieutenant, but I'll still want that gun back."

Alex turned to check on Sam, Adira and Zach. Their suits were heavily marked from the blast, the ceramic plates over the shoulders and armadillo scales down over the lower back scarred and pitted. They'd been lucky. As Alex was running his fingers over the back of his helmet to check for damage from the stone shrapnel, he felt his SFPDA comm unit vibrate in one of the pouches at his waist. The Hammer wanted to talk.

"Sam, get the men to drag all these bodies back into the tunnels, and see if you can resurrect that tent over the entrance," Alex said. "Clean the perimeter. I'll update HQ and receive orders."

He walked away a few paces into the dark and cold desert air. He pulled the miniaturised military PDA device out and switched it to wirelessly receive into his helmet comm. The signal was clear and strong, already piggybacking over the strongest communication grid it could find while frequency-hopping to avoid detection.

O'Riordan was pulling one of the bodies into the mouth of the tunnel when he spotted something small in the sand. He nudged it with his toe to bring it to the surface—a human finger. It must have been blown off one of the Takavaran by Hex's laser when he moved it to a broad-beam pulse. He bent and picked it up, and looked at it for a few seconds before he glanced across at Adira. She had her back to him while she talked to the young scientist. A hundred possibilities ran through his mind.

"Don't even think about it, Irish," Rocky said. He was watching with his hands on his hips, plainly he'd read the redheaded HAWC's mind.

O'Riordan saw Alex near the woman and gave up his plan. "I know where I'd like to fucking stick it," he said. He threw the finger to the sand and ground his boot over it until it was buried inches below the dry desert surface.

"Did we have to kill them all?" Zach was saying to Adira. "Couldn't we have just knocked them out, or shot them in the leg?" He had his arms wrapped around his torso and shivered slightly as another body was dragged past him.

Adira shook her head. "Them or us, Zachariah. This is

the real world and how it works—very different from the lecture theatre, yes?"

Zach shrugged his shoulders and let his arms drop. "It feels wrong."

Adira grabbed his upper arms and looked up into his face. "Sometimes you have to fight. Sometimes you need to defend yourself and others." She shook him slightly. "When the time to fight comes, what will you do, Zach?"

"What is your status, Arcadian?" said Hammerson into Alex's helmet comm.

"Twelve bad guys down. Good guys still unannounced. Target site is confirmed as ground zero for gamma pulse and gravitational distortion. Nothing remains in operation. Party has gone elsewhere."

"Attention. Party has now been reacquired—secondary pulse detected. Partially shielded gamma signal confirmed; coordinates being sent now. Further instructions on rendez-vous with blue doves. Beach holiday now extended. Good luck, Arcadian. Over and out."

Alex signed off and looked at the SFPDA. There was an attachment that opened to supply the coordinates. A map appeared—their current location was circled in red, another circle appeared to their north, and a line connected them. A name appeared: Arak. Alex knew the blue doves were the Israelis, so obviously Mossad had more information to share with them. He called Adira over.

"We're being redirected. Tell me about Arak."

Adira made a guttural sound in the back of her throat and rolled her eyes. "Smallish city in the Markazi Province, just under 500 miles to our north."

Alex couldn't help groaning.

"If we take the new highways, about one day," she told him. "But there are roadblocks. If we take back roads, several days and we will need an SUV. The fastest and safest way for us is to meet the returning supply train from Bushehr. It's fast and cuts right through the Zagros Mountains. We need to jump off at Kashan and then trek west up into the Markazi. Should get us there in just over a day."

The clean-up was complete. Seen from the air, the inter-action was now completely erased. Alex checked his watch: 0200 hours. It had all started and finished in three hours—not bad. They still had about four hours until sun-up—they needed to make use of it. He looked across at the truck one of the Takavaran squads had been resting under. "Irish. Get that truck working ASAP."

He turned back to Adira. "Now, where do we meet that train?"

# Twenty-five

The president was coming.

Ahmad Al Janaddi was sweating profusely from the pressure of a thousand unfinished tasks. Even though Moshaddam wasn't due for a few days, he needed to have the facility rebuilt in time to conduct a third trial to finalise the calibration of the test openings—or "Judgment Events" as the president had instructed they now be called. The scientist was a little unnerved by how Moshaddam so smoothly intertwined religion and science. He spoke as if every successful test was a prophecy straight from the holy book.

Al Janaddi thanked Allah that they had refined the rebuilding process, with many of the pieces prebuilt for fast installation. The entire acceleration chamber could now be recreated and operational within twenty-four hours. The latest test must occur today, without fail, and then they must be ready to rerun by the time the president was on site. Since Moshaddam had announced he was coming, the schedule had become immutable. Al Janaddi didn't doubt for a second that all his successes would count for nothing if he were seen to be slow in responding to a direct order from the president.

Installation of the new silver sphere was almost complete, and the circular line marking the edge of "Allah's Gateway" was already in place. There would be just a single traveller this time, and the president had personally provided the blueprint for the design of a six and half foot lead capsule that was to be fully constructed and in place before the next test run. Inside the hermetically sealed pod, which weighed many tons, there was room for a man to stand comfortably. In addition, it held black box-type recording equipment, homing beacons and communication devices. Theoretically, when the traveller returned, he could be detected and retrieved from anywhere in the world.

The computer simulations were very encouraging; it now looked possible to control the size of the Judgment Event and even its duration. This was the most important step in being able to design a harness for the powerful gamma radiation emissions—a repository to actually store the enormous cosmic energies. Al Janaddi smiled to himself. Already he had achieved more than dozens of scientists working in laboratories around the world. If only he could tell someone . . . If only he could tell *everyone.*

Al Janaddi was a talented scientist and a man with great dreams. Like every science professional, he imagined the ultimate recognition of his work—a Nobel Prize for science. It had proved to be more than a dream for one Iranian. Shirin Ebadi had been awarded the Peace Prize in 2003; she had been showered with wealth and was now treated as a national hero.

Al Janaddi closed his eyes and dreamed for a moment. Success and recognition could bring him many fantastic things—enough money to buy his mother a new house with heating that actually worked in winter, a new car for his lazy brother—just a small one though. A holiday for himself, maybe even to America; it would be worth it, even if he had to have a Republican Guard accompanying him everywhere.

*Ahh, what would it be like to live in America with so much freedom?* He daydreamed some more: *Hello, I live in New York. Hello, I live in Texas. Hmm . . .* He breathed in through his nose, a smile just touching his lips as he imagined the Norwegian gold medal being hung around his neck while the world applauded.

He opened his eyes and made a guttural sound in the back of his throat as the image of that disgusting creature in the containment cell ruined his beautiful daydreams. *It wasn't my fault,* he thought, pushing harsh reality and its side effects to one side as he returned to fiddling with some software refinements. He still had much work to do.

On Al Janaddi's instruction, his fellow scientists and the attending technicians went through a final operational program while he reviewed the facility's image recorders, transponders and other electronic sensory equipment. New equipment had been added, which, they hoped, would contain the dark matter and stop it evaporating so rapidly. More refinements were still on the drawing board and would be engineered following this test; every run now was an opportunity to learn more about the mysterious anomalies they were creating. It was all in order—they were ready.

Al Janaddi stopped flicking between cameras when he reached the sphere room and stared at the lead capsule standing in the semi-gloom of the chamber. He had made one adjustment to the president's blueprints, more as another option for retrieval of the capsule than as any form of improvement. A large half-ring had been welded to the back of the capsule; attached to it was an inch-thick titanium cable that snaked away to be bolted securely to an industrial winch on the wall. An extra 500 feet of cable was coiled at the base of the wall—hopefully enough to allow the traveller to enter the black hole far enough to obtain meaningful data, then be reeled back in like a fish.

Al Janaddi flicked the image feed to a small camera inside the lead capsule. The old cleric who had volunteered for the test looked almost rapturous at his imminent departure through "Allah's Gateway." The promise of a personal meeting with God followed by eternal life in Jannah was irresistible to any man of faith. Al Janaddi wondered whether the cleric would be so composed if he met the distorted remnant of humanity that moaned and slavered in the tunnel complex below.

He raised his voice without turning. "Green light in sixty seconds." This time there was little enthusiasm, just nods and one weak "*Allahu Akbar*" from a younger technician. Al Janaddi lowered his visor and initiated the particle acceleration lasers—once again the lights dimmed.

As before, faster than human vision could comprehend, the sphere room disappeared into a nothingness so black it hurt the eyes and confused the consciousness. This time, however, the event was suspended and didn't dissipate so quickly. Encouraged, Al Janaddi levered up the accelerator just one notch on a dial that held over fifty calibrations. Immediately, a wave passed through the laboratory that made his fingertips tingle and caused his stomach to threaten to erupt. He checked his dials—no radiation leakage, but his small screen clock seemed to have slowed.

The capsule was gone. The thick cable fed out with a surprising slowness into the black emptiness—a loop every twenty seconds, as if the capsule were on a sedate and comfortable voyage.

*Excellent, just one more*, Al Janaddi thought, and pushed the dial up another notch. In an instant all the lead shielding started to warp out from the walls and ceiling. Red lights flashed and a siren screamed a warning that the gamma particles were threatening to explode out of the complex. The scientist sucked in a frightened breath and eased the lever back, allowing the event to stabilise for another moment.

"Merciful Allah, that was close. Now let us see if we can bring him back . . ." Al Janaddi pressed the winch button and, with a deep whine, the loose cable was drawn up from the floor. After the slack was taken up, there was a thump and the whining changed to a deeper grinding noise.

*Achhh!* Al Janaddi switched the winch off, and was deciding on his next move when an even more ominous sound started within the chamber. The cable leading into the cold blackness, already piano-wire tight, moved up, then down, grinding and shrieking as it wrenched against the winch ring. The cable thrummed, as if something was hauling itself grip over grip along the metal cord. As Al Janaddi watched with an open mouth, he couldn't help but be reminded of when he was a boy, fishing with his father, and they had hooked a big shark. The fishing line had done something similar before they cut it free. "Never bring a shark into the boat," his father had said in a low voice as they watched the cut line whip over the side.

*Never bring a shark into the boat.* Al Janaddi quickly hit the disengage button. Now free, the cable thrashed away into the dark pool almost faster than his eye could follow.

He switched off the acceleration beam and the Judgment Event dissolved as fast as it had appeared. He looked around at the lead-lined room and sucked in an enormous breath, realising he had forgotten to breathe. The shielding over the command centre had held, otherwise he and his technicians would be melted flesh or would have been dragged into the black hole's corona. He sat down and wiped cold perspiration from his brow—he needed better technology to hold and manage the event.

He checked the other monitors; in the previous test runs, the subjects had been returned almost instantaneously. But of the elderly cleric there was no sign, no signal, nor any images. Either the recording equipment inside the capsule had short-circuited, or the man and capsule were no longer on the planet.

Al Janaddi thought again about the behaviour of the cable. He suspected the little cleric was gone for good.

The creature stopped its slow, insidious movement through the sand. Small glands in its head sensed the slight radiation pulse that had leaked out of the containment sphere facility, and it remembered the same feeling just before it was wrenched from its home.

It raised itself up; sand falling from its armoured plating. Its unearthly vision allowed it to see electromagnetic and X-ray waves travelling across the ionosphere. Its fan-like protuberances waved in the air, scooping molecules from the atmosphere to sample and taste. It could detect the heavy radioactive particles and was drawn to their source—the Jamshid II laboratory.

It reared up on its four powerful hind legs, each bristled point digging into the crusted sand, and called again to its own kind across the desert floor. It held immobile for a few seconds—as before, there was no reply.

The sun glinted off the waxy, mottled shell as it drew in

the sensations of this new world. The armoured exoskeletal plates had been compacted together to preserve precious fluids within its body, and its bullet-shaped head was drawn back into the bulbous hump across what could pass for shoulders.

As two black chitin-covered eyes extended on the end of eyestalks, the plates opened out, and its upper body flared open briefly to dislodge more particles of the annoying dry sand. The creature flexed, and the open carapace revealed an underbelly that carried two enormous curved claws—each covered in rows of teeth and ending in a blackened talon. Below these lethal daggers were row upon row of numerous smaller thoracic limbs that slowly undulated. A slight clicking could be heard from the sharp tips whenever they struck each other in their wave-like twitching. Further in, greasy flaps and tendrils hung, coiled and furled amongst the rows of dark green armoured tiles. The carapace shuddered, and then closed across the thing's hellish appendages.

The fan-like tongue flicked out again and its head swayed slightly as more of the radioactive particles bathed its sensory organs, and it turned to face the direction they were coming from—perhaps there was a way back to its home.

It dropped to the sand and sped towards Arak and the sphere chamber.

# Twenty-six

Hammerson read the information brief quickly. Another radiation pulse—weaker, but still heavy gamma and little else. This one again from the small city of Arak at the foot of the Markazi Mountains. Whatever they were doing there certainly wasn't finished.

Hammerson pressed the button on his phone. "Annie, get me Major Harris at Space Strat. Then put a secure call through to Moss-1 for me."

Right now he needed two things: some thermal images from around Arak to get an idea of what Alex was walking into; and to speak to his old friend General Meir Shavit. Mossad needed to be kept in the loop.

Hammerson would trade what he had with the Israelis because he needed to know what they were thinking and what they were planning. The constant radiation emissions coming from central Iran would be worrying the hell out of them. He could only keep them on a leash for so long before they decided to take matters into their own hands. He needed to give his team time to secure the technology before the general decided that the best way to deal with the problem was to incinerate everything.

Hammerson knew that most of the Middle Eastern countries tolerated, distrusted or downright hated each other. But nothing would unite them quicker than an attack from Israel, and somehow it always ended up being America's fault. *Life was a lot simpler when they just burned our flags*, he thought as the call was put through to his desk phone.

* * *

The HAWCs and their Israeli companions leapt onto the slowing train just outside of Shiraz. The dilapidated diesel locomotive was returning to northern Iran with oil refinery equipment and supplies for one of the new drill platforms at Babol on the Caspian Sea. There were no passengers and the train was unguarded, so the HAWCs found it easy to enter the packed cargo carriage without being detected. From time to time they would open the door a crack for fresh air and to check their surroundings, but that was all—the bone-chilling wind that blew in off the mountains discouraged any sightseeing. Sam managed to track their progress on his GPS unit and called out their speed and position every few hours.

Even in the bitter cold of the unheated car, they rested. Until they reached Kashan, the fate of their mission rested with the train driver and good luck. Alex knew that if the bodies of the Takavaran weren't discovered at Persepolis, they still held the element of surprise. From what they'd seen so far, they'd need it.

In the corner of the carriage, a tiny mouse scurried up to a crate and started to gnaw at the wood. In no time it had opened a hole the size of a fingertip and squeezed through, returning a few seconds later with what looked like a coffee bean. Alex smiled. *Just a tiny opening—that's all we'll need too*, he thought.

Adira woke from a light doze and half-opened her eyes. She sat with her back against a crate and her arms folded on bent knees; she lifted her head slightly to rest her chin on the arch made by her arms. Dawn light was beginning to squeeze through cracks in the carriage walls and she could make out the form of Alex Hunter sitting opposite her, his large frame striped with the morning's early glow. She smiled as she watched him try to feed a little grey mouse something he had found on the floor. She went to look away, but found her eyes kept being drawn back to the man—so she gave up and studied him.

He was handsome, but she knew plenty of good-looking

men. He was dangerous, but also honourable—and right now he just looked so . . . normal. It was impossible to think that he was part of some secret American experiment. But she had seen him do things that were not possible. What was the Arcadian? What would happen to Alex Hunter if she betrayed him to General Shavit, to the Mossad hierarchy?

She took a breath, then exhaled quietly through her nose. *Why this one?* she thought, and smiled again as she saw him whisper something to the small creature at his feet.

Alex felt a bead of perspiration run down the side of his face. As the sun climbed higher, and the Zagros Mountains fell far behind, the temperature had risen rapidly in the carnage. What had been a freezing wooden box as they passed through the mountains had quickly becoming a foul-smelling roaster.

The HAWCs were relieved when Sam called their position as being just ten miles out from Kashan. Rocky pulled open the door and filled their carriage with sweet-smelling, dry desert air. Adira leaned out of the car, looking up and down the track, and called for them to get ready. The train slowed from its top speed of around sixty miles per hour down to thirty to negotiate a bend—"Jump!" Adira yelled. One by one, like parachutists leaving a plane, they leapt and rolled into the hard-packed soil. At twenty miles per hour, there were no comfortable landings.

Sam took charge of Zach, forcing the young man to roll with him so he didn't break any bones on the landing. They all stayed low to the ground until the train was several miles away, then got to their feet. In the distance, they could see the train heading for a small city nestled among clumped wild date palms and tall trees—a small haven of green in the dry sepia and brown of the desert.

"Kashan is one of the small oasis cities," Adira said. "A peaceful place of gardens and poets, and we have good people there." She turned away from the verdant town setting and nodded west. "That's where we need to go. About sixty miles to Arak—ten to twelve hours on foot."

Alex surveyed their position and the parched land to the west. There was no road, no path. It was just after 1100 hours and the day was cloudless and dry. Thankfully, the temperature was fairly mild for around here—only 100 degrees. *A walk in the park*, he thought.

"We'll do it in eight. Let's go." He led them out in a trot.

They had been moving fast for nearly five hours when Alex called a rest break. They would stop for forty minutes—ten minutes for food and then fifteen minutes of rest each—one team on, one team off. Hex, Irish, Rocky and Adira rested first, then Alex, Sam and Zach. Alex saw Zach pass out instantly, but he let the young scientist sleep; he couldn't imagine what Zach's body must feel like after all the exertion. A few miles back he had seen Adira help him with his pack—he would allow it this time only. Even Alex's supercharged body needed to repair itself. He ate some dried beef and then slept. For fifteen minutes the world went away.

His body rested, but his mind worked—dark memories slithering up from its depths. Beneath his eyelids his eyes moved back and forth, searching, hunting, trying to see in the murky darkness of a cave. The creature had him again, its tentacle was wrapping around his body, its curved, razor-sharp talons were embedding themselves into his back and neck.

Alex woke with a roar that caused all the HAWCs to draw their weapons and crouch in defensive positions. Adira had both her Baraks drawn and aimed towards Alex. The snake fell from his neck and started to slide away into the desert.

Adira leapt at it and put her boot on its neck, then reached down to pick it up. "*Yaarsh* . . . did it bite you? This is a saw-scaled viper—deadly."

Alex had taken his helmet off to rest and also unzipped the collar of his suit. He reached up and felt his neck—his hand came away spotted with blood. Perhaps the pulsing of an artery had attracted the snake, or maybe it was just pissed off in the heat. Alex felt his head start to throb with a deep ache that made his eyes hurt.

"Yeah, it got me," he said. "What type of venom?"

Sam kneeled beside Alex, opening his upper eyelid to peer at the white around the pupil.

Adira drew one of her knives and pressed the back of the snake's head, forcing its mouth open. She used the knife to bring out its fangs and pushed upwards. Venom should have squirted from the extended fangs. Nothing came.

"*Shishza!* It's dry," she said. "You must have got a full dose. This is one of the Middle East's deadliest snakes—proteolytic venom, haemotoxic; painful and deadly. If the bite was on a limb, rapid amputation would be recommended. You need antivenene and about several pints of blood in a field transfusion." She jammed her blade roughly back into its sheath and squeezed the snake's neck in her fist.

Alex pressed his thumbs into his eyelids and shook his head. "A week on the beach would be nice too. Don't worry, I think I missed the full dose. I'll be okay, but I'll need to rest up a bit. Hex, you take your team out immediately and we'll catch up on the way. You know what to do."

Hex nodded. There would be no questioning the decision—the boss's orders were always followed. Rocky and Irish kitted up and prepared to leave.

Adira looked at the snake and said something in Hebrew. She changed her grip, twirled the short body once around her head and then used the momentum to flick it bullwhip-style. The viper's head exploded off its body in a spray of scales and blood, leaving Adira holding a writhing pipe of snake flesh, which she flung out into the desert.

She looked down at Alex almost angrily and said, "*Lehitra'ot*, Alex Hunter. I hope I will see you again." She turned away, her fists balled, still muttering to herself.

Alex knew they didn't have any antivenene, and they certainly didn't have the time or equipment for even the roughest field transfusion. He also knew he had received a full dose of the poison—he could feel it in his system. He had to trust his body to combat the venom by itself, but for that he needed to sleep.

He spoke to Sam quietly. "You need to knock me out for two hours while I rest. I'll be okay—you know that, Uncle."

Sam nodded and knelt down beside him, turning Alex's head to look at the small wounds on his neck. "Two hours, huh? Sixty milligrams of benzodiazepine should do it. Anticonvulsant and muscle relaxant. I can put you out for around that long—the rest is up to you. But, ah, I heard Ms. Senesh—she did say amputation was an option. Might be quicker—it is only your head we're talking about, after all."

Alex chuckled. "Just keep an eye out for more snakes, will you, or next time I'll make you suck the poison out."

Sam gave Alex the sedative, and he lay down with his head and shoulders in the shade of a small spiky bush. He sucked in an enormous breath and closed his eyes. In a minute he was breathing deeply.

Sam noticed that the veins around the snake bite on Alex's neck bulged like fat worms fighting under his skin, and the bite itself was weeping clear liquid. *There's a war going on in there*, he thought. Sam was one of the few people in the world who knew what the Arcadian was capable of. He had seen Alex perform feats that had left elite soldiers gaping. For most, the Arcadian was a Special Forces myth, but to a few—a handful of scientists, the most senior brass in USSTRATCOM, the Hammer and Sam—he was a miracle.

Sam caught up with Adira as she was heading out with Hex's team. "Ms. Senesh—that snake . . . What's Captain Hunter in for?"

Adira looked over at Alex's sleeping form. "Without treatment . . . if he's lucky, some swelling, pain, maybe blindness and some loss of motor functions. Then he'll probably go into a coma and die. If he's unlucky, he'll bleed out internally and die in great agony. This type of viper has killed many of our soldiers on desert missions; they're active day and night, aggressive and deadly. Captain Hunter's strong, but I don't think you'll be catching up with us anytime soon,

Sam Reid. I can get him to Tel Aviv in a day—just say the word."

Sam shook his head slowly. Adira narrowed her eyes and shrugged. "*Behatzlacha*, Sam Reid." She looked once again at Alex. "Was . . . is he the Arcadian?"

This time it was Sam's turn to shrug. "Good luck yourself."

Adira nodded and turned away, then paused as the response to her Hebrew comment registered with her. She gave Sam a fleeting smile, then joined Hex and the Red team.

Sam watched her go, then called Zachariah over. "Keep an eye on him—I'm going to have a quick look around. Make sure nothing else bites, stings or pecks him while he's out!"

Zach looked down at the unconscious HAWC leader and placed his hand just above his forehead. Sam knew Zach didn't need to touch Alex's skin to feel that he was on fire. Alex's body temperature always ran a few degrees hotter than any normal man's—it was his furnace-like metabolism operating at full throttle all the time. Now, with the deadly toxin in his system, he was burning up.

Sam could see Alex's eyes flicking back and forth under his lids as his body fought the poison. He remembered Adira's Hebrew word for luck: "behatzlacha." *Yes, he'll need it*, Sam thought.

Alex had loosened his grip on the rope for only a second and had flown off the swing to land face first in the loosely packed earth. His head hurt and his mouth was full of dirt. He looked up at his father, trying to decide whether or not to cry.

Jim Hunter smiled and brushed the earth from Alex's forehead and cheeks. "You're not hurt, you're strong," he said.

Alex nodded and reached out to touch the scar on his father's left brow. "Did that hurt, Daddy?" he asked, his stubby little finger tracing the shiny, pink crescent.

"Yes, but only for a second. The trick is to be stronger

than the pain. It always goes away, and then you're left with a small scar and a big smile."

"I'm stronger than the pain," Alex repeated, deciding not to cry after all.

His father hugged him and he felt the strong hands on his back. But his father wouldn't let go and the fingers were starting to dig in. Alex tried to push away, but the grip became impossibly tight . . . and sticky now, congealing all around him.

Alex lifted his head and saw that he was a man again, not the little boy of a moment ago, and his father had changed . . . it was no longer his father holding him but the tentacle of a creature he had last battled with under the Antarctic's ice.

He felt the dagger-like tusks enter his chest, his back and sides. His whole body was being crushed and pierced. His strength was failing him, falling away like dry leaves. The pain was unbearable. *You're not stronger than the pain; you never were. Pain always wins . . . it always wins.* The words repeated over and over in his head.

Alex opened his mouth to scream as he felt the bones crumble beneath his skin. His flesh was peeling away and he was falling. He knew that when he hit the bottom he would die. Blackness slammed shut on him like the lid of a coffin.

# Twenty-seven

The sun was sinking towards the Markazi Mountains and the temperature had dropped to a pleasant seventy degrees. Zach was leaning up against a warm rock, dozing. He held a slim water canteen loosely in his hand, and a long string of dribble created a glistening river from his slightly open mouth and down his shoulder. His glasses had slid to the end of his nose.

A tall shadow fell across him and a hand grasped his shoulder.

"Whaa—?" Zach opened his eyes; then had to blink twice and push his glasses back up before he could speak. "*Yoish!* You're alive . . . I mean awake."

"You're losing water; cap your canteen," Alex said.

Zach blinked once more and looked up at the HAWC captain. The man's hair was damp from perspiration, the snakebite wound was now just a couple of small pink marks on his neck, already healing over. "Uh, how do you feel?" Zach asked.

Alex ran his hand through his hair. "Like I'm hungover and thirsty as hell. What's our status?"

"Ahh . . ." Zach looked around, not exactly sure what to tell him.

"I'll take that one," Sam said, walking up behind Zach and handing Alex a water canteen. While Alex drank, Sam looked at the wound on his neck and nodded. "Looking good."

Zach stood to take a closer look at the near-healed wound. "So the snake didn't inject you with all its venom, after all?"

Alex turned away and said over his shoulder, "I was lucky this time. Sam?"

Zach could have sworn Sam was wearing the hint of a smile as he began his report.

Hex's team had made good progress to the Arak Jamshid II facility—they were over two hours ahead and expected to rendezvous with Mossad agents for a briefing before entering the city. They'd encountered no Takavaran, nor had there been any signs of pursuit.

Alex nodded. "Good. I need something to eat, then we go. Two minutes—be ready, gentlemen."

Adira held the HAWC monoscope to her eye and looked into the high areas of the Markazi Mountains. The scope was a matt black tube with a rubber cap on the end for fitting snugly over the eye. It sat in the fist comfortably and its image enhancers magnified thirty times with an infinite range. She pulled the device away from her face and looked at it admiringly. *Better than anything back home—think I'll keep it.*

She replaced the scope in its pouch and breathed in the desert air. She felt strangely flat and shook her head at a creeping thought: *he's probably already dead by now.* It was perhaps a good thing. Alex Hunter was becoming a distraction from her primary mission. And if he was the secret Arcadian, or part of that project, she now felt free to give a full briefing about him when she returned. Yes, his death was probably a good thing.

She took another breath; the hollowness in her stomach was still there . . . and maybe something else. "*Achhh*, stop haunting me, Alex Hunter," she said softly as she looked towards the city of Arak.

Ice-capped peaks to the west framed the ancient settlement; everywhere else it was surrounded by vast arid plains that looked barely hospitable. Adira knew the city had a large lake at its edge. This was the Nemisham Lake—beautiful, but its inviting waters were a cauldron of toxic chemicals that steamed with skin-stripping acids. *Like the country itself*, she thought, *alluring and dangerous in equal measures*.

A Mossad agent appeared out of the desert like a wraith, spoke in hurried Hebrew to her, then vanished just as quickly in the wavering heat haze. This was what Adira had been waiting for. She stood looking at Arak for a further moment, then returned to the HAWCs.

"The laboratory is hidden on the outskirts of the city, in a labyrinth of ancient caves," she told them. "They've been posing as archaeologists carrying out significant restoration work on the Sassanid Dynasty statues deep inside the caves. They've been digging for years; there's no telling how deep they are. We can't take them head on or covertly. The place is heavily fortified and guarded by the regular Iranian Army. Worse, my men tell me there are many squads of Takavaran Zolfaghar now in and around the facility."

Irish blew air through his lips in disdain. "Yeah, those guys were real tough," he sneered.

Adira tried to ignore him, but there was something about the man's attitude that made her want to lash out. "I think you were lucky Hex was back there for you, Lieutenant O'Riordan, or you would be just another dead animal drying in the desert."

"Fuck you," Irish spat.

Adira smiled and went on. "There may be another option— another way into the Jamshid II facility that is unknown to the Takavaran. There is a cave opening high within the Markazi Mountains; the locals avoid it because they believe it is filled with demons. My people believe it's not guarded, so we may be able to use it to break into the facility."

"May be able to? Possibly unguarded? That's all we got to go with?" Irish said scornfully. "We don't have a lotta time to invest in maybes right now. Pretty soon they're gonna know we're here. We get our backs to the wall in a freakin' cave and we're dead meat."

Adira and O'Riordan took a step towards each other and Hex moved in between them. Adira suspected O'Riordan was a man who didn't like any opinion other than his own.

She looked at him steadily around Hex, holding back the Hebrew curse and keeping her voice calm and even.

"That's right, Lieutenant O'Riordan. Best intel we've got. The alternative is a direct assault—go head to head with an unknown number of Iranian Special Ops. We could be bogged down for days . . . and the only reinforcements arriving will be theirs. How much time did you say you wanted to spend here, Lieutenant?"

O'Riordan locked eyes with her, then spat onto the sand and walked off swearing under his breath. She smiled; she'd made her point.

Adira gave the cave coordinates to Hex and a description of the entrance. It was distinctive because of its guardian: a ten foot tall decaying statue of a long dead king.

Hex nodded and turned to the HAWCs. "Rocky, send a squirt to the Blue team. Irish, we move in three minutes for the cave."

Though the team had direct communication via their helmets, from now on they would use coded information squirts, especially in open terrain. If there were Iranian Special Forces close by, they might be able to pinpoint a foreign signal coming from the desert—with or without the frequency jumpers. The "squirt" was almost instantaneous and technologically invisible. Rocky simply used a text-based messaging format in his SFPDA, which, when sending, was coded and compressed and bounced off any local satellite it could find. He sent Alex information on the Takavaran, the cave system and its entrance, and their operational status. Within minutes, the message was received and acknowledged: they were good to proceed.

Hex checked the ground-based radar strapped to his forearm while Adira scanned the near horizons with her scope. They looked at each other and Adira raised her eyebrows. Hex mouthed *okay* back to her—no movement or metallic readings in a two-mile radius. *Good as it's going to get, time to move*, Adira thought.

It would be a ten-mile jog to the cave in this dry heat and they needed to remain alert at all times. She was tired already, pissed off with the redheaded HAWC, and they hadn't even got to their objective zone yet. She sucked in a deep breath and began to run.

Zach saw Alex receive the information squirt. The HAWC read for a few seconds, then turned to him and Sam and spoke briefly about the potential force of opposition, their destination, and the cave system they would use to try and enter the Jamshid II complex. Zach was intensely interested in the further gamma-pulse readings emanating from a live Jamshid site and couldn't wait to actually see what technology the Iranians were using. But he was tired, his elbows throbbed from the jump from the train, and his stomach still ached from the buffeting he'd taken strapped to Sam for the HALO jump.

"Uh, how do we get there?" he asked, spinning around as though expecting to find a taxi to hail.

Alex looked at Sam and smiled. "Speed formation. Uncle, you'll be taking us out. And you, Dr. Shomron, suck in some air and take a big swill of water—you'll need it."

Sam quickly checked for any loose equipment on his suit and lowered his visor. Alex grabbed Zach by the elbow and checked his suit for loose equipment too.

"The speed formation is the optimum way to cross a hostile terrain on foot," he explained. "We run in single file, and each man takes a turn in the lead to absorb the wind resistance and allow the man behind to 'rest' in his lee. The rest only saves a minuscule amount of energy each time, but over many miles it makes a difference. It's all we've got, and we don't have a lot of time."

*Many miles* was all Zach heard. "I . . . ah . . . I don't think I'll be able to keep up, Captain Hunter."

Alex put both his hands on the tall, skinny scientist's shoulders and looked him in the face. "You'd be surprised what you can do if you try, Zachariah. I remember a young man who probably didn't think he could jump out of a plane at 35,000 feet or climb down into a pitch black elevator shaft a while back."

Zach knew Alex was waiting for him to make some sort of positive response, but there was no way he could speak as his voice would betray the lack of confidence he felt.

After a few more seconds, Alex nodded in understanding, "It's okay, I'll take your shift out in front. I'll carry you if I have to, but I'd prefer you give it all you've got, all right?"

Zach nodded, still unable to speak. Alex slapped him on the shoulder then pulled down his visor. Zach sucked in a huge breath and slowly slid his visor down as well.

Dozens of miles apart, two small camouflaged teams, looking like sand-coloured cyborgs, ran across the dry and spindly Markazi landscape.

A little over two miles from the Blue team's position, a small four-man Takavaran team monitored their surveillance equipment. They were on a two-on, two-off shift rotation so they had eyes and ears on the desert for an unbroken twenty-four hours. They had with them a traditional nomads' tent constructed of sun-bleached canvas and animal hides, to give them the appearance of a small band of traders resting before entering the city for a day's commerce. Inside the tent, the antiquated gave way to high tech, with guns, explosives and ammunition lined up for quick access next to surveillance, communication and monitoring equipment. An electronic eye kept watch on their surface surroundings: day or night, nothing would cross the desert within a mile of their patch without them knowing.

Or so they thought.

A hundred feet from the men, the dry, dusty surface of a hump of earth broke open. A sharp proboscis lifted in the air and fine, boneless tendrils protruded, waving back and forth as they tasted their surroundings. Anyone watching might have mistaken them for the petals of a colourless fan-like flower gently waving in the breeze.

The creature had detected the slight footfalls of the men and the hum of their electronics from many miles away, but it was their body fluids that had been an irresistible magnet. The creature's hunger flared—it sensed two of the organic beings were sleeping and decided to approach these first. The pale fan folded and the proboscis withdrew below the ground. The earth lifted slightly as the mound moved towards the tent and disappeared under its edge.

Abu Tayib woke to an intense pain in his shoulder. When he went to sit up, he couldn't. He could open his eyes and his mouth, but his limbs weighed a ton, as if he were drugged. He concentrated all his strength on his arm and managed to raise it a little—just enough for him to catch sight of . . . But this arm couldn't belong to him—his arm was burly and covered in shiny, black curls of hair, while this limb was shrunken and withered. The pain intensified and he tried to scream, but all that escaped his cracked lips was a feeble mewling.

From under the sand, the creature had inserted its feeding spike up into the sleeping animal and injected it with a natural sedative designed to immobilise it. It also injected a substance to liquefy the organic matter it found within the soft outer casing. The absence of a hard exoskeleton meant the creature was quickly able to penetrate the body and soften the muscle, cartilage and even most of the bone. Abu Tayib was literally being liquefied and drawn down the feeding spike into the belly of the monster below the sand.

Yusuf Ayyub and Tawbah Siluf entered the tent to wake their sleeping Takavaran brothers. After a long boring shift they were looking forward to taking their turn on the sleeping rolls. At first, they didn't comprehend what they were seeing. Abu Tayib seemed smaller somehow.

Yusuf pulled back the bedroll covering and blinked; it looked like a shrivelled monkey had been placed inside his comrade's robes—stick-like arms and legs attached to a mottled, collapsing diaphragm. Yusuf nudged the thing with his foot and the head slowly turned towards him. A withered black tongue came out of its mouth—the thing was still alive and trying to speak to him.

"*Al-Muhaimin*." Yusuf spoke one of Allah's secret names

as the Protector of Men, and stuck his knuckles in his mouth. He had seen men blown to pieces, or tortured in ways that would cause normal men to loosen their bowels from fright. But this was something else, so horrifying that it tore at his consciousness.

Tawbah pulled back the covers on the second bedroll and found the other agent in a worse state. He was even more desiccated if possible, just a small sack of bones and tendons. Even the orbs of his eyes had been drained of all their fluids.

Both men were about to flee when Abu Tayib's collapsed body was thrown to the side. What rose from the ground froze the two soldiers in terror. Yusuf thought perhaps they were already dead and had been cast into Jahannam, for this was surely one of the foul beasts of the pit sent to torment the souls of the unbelievers.

In a sinuous motion, the creature lifted itself from the hole below Abu's bedroll and stood on powerful, segmented legs bristling with insectoid hairs. A rain of sand fell from it as its cuticular exoskeleton front flared open, exposing many smaller legs. It was far quicker than a creature of its size and bulk should have been, and immediately enveloped Yusuf. While holding him close to its body with its many legs, it shot out a long curved claw to cleave the head of Tawbah.

The creature lowered itself and its struggling prey to the ground, its eyestalks swivelling around to fix black, glass-like bulbs on the terrified man. Its pointed head broke open at the front and its gristly mandible apparatus spread wide to allow the feeding spike to extend slowly into Yusuf's chest. The Takavaran vomited as he realised what had happened to the sleeping men—and what was about to happen to him.

# Twenty-eight

After jogging for just three miles, Zach collapsed. The temperature in the open Markazi desert had been known to reach over 170 degrees. It was nowhere near that yet, but for the untrained Israeli scientist it was still far too hot and dry to stop exhaustion and dehydration from knocking his legs out from under him. Alex took a quick look at the thin, young man, gave him a sip of water, then lifted him onto his back as if he weighed no more than a child.

Sam didn't even bother offering—he knew Alex had far more stamina and strength than him. If need be, Alex could have carried them both. Both HAWCs increased their pace now that they didn't need to keep it in second gear due to the young scientist.

They still had a long way to go.

After about twenty minutes, Zach felt a little better. His eyesight had stopped swimming and he was less nauseous, but bouncing along on Alex's back didn't make for a comfortable ride. His head throbbed every time the armoured plates of his own suit banged into Alex's shoulder shielding as the HAWC pounded across the sand.

Sam was taking his turn out in front again, and Zach marvelled at how effortless he and Alex made the desert crossing look. In between the armour plating, the HAWCs' suits stuck to their bodies, probably drenched in perspiration. *They'll need to stop soon to drink*, Zach thought. But as yet both men looked powerful and relentless.

Zach could feel a rash beginning on his neck where the material met his bare skin. His suit didn't fit right—it bagged on him and made him look like a skinny kid playing dress-ups in his father's work clothes. He remembered what his Uncle Mosh, Aunt Dodah's squat husband, used to say to him almost every week: *You need more muscle, Zachie.* Uncle Mosh was forever trying to encourage Zach to get his head out of the books and do more exercise. *You'll need muscles as well as brains when you grow up,* he used to tell him. Uncle Mosh had played football at high school and got around in a white singlet in even the coldest weather. Though he only owned a carpet-laying business, he used to waggle his finger in Zach's face and say, "The brainy kids never get to do anything interesting. They just sit at a desk all day and write boring papers."

Zach watched the hard-packed desert earth pass rapidly beneath Alex's feet and his mind travelled back to the Persepolis ruins and the unbelievable physical distortion evidence he had seen. He had hoped the first gamma release was just some form of accident, but he had overheard Captain Hunter talking to Adira about a further radiation pulse. He hadn't really believed anyone would actually try to harness the strange forces involved in black holes and dark matter—everything was so theoretical, so dangerous. They just didn't know what they were dealing with. It was a little like looking for a landmine in the dark by banging the ground with a hammer.

Zach liked to think he was equalitarian when it came to politics, race and religion. Everyone was equal; everyone had the right to be heard. But what if Adira was right? What if it was possible to turn the power generated by a black hole into a weapon? Would he want Israel to have that weapon? America? Worse, someone like Moshaddam?

*You're right, Uncle Mosh,* he thought. *We brainy kids never get to do anything interesting.*

He contemplated asking Alex to let him down so he could try again to keep up with the HAWCs. But Alex accelerated to take the lead from Sam, and after a few more seconds of watching the speed with which the HAWC leader

travelled across the dry desert, Zach decided another few
minutes' rest wouldn't hurt.

Both HAWC teams were closing in on the Sassanid Dynasty
cave. Hex's Red team was less than four miles out, and the
Blue team about double that as Alex had to travel in a slight
loop to skirt the city. Night was closing in and the temperature was falling. The cooler air was easier on the straining
soldiers, but they were all exhausted. They planned to rendezvous and rest about a mile out from the cave.

Twilight was turning to night as O'Riordan slow-jogged
at forward point in the line. He should have been taking sensor readings every few hundred feet, but instead his mind
kept travelling back to the woman kneeling on his chest and
pinching his windpipe. *Try that again, you bitch, and you'll
wake up in fucking traction*. He spat dry, sticky saliva out
into the desert.

Behrouz called to his Takavaran partner—there was motion
on the sensor. The other Takavaran positions were logged
into the grid so they knew immediately that it wasn't their
own people. This was an unidentified incursion. It was as
their Commander had said: *They will come*.

Behrouz woke his two other team members, and com-
municated the presence of the unidentified contact to headquarters so the nearest teams could be immediately dispatched
as backup. They were under instructions to take the intruders alive, or at least one of them. Behrouz knew that
didn't mean they couldn't have a little fun first. He hoped
they were tough—Mossad or any enemy Special Forces
soldiers were best. He loved it when they held out for a long
time, giving him the pleasure of inflicting more and more
pain and degradation before they finally broke or their
hearts gave out.

He checked the motion sensors again against the updated
grid—at the rate of approach, the intruders would arrive only
minutes before the next Takavaran team—*perfect*. Behrouz
sent the information to the other teams so they could approach

from behind and squeeze the enemy in a pincer movement. There would be no escape.

As O'Riordan approached a tumble of boulders, his mind continued to work on his team's failings instead of his environment. He cursed Rocky Lagudi for doing nothing to help him against Adira. He swore revenge on Hex for making him look bad with that fucking space gun. Even Captain Hunter had managed to get himself bitten by a fucking snake—some great leader he turned out to be.

He looked up and noticed it was now night-dark and the boulders were closer than he expected. He ignored them, turning his mind to the young Israeli professor and what was annoying about him.

The first high-calibre bullet took him in the chest and the second in the gut. The powerful impacts kicked him backwards off his feet and he sprawled groggily on the rocky ground. His ceramic plating had defrayed and absorbed much of the force, but two of his ribs were painfully smashed. He shook his head to clear it and rolled fast.

Even though the high-powered rifles had silenced muzzles, the Red team knew where the fire was coming from and spread in a standard defensive formation. Rocky Lagudi pulled a small thermal scope from a slot in his belt and held it to his eye. He'd just caught some of the phosphorescent movement of a warm body in the dark when a bullet splintered the rock in front of his face.

"Takavaran," Adira whispered.

Hex nodded; they had just walked into an ambush. The Iranians would already be calling in backup. Not good, not good at all. And no time to be pinned down.

Irish had managed to drag himself back behind a rock—he would have to pull his weight regardless of his injuries. Hex made rapid hand signals to the HAWCs and Adira to prepare for an offensive spike-and-spread attack—two go up the centre and fan out, leaving a cleared tunnel for the next two to come up the middle and fan again.

Hex held up one finger—*hold one minute*—and pulled the M24 A3 from over his shoulder. He quickly slotted a nightscope down the rail and leaned around the rock. One of the Takavaran noticed the slight movement and brought his own sighted sniper rifle down and focused. It only took him 1.7 seconds—too long. The large slug entered his forehead and removed the entire back of his skull, spraying blood, bone and grey-green brain matter over the sand behind him.

*One less bad guy.* Hex replaced the gun over his shoulder and drew a shortened M9 pistol, then held up five fingers: *four, three, two . . . go!*

The bullet took him in the back of the shoulder, just under a ceramic plate, and passed up through the flesh to shatter his clavicle. A stun grenade went off next to Rocky Lagudi and knocked him to the ground. His helmet and armour plating protected him from most of the blast, but he probably felt like a man swimming to the surface from under fifty feet of water. The second Takavaran squad had arrived—the Red team were now sandwiched, exposed and outnumbered.

"Call it," Hex yelled to Adira.

She fired twice more into the dark, then pressed her back against a sheltering rock and pulled her SFPDA from her belt. "Ambush, three dents," she said quickly into the tiny flat device and immediately sent the squirt. The device would code it and attach the coordinates. She let the comm device drop and pulled her other sidearm from its holster.

She whispered something to the sand, sucked in a deep breath and then stood up between the two Takavaran squads, one Barak held out at twelve o'clock and the other at six. The two guns barked loudly in the dark.

Alex lowered Zach to the ground and motioned for Sam to do a 360-degree scan as he knelt to decode and read the unexpected signal. As he listened to the brief message and absorbed its meaning, a pain started to bloom in his head. He listened again to the three words, hoping that he'd misheard them . . . he hadn't.

"Shit. Red Team's been engaged—three injured already."

Three down out of four was an unacceptable loss when they hadn't even reached their primary objective. He should have been with them; he shouldn't have split the team up again. The knot of pain in his head unfurled and started to grow. *They're lost in the dark again*, he thought as a red mist rolled across his consciousness.

Zach came closer. "Is Adira okay?"

Alex didn't hear him. His hand curled into a fist on his knee as another wave of blinding pain washed across the inside of his head. He grunted, crushed his eyes shut and banged his thigh.

"Are *you* okay, Captain Hunter?"

Zach reached out to touch Alex's shoulder. Alex's hand came up quickly, grasping Zach by the wrist and lifting him off the ground. He shouted into Zach's face, "I wasn't there! I wasn't there again!"

He dropped Zach and pressed a fist into his temple. Zach stepped back, visibly terrified, and Sam pulled the young Israeli behind him.

"Boss? Alex?" he said evenly, keeping a few paces back from his friend and senior officer. He tried again. "Alex?"

This time Alex heard Sam's voice. He turned to look at the large HAWC, and saw him shielding a white-faced Zachariah. He blinked and handed Sam the communication device so he could see and hear the information for himself. "Three dents, Sam. I should have been with them."

Sam ignored the self-recrimination and pain in Alex's voice. He looked at the coordinates delivered with the message. "They're not far from here . . . not for you."

Alex looked at Sam, and then shook his head. "I'd be leaving you and Zach exposed."

Sam handed back the device, "We're clear, they're not. From a strategic perspective, if they're all wiped out, our chances of success on this mission decrease by sixty per cent. If any of them are captured . . . well."

"Yes. You're right—you're always right. I'll call it when I

know what I'm dealing with." Alex took the device back from Sam, trying hard to ignore the temptation to listen to the urgency in Adira's voice once again.

"Rescue or retribution." Sam gave Alex a grim smile.

Alex nodded and looked to the distance. He hated to leave Sam alone with just the young scientist for backup, but Sam was right—they needed the other HAWCs' firepower. They couldn't afford for them to absorb any more losses or, worse, be taken. Of all the team, Sam was the one HAWC Alex could trust to complete a mission, with or without him.

Alex checked the Red team's positions. They were about six miles away as the crow flies—a lot of distance in dark, unfamiliar terrain; an impossible distance for any normal man.

He turned back to Zach and Sam. "Double-time to Red position, and I expect you to keep up, Dr. Shomron."

"Good luck," Sam said, and held out his fist. Alex punched it with his own.

Alex turned to the desert and drew in a long breath. He knew what he was capable of, but it would still probably take him too long. Ever since Roger Bannister broke the four-minute mile in 1954, humans had managed to whittle the time down by a few seconds every decade; the world record stood at around three minutes, forty seconds now. Human physiology and evolution would not allow humans to go much faster—not without the assistance of chemistry, surgery or both. Alex had six miles to cover, and knew he had to get there in less than fifteen minutes with enough energy to enter battle. Any longer and whatever was happening to his team would be long over. He nodded a farewell to Sam and Zach and sprinted off into the darkness.

# Twenty-nine

Adira had heard the joyous note in the Takavaran's voice as he relayed their success to their mission coordinator. She had no illusions about what would happen to them now they were in the hands of the Takavaran Special Forces. They would be tortured, interrogated and then disposed of. A quick and glorious death was not going to be an option.

O'Riordan and Lagudi were some distance from her, their hands tied behind them and their legs tied out in front. She had been forced to watch as her teammates were savagely beaten. She knew the Takavaran hoped she would be unsettled or angered, and so she sat there and watched, as unflinching as stone. To do otherwise would have simply prolonged the beating. Now the HAWCs' faces were puffed and bloody, and Lagudi's lip had a deep split that would need stitches. She was sure that the only reason they hadn't fought to the death was because she was with them, and that made her angry. In Mossad, men and women were equal—no excuses or handicaps: fight or die.

She had taken several bullets into the mid-section, none of them penetrating the ceramic shielding of her suit. When one of the Takavaran had turned her over, she had delivered a flat-handed strike to his nose that had shattered the bridge with a sound like breaking twigs. But she had mistimed the blow—it should have driven his septum up into his brain and killed him instantly; instead all she had managed was a very bad break. She was annoyed with herself for that. She could see the man now, his nose and lower face still smeared with dried blood. He had to let his mouth hang open to breathe and must be in a lot of pain. *Good*, she thought.

It had needed three of them to take her down, and they'd only realised she wasn't a man after they tore the helmet from her head. The look on the face of "bloody-nose" was worth the coming pain. First his nose smashed, then his honour—to be knocked down by a woman! *Ha!* His comrades would mock him for years.

Hex had been bound to a chair and stripped so the Takavaran could examine his suit. His pale grey eyes seemed to shine from his bloody face. The bullet wound in his shoulder had been sealed shut with a burning stick—not out of concern over his wellbeing, but to stop the blood loss so they had plenty of interrogation time with a conscious prisoner.

Hex was refusing to respond to the questioning, addressing the Iranians first in German, then French, then Danish. Anything but English—there would be no easy clues to their origin from him. Adira remembered an ancient Hebraic saying: *Giborim noflim kodem*. Loosely translated, it meant *Brave men die first.* She bowed her head forward onto her knees and closed her eyes—things were about to turn ugly. She touched her rear wisdom tooth with her tongue and felt its plasticised cap. Field cyanide capsules were only used by a few agencies in the world—Metsada was one of them.

The man guarding Lagudi and O'Riordan was examining a small steel box drawn from Hex's suit. Adira knew the spider explosive would only key on one of the HAWCs' DNA signatures; it would remain inert in the Iranian's hands.

"What is this thing?" the Takavaran soldier asked in thickly accented English. The HAWCs were like two blood-spattered stones. He smashed Lagudi in the face with the box and kicked him in the side of the head. He repeated his question and got the same stoical response. He backhanded Lagudi, his fist making a moist sound against the stocky HAWC's blood-wet face. Rocky's head bounced left and right with each savage blow, always coming back to centre; always remaining emotionless and silent.

"You will give us much enjoyment, tough little man," the Takavaran said. He went to kick Lagudi again, but noticed that the others were about to notch up their interrogation of Hex.

Adira followed the Takavaran's gaze, to see one of the Iranians approaching Hex with one of his own blades. Hex stared straight ahead. She looked away when she saw the man moving the blade towards Hex's face. When she had the courage to look again, the Takavaran soldiers were laughing and a ragged hole had appeared in the meat of Hex's cheek. They did the same to the other cheek, pushing the laser-sharpened blade in and turning it. Hex's eyes stared grimly ahead but Adira could see the chair vibrating as he squeezed its arms tightly.

She looked at the other two HAWCs: O'Riordan and Lagudi were staring straight ahead. Adira knew their minds would be working out how to inflict terminal damage on their captors before they too found themselves bound in that chair.

The HAWCs and Adira now wore nothing but their underwear. All their equipment, outer clothing and shoes were in a pile before them. They had been searched roughly—in Adira's case, less as a security process and more as an opportunity to run rough hands over her breasts and between her legs. She had expected this, and had been pleased—the more they focused on her body the less they did a proper search. As long as they thought she might be an American, they didn't regard her as the same level of threat as the men. Pirated satellite television programs had fed the Takavaran a glamorised and pampered image of Western women—whether they were combat-trained or not.

She stared straight ahead as her hands worked behind her. The plastic binding joining her wrists dug into her skin, but the pain was insignificant and a simple investment in her escape. From between the fibres of the waistband of her underwear she pulled free a thread of wire roughly six inches long, one side smooth, the other serrated with razor-sharp teeth.

She heard footfalls in the dark sand and froze. There was a command in Farsi for her to look up—she ignored it. It came again in English and she ignored it again. A boot caught her on the cheek and knocked her backwards. The soldier grabbed her and returned her to a sitting position. Adira didn't have to see his face to know it was the man whose nose she had smashed. She could tell by his thickened voice and the way he had to stop talking now and then to breathe heavily through his mouth. He forced her head towards Hex in the chair—she was to witness his torture. She knew this game well. They assumed that an American woman would break while watching the physical mutilation of her male companions.

The Takavaran loved fire—it could deliver the threat of pain just as equally as it could inflict disfiguring torture. Both were useful. One of the Iranian Special Forces men approached Hex with a large canister and uncapped the lid. Even from where Adira sat under guard, she could smell the fumes of the gasoline in the still night air. The Takavaran said something to the bound HAWC and leered viciously, but obviously didn't expect a response. Hex had endured the torture without a single cry, and Adira marvelled at his bravery and training. *These HAWCs are worthy warriors*, she thought. Then Adira noticed Hex making one small movement—he slowly closed his eyes.

The man holding Adira yanked her head back roughly and whispered in her ear in Farsi, "Each time it will be worse, until it is your turn. I promise I will make your pain last a long time, and before you finally die, you will be our whore many times."

He looked again at the figure in the chair and laughed. While his attention was drawn to the torture, he didn't notice Adira's hands sawing back and forth behind her back, using the looped wire to cut through her bonds.

The *whoosh* of the flames startled her. O'Riordan and Lagudi could have been statues, but in the glow of the flames she could see their muscles working in tiny movements, testing their bonds, seeking any give in the toughened synthetic material. She looked one last time at Hex and felt her anger swell as the young man sat unflinching while his body was consumed by fire. He was not yet dead—she could see his hands curling and uncurling from the pain. *Just another second and you will not die alone, brave one, this I swear.* She could feel the binding at her wrists begin to separate.

Alex stumbled as a sensory image washed across his mind: *his men were dying.* A trickle of blood ran from his nose and he wiped it away as he ran. He could sense the pain of the torture before he heard its sounds. He couldn't determine who was in such agony, but he knew it was one of his own. In the past, Alex had felt anxious every time he had developed a new ability—he had no idea where it would stop. But not this time; this time he welcomed the change and didn't fight or question it. The sensation of agony was like a beacon drawing him to his captured HAWCs.

He was still three miles out. He increased his speed, hoping he got there before the agony ended in death. He knew that the little time the Takavaran had had with the Red team meant they could only inflict physical torture. Though abhorrent, it wouldn't leave the same inner scars as psychological or chemical torture—both of which caused wounds that sometimes never healed.

About half a mile away, he saw flames explode skywards and knew from their colour that something biological was part of the inferno. *No! I'm too late.* Another fire began to burn—this one inside him.

He increased his speed for the last few hundred feet, then flattened to the ground, crawling to the top of a small rise to survey the scene below. He gulped in air and allowed his heartbeat to slow while he took everything in: O'Riordan and Lagudi bound and guarded by one man; Adira being held by another. Standing around the flames were five large black-clad men, jeering at Alex's youngest HAWC, Hex Winter, who was burning alive.

Alex gritted his teeth to stop himself screaming in rage at the brutal scene. His training as a HAWC demanded that in

the face of insurmountable odds his primary objective was
to disengage and complete the mission. There should be no
rescue missions that might jeopardise the final success of
the objective or endanger the primary group—better to
sever the injured hand and save the entire body. But for Alex
Hunter, the Arcadian, these were not insurmountable odds.
He was writing new rules of battle as his skills increased.

One of his hands curled around a smooth, round stone
the size of a golf ball. It had been smoothed and rounded by
a millennium of tumbling at the bottom of a long-disappeared
stream as it worked its way down from a mountain run-off.
A lightning bolt of chemicals shot through Alex as he felt
his body surge with anger and power. The hard stone in his
hand exploded from the pressure he was exerting on it.

Alex had conditioned his mind to deal with the rages. He
had been trained to use sensory triggers to help him chain
the furies deep within him, or send them back after they had
burst forth. The green apple scent of a lost love's hair, or the
sound of surf crashing on an empty beach, could stop him
destroying everything around him. The rage was becoming
easier to deal with now, easier to manage, but there were
times when it was released unexpectedly; or when he released it on purpose . . . with deadly intent.

Alex saw Hex's hands curl from pain; saw the men jeering and joking as they watched him burn. He had time to
loose one pulse from the laser before he dropped it to the
sand. It found its target and the young HAWC's agony came
to an end.

There was a voice screaming in Alex's head as the world
turned red around him: *Obliterate them all!*

Just as Adira was about to turn away from the agonised
figure in the chair, a small hole appeared silently in Hex's
forehead and his head slumped forward.

Adira held her breath as something hit the camp like a
runaway truck—three Iranian agents who had been standing together were flung twenty feet into the air and another
was lifted and broken in midair like a doll.

The Arcadian had arrived.

* * *

Alex was becoming more familiar with what his body was capable of on a daily basis: what his physical frame could withstand, and what his speed and great strength could inflict upon another being. He aimed all that power, force and aggression at the huddled group laughing and jeering at Hex's burning flesh.

If Alex had been thinking a little more clearly, he may have taken the men down with the KBELT laser—a single shot to the head or heart would have burned a hole clear through bone and flesh. Logical, fast and clean. But by then, he wanted more than just the quick take-down. There was the need to hurt, to feel their pain, to see them acknowledge his revenge. There was no finesse in his battle strategy, just a clenched-fist charge and impact.

The first three Takavaran he simply rammed with his head down, like a six-foot bowling ball, throwing the human-shaped pins backwards into the rocks, crushing the spine of one and incapacitating the other two. He turned and lifted the fourth over his head, his strength and rage peaking. The man's backbone, sinew and cartilage were compressed and then sheared in two by thousands of pounds of pressure being exerted on his frame as Alex's hands came together. He flung the broken body at the fifth man as he attempted to escape into the darkness.

Alex's rage had urged him to action before he could formulate a battle strategy, and he realised his intervention had put his other team members' lives in danger. He needed to neutralise the agents guarding Adira and his men.

The soldier next to the two bound HAWCs had seen enough—an armour-plated giant had landed amongst his fellow Takavaran and brushed them aside like they were no more than children. To the terrified Iranian Special Forces soldier, Alex looked like an ancient Persian demon of vengeance. Mere bullets would not stop this beast from Jahannam. He decided to run, but before he fled into the desert he had one final gift for the HAWCs. He pulled a fragmentation grenade from his belt and dropped it next to the bound men.

Rocky saw the live grenade fall to the sand beside him. All he could do was groan and turn his head.

Alex also saw the grenade drop and did some quick calculations: probable high-power fragmentation device—ten-foot kill radius, thirty-foot wound radius. Flechettes—notched wire or ball-bearing fragments—and now two seconds till detonation. He dived across the fifteen feet that separated him from the deadly explosive in a single motion, grabbed the small metal globe and swung his arm faster than a normal eye could see.

The grenade flew out into the dark—and was just twenty feet from his hand when it detonated in a powerful concussive blast that dispersed flechettes in all directions. Alex, who was standing between the blast and his men, was knocked backwards to land on top of his bound HAWCs. Tiny razor-sharp metal stars thudded into his suit and raked across his helmet visor.

Adira's captor was preparing to flee when he saw Alex knocked backwards by the blast. His blood-encrusted mouth broke open into a grin and he let Adira's hair go so he could draw his weapon.

Alex shook his head to clear his vision, and saw the man step forward and aim his gun at his face. If he put a bullet into the weakened visor at this range Alex knew he was finished. The Takavaran's finger started to depress the trigger when he was quickly spun around. Adira was on her feet, shredded plastic hanging loosely from her unbound hands. She stood before the open-mouthed Takavaran in blood-stained underwear, yelled something at him in Hebrew, then brought her hand up and into the man's already swollen nose. There was no light twig-snapping sound this time, more a deeper thump as she finished the job she'd set out to do earlier. The man fell like a tree in front of her, dead before he hit the cold, dark sand.

Alex got to his feet and looked into the darkness where the remaining Takavaran had fled; there could be no witnesses. His enhanced senses allowed him to pick up the rapid footfalls of the fleeing man even though he was moving at speed and nearly a mile away.

"No! They have already called in our capture, so we must leave the area before more Takavaran teams arrive." Alex heard Adira's voice, but it sounded distant.

He faced the desert and listened to the running man getting farther away, and the voice in his head screamed at him to hunt the man down and tear him to pieces.

"No!" came Adira's voice again, from right beside him.

He closed his eyes and drew in a deep breath. He heard the sound of waves on a beach. He inhaled through his nose and smelled sea salt, drying sand and the scent of green apples. He forced himself to relax. His breathing slowly returned to normal and the chaotic storm in his brain calmed. When the bloodlust had dissipated enough, he opened his eyes.

Adira was right: it was time to go.

He drew a shortened Ka-Bar blade and sliced through O'Riordan's and Lagudi's restraints. Adira noticed that Alex's upper arm was damp with blood and went to say something to him about it, but he turned away and barked angrily to the HAWCs: "Rekit, soldiers. We leave in sixty seconds."

Adira scrambled along with the HAWCs to get back into their, armoured suits and recover as much of their weaponry as they could find. There were no apologies, no thanks. For now they simply needed to evacuate the area and complete their mission.

Hex's remains had collapsed into the fire, and Alex let them burn. Hex's soul had long left his broken body.

# **Thirty**

Early evening in the desert of Iran was a busy time for nocturnal creatures. The sand was still warm, and snakes, scorpions and spiders were out hunting lazy insects or rodents not yet in their burrows for the night. The Corsac fox silently wound through the spindly brush, its enormous bat-like ears listening for the smallest footfalls of its prey; and massive owls lifted snakes and rodents from the desert floor. By late evening, the sand would be cool and the air temperature near freezing; the desert would be silent and still.

Sam was moving carefully through the twilight. For a large man, he trod as silently as the other night predators. He stopped and turned to motion Zach to lie flat to the ground; his scope had shown him an encampment ahead, probably desert traders, but possibly an ambush. He could make out the glow of flames in the distance, but could not detect any movement or thermal signatures other than the small fire. He would have preferred to skirt the camp, but a small human-like form slumped in front of the open flap of the tent had attracted his attention. *Might be a kid*, he thought, *it's too small to be a man.* He observed the prostrate form for three more minutes, but with no heat signature he had to assume it was dead. He would still be cautious though—it was possible the bodies were booby-trapped.

He crawled back to Zach. "We need to check something out, son. Could be an ambush, but I'd still feel better if you were close so I can keep an eye on you."

Zach nodded quickly, but his eyes were round and he looked nervous.

Sam moved from cover to cover—a low bush here, a mound of sand there—alert for noise, vibrations, or anything else not in keeping with the night-time sounds of the desert. He had Zach draw his pistol to cover his back, but knew that in a firefight the scientist was only there to draw his share of the attention or make some noise so Sam could target and destroy the enemy.

There were no wires on the ground and his scope didn't pick up any laser trip lines. Sam moved to the tent and ducked his head in—odd smell, but no movement. Three small bodies in oversized crumpled clothing. He called Zach in as he began to examine the tent further.

"*Phew!* What's that smell? Sort of a sweet vinegar . . . *yeech*." Zach held his hand over his nose as he joined Sam, who was bending over one of the small figures.

"What do you make of this?" Sam said, using the muzzle of his gun to turn the face towards Zach; he was taking no chances by using his hand to touch the body.

It might have been a man once, but now it was barely a humanoid shape: four feet in length with skin the colour and consistency of tanned leather. At first Sam thought the eyes had been removed, but on closer examination he could see small, shrivelled balls like dried raisins inside the collapsed sockets. He pressed his gun barrel a little harder against the skull and it collapsed inwards with a puff of dry powder.

"What the hell could do this?" Sam looked up at Zach, whose face was screwed up in an "I reserve the right to throw up" expression.

He was about to move on when he noticed the small circular hole in the man's chest. He went from body to body and found similar holes in all of them, either on their front or back. The only exception was a mutilated corpse with its head cleaved in two. From the excoriated remains, Sam could see that the insides of the body—all moisture, muscles and organs—had been somehow removed. Even the fluid and marrow from the bones had been extracted, leaving odd structures like brittle cobwebs. The cadavers were just empty cases.

Zach had both hands over his mouth and talked nervously through his fingers. "I've taken hundreds of biology classes on a hundred different subjects and I've never come across or even heard of anything that could inflict this type of damage on a human body. These men are totally devoid of all fluid. Even if it *was* a type of bleed-out virus like ebola or hanta, there would still be traces of the fluid leakage everywhere. The desert is extremely dry, but for this effect they would have needed to be in the direct sun for months."

Sam nodded. "But the fire outside tells me that whatever happened here only occurred in the last few hours."

He looked around the tent quickly and quietly, checking maps, inside boxes and turning over blankets. "Over here," he said. In the corner of the tent was a hole about three feet wide where the sand had erupted around its edges. This was the source of the smell, and it made even the battle-hardened HAWC hesitate. The hairs on the back of his neck rose slightly.

He pulled a small pencil torch from his pocket and shone the beam into the hole. It wasn't deep and trailed away outside the tent. He moved the torch closer, leaning forward as he did. The edges of the hole were greasy and coated in a waxy substance. This close, the smell was overpowering. On his knees, he leaned closer.

"Don't!" Zach's voice was so sudden and sharp it made the large HAWC jump. When Sam looked up at him, he seemed about to faint.

Sam turned back to the hole and spoke over his shoulder. "Could it be some sort of tunnel—like Hamas uses along the Gaza?" After a few seconds silence, Sam answered himself. "I didn't think so either."

Zach had his thin arms wrapped around his body and refused to come any closer to the pit. "Night bugs," he said.

"What?"

"Night bugs. When I was a first-year student I had to share temporary accommodation in a low-rent suburb with about ten other students. The beds were infested with night bugs. That smell reminds me of the stink."

Sam had seen enough. "Let's get the hell out of here."

It was cooler now and the creature could travel over the surface without fearing the crushing heat of the yellow sun. It felt stronger after feeding on the small fluid-filled animals; they were soft and slow, with no defensive claws, teeth or stingers. The creature could survive here; its kind could rule here.

It stood again on its powerful jointed legs, lifting two-thirds of its body from the sand and extending its shivering eyestalks. Its bulbous, chitin-covered compound eyes enabled it to see ultraviolet, infrared and polarised light, and its multinocular vision gave it almost unlimited depth perception—mandatory in its own dim and vicious world where it was the alpha predator.

It called once again to its kind, and waited. After a few barren minutes it dropped back to the sand. Its landing startled a sand viper, which struck out at the larger creature. The snake had no chance of penetrating the arthropod's inches-thick armour plating and its strike got a defensive reaction from the creature—a lightning-quick jet of its saliva. It was the same fluid the predator injected into its prey, which liquefied organic matter so it could be easily drawn up by its feeding tube. Concentrated, however, it had another defensive use—the combination of formic and caprylic acid, mixed with dozens of other unknown enzymes, made the saliva a strong biological corrosive.

The snake fled quickly, winding its way across the cooling sand, its body already starting to dissolve and leave a trail of scales and liquefied flesh in its wake. The creature watched the small animal flee: it was too small for a meal and no threat. It tasted the air once again and continued its scrabbling movement across the dark desert sand.

# Thirty-one

Alex's head shot up and he raised his hand in a closed fist gesture meaning an immediate halt. He made a chopping motion left and right and the HAWCs spread to either side of him and took cover.

Something was out there; something he had never heard before. The scream was below the range of normal human hearing. It made his skin crawl. He waited for it to be repeated, but nothing came.

Alex waited a few more moments and tried to open his senses—but still nothing came. *There's something out in the dark*, he thought, and a sense of unease settled in the pit of his stomach.

He shook his head and pressed his comm stud. "Sam, come in." Change of plan; he'd bring the teams together now.

When Zach and Sam had caught up with Alex and the others, the reunited team took the opportunity to share their experiences. Alex gave them a short rest stop, and Zach took his boots off. Alex saw that his toes and heels were rubbed raw, and then rubbed again. *Good on the kid for not complaining*, he thought.

When Alex heard the discussion turn to the details of Hex's execution, he walked away—he didn't want to hear it all again. The few moments of solitude gave him the opportunity to take a quick inventory of their situation. He had one man down, two injured but operational, the Iranians now alerted to their arrival and potential position, and something moving out on the desert flats that worried the shit out of him. They were still on schedule, but things were definitely not getting any easier for them. *Ahh, every day above ground is a good one*, he thought.

He decided they could afford to rest for twenty minutes now, and then have some longer downtime when they got to the cave mouth. The two teams had been running for several miles and he knew even his strongest HAWCs were exhausted—and he couldn't carry them all.

Adira intercepted him as he rejoined the group. She touched his arm. "You're bleeding, Captain Hunter."

A flechette had grazed his upper arm just above the bicep, managing to part the toughened para-aramid synthetic fibres of his combat suit. Alex had patches in his kit to glue tears together to maintain the biological and thermal seal—and he wasn't worried about his flesh.

"It's nothing, I heal quickly," he said.

"You certainly do. Not many men can slay two Takavaran squads with their bare hands. You should be dead—not least from the viper's bite, Captain."

She reached up to try to check his injury again. Alex turned slightly so she wouldn't see the wound and instead grasped her hand before she laid it on his arm. He held it for a minute and smiled into her eyes. He could see the intelligence and strength in those dark pools. As a reflex she reached up and laid her other hand over the top of his and smiled, blushing at the same time.

"Alex," he said. "Call me Alex."

He looked down at her small hand and for the first time noticed the tiny blue star on the skin between her thumb and forefinger. *Brand of the fighter*, he thought. He smiled again, then moved away to talk to Sam.

*Achhh, wake up,"* Adira told herself sternly. Her heart was beating in her chest and she could feel the heat in her cheeks. She had crawled into pitch-black terrorists' tunnels and kicked down doors under enemy fire, and here she was with shaking hands because the handsome captain had smiled at her.

She didn't even know him, and perhaps never would. Still, after seeing him in battle, she couldn't help feeling he was different from any man she had ever known.

Adira was a warrior herself; she had never married, and rarely dated. *Who could ever keep up with me?* was the little excuse she used to justify the lack of close relationships in her life. She rarely even saw her family these days; her closest link with them was her contact with her uncle, General Shavit, but they hardly ever spoke of personal things. She wondered now how the general had managed to have a wife and his own family while still focusing on his military career. Or perhaps it was different for a man. Adira was respected as an equal in the Israeli military, but would that equality remain in married life?

She looked at the broad form of the HAWC as he walked away.

How would Alex Hunter treat his woman, she wondered. As an equal or as some fragile being who needed his protection? She shook her head. Her job wasn't to daydream about good-looking American soldiers; it was to discover this secret weapon the US military had developed and pass that information on to Mossad.

*If you're not the Arcadian, you should be*, she thought as Alex made his way over to Sam Reid.

In all her time in the army, and now Mossad, Adira had never disobeyed an order. But the thought of submitting Alex's name to her superiors felt like a betrayal of him . . . and herself. Besides, the report would be premature—what good was the end result without learning how that result had been achieved? *Not yet then*, she thought, *not just yet.*

"And you can call me Addy," she said under her breath.

Alex's powerful hearing picked up Adira's words and he smiled back at her over his shoulder. *Addy, nice name*, he thought.

He slapped an adhesive patch over the tear in his suit and crouched down next to Sam and Zach.

"Never seen anything like it, boss," Sam reported. "Those

men were shrunk down to the size of five year olds, just
empty bags. Even their eyes were shrivelled down to Cali-
fornian raisins. And another thing—they all had these
thumb-sized holes in them, but I don't know what type of
weapon could cause that."

"Could it have been a laser?"

"Doubt it. No burns to the clothing or cauterisation of the
flesh; just shrivelled bodies with a single small hole . . . oh,
yeah, and a bad smell."

Sam looked worried and Alex didn't like it. There wasn't
much the man feared—something had rattled him.

"Describe the smell," he said.

Sam's gaze seemed to turn inwards as he took himself back
to the tent for a few seconds. "Vinegar, sugar and almonds . . .
musty-sweet, disgusting. Animal, but not." He sat quietly,
deep in thought for a few seconds.

"Uncle!" Alex brought him back. "What else—any
tracks?"

"Nothing except the Iranians' footprints. All the action
occurred in the tent. There was a hole in the corner—big
and deep, all the dirt pushed upwards. My guess is something came up out of the ground, ambushed them, then went
back down the same way. Maybe they were shot full of some
toxin that destroys blood cells. Or microwaved—I've heard
the Chinese are refining a microwave weapon that cooks
you from the inside out. But one thing's for sure, those men
hadn't been dead for very long—their fire was still burning
down when we got there." Sam shook his head slowly and
ran his fingers up through his hair. "Maybe radiation poisoning, maybe a hundred things I'm just not thinking of. But
I'll tell you, boss, nothing I know of works that quickly, or
does that to flesh and bone."

Alex looked across at Zach who was sitting on the sand
with his feet and legs drawn up to his chest. He anticipated
Alex's question. "No, not radiation. Even a mega-sievert blast
wouldn't cause that type of damage. Blistering, skin vapori-
sation, cell destruction and DNA mutation, yes, but not
that sort of physical . . . desiccation. Besides, there was no

secondary irradiation or any trace of lingering particles—so, no, not radiation. I think it was something biological—did you tell him about the night bugs?"

"The what?" Alex looked from Zach to Sam and then back again when Sam shrugged his shoulders.

"This might be totally unrelated," Zach went on, "but I've smelled something like that before, when I was in a student share hostel. It was the odour of a night-bug infestation—I believe you call them bedbugs. Entomology is not my area, but night bugs give off a distinctive sweet smell from the abdominal scent glands—only detectable by humans when they're in large numbers."

Alex raised his eyebrows and looked at Sam. The big HAWC motioned with his hand back to Zach. The inference was clear—*it's his story, let him tell it.*

"You think bedbugs did this?" Alex asked.

"No, of course not. That would be crazy." Zach looked down at the ground and knitted his brows. "Crazy," he said again.

*But not crazy enough for him to voice his concerns and be clearly affected*, thought Alex. He also noticed Sam never once contradicted the kid.

"Okay. Sam, lay out a few seismic sensors. Don't want anything creeping up on us—man or bug."

Alex stood up and had turned to leave when Zach spoke again. "One more thing—these parasites live on blood and bodily fluids. And the bodies were . . ." He shrugged.

Alex looked at him silently for a few seconds, then nodded and disappeared into the dark. He tried to pick up any sign of the mysterious presence out there in the desert, but all seemed silent and still.

# Thirty-two

The HAWCs were now a few miles out from the Sassanid cave and just as many again south of Arak. An hour ago they had received an information packet from Major Hammerson telling them that further gamma pulses, just slightly smaller than those from the Persepolis site, had been detected in Arak. It confirmed they were on the right track.

It was dark now, and cloudless, and the day's heat had quickly fled, leaving cold stars glittering like brittle chips of ice on a thick, black blanket. While the others took some much needed rest, Alex prepared to do a perimeter sweep. He had only taken around fifty steps from the group when the wave of pain and nausea passed over him. He put his hands to his ears in an attempt to block out the subsonic assault to his brain. The eerie alien howl caused him agonising pain, and for a brief moment he felt the furies strain within him again—he wanted to fight. He crushed his eyes shut and breathed deeply until he calmed. But after the pain subsided, the unease remained. This time the strange scream had come from nearby. Way too close.

From the darkness he looked back at the group. O'Riordan had his suit down to his waist and was injecting a cocktail of steroids and tromadiene directly into the purple trauma area on his side. His ribs would stay broken until he returned home, but at least he wouldn't feel it. Lagudi had a massive split lip, which he'd stitched himself; he'd lost a tooth and one of his eyes was the colour and size of a ripe summer plum. He'd told Alex he felt better than he looked. Alex saw him turn to O'Riordan now, "You see the captain take out those Takavaran guys? He was unbelievable. No wonder I couldn't knock him down back at base during the exercises. He was just playing with me."

"So what," O'Riordan sneered. "The guy's a freak—he was probably hopped up on some drug."

Alex realised the two men thought he couldn't hear them from this distance.

Lagudi blinked at O'Riordan's response and touched his bloated lip. "Bad business about Hex—not a good way to go out."

"Yeah, well, he was the team leader and he walked us into a freakin' trap. That could've been all of us on that bonfire."

Lagudi exploded. "Are you shittin' me, man? Did you see them Takavaran guys—they were no slouches! Could you have done better? Anyway . . . I seem to remember you were the man out at point."

O'Riordan's tone became belligerent. "I was out in front doin' my job, but he was leadin' us! He's supposed to be one of those experienced super HAWC soldiers, but we ended up being led into a stinkin' ambush. It was bad luck it turned out like it did. But you know what—some days you're the dog and some days you're the hydrant. Like I said, it coulda been all of us."

O'Riordan went to walk away, then spotted Alex standing about fifty feet out in the black desert, staring at him. The HAWC looked back for a few seconds, then shrugged and continued on his way. Clearly, he had no idea he'd been overheard. Alex felt the rage begin to build in him again, but summoned the sound of waves crashing on sand to calm himself. O'Riordan would keep.

While he stood staring out into the cold and dark desert, Adira walked over. She took a sip from her water canister, wiped it and offered it to him. "How's the headache?"

"It wasn't a headache—it was something else, a sound, but it's gone now." Alex turned to her. "Have you ever heard fingernails down a blackboard? It was like that—unpleasant and weird. But very low frequency, not like anything I've ever heard before." He went back to scanning the dark horizon, as if keeping guard.

"I didn't hear it, and I know most things in this desert. Can you describe it to me?" Adira was looking intensely into his face.

Alex looked down at her and saw the concern in her eyes. How could he describe it to her though? How could he get her to understand it when he didn't understand it himself? The mental pictures didn't make sense, and neither did his ability to "see" them. The sound had conjured images of sharp alien cliffs rising from a moist valley floor. Of pale grey bulbous-headed plants leaning over wet sand, and a sky that was orange, punctured by a weak blue sun. The images had jumped into his head with dizzying speed and left him dazed and confused. The call was a longing for that world; a lament of loneliness, and then of anger and frustration.

Alex shook his head slightly. He knew he should be telling Hammerson or Medical about these new changes in his abilities, but he worried that they would confine him to the base for more tests. And he wasn't sure anymore whether the tests were making him better or worse.

He turned away from the dark to look at Adira again. "Describe it? I couldn't even try. It wasn't remotely like anything I've ever heard. Like I said, it was weird."

Alex compressed his lips and breathed out through his nose. The weird scream from out of the desert, Sam's description of the drained Takavaran corpses, and now the sense of danger close by made him feel he needed to be constantly vigilant.

"I need to walk the line. Would you—"

"Yes, and thank you for asking," Adira jumped in.

Alex had been about to suggest she head back to the group. He smiled. *Might as well take her with me—she'll probably tag along anyway*, he thought. She was obviously a woman who was used to doing things *her* way. She returned his smile with a raised eyebrow. "No holding hands on a first date, okay?" she said with mock seriousness.

Alex laughed. He couldn't help liking her.

Adira liked his laugh. Although she was tired and could have done with the rest, she was determined to learn more about Alex Hunter. He intrigued her. She needed to understand him—who he really was, and how he was able to do the things that she had seen him do. She should have sent that information back to her headquarters immediately, but she felt that knowing *who* he was was less important than knowing *how* he got to be that way. This rendered the information incomplete. She almost believed the rationale herself.

She stole glances at him as she walked beside him in the cold, dark desert. She had seen him clutch his head in agony. She didn't like to see him in pain, but was in some way glad that he could acknowledge a physical sensation. She had started to think there was something not quite human about him, marvelling at his indifference to wounds and fatigue. Adira knew Mossad's training was comparable to that of any special forces around the world, but Alex Hunter's skills made Metsada, Kidon and even his own HAWCs look like ordinary infantrymen.

Apart from General Shavit's reference to the Arcadian, and the few details from the stolen American report—passed on to her by one of her agents in the past few days—she had little to go on. Other than his "creators," no one, it seemed, knew who or what the Arcadian was. Most of the international spy networks had had to put it down to American myth-making, but Adira knew the Arcadian was no myth—the report and the man beside her proved that.

She remembered the impact when he had struck the group of Takavaran—their broken bodies had flown through the air like empty sacks. He had destroyed half a dozen deadly Special Forces soldiers without firing a shot. She recalled some of the analysis from the stolen report: "Potential ability to change lethal battlefield dynamics." *Yes, he would*, she thought. *Alex Hunter in battle would change the rules of ground combat.*

Adira looked again at Alex as he turned to listen to something out in the dark. *What would it be like if Israel had men such as he to patrol our borders? We could all sleep soundly again at night.*

Her brows knitted as she remembered another line in the report: "subject displays sporadic periods of lethal instability." *Lethal instability*, she repeated to herself, *what does that mean?* She knew all about battlefield psychosis, instability and trauma—she could see none of them in this man. He looked strong, in control . . . and stable.

She looked at his jawline, and then his mouth. An image formed and she looked away quickly, and put a hand over her own mouth to hide her smile. She had seen herself kissing him.

They stopped next to a large rock, and Alex took his glove off to lay his hand on its flat surface. To Adira it probably looked like he was testing the stone for residual warmth in the cool night air; in fact, he was feeling for vibrations. He didn't plan on hanging around here long enough to plant more seismic monitors, but he still didn't want anything tunnelling up into their camp.

Adira sat back against the rock and turned her head up to see his face. "So what does Captain Alex Hunter, codenamed 'Arcadian,' do with himself when he's not saving the world on the other side of the planet?"

Her smile was disarming and Alex was sure it had made fools of many men before. He still found it hard to believe she was a lethal Mossad agent with quite a few kills on her sheet. He ignored the Arcadian fishing expedition and decided to play along.

"Right now, I miss clear blue water and lying on a white sandy beach." He drew in a deep breath as if to inhale the images that were forming in his mind. Just saying the words out loud made him think of sun-dried shorts, sand up to his ankles, the feeling of slight sunburn and a crusting of salt on his shoulders. For a moment, he could almost see the beach towels hanging over a wooden porch railing to dry.

"Plenty of sand here, Alex." She grinned at him. "If you hadn't noticed, we have truckloads of it in the Middle East. Now let me see, there's no ring on your finger—anyone lying on the beach waiting for you at home?" She raised her eyebrows.

"Once, but not anymore—too many missions, too many nightmares. Makes it hard to sustain a relationship, let alone talk about long-term plans, when you can't even promise to come back from the next project." His face turned stony and he changed the subject. "Come on now, your turn. Tell me about Adira Senesh, brilliant young Mossad torpedo."

She put her hands on her hips. "Torpedo? Hah, I thought I had a little more shape than that. Well, let's see, I do competitive archery some weekends, and I'm a member of the Tel Aviv shooting club."

"Rifles?"

"No, twenty-two calibre target pistols. I could have competed at the Olympics, but my career with Mossad overtook everything." She was quiet for a moment, then cocked her head slightly at a thought. "I like horse riding." She looked at him quickly as though to check he wasn't about to make fun of her. When Alex didn't, she went on. "I have a horse called Vulcan, he's an Appaloosa. I ride him along the water's edge at the Sea of Galilee, or sometimes up to the views of the Golan Heights. Do you ride, Alex?" She leaned across and looked into his face. Her brows were knitted, as though the question was the most important he would answer today.

"Yes, but not as much as I'd like to. Hey, running, horse riding, archery, shooting—not much of an action girl, are you?" He raised his eyebrows and smiled.

He saw her lips part to say something else when the subsonic scream rang out again—closer this time. Alex turned away and gritted his teeth, trying to focus on its whereabouts. This time he could tell it wasn't coming from a mechanical device due to the organic rise and fall in the modulation. It wasn't just a random screech either, it was a call—too crude to be called a language, but definitely something trying to communicate across the dark landscape.

This mission had long moved past being weird; now it was starting to get damn creepy. Alex watched the dark desert for a moment or two then looked up at the stars. He checked his watch and pulled his glove back on. He had to get them moving again.

"Time to get going, Ms. Senesh."

"Call me Addy."

"Okay, time to saddle up, Addy."

The creature stopped once again to sample the air. The gamma particles in the slight breeze drew it along an invisible path. It had felt again the tingling warmth of the radiation and remembered its own world—the warmth, the humidity, and its own kind.

It climbed a small mound and raised itself up—a massive column of razor claws and armour plating, silent and still as the trunk of a mighty tree. Both eyestalks swivelled and the three bulbs in each focused on the distance. Its eyes searched the horizon and found tiny flaring dots moving across the sand—infrared images of warm bodies.

Its mandibles opened and closed with a sticky viscous sound and it dropped back to the sand. Hunger was gnawing once again at its core.

It increased its pace to catch up with the small moving figures.

# Thirty-three

The HAWCs reached the cave at about three in the morning. From their position, crouching at the base of an old rock fall, they could detect no movement, thermal presence or any sound coming from the cave.

Alex went alone to stand in the enormous mouth of the ancient cave. The primitive smell of the tunnel ahead threatened to overwhelm him, and though he couldn't discern any threats to his team, he found it difficult to take another step forward. He'd lost an entire team of HAWCs in a cold dark maze below the Antarctic and it still haunted his dreams. He'd never suffered from claustrophobia before, but the idea of entering another cave system was making him feel tense and uneasy.

Alex shook his head as if throwing off beads of cold water, then took one step, and another. Limestone coolness flowed from the tunnel's depths and he knew there must be a vast labyrinth deep in the mountain. He stopped and marvelled at the giant statue standing guard at the entrance: a colossal, scowling warrior holding a sword as tall as a man.

Adira came and stood beside him. "Shapur the Great—a warrior king and the mightiest of the Sassanid rulers. He brought wisdom and peace for his entire rule. His statue has stood guard over Arak and this land for nearly two thousand years."

"We could do with a few more leaders like that today," Alex said. "Let's get inside; we can rest for a while." He turned to the group. "Irish, you and I will take first watch outside. Sam, Rocky, you're up next. Ms. Senesh and Dr. Shomron, please get some rest as you'll be needed to guide us into the facilities."

Alex saw O'Riordan stare at him for a moment, then blink and turn away. *Looking forward to that, aren't you, buddy?* he thought.

He'd purposely chosen O'Riordan to do the first watch with him. He figured Irish must have been affected by what happened to Hex—who wouldn't be—but the man needed to put it aside, and, if he had any residual anger, channel it into his mission. Everyone dealt with loss or failure in a different way. He'd heard Irish's comments about Hex—blaming others was a weak but standard defensive mechanism that kept the blamer's ego and reputation intact. Still, that didn't mean that person couldn't learn from the experience. For the last few hours, Irish had seemed withdrawn. Alex wanted this one-on-one time to see if he could open him up a little.

They took a position just twenty feet from the mouth of the cave that provided an unbroken view over the Markazi Plains. They sat with their backs to a sheer rock face that rose 100 feet into the air. Alex broke off a piece of hard tack and handed it to the redheaded HAWC, who shook his head. Alex popped the tack into his own mouth; he lived on the stuff while on missions—it was lightweight and provided him with concentrated protein. His supercharged metabolism burned up protein twice as fast as a normal man's did, and he often lost several pounds on a mission. He needed his fuel.

"So, enjoying the new squad, Lieutenant?"

"Has its moments," O'Riordan said and turned away, signalling a distinct lack of interest in the conversation.

Alex could tell there was something burning inside the man and he was determined to draw it out before they entered a potential conflict zone. "Oh yeah, you got that right," he said. "Lieutenant Winters certainly had his moment. What do you think he'd want to say to you if he was here now?"

The question took O'Riordan by surprise. He looked

briefly at Alex and then skywards for a few seconds before shaking his head.

Alex pressed him. "Think he might have some advice for you? Want to tell you something? Come on, Irish, use your imagination. What would your team leader want to say to his point man after being tied to a chair, tortured and then burned alive?"

O'Riordan was still shaking his head, as if to distance himself from the other HAWC's savage death. His teeth were clamped shut, but suddenly they sprang open and a string of obscenities spewed out. Eventually O'Riordan got himself under control and answered the question. "He'd fuckin' say, 'You got me killed!' But I didn't—that asshole committed suicide the moment *he* walked *us* into the trap." He threw a handful of pebbles and scree out into the desert and folded his arms, still muttering curses to himself.

Alex studied the man. He could tell that Irish didn't believe it was Hex's own fault he'd got killed; it was just that he didn't believe he was to blame either. "Okay, tell me what happened, soldier. I wasn't there."

O'Riordan described the ambush, laying all the blame squarely at Hex Winter's feet. He reckoned they should have had two out at point, or at least a man at long point, given they knew there were hostiles in the vicinity. Besides, what good was a man out at point when they got hit from behind at the same time? Hex should have had them *all* monitoring their electronics in the dark rather than relying on their own senses. They knew there were Takavaran squads spread out in the desert, and they'd managed to find not one but two.

"Look, Captain, Hex paid the price for his mistake and it was fuckin' bad luck, but we all coulda been wiped out. Sorry, but that's it."

Alex kept his expression unreadable as he listened. He knew that if he asked Rocky Lagudi or Adira for their take on events, he'd get a different version, but then they hadn't been out at point. In Alex's experience, an effective ambush meant maintaining maximum concealment to allow the point man to walk his team into the prime killing zone, then to open the box and rain hell on them all. Why kill one when you could kill the lot? Alex knew that about ambushes, and O'Riordan should have too.

"Bad luck, was it? Listen, soldier, you were at point—that means accepting the most exposed position in a combat military formation. You're the lead man, the spearhead, the one advancing the unit through hostile or unsecured territory. The one with a need for constant and extreme operational alertness. I can't know what happened for sure, but every time someone says 'It's not my fault,' it just makes me look at them harder. Says to me they think they've got nothing to learn."

"For Chrissake, I was lookin' out," said Irish angrily, "I was alert, I was doin' my fuckin' job. Those mooks just came outta the dirt. I'm only here 'cause I reacted quickly. I know how to look out for myself and for the fuckin' team as well. No one ever looked out for me, and I reckon no one ever—"

Alex felt a moment of anger wash across him and he punched the ground in front of the redheaded HAWC so hard that sand fell from the cliff face down onto O'Riordan's head. The man's intransigence was beginning to infuriate him, but he forced himself to push down the anger. He knew Irish might not have been solely to blame. Bottom line—it was because Alex was miles away, incapacitated, that they had walked into the ambush. If Alex hadn't been flat on his back, Hex might still be alive.

Alex sat back against the wall and closed his eyes. "You know, Lieutenant, every single time I'm out in the field I learn something new. Use what happened to Hex as part of your education and next time you may avoid the ambush— for yourself or for all of us."

Alex had faith in every HAWC that Hammerson sent him. They were the best of the best, the highest-trained soldiers on the planet, but they were still human and that meant they would make mistakes. In this business, mistakes didn't mean a pay cut, demotion or a dressing-down from the boss; they meant death, and for Hex it had been a painful one.

*All those men torn up under the Antarctic ice, and now Hex. I can't lose anymore*, Alex thought. *Gotta complete the mission and get everyone through this time.*

He opened his eyes and looked across at O'Riordan. Irish still had a pained look on his face, but he nodded and held out his hand. Alex, surprised, grasped it and shook it.

"Nah, I want some of the hard tack. Looks okay."

Alex laughed briefly and handed O'Riordan some of the dried beef, then pointed with his thumb to the cave mouth. "We're probably going to need to punch through into the underground laboratory—without so much as waking a mouse. Think you can do it?"

O'Riordan pushed the beef into one side of his mouth and gave Alex a half-smile. "Walk in the park, Captain." He picked up a piece of loose rock and rubbed it with his thumb. "This entire mountain is Doran granite, felsic crystalline type. Very hard but very brittle. I can design a shaped symmetrical implosion assembly usin' RDX cyclonite. It'll give you about 400 kilobars of nearly noiseless blast pressure exerted on a rock wall of your choice—it'll just crumble away to dust in front of us. Wake a mouse? Shit, I won't even wake the ghosts."

Alex was unsure whether he had crossed any bridges with his new HAWC but was satisfied with the man's expertise and confidence. "Good man. I hope you decide to stay with us after we get home."

Alex looked out over the darkened valley; sunrise was gaining on them. They needed to be well inside the cave system before daylight. *Better check in with the big guy*, he thought.

He walked a few paces away from O'Riordan, pressed a few buttons on his comm set and pushed it back into his pocket. Electronic pips and squeaks sounded in his helmet speaker as the signal bounced around the local networks and passed through numerous coders and firewalls before the gravelly voice of his commanding officer came on the line.

"Go ahead, Arcadian," Hammerson said curtly.

The devices were meant to be field secure, but both men

knew not to stay on the line too long or to give identifiable information.

"We're at insertion point," Alex said. "Expect full entry within two hours on 'Go' order. Expect hostile reception. Good guys are one down and two with minor dents."

There was silence for a second and then Hammerson said, "You are 'Go' for entry."

Alex should have signed off but was still concerned about his ability to execute the breadth of the order. "Order clarity?" he asked.

"Orders unchanged. Obtain 'black' technology and await orders for extraction. Do not allow blue doves to obtain technology under any circumstances. Destruction *only* if retrieval impossible. Repeat: retrieval is priority. Orders are from highest authority. Proceed. Out." The line went dead.

*Highest authority? Why are they looking over my shoulder?* Alex wondered.

He was heading back to the cave mouth when he stopped—something didn't feel right. There was danger, but he couldn't tell from what or where. *Must be the cave that's still got me spooked*, he thought. He turned slowly on the spot. The sensation of danger remained, but now it was coming from behind him. He ignored it and walked slowly back to O'Riordan.

# Thirty-four

Thunder, as though from a thousand storms, was all around him as he floated in space. He was looking down at Earth. As he watched, a black canker appeared on the yellow desert of the Middle East and spread rapidly. Land mass, rivers, mountains fell into it and still it continued to grow. The continents started to slide across their crustal shelves, and the mighty oceans began to pour into the dark vortex. The black hole was free.

Even from his great height, he could hear the billions of voices screaming.

Zach sat up quickly, and shook his head to clear away the image. He wiped his forehead and eyes with his sleeve— both perspiration and tears streaked his face.

"No, no, no . . ." he said softly. "It's not real. It must never be real."

Adira sat up and rubbed her face with her hands. She had lain down and closed her eyes, but had been unable to sleep or even relax. She could feel her body humming in anticipation— she would fight soon, she could feel it.

She glanced over at Zach. His face was shiny with moisture; it looked like tears. "What is it?" she asked, but he waved the question away.

She shrugged, undid her pack and opened a couple of small silver-foil packages of food. There were no luxuries in the field, just water, chocolate, hard tack, vitamin and mineral supplements—minimal weight, no cooking and no debris to leave behind. Breakfast was fuel, nothing more.

With a faint glow just picking out the distant line of the horizon, it was time to enter the cave. Adira had been in Middle Eastern caves before—every one of them was known and well used. This land was ancient and civilisations had been living in and around these caves for thousands of years. She knew they couldn't expect to have the place entirely to themselves; she just hoped the climb to the cave mouth discouraged the local villagers from visiting too often.

Lagudi was down on his knees sweeping the ground at the entrance to the cave to remove their footprints, while the others were rechecking their equipment. They wouldn't switch on torches until they were well inside the cave system so that no light leaked out from its depths.

Inside, Adira could feel the weight of the ages pressing down on her in the blackness. A slight cool breeze drifted past, tickling her nose with its dusty dryness. She spoke softly in the dark: "An old cave, but they're all old in this province. Depending on the geology, they could be hundreds of thousands or millions of years old. Some—"

"Some can be wet, some can be cold and frozen, or dry as dust. They're all old, they're all different and they're all dangerous. I've spent some time in caves before. Let's go."

Alex was unusually abrupt and Adira wondered what had happened to him in a cave that had affected him so deeply.

About 100 feet into the cave, Alex turned on his torch. In quick succession the HAWCs, Adira and Zach turned on their own flashlights. They were walking in complete silence, and would continue to unless Alex spoke first or they needed to warn of danger.

The cave was large—about fifty feet in diameter—and as powdery dry underfoot as the desert they had just come from. Their waving torches illuminated a fine mist of dust motes dancing in the light beams.

"*Yoish!* Look at this." It was Zachariah, breaking the rule of command. They followed his light beam across a massive relief carved into the wall. Soldiers in battle, armies with chariots and nostril-flaring horses were shown in beautiful detail. The scenes changed as they moved along, showing subjects paying homage to a king—infantrymen with great swords saluting him; unarmed people paying tribute. There were also scenes of torture: enemy soldiers having their limbs hacked off, eyes gouged or tongues ripped out or being torn apart between muscled oxen.

"The reign of the great Sassanid King Shapur," Adira said. "We met him out the front. This looks like his victory over the Roman Army under the General Glauxus. He captured the Roman general and sent his head back to Rome stuffed with snakes as a warning to the emperor to stay out of Persia—and the Romans did for another hundred years. As I said, he brought peace to the land; I just didn't say how."

"Yeah, I see now where those Takavaran freaks get their pedigree from." O'Riordan was holding his torch up to a Sassanian soldier pulling out another warrior's eyes with a long curved hook.

"This was, and unfortunately still is, a very brutal land, Lieutenant. That is why we Mossad agents are rarely taken hostage. Death is preferable to an evening with the Takavaran."

Adira joined Alex, who was shining his torch on some raised characters low down on the stone relief. "Don't ask," she said. "I don't know. These symbols, language, or whatever predate everything else in the Middle East, and are found deep in many of the caves in these parts. Legend has it that they were left as a record by some race that arrived by sea at the dawn of time. Unfortunately, no one has ever drawn out their meaning. The local people believe they are the words of angels."

Alex traced the raised petroglyphs with his fingers. "I've seen these before, and I know a professor who would love to spend a few hours with them. He turned his head slightly and spoke over his shoulder. "Uncle, anything yet?"

Sam Reid consulted a device that looked like a complicated flashlight with a small flat screen on its upper surface. Zach was hovering at his shoulder, obviously attracted by a new piece of technology. "Portable ground-penetrating radar," Sam explained. "The technical design's similar to a diver's imaging sonar system, but it's modified to use geophysical radar pulses to scan through hard surfaces. It's a bit like reflection seismology except that it uses a combination of acoustic and electromagnetic energy—different densities, different colours. Simple really."

Zach looked impressed. "Swiss?"

Sam grinned. "Nope, Sam Reid GPR special. It's my modification. Maybe I'll swap you for your miniature Geiger some day."

He checked the device again then reported to Alex. "Nothing yet, boss, just solid stone."

"Keep at it, soldier," Alex said. "Find me that door."

They continued on into the dark, dry cave.

The creature halted and rose up again on its pointed rear legs. The fan-like protuberance extended almost delicately from between its mandibles and waved gently in the direction of the small animals—their trail was becoming stronger.

Hunger gnawed at its gut. Its liquid diet meant food was ingested and assimilated quickly, and it needed constant nourishment to sustain its powerful body. It was developing a preference for the fluids in the tiny beings that inhabited this strange place.

The creature dropped to the ground and vented several tight foul-smelling packets from its abdomen, each resembling a large black egg. It was excreting waste to make room in its long, complicated gut. It was preparing to feed.

Hammerson gripped the slim white phone in his oversized fist and delivered his message in his usual economical fashion. "Unit has achieved target proximity. Expected retrieval of 'black' technology in twenty-four hours."

He listened for a few seconds to the voice on the line,

then nodded. "I agree, sir, it's too dangerous to leave in less moderate hands. Either we'll own it, or no one will."

His eyes narrowed slightly. "I don't agree, sir. The Arcadian will succeed. There'll be no need for a heavy strike."

The major placed his other hand on his forehead, then ran the fingers up through his iron-grey crew cut. "Yes, sir. Roger that."

*Fuck it.* He banged the handset into the cradle so hard that a chip of plastic flew off it.

He turned his computer screen around and looked at the live satellite images of the Iranian night-time desert. He flicked between light-enhanced and thermal imaging, easily picking up his team from their SFPDA signatures. He could confirm they were at their destination, and the scattered non-friendlies didn't seem to be making any movement towards their position. *Godspeed, son,* he thought.

He flicked through a time sequence over a five-minute period, speeded up so it looked a little like a darkened movie with red dots signifying body heat. *Strange.* Something to their south looked to be closing in on them, but it gave off no residual heat. Hammerson switched to the light-enhanced pictures and zoomed in on the high-resolution image.

"Holy shit, what the hell is that?"

A nine-foot-long creature was snaking towards Alex's position. He reached for his keyboard and began typing furiously. He needed to warn his HAWCs they were about to receive some company—identification unknown, assume hostile.

Hammerson pressed send. His message would be immediately bounced off the high-speed communication satellites and delivered in real time to Alex's SFPDA. A small, amber circle turned on his screen as the message was delivered. He waited for it to turn green, signifying the message had been received. It continued to turn, and turn . . . then stopped and went red. A message appeared below the red circle: *Destination device out of communication radius.*

"Shit—they've gone in."

Hammerson stood up so quickly his chair crashed back against the wall. A dozen options raced through his head, and each was rejected just as quickly. He could do nothing but wait. God, how he hated to wait.

# Thirty-five

Ahmad Al Janaddi buzzed around the command room shouting instructions into various microphones and snapping at any technicians not quick enough to get out of his way. The president's helicopter was only about an hour out and there was a risk they wouldn't be ready to conduct a complete test in his presence. That would be a humiliating experience, and one the president would not forgive quickly.

Moshaddam had ordered the scientist to present an overview of the devastating potential of the sphere, and then he wished to witness another run, with the inclusion of an additional lead capsule. Al Janaddi wondered who the lucky person would be this time. He shuddered at the thought of what had happened to the last poor soul who had entered one of those capsules—perhaps he was now at the bottom of the Mariana Trench, or even deeper—at the very core of the Earth. *Achhh, it is a terrible waste of life*, he thought, *and also a distraction*. Here he was harnessing one of the greatest energy sources known to the universe, and the president wanted to play at human experiments.

Al Janaddi sighed and leaned on his knuckles on the desk. He had achieved the equivalent of splitting the atom yet it seemed to mean so little. *In any other country*, he thought. *Why was I not born in any other country?*

The creature halted at the base of the steep incline below the mouth of the cave. The large flat carapace plates on its back were a greasy, mottled green in the dawn sun. Sensory hairs running over its head bristled as it tested its surroundings for danger or prey.

The stone giant standing at the mouth of the cave was discarded as a threat. Even though its form was menacing, it gave off no life energy. The creature's complex arthropodic eyes could see the warmth emanating from the pebbles O'Riordan had tossed from his sentry position and blurred footprints in the sand. Though the sand had been wiped clear, residual thermal energy remained just below the surface and presented a glowing pathway for the creature to follow all the way into the cave.

It shot into the opening at a startling speed, staying close to the ground as if it were inhaling the scent of the prey it followed.

"Bingo," said Sam. "I've got various densities thinning into a large hollow, which stretches hundreds of feet in all directions. Deeper in, I also read multiple alloy signatures in a plated structure—that's got to be metal sheeting, man-made. Here's your door, boss. Irish, do your thing." Sam turned off the GPR, fitted it snugly into a pouch on his suit and nodded to O'Riordan.

The redheaded HAWC withdrew a long Ka-Bar blade and knelt up against the wall, closed his eyes and placed his ear to the cold, dry stone. He gave the rock a single tap with the knife's steel pommel. Satisfied, he stood up and resheathed the blade. "'Bout a foot of crystalline granite. Gimme six minutes."

Alex took off his pack and the KBELT and laid them on the ground. "You got three," he said, and nodded to the others to take a brief rest too.

O'Riordan gave a grim smile. "Thought you'd say that. Three it is."

He removed his pack, withdrew several small tubes and canisters and placed them carefully on the cave floor. From one the size of a toothpaste tube he squeezed a two-foot "X" on the wall. He turned and looked at Adira with a blank stare while he waited for the explosive to dry. She rested her hands on the butt of each of her guns and smiled. O'Riordan shrugged, turned back to the explosive and stuck a small metal spike into the centre of the "X." He fiddled with some pin-sized dials on the spike, then lifted a canister from the ground and sprayed the wall. Pillows of foam grew to cover the entire two-foot section of the wall he'd been working on. He repacked, stood up and turned to the team.

"Gel-based C4—twice the boom for half the bucks. I've coated it in military styrocrete, which should muffle the noise and direct more of the blast wave into the stone. In case I'm wrong, it's best if you don't stand there—ya got ten seconds." He laughed and ran towards the mouth of the cave.

"Shit!" Lagudi ran after him and disappeared around a bend in the stone tunnel.

Adira and the others followed, with Alex jogging at the rear, shaking his head. From behind them came a sound like dry wood cracking, followed by tumbling rocks.

Alex rounded the bend into a frozen silence and a scene from one of his worst nightmares.

Framed in the mouth of the cave, gently lit by the creeping dawn sunlight, was a scorpion, spider, crab—all of them, and none. Its shape was everything that made you pull your hand from beneath the log, when you felt the touch of many unseen legs on the back of your fingers. But now standing before Alex that horror was amplified in both its size and grotesqueness.

The creature stood like a living pillar of mottled green shell and bristling insectoid hairs. Its upper body was thrown open to reveal two powerful spiked limbs and dozens of smaller appendages that moved and clicked as if in mad anticipation of some feast to come.

Eyestalks like ropey tentacles swivelled towards Alex, and black bulbs delivered a soulless, unblinking stare that was all the more hideous for their lack of life or emotion.

There was a blinding pain in Alex's head as a scream tore through his mind. It was an attack cry and it hadn't come from anyone on his team.

"Fire!" Alex ordered.

He was first to pull his gun, followed by Adira, Sam and then Rocky. Bullets sprayed towards the creature, the impacts sounding like heavy hail on a tiled roof. Its cartilage plates clamped together in defence and the gunfire did little damage to its body.

Irish ran to squeeze between the tumble of rocks and the creature that was blocking the middle of the cave. Perhaps he was trying to draw the thing out into the open where they stood a better chance. But it moved quickly, beyond anything they had ever encountered, its hardened legs clacking as it raced towards the running man.

Only Alex saw the large serrated claw fire out at Irish—the movement was too fast for normal human vision. The blow lifted the HAWC off his feet and smashed him into the wall. His pack went bouncing off his body and skidded in the sand of the cave floor.

"Damnit." Alex fired again and again at different angles, but with the same lack of result—the creature just compressed itself down behind its thick carapace plating. He could see there was little damage and the monster wasn't going to retreat.

It moved sideways across the cave mouth, staying low against their fire, only fully opening its thorax to display its grasping claws when it was close to Irish's fallen body. The thing had started to drag Irish towards it when Adira ran forward with both her guns held out together, firing a stream of jacketed lead bullets in an accurate but ineffective attack. At least the creature had stopped its attempt to spear the HAWC.

"We're hurting it, but not enough," Alex yelled over the gunfire. He guessed they were little more than an annoyance to the large arthropod. It swung back towards them and he saw its body compress slightly—like the way a spring coiled before it was unleashed.

"Sam, get Irish and pull him back. That's an order," Alex shouted.

He heard Adira's guns click on empty chambers and saw her step back to reload. As she moved, the creature's eyestalks swivelled in her direction. Alex heard the unearthly scream in his head again as the thing shivered in preparation to attack.

"Oh, no, you don't."

Alex dived and grabbed Adira, rolling her away from the creature, then he physically threw her out of the way. She hit the sand near Sam who grabbed her and yelled into her ear, "We gotta get Irish."

Alex came up firing again, moving in front of the creature to distract it, betting on his own speed to keep out of its killing range. He looked quickly over his shoulder and saw Adira pull her arm free from Sam. A brief spasm of anger crossed her face. For a split second Alex met her eyes and he knew she understood what he needed her to do. She and Rocky grabbed the fallen HAWC, while Sam took Zach by the upper arm and pulled him back deeper into the cave.

"Okay, ugly, let's see what you've got." Alex pulled his helmet visor down and reached over his shoulder for the KBELT. His hand came back empty. "Oh yeah, that's right." It was back near the place where O'Riordan had punched through into the new cave.

The creature moved and Alex dived. He felt an impact to the back of his head and something warm on his neck. He kept rolling and wedged himself into a small crevice, barely wide enough for his body, and kept moving back into the narrow passage. He felt up to his helmet casing and it came away in two pieces. The creature's claw had sliced the hardened ceramic in two, but only just managed to graze the back of his head. Already the trickle of blood had dried and the wound was scabbing over.

Alex raised his gun as the thing moved slowly towards the gap in the rock. Its foot-long eyestalks extended into the crack—hanging there like a shark's dead eyes. It was dark, but Alex knew the creature saw him clearly. The sickening smell of sweet vinegar filled the crevice. *Night bugs*, Alex thought, remembering Zach's description of the smell. Slowly, almost gently, the monster extended one of its claws. It telescoped on a double hinge and the large serrated blade hooked forward, falling just inches short of Alex face. The long eyestalks reappeared and shivered for a moment.

Alex lowered his gun and exhaled. "This ain't gonna end well, is it?"

The stalks withdrew and the creature repositioned itself to try again. This time the claw came further, and as the serrated blade started to unfold Alex grabbed it and held on.

Visual images punched into his mind: once again he saw a heavily forested landscape—its strange colours rendered even more incredible by the orange hue of the sky and a low blazing sun of the deepest blue. The images vanished as the thing tugged against his grip. This time it was the creature's emotions that Alex sensed—they were raw and primeval—all about anger, killing and dominance.

It pulled harder and Alex skidded forward a step. The thick bristles and large inward-curving teeth on the claw gave him a good grip and he wedged his shoulders sideways to further cement himself into the crack in the rock. But the strength of the thing was unbelievable. Alex exerted all his own strength and pulled, but the creature pulled back even harder. Thoughts of snapping off the claw evaporated as he analysed the extraordinary density of the waxy, chitinous material. The monster had obviously evolved to combat things a lot more formidable than Alex.

Alex tightened his grip and decided on one last almighty twist. Before he could move, the creature drew back its entire body and pulled him out of the crevice like a cork from a bottle. Alex had no time to react; he was whipped free and flung against the cave's wall. Without his helmet, the side of his head impacted with the cold stone and he crumpled to the floor of the cave unconscious.

O'Riordan had done his job well—there was an almost perfect hole in the tunnel wall, three feet around and so clean that it could have been cut by machinery. The HAWCs stepped through, Rocky and Sam dragging Irish between them, but Adira held back.

"I'm not a HAWC," she said. "You must follow your

captain's orders, Sam Reid, but I don't have to. I shall be back shortly."

Adira picked up speed as she raced back down the tunnel, pulling both her reloaded Baraks from the front holsters. She rounded the bend and cursed when she saw what lay before her.

The creature had Alex's body pinned to the ground. One of its large jointed legs was digging into his back, only the armadillo plating stopping it from piercing him completely. Its twin eyestalks swivelled around to peer at Adira then back to Alex. The creature leaned forward. Its mandibles opened and a spike like an oily black spear slid out towards Alex's exposed neck. Adira had a pretty good idea what was about to happen.

She screamed at the beast as she raised both her guns and charged. The Baraks were loud and the impacts hard. She aimed for the creature's head and was momentarily rewarded when it pulled the tube back into what passed for its face and stepped off Alex's body.

Adira knew that if the creature could best a warrior like Alex, then she would not stand for long if it attacked her front on. She looked around and saw Alex's destroyed helmet . . . and O'Riordan's backpack. She dived for the backpack.

The creature remained immobile. Perhaps it knew that she couldn't do it much harm, or perhaps it was hungry and wanted to stay close to its next meal. Whatever the reason, it gave Adira the few seconds she needed to dig around in the backpack and pull out the tube of C4 gel. She holstered one of her guns, thought for a second, then simply pulled the top of the tube open and squeezed a large lump of the sticky gel into her hand until she had a mound the size of a pool ball. She sucked in a breath, gritted her teeth, and sprinted at the creature, flinging the sticky ball at its back. She had no time to be careful of Alex; she just hoped the thing would shield him. And if it didn't work, they were both as good as dead anyway.

The ball stuck; the creature didn't even bother turning. It was once again lowering its head towards Alex's neck.

Adira slowed, aimed at the blob and fired.

The result was more than she'd hoped for. The high-energy explosion kicked the creature twenty feet down the tunnel. It immediately righted itself, but seemed disorientated. Staying low to the ground, it scuttled away towards the mouth of the cave.

It was the only chance she was going to get. She sprinted for Alex, grabbed him under the arms and dragged him back towards the team.

# Thirty-six

Zach stood back against the inside wall, watching as Rocky gave O'Riordan a sip of water. O'Riordan grabbed the bottle, pulled off his helmet and poured some over his short red hair, mumbling something about a car crash as the water ran down his face.

"What happened? How'd I get here?" he said, shaking his head and flinging droplets to the dry cave floor.

Rocky took the water canister from him. "Ms. Senesh and the boss ran defence for you. She stopped it skewering you, and then the boss distracted the . . . uh . . . thing to give us time to pull you out.

O'Riordan rubbed his hands through his hair and looked around. "So where are they now?"

Rocky glanced at Sam who just gave a shrug.

"Ahh, fuck it." O'Riordan closed his eyes and tilted his head back.

Rocky looked down at the cave floor, then quickly back up at Sam. "I think it was guarding this place," he said. "Maybe the Iranians were controlling it somehow? Or maybe it lives in the caves—like a dinosaur, or a demon. Hey, maybe there are more in here."

"Great. Let's all go fucking insane as well," O'Riordan sneered, grabbing the water back from Rocky.

"Dr. Shomron," Sam said, and Zach jumped at the sound of his voice. "What the hell was that thing?"

Zach frowned—for a moment, he was having trouble remembering what he'd seen. It was as if his mind was trying to shut the image out. Slowly, however, the monster formed in his mind, but refused to be categorised.

"I've no idea," he said. "I'm in physics and that's outside my area of expertise. I really—"

"Just have a fucking guess, genius. This is your shit-suckin' stompin' ground," O'Riordan said, glaring at him as he got slowly to his feet.

"Urn, ahh . . . I think, um . . . non-indigenous, I know that much. Mutation maybe? If they've been using high-energy radiation here then it's possible there's been some kind of corruption at the cellular and nucleic acid level." Zach put a knuckle to his lips and thought for a moment. "Unless . . ."

"Contact." Sam whispered. He'd been peering through the hole looking for any sign of Alex or Adira. He pulled his sidearm and spoke quietly over his shoulder. "Soldiers, go to red."

Rocky and Irish fanned out into a defensive position on either side of the hole in the wall. Zach felt his stomach lurch at the thought of the large creature pushing through the tunnel while they were trapped inside. He backed up until his shoulders touched the dry wall, his teeth locked in a grimace. He couldn't stop his hands dancing at the end of his arms, even when he held them up in front of himself.

"Rocky, eyes out. Irish, with me," Sam ordered.

He leapt through the hole, quickly followed by O'Riordan. Zach tried to back up even further as he heard a sliding sound coming closer.

"*Heeey.*" Rocky placed his pistol back in its holster and leaned through the hole. When he stood again, Zach could see that he was supporting the upper half of an unconscious figure. The man's helmet was off and, despite the dirt and dried blood, his face was clearly recognisable as the HAWC captain's. Zach felt as if a giant sack of stones had been lifted from his shoulders. He stepped forward to help.

Adira bathed Alex's face. Her movements were soft and she spent more time washing the dirt away from his forehead and cheeks than was probably necessary. *Nice face*, she thought.

"I think you have many lives, Alex Hunter," she said as he opened his eyes.

Alex sprang to his feet and looked around. "Where is it?"

Sam grabbed him by the arms. "Easy, boss. Ms. Senesh gave it an explosive kick up the ass and it ran out of the cave. Rocky and I went back to scout the skirmish zone; there's nothing there now."

Alex looked at Sam for a few seconds, then towards the hole. He seemed to be listening. He swung back around quickly. "We're out of here—now. Sam, take 'em in."

"Roger that, boss. Rocky, take point. Dr. Shomron, I want you with him to check for any further radiation traces. I'll take left; Irish, take right. Let's go, soldiers."

Adira pulled one of her Baraks from its holster and let it hang by her side. She watched Alex as he walked back to the hole and swung his head through. Again he seemed to be listening. After a second he shook his head and pulled two metal boxes from his belt pocket. He typed some instructions into each, then stuck one to the outside and one to the inside of the hole.

"It's still out there, isn't it?" she asked.

Alex looked at her. "Yeah, it's close. We'll just leave it a little surprise." He grinned and nodded at the little metal boxes. "Come on."

The tunnel was like a tomb; not a drip, a rustle or even the hushed whisper of a breeze broke the silence. Out at point, Lagudi was moving forward quickly and carefully. Zach, on the other hand, seemed to find every single piece of fallen debris, mound of dust or broken rock shard. He had a small flashlight, but they mainly relied on Lagudi's barrel-mounted torch for illumination. Though it had a powerful beam, it created a pipe of light that left much of the peripheral darkness untouched. After what they had encountered in the outer tunnel, that was way too much shadow for Zach's liking.

They came across the skeletons about ten minutes along the tunnel—mummified cadavers scattered on the dusty floor, their parchment-like skin drawn back from gaping mouths. *Yeerk*, thought Zach. Skeletons always unsettled him. The tendons in the jaw shortened as the body decomposed, and in a dry atmosphere this process pulled the mouth wide, making them look as if they were screaming. Patches of long wispy hair were still attached to some of the skulls. Zach shivered and looked away. He knew that it was a myth that the hair and nails continued to grow after death; it was just that as the body dried and shrank, the hair seemed longer by comparison. Basically, dead was dead. But still . . . *yeerk*.

Rocky held up his hand. "Let's wait for 'em."

Zach nodded and jammed his hands into his pockets to keep them still. They didn't have to wait long. In a few moments torchlight coloured the tunnel walls as the team approached.

Adira went down on one knee beside the closest skeleton. "Not old—no more than five years, I'd say, maybe even less."

She went through its pockets and found a few hundred rials, a comb and what was once probably an apple wrapped in a handkerchief—a final meal never eaten. She moved quickly to the next, whose tattered jacket gave up a wallet. She checked its contents. "Faribez ibn Yousef—a student at Tehran University . . . hmm, one too many student protest rallies, I'd say. Head shot, ribs shattered from gunfire. These guys were executed."

O'Riordan lit up the wall behind them—it was scarred by dozens of bullet impacts. "I'd say they were lined up and gunned down right here."

Adira nodded. "I think they're probably Iranian, maybe prisoners or dissidents who were made to work on the hidden facility and then disposed of when their work was completed—dead men don't talk. A lot of people go missing in Iran for the most basic misdemeanours."

"Bad for them, but good sign for us," Alex said. Means we must be close. Rocky, continue on—fast and quiet."

Zach noticed that as Alex moved them on, he kept looking back over his shoulder, squinting into the darkness.

The creature clung to the cave wall, compressing itself down so it looked like an enormous spiked barnacle, its heavily armour-plated back to the cave's interior. The thunderous sound of the explosion had startled it. It had never felt an impact like it, or such searing heat.

It waited for the next attack. Hours passed before it extended its eyestalks again. No great creature stood waiting to deliver the killing blow. It scuttled down from the wall.

The small creatures had disappeared, their heat trails vanishing further into the tunnels.

There was no danger now; there was just the hunger.

# Thirty-seven

The creature reached the hole in the tunnel wall. The small animals had passed through it and away into another cavern.

As it moved closer, a light winked on in a small box at the base of the wall. Spidery legs shot out of each of the box's sides and it scrambled towards the monster. The creature pointed its long black proboscis at the scuttling explosive and, with unerring aim, splashed it with corrosive saliva. The box continued for another second, slowed and then started smoking. In another instant it was a puddle of rainbow-coloured electronics and liquefied steel.

As the creature placed one of its thick exoskeletal legs on the rim of the hole, a light sprang on in the other box. This device had a different calibration—it did not wait. The explosion blew the creature backwards, spraying a fifty-foot circle with metal shrapnel and collapsing the ancient cave wall. Hundreds of tons of granite rained down, sealing the small hole and partially burying the monster.

The booming thump echoed along the tunnels, bouncing away into the distance until it was no more than a whisper. For seconds, silence returned to the Sassanid cave, then a car-door-sized sheet of granite was thrown into the air and other large stones were pushed aside like empty boxes as the creature flipped over onto its segmented legs. Its thick cosmoid scales were barely pitted by the explosive's tiny jagged missiles, and the crushing impact of tons of stone had stunned it for only moments.

It cautiously approached a section of flat wall away from

the rockfall, then struck out with one of its raptorial claws at an acceleration of over 10,000 gravities and nearly twenty-five miles per second. There was a boom as the shock wave travelled up and down the cavern, and a sharp echo continued for many seconds afterwards. But the granite's crystalline molecular structure held.

The beast reared up on its four powerful rear arthropodic legs. Its upper carapace unfolded to expose its twin attack claws and the numerous smaller thoracic limbs used for grasping prey. Multiple antennae and fan-like whips waved in the air as if it was deciding on its next approach. Its eyestalks lengthened and moved independently of each other as it investigated its options. One eye swivelled towards the interior of the cave, followed by the other. It had decided.

A faint breeze wafted down the tunnel, carrying with it the scent of the small animals the creature was following and the irresistible radiation trace that had initially drawn it here. It sensed there were other openings that would give it access to the tunnel; its dorsoventrally flattened body could compress down and slide through the tightest crevices.

It dropped to the ground and sped into the dark, its chitinous legs making a clicking sound as they rubbed against each other in its haste.

Alex saw Zachariah jump from the explosion, and his HAWCs stopped in their tracks. All eyes swung towards him and then back down the tunnel. No one spoke; everyone listened. Alex knew they were all aware of what that detonation meant—the thing was still coming.

Adira tried to catch his eye and he ignored her to turn back to the dark tunnel. He cleared his mind; it was still there, but further away now. Satisfied, he swung back with a grim smile on his face. "Okay, people, the back door is closed. Only one way for us now—forward."

Rocky didn't seem to hear; he just stood looking back down into the darkened passage.

"Let's go, Rocky." The sound of Sam's voice brought him

back, and he trotted out to point, Zach shuffling a few feet behind.

After a few more moments, the small team came to a dead end—a wall made from huge blocks of stone. Alex could hear the hum of machinery, probably air conditioning.

Lagudi knelt and pressed his ear to the wall. "I can hear something that sounds like a washing machine."

"Maybe it's an Iranian laundry." O'Riordan laughed at his own joke and examined the wall. "Looks like cinder block with a substandard mortar mix. Just need to disintegrate the mud around these stones and we should be able to pull 'em out by hand." He felt in one of his suit pouches. "I just got enough boom gel left to do a ring charge—it'll give us a high-energy vibration over the bricks in a four-foot area. It'll shake 'em loose like Granma's teeth. Gimme five minutes." He looked at Alex. "Okay, three."

Alex walked over to Zachariah, took him by the arm and led him a few feet away from the others. "Dr. Shomron, remember back at the base when you described the German scientist's body as being washed back into our universe? If *he* hadn't been washed back, then is it possible that something else could have come in his place—to restore some sort of universal balance?"

"Sure. It's all theoretical, but just about everything is when you're talking about black holes or dark matter anomalies," said Zach with a shrug.

"Even theoretically how is that possible?" Alex asked. "How does something come *out* of a black hole—I thought matter only went one way?"

"From what we know so far, that's true. Once you pass the event horizon, there is no return of anything—matter, heat, light, colour, nothing. But there is another theory that says black holes could be doorways, portals; that they are only one side of a wormhole. I, for one, certainly don't think that matter is destroyed—or even can be. For over 100 years we've had a theory of mass conservation—you know, that matter can't be created or destroyed. Sure it's being challenged now, but my view is that the theory is still sound if you re-gard our planet, solar system or universe as just bigger closed systems."

"Okay, but a wormhole—you mean like a warp-in-space-type wormhole?"

"Yes, but not just in space—in time and even between dimensions. And warp isn't really the right term. It's more like a short cut—a quick way to traverse two points in space and time in our universe, or between multiple universes. A more scientific term is a space–time topological nontrivial tunnel. But I actually like 'wormhole.' I'm pretty sure that's how Hoeckler ended up in your backyard, through a worm-hole." Zach nodded to himself as he spoke, his hands work-ing as if he held a pencil and was drawing mathematical equations in the air. "It's my theory that there's an *osmotic gradient* that operates between existences. Matter is univer-sally balanced, and if the concentration in one existence is suddenly upset, then the *system* will try to restore the bal-ance by some means. Like a swap or transference from one to the other. In fact—"

"Okay, okay, I think I understand," Alex said. "Now the million-dollar question—could something have been depos-ited here through the opposite end of a wormhole? Some-thing . . . living?"

Zach looked at Alex with a creased brow, then slowly his eyes widened. "You think . . . Yes! Yes, of course, on paper, sure. I was starting to think the same thing. It couldn't have been a mutation as it was too complete, too efficient. There was nothing about it that inferred deformity—more . . . precision."

Zach stepped in closer to Alex and grabbed his upper arm. "This is bad, very bad. This means they're opening black holes and sending matter through . . . and somehow allowing matter to be pulled back. This is beyond danger-ous. What if they pull through some type of infection, or a universal parasite plague? Not to mention what the black hole itself will do. We need to shut this off immediately. We need to destroy it."

Alex patted Zach's shoulder. "Just help us find it first, Dr. Shomron. Then we can decide what course of action to take."

A low-frequency hum followed by the sound of sand raining down signalled the end of their conversation.

"I think we have a breakthrough, so to speak," Alex said with a grin. "Let's see where we're up to."

He moved back to the group, leaving Zach standing in the dark. Alex didn't need to see the scientist's face to know it was troubled.

The HAWCs worked quietly and efficiently in the darkness, removing the cinder blocks until they had a hole roughly four feet across. They held their position, waiting, listening for the slightest sound of habitation. After a few minutes, Alex nodded his head to proceed. They broke through about five feet above a dirty moist floor in a tunnel lined with pipes. The cool air was like a balm against their perspiration- and dust-streaked faces, but there was no time to rest. The whine of the air conditioning was louder now that they were through the wall. Faulty fluorescent tube lighting cast a white flickering glow every dozen feet along the tunnel.

Lagudi went through first and shot ahead to provide forward cover. One by one the others slithered through, with Alex last. He lifted O'Riordan up above his head so the HAWC could turn off the light tube near the hole in the wall so the breach was less noticeable.

The HAWCs moved quickly down the tunnel in single file until they reached a nexus of corridors. The Iranian signs were meaningless to everyone except Adira, who pointed to one that indicated both elevator and exit.

They avoided the lift—if they were being pursued, no one wanted to be caught in a steel box jammed in a vertical concrete pipe. The solid wooden fire door they encountered was old-style and low-tech. The heavy frame and solid steel lock casing was sealed tight; tough luck if there was a fire. Lagudi reckoned he could pick it in under two minutes. O'Riordan said he could blow it open in one. Alex shook his head and took the handle—he exerted a gradually increasing enormous pressure to the frame and was rewarded by a soft splintering sound. The door swung open.

"Hey, must have been unlocked," he said, and winked at Sam who gave him an *oh really* look.

The HAWCs were now travelling blind; neither the American nor Mossad information networks had been able to obtain any intel on the inside of the Jamshid II facility in Arak. Alex knew they didn't have time to do a floor-by-floor sweep of the multi-level facility, so he based his judgment on a Western military design—first level for meeting rooms; second level for scientifics, where there was probably more shielding; lower levels for storage and perhaps staff quarters. "Level two," he told his team.

They went up the stairs like wraiths. They only halted when they heard the elevator coming down, but it continued past their position and so they resumed their rapid climb.

Al Janaddi was in the sphere room, shouting instructions, when a guard interrupted him.

"Professor Al Janaddi, one of the motion sensor alarms has gone off down in level five," the young bearded soldier informed him. "There's movement in the eastern sub-basement."

"*Achhh*, what now?" snapped Al Janaddi. "I can't deal with everything personally. It's probably rats—send some of Bhakazarri's madmen down there to shoot them. I'm busy!"

The man spun on his heel and left. Ahmad Al Janaddi was about to turn back to his monitors when he paused—could it be the intruders that the Takavaran were meant to be guarding against? What if they were American agents come to steal his work? Maybe they knew its potential and wanted it for themselves.

He tapped his pursed lips with a stubby finger. They wouldn't need to steal it—he would gladly trade it to go with them. After all, he was the secret to the process, not the machines. He just had to make things a little easier for them.

The sub-basement didn't have electronic locks, but every-where else . . .

Al Janaddi looked quickly over his shoulder. No guards were in the room and all the technicians were deeply en-grossed in their preparation for the test run. His fingers flew over the keyboard and he dived into Jamshid II's electrical security grid. *Just a few open doors should help*, he thought as he changed the small green security lights to red.

Although he couldn't hear the whirr of the electronic locks being disengaged, he imagined it occurring through-out the facility. The doors were now open for everyone . . . and everything.

Al Janaddi shut the screen and glanced over his shoulder once more. Satisfied, he smiled and then moved his lips to practise again. "Hello, I live in New York. How are you?"

"How are you doing? I live in New York."

"Howrya doin?" I'm a NooYarka."

# Thirty-eight

It didn't take long for the Takavaran to find the break in the wall. Of the fifty soldiers deployed to the inside of the Jamshid II facility, ten had been sent to the lowest level. Now Makhmoud Ajhban, the squad leader, called in to report the wall intrusion to the unit leader, who ordered all his men to break into ten-man teams and perform a floor-by-floor search.

Ajhban sent eight men through the hole to investigate if there were any more enemy agents inside. He hoped so; he would put his men up against anyone or anything. The tall Takavaran was looking forward to breaking the boredom of what had, up to now, been a babysitting job in the middle of the desert.

The eight men cautiously entered the tunnel. They only had small handheld torches against the darkness, which enveloped them like a velvet curtain once they had moved away from the hole in the wall. Akhbin Ramsheed crouched down and examined the floor of the cave. Multiple footprints led back into the dusty tunnel: a party of at least five, perhaps six, military men; all large, with one exception—a youth or maybe a woman. He smiled at the thought of capturing a Western woman.

The Takavaran passed through the skeleton room without stopping—these men had witnessed violent death a hundred times and a few more cadavers didn't interest them. They stopped at the rockfall and looked in silence at the tracks that disappeared into it. Ramsheed felt the cool granite—the ancient rocks were newly broken. *Just blown*, he thought. His neck prickled and he looked around and sniffed. There was a lingering sweet smell, like overripe fruit and vinegar.

It was then they heard the clicking, like furiously working rug-picking sticks. Ramsheed gave a small signal whistle and the men moved into a back-to-back defensive formation, torches placed on top of their handguns and held in front of them to throw weak yellow pipes of light into the gloom.

The creature was already there with them, standing motionless just a few feet from Ramsheed. In the dark he had mistaken it for a large stalagmite. Even when he shone his torch full onto the gigantic, glistening frame his brain refused to comprehend what he was seeing.

A huge claw shot out and cleaved his body from the navel up. His fellow soldiers were bathed in a warm spray of blood.

The men fired instantly, but their bullets glanced ineffectively off the hardened carapace plates. A single bullet penetrated between the gristly jointed segments on the monster's slightly softened underbody—the projectile was not large enough to cause any significant trauma, but the spark of pain inflamed the creature. It moved at a blurring speed into the midst of the unit, spitting its corrosive venom and striking out with its claws until six bodies lay in pieces or liquefying on the tunnel floor. The remaining two men ran for their lives towards the hole in the wall. One managed to dive through, but the other was grabbed in a deadly embrace.

The creature's mandibles parted and it extended its feeding tube and inserted it slowly into the soft skin at the base of the man's neck. His hellish screams changed to a strangled, wet gurgling sound. Already his face and torso were beginning to collapse as his insides were liquefied and sucked out from his body.

Makhmoud Ajhban struck the jabbering man full in the face to try to make him more coherent. He had no time for this; he had heard the gunfire and the screams from inside the tunnel and he needed information. Spittle was running down the terrified Takavaran's chin and his eyes were like those of a horse about to bolt. He was babbling about Azih Dahaka—an ancient monster from Persian stories to scare children and old goat-herders on dark nights. Azih Dahaka, the stinging dragon, was a fearsome demon from the time of creation, a horn-headed monster with the tail of a scorpion and a great armoured body. It was said to eat men and horses and would eventually destroy the world. Azih Dahaka had been defeated in battle by a great warrior who blinded him and chained him beneath a mountain.

Ajhban was about to strike the useless man again when a small sound from the opening in the tunnel wall attracted his attention. Two, foot-long eyestalks came through the hole, followed by a waxy, insectoid head that was sharp at one end and telescoping out from under an enormous armoured hump.

The thing's dark green shell was spattered with fresh blood, and as Ajhban watched, a vertical split at the front of the face broke open to reveal the tip of a black spike that eased out and back. As the barb re-entered, more blood dripped from the dark bristled maw. The black bulbs of its eyes fixed on the two remaining Takavaran, and it climbed through into the passageway and perched upside down on the ceiling like some sort of a giant flattened cockroach.

Ajhban had seen enough. He threw the convulsing soldier roughly to the ground and turned to run.

The creature dropped down on the fallen man and snatched up his body. The front of its torso opened and a series of smaller thoracic limbs held the struggling soldier tight against its plated chest like a parcel of meat. The whole time its eyestalks were on the squad leader as he sprinted down the corridor. For a hunter, fleeing prey was irresistible. It shot after the running man, knowing it could catch him with ease.

The solid white door from the stairwell into level two had no lock, just a bar embedded in a steel plate. It opened easily when Sam pulled lightly on the handle. The HAWCs went through fast and fanned either side of the doorway.

All quiet.

They were in an immaculate corridor with gleaming white tiled walls and a ceiling that had recessed lighting every few feet, giving it a surgical brightness. *Good, means we're either on the right floor or very close*, thought Alex.

"Stay alert," he ordered his team. He knew that the better the facilities, the better the security—and he expected it to be formidable here, given what they had encountered at the Persepolis facility. He motioned them to proceed.

Jamshid II was based on a circular silo design: most of the important rooms were in the centre and the exits and storage on the outside. He knew that if they continued along the curving corridor they would eventually return to where they'd started—no corners or dead ends. Great for surveillance, not so great for Special Forces insertions.

Alex held up a clenched fist to signal the team to halt. Guns pointed up and down the curving corridor as the men waited for his signal to proceed or withdraw. Adira stepped in front of Zach to keep him sandwiched between the wall and herself. Their breathing slowed; all was still and silent.

Alex could sense something. The floor wasn't empty—he'd expected that—but the presence was . . . strange. He was relieved to sense that it wasn't the monster, but something human, or almost human. It seemed captive or somehow bound. Alive, but not fully living; tortured and longing to . . . not exist.

*Maybe a prisoner; could be useful.*

Alex cleared his mind and listened more intently; breathed in his surroundings. He closed his eyes and pushed out further. He grunted softly: *it hurt*. The pain surged through his head like a red tidal wave and washed down the back of his neck. An image formed then faded, and the contact dissipated like a dream.

Alex slowly breathed in and out. Gradually, the raging fire in his skull weakened and died down to smouldering embers. He opened his eyes and blinked. It took a few seconds before his vision cleared.

"Are we okay, boss?" Sam whispered beside him, keeping his eyes on the corridor.

"Fine. Stay alert—there's someone ahead."

Alex motioned to proceed and the team crept forward, staying flat to the inside wall.

There was door after door and little else. Alex was confident that, between them, Sam or Irish could open any barrier they came across. But so far nothing was locked. For ten minutes the HAWCs went down the corridor checking rooms—they found nothing but empty storage rooms and plain square cells containing a bed, toilet and sink. None of them looked like they'd ever been used.

Until Lagudi opened one of the doors.

"Jesus Christ!" He fell back out of the doorway and scrambled to the opposite wall, his gun held out in front of him. With his other hand he crossed himself and then pointed.

Alex drew his gun, pointed at Sam and O'Riordan and then in both directions along the corridor. Each posted himself at opposite ends of the stretch of corridor, ten feet from Alex and the rest of the team.

Rocky had gotten to his feet and was breathing fast. Alex gave him a look that made the stocky little HAWC nod and mouth *I'm okay*. He still kept his gun on the open door.

Alex could feel waves of self-loathing and anguish pouring from the room. *Our captive*, he thought as he stepped over the threshold.

Though it was dark inside, a harsh band of light from the corridor lit something that was propped up on the bed. It was barely recognisable as human; its mass glistened redly, as if a thousand arteries had ruptured and bathed it in sticky blood and other bodily fluids. It quivered, probably in fear.

It took all of Alex's resolve to look the being in the face. If it hadn't been moving, he would not have believed it had ever been alive. Its body looked torn and stretched, as if it had undergone terrible torture. Its tongue protruded like the cap of a huge mushroom, and a soft mewling emanated from the broad slit of its mouth.

Alex holstered his gun. Almost immediately the thing began to raise itself up. Alex slowed his breathing again, not only to settle his nerves but also to reduce the intake of the foul smell in the room. Now closer, he could see that metallic fragments were embedded in the creature's flesh; not shrapnel but something that seemed fused into it. A long thin appendage—Alex thought it might be an arm—lifted towards him.

"Can you understand me?" Alex asked, holding out his hand. The limb, reddish-white, brushed his fingertips . . . and an image began to form in Alex's mind.

"*Ai-yish!*" Adira had entered the room. She hissed something more in Hebrew then drew her gun. Alex swept his hand up quicker than she could move, knocking the weapon out of her grasp.

His contact with the misshapen form was broken and it collapsed back like a wave on the shoreline.

Alex turned to Adira. "It's . . . he's not dangerous. Get Dr. Shomron in here."

Adira stood transfixed for a moment, revulsion pulling her features into a grimace. Alex handed her gun back. "And you wait outside," he told her. She made a guttural sound in the back of her throat and left.

Zach came into the room quickly, stumbling slightly. Alex guessed that Adira had given him a little push to help him make his mind up about entering. He stood there with his mouth open and stared for several seconds before whispering, "*O Elokim Yerachem*; oh my God. Do . . . do you think he understands us?"

"I think so, but I doubt we'll ever understand *him*. His mouth doesn't work properly."

Alex stepped forward and the thing rose up slightly, drawing back into the corner where the walls met. He made a gesture of reassurance and said to Zach, "Could this be the result of proximity to a black hole?"

Zach put his fist over his nose to mask the smell. "Yes, spaghettification—the theoretical elongation of the atomic structure of matter. Just astrophysics conjecture, really . . . I used to think." He shook his head. "He shouldn't even be alive. Forget about the gravitational deformity—he should have been radiated down to a molecular disintegration point. He must have been shielded from the worst of it somehow. He's lucky to be alive."

Alex looked at Zach with a creased brow and the young Israeli realised what he'd said. "Sorry, I didn't mean lucky as in—"

"Doesn't matter, forget it. Was this an accident, do you think? Some sort of side effect?"

The miserable being was once again reaching out with its long, raw-looking appendage. Alex's fingers touched the fleshy tentacle as it waved towards him.

"It's an effect, sure," Zach replied, backing up as Alex and the creature made contact. "But I don't yet know enough about what they're doing to know whether it's a side effect or the end result. The thing is, the colossal forces they're playing around with could wipe most life from the planet, with any survivors being left . . . like this."

Zach backed up some more. "Who was he?"

Alex felt a soft wetness as the long wet tentacle stuck to his fingertips. "Maybe a test subject; a volunteer—who knows? Some people sacrifice their all for what they believe in."

"Yes. Yes, I understand sacrifice," Zach said, near the door now.

An image flashed into Alex's mind—so clear that the event could have been occurring right before him. A young handsome man in a blue, cheaply cut suit, a stiff white shirt and no tie stood beside a girl with beautiful honey-coloured skin. A scarf of royal blue covered her hair. The man looked down at her and smiled as he felt her squeeze his hand. Alex felt the man's emotions: a love so strong that it made the wave of sadness that came next all the more pitiful.

The image dimmed, there was a moment of nausea and pain, then darkness as dead and cold as the void of space.

Light came again, but changed, warped and unclear. The man was back and alone, and not even a man anymore.

Alex went to drop his hand, but the long thin whip held on tightly. The man wanted to impart one last image. Alex looked into the milky, elongated eye and nodded his understanding.

"Thanks, Dr. Shomron," he said quietly over his shoulder. Join the others. I'll be out in a moment."

When Zach was out of the room, Alex drew his longest knife from its scabbard and stepped forward.

# Thirty-nine

Alex came out of the room with a face as hard as a tablet of stone. There was blood on his sleeve and he could feel a deep anger burning within him. Not because of the merciful act of execution he had just performed, but directed at the people who had first caused that poor man's terrible injuries and then kept him alive, imprisoned and wallowing in his own filth. *This black-hole technology is not a good thing for any country to possess*, he thought.

He made a small twirling motion in the air and pointed back to the doorway they had first come through. The HAWCs immediately holstered their weapons and headed silently and quietly for the exit. The second floor was clear, so there was less need for caution and more for speed. Sam grabbed Zach and pulled him along.

As the HAWCs rounded the final bend in the corridor, there they were, pouring from the elevator—the ten Takavaran that had been assigned to sweep this floor for the intruders. They fanned out to cover the stairwell exit door as well, then stopped as they saw the Americans.

Time seemed to stretch as surprise momentarily froze both forces. Under Alex's command, the HAWCs reacted first. He ordered them to charge the exit rather than retreat the way they had come—they couldn't afford to get trapped and bogged down in a firefight on this floor.

As the HAWCs streaked towards the door, the Takavaran drew their weapons and sped to meet them. None of them bothered to call the contact in.

Lagudi was through the door first, then Sam—with Zachariah under his arm to make sure he kept up with them—followed by O'Riordan, who stopped briefly to hold the door ajar for Alex and a lagging Adira.

Adira was quick but she couldn't match the HAWCs for speed. She was gaining on the doorway when a bullet struck her high in the shoulder. Her armour plating protected her from the penetrative force of the projectile but not its energy. She was lifted sideways and thrown into the wall, striking it with her cheek. She fell to the ground, not unconscious, but groggy and disorientated.

Alex yelled to Sam to secure their climb to the next floor up, then knelt beside Adira. He lifted his gun and fired twice as the entire Takavaran squad filled the corridor. Two bullets, two head strikes, two down, but a third man had thrown an incendiary grenade. For Alex, time slowed as he watched the dull metal canister approach through the air in a lazy somersault.

He calculated his options: he knew where the grenade was going to fall, he knew how much time he had until it detonated and also how long it would take him to get to the explosive. He could see the Takavaran from the corner of his eye, either flattening themselves against the wall of the corridor with guns drawn, or retreating from the blast radius. Alex absorbed all the information and knew he could not neutralise the grenade and still keep Adira covered from gunfire while she was stirring groggily on the corridor floor. He made his decision.

In a single lightning move, he picked up Adira, hugged her to his chest and wrapped one large arm around her head and ears. The other arm he threw over the back of his own head, which he dipped as far as it could go below the heavily shielded back and shoulders of his suit. He leaned into the wall, bracing himself and presenting only his armoured upper body to the Takavaran and the small explosive. He felt the bullets thud into the plates across his spine—each powerful blow making him grit his teeth with pain and anger. He felt a door opening within him—and a voice that sounded like his own screamed from its depths.

The blast erupted. Alex's back and neck were smashed with thousands of pounds of percussive blast and scorched by a boiling plume of orange and white flame. He could feel the plating and specially strengthened material of his suit separate and begin to burn, but he didn't care. He was alive and so was Adira—for now. He knew that he had only a few seconds before the smoke cleared and the Takavaran would once again have them in their sights. He could not protect Adira forever, and another blast, even closer, would finish them both.

Alex guessed the Takavaran would think there were no survivors—how could there be after the proximity of the explosion. For a few seconds he still had the element of surprise. *My turn*, he thought.

He pulled his weapon from its holster and took one of Adira's from hers, then he turned to the smoke-filled tunnel. His enhanced vision picked out the images of the Iranian Special Forces soldiers clearly even though he was still invisible to them. He laid Adira down, and as he did he noticed that his arms were shaking—not from fear or from the strain but from the rage that was building in him. He needed to focus and release it—now.

The Iranians moved cautiously into the centre of the corridor, some reholstering their weapons. With the flaps of his shredded and smoking suit billowing up behind him Alex came out of the smoke like a flaming juggernaut. Two Takavaran went down with precise bullet wounds before they had even closed their mouths from the surprise, and then Alex was among them, using his guns as clubs to crush their skulls and break their bodies like kindling.

Of the ten Takavaran that had entered level two, soon only four remained. Their retreat was panicked and wildly disorganised as they scattered along the corridor. One man stood his ground and fired at Alex, but his shots had no chance of hitting the lightning-quick HAWC.

Alex pursued the fleeing men, snatching up the firing Takavaran as he went and launching him spear-like at the backs of the running soldiers. The flying body slammed into a steel door just as the last three men passed through it, leaving a small dent and a large red streak on the metal.

Alex covered the ground to the closed door in seconds, then stopped, his hand resting on the steel handle. *Wait!* He couldn't follow them, even though his rage was driving him to track them down and obliterate them. He could not indulge in his bloodlust while his mission was incomplete. He struck the door with his closed fist, leaving another dent in the steel and causing a booming clang that echoed along the corridor. He inhaled deeply and exhaled through clenched teeth. His breathing and heart rate were returning to normal. He planted a spider on the doorframe and sped back to where he had left Adira.

Halfway back he almost collided with Sam.

"No time for sightseeing, boss," Sam joked. "Next floor up is where we need to be."

Sam was trying to keep his cool, but Alex was a vision from hell—his suit was burned and tattered, and the ceramic plating across his back was completely gone. The front of his suit was intact, but the chest and abdomen plates were scarred and pitted from shrapnel and bullet impacts.

Alex looked briefly down the corridor and Sam noticed the skin on his neck was pink and raw. His forearms were wet with blood, and his eyes glowed out of a thickly blood-streaked face. None of it appeared to be his.

"We've got Ms. Senesh," Sam went on. "Other than a headache and swollen cheek, she's going to be fine. She said she wants her gun back."

Alex laughed humourlessly. "Just introducing myself to our hosts, Uncle. They didn't seem happy to see us."

Alex reloaded his pistol and reholstered it, then stuck Adira's Barak into his belt. He looked down at his bloody hands and wiped them roughly on his pants. Sam pulled his gun-cleaning cloth from a pocket, handed it to him and said, "Face."

Alex took the cloth and wiped it over his eyes. When he

opened them again, they were still dark and grim, the pupils fully dilated—Sam could tell Alex's miraculous chemistry was fully charged.

"All right, soldier," Alex said, "I guess we've announced we're here. Time to show them some war."

Around the bend of the corridor an explosion sounded. Alex looked over his shoulder. "Always liked spiders," he said. "Let's go."

Irish O'Riordan draped an arm around Adira's shoulders as she sat forward and sipped water. With a damp cloth he wiped the blood from a graze on her cheek. He quickly looked around to see if anyone was watching or listening. "You're okay," he said. "Took a heavy knock, but the cheekbone's fine and I don't think there's any concussion. I got some pain-killers."

She shook her head and slowly got to her feet, still leaning on him for support.

O'Riordan looked over to where Rocky and Zach were checking the stairwell and whispered to her, "Thanks, Ms. Senesh, for . . . ahh . . . pullin' me out down in them caves back there. Look, I don't know what happened, but the guys said you stopped that thing from makin' me shish-kebab—"

She put her hand up to stop him speaking. "You would do the same for me. We are more alike than you think, Francis Irish O'Riordan."

Irish felt his face go hot. He just nodded.

# Forty

Ahmad Al Janaddi swore in Farsi as he looked at the security console. Warning lights flashed and alarms screamed all over the complex—intruder alerts, motion sensor activity in areas that should have been empty, fires burning in level five and now level two. *Too much noise*, he thought. He flicked off as many alarms as he could control from his console, and gradually the clamour receded and the pulsing red lights returned to green.

The scientist stood back from the desk, narrowing his eyes as his mind worked. It would be best if the president remained unaware of what was going on until the Americans had things under control. And if they somehow managed to capture the president, then *no one* would dare to attack them. Al Janaddi smiled; he could actually be living in America soon. The thought made him tingle from his chest all the way down to his toes.

He was turning away from the console when his face fell. *What if it isn't the Americans? What if it's the Israelis? They'll kill us all.*

He reached for the phone on his desk and spoke rapidly, slamming the receiver down when he had finished. He had instructed his security detail to report to him immediately when they sighted the infiltrators. If they were Americans, he would guide them right into the sphere room. If they weren't, he'd simply resecure the facility and trap them on one of the floors where they would be taken care of by the Jamshid II security personnel or the fanatical Takavaran.

President Moshaddam was touching down in fifteen minutes and Al Janaddi anticipated they would need at least an
hour to run the Judgment Event demonstration and complete
the president's tour. *Allah, give me speed.* He needed more
time, but dared not try to stall the president. The man seemed
able to look into one's very soul and smell deception. There
was nothing he could do now but pray he had made the right
choice.

Al Janaddi walked slowly to a white cabinet set into the
wall and pulled open one of the lower drawers. He knew that
if he had made the wrong choice, he was finished. If he
chose right . . . well, best to be prepared. Keeping his back
to the room, he reached in and selected a small thin device
the size of his thumb, which he had in the palm of his hand.
He stood and pushed his fists into his coat pockets, then
sauntered back to his console with stiff legs. *Calm down*, he
thought. He pushed the mass storage device into the master
console's port. A dialogue box, *Save Y/N*, appeared on his
screen. He half-turned, his right eye straining to use its peripheral vision. Satisfied that no one was watching, he turned
back and clicked "Y." A bar appeared on the screen and
started to climb like a thermometer left out in the summer
sunshine.

It took only a few minutes, but to the little scientist it was
as if time had slowed and the screen was screaming out his
deceit in phosphorescent green.

"Oh, merciful Allah, watch over me," he whispered softly
as the data save completed. He quickly pulled the device
from the console and pushed it back into his pocket.

Al Janaddi straightened his back. He felt a little unsteady
on his feet, and as he swallowed he tasted bile in the back of
his throat. He turned slowly, trying to appear as normal as
he could, and met the eyes of one of his technicians. He froze
and stared. The man nodded and made a thumbs up gesture.
Al Janaddi returned the gesture and leaned against the desk
behind him, lest his trembling knees throw him to the floor.

He sucked in an enormous breath. *Stay calm. Things
must appear normal*, he told himself. *The president must*

*be fully occupied; everyone must be fully occupied.* He watched the technicians putting the finishing touches to the sphere room and undertaking the final checks to ensure all was ready in time for the president's arrival. Each time a Judgment Event was undertaken, the damage was an almost perfect circle over 500 feet in diameter. Each time they re-built, they learned new ways to speed up the reconstruction process. Rather than refill the hole, they simply built across it, suspending the flooring of the vast chamber on replaceable metal beams covered by wooden planking with a thin layer of spray-on concrete for additional strength. A rubberised sealant was then applied, giving it the appearance of permanent flooring. The new structure had more than enough strength to take the weight of the sphere and the lead capsule, and was now replaceable within twenty-four hours. The laser-enhancement spheres were now preconstructed and could simply be attached and reintegrated with the supporting electronics each time. Al Janaddi gave a half-smile. *It was a fully disposable laboratory—just add some martyrs and a few billion rials and you were ready to go.*

A new lead capsule was already in place, constructed according to the president's design. The exterior had been decorated with Persian prayers and the names of the prophets, all swirling in beautiful calligraphy over every inch of the capsule. Inside was the homing beacon and communication equipment, although Al Janaddi doubted they would ever be of use. There was one more special addition to this particular capsule—a shoebox-sized padded container for an as yet unknown item. The president had inferred that he would be bringing a guest with him who would be travelling in the capsule. *Oh, lucky man*, thought the scientist.

He pursed his lips as he thought of the result of their first test, locked away in the containment room. Once the president had gone, he would have the poor thing put out of its misery and its remains cremated. He shuddered at the thought of the creature and marvelled at how it managed to keep on surviving when its organs and body were so grotesquely distorted. He didn't understand why the president wanted it kept alive. It would be best to have that mistake well and truly dealt with before his Nobel Prize. *Ahhh, life will be good then.* If he could only get through this one final demonstration to his fanatical president.

The creature followed the thermal traces of the HAWCs' footsteps across the cold sub-basement ground and quickly found the doorway to the stairwell. It needed to compress its segmented exoskeleton to fit through the frame as its broad, flattened body was not made for the tall and narrow structures these smaller animals seemed to favour. Its eyestalks swivelled to take in the small space and the stairs to the next levels. It sensed danger, but couldn't detect any movement or sound from the stairwell.

It moved forward warily, and had just placed one sharp leg on the bottom step to test its purchase when two small boxes fell upon it.

The explosive spiders had been placed high on either side of the doorframe, and had been activated by the creature's movement. In a microsecond they scanned their catalogue of friendly signatures and didn't find a match—unsurprising, as the creature's strange physical signature could not have been categorised by any but the most demented of military programmers. The spiders leapt from their ambush placement to land on the flattened, heavily armoured back.

For a being that weighed several tons, the creature moved with an unnatural swiftness—perhaps due to the lighter gravity of earth, or to an exoskeleton that allowed more surface area for muscle attachment. It lashed out at the little boxes faster than any human eye could follow, crushed one as if it was no more than silver foil.

The second exploded on its back carapace, causing it to wheel around in anger then rear up in defence. The small explosive charge created little damage to the creature's hardened procuticle—it had evolved under a different sun and was suited to conditions far more arduous than those of this benign planet. But there was a consequence of the charge, and not one the HAWCs could have expected. It ignited in the monster a primal fury that would not be satisfied by merely feeding on the small creatures it searched for. Now it wanted to rend them to shreds.

Five flights up, the subsonic scream of rage smashed into Alex's brain like a spike, He winced and shook his head to clear away the blinding fog of pain. They were about to be squeezed, and he for one preferred the potential human danger behind the door to what was about to climb those steps.

The sound of the explosion caused the team to halt and look to Alex.

"Sam, Rocky, get us through that door—now," he ordered.

He peered over the railing; smoke was still billowing around the bottom of the stairwell five flights below and he could see nothing moving in the hot fog of the explosion.

"Irish, watch our backs."

O'Riordan nodded, stepped down a few stairs and looked over the railing. He smiled; the redheaded HAWC seemed to be looking forward to the coming battle.

# Forty-one

President Moshaddam was accompanied by the leader of the Islamic Guardian Council, Mostafa Hossein, and four of the largest bodyguards Al Janaddi had ever seen. Each wore a black suit, carried a sports bag and looked to be hewn from a slab of dark granite. They all moved with an extraordinary silence that belied their six-and-half-foot frames. Their eyes seemed totally devoid of any human emotion, like obsidian buttons.

Al Janaddi's face was flushed as he welcomed the president and his guest. He showed them to the facility's meeting room, where refreshments were waiting for them, then launched into the update briefing the president had requested beforehand.

"This is our grandest achievement," he began. "I have . . . er, Iran has gone beyond the creation and stabilisation of a Judgment Event—a magnificent feat on its own. We now possess the ability to capture and store the powerful gamma radiation itself. No other country has this technology, my President, not the Germans nor the Russians nor even the Americans. This magnificent and powerful energy source will free Iran from fossil fuels forever."

He looked at the president, waiting for a response, but the man remained stony-faced. Al Janaddi felt the excitement ebb from his belly. Perhaps he needed to explain in a little more detail what a triumph he had achieved, how he had turned a scientific impossibility into reality. He took a deep breath and continued. "My President, let me explain the con-

cept behind this accomplishment. Man has been trying to
harvest the sunlight since the time of the Pharaohs—and
indeed the Egyptians managed to capture the sun's rays using polished copper discs to light the corridors deep within
their pyramids. Today, we use photovoltaic solar cells to trap
and store radiation from the sun and turn it into energy."

Moshaddam had closed his eyes in an open display of
indifference. Al Janaddi decided to get to the point. He
reached for a glass of water and raised it shakily to his lips.
He swallowed, cleared his throat and continued.

"My President, where I have achieved the breakthrough
is in applying the principles of storing solar radiation to capture the more powerful gamma rays. I have devised a thermoelectric power cube that is fuelled by the particle heat of
the gamma radiation created by the Judgment Event. The
quarter-inch cube is made of porous copper and covered in
micro-thin film arrays of thermocouples mounted on all six
faces of the cube, which convert the radiation heat into elec-
tricity. These cubes, though tiny, have a retention half-life of
eighteen years and potentially can store and release nearly
300 gigawatts of power each."

The ongoing silence from the president was crushing. Al
Janaddi licked his lips and was about to forge ahead when
Moshaddam held up his hand.

"Ahmad Al Janaddi, do you know of the Yawm al-
Qiyamah?"

Al Janaddi nodded slowly, though his mind was scram-
bling to remember the details. Like all Muslims, he had read
the Qur'an, but he could not remember the specifics of every
individual sura.

"And do you believe in it?"

The president was watching him like a snake watched a
mouse. Al Janaddi hesitated. He knew that Moshaddam believed the Qur'an directed his life and the entire world around
him. If a plane fell from the sky, it was written. If a king was
toppled, a sandstorm struck, or a car hit your brother, it
was all written in the holy book. You just had to interpret it
correctly—and it was said that no one could interpret it like

the president. To him, the Qur'an was more than just a religious book; it was the key to everything—past, present and future.

The president didn't wait for a response. His lips curled up slightly in a smile and he spoke slowly and lovingly, as if to a child. "The Yawm al-Qiyamah is the Last Judgment and belief in it is fundamental to our faith. The trials associated with it are transcribed in the seventy-fifth sura of our beloved Qur'an. You, me, every Muslim, every non-Muslim, every human being, will be held accountable for their deeds and will be judged by the one and only god, Allah."

Al Janaddi remembered the sura, but couldn't understand why the president wanted to discuss it now.

Moshaddam placed his fingertips over his eyes, then his lips, then brought his hands together as if in prayer. He was still smiling as he spoke. "Whether you call it the Day of Resurrection, the Day of Judgment, the Day of Reckoning, or even the Day of Distress, it is now upon us, my friend. At a time preordained, and when the people least expect it, Allah will give permission for the Yawm al-Qiyamah to begin. The archangel Israfil will sound his mighty horn, sending out a blast of truth for all mankind and a warning to unbelievers to prepare their soul for judgment. I know this to be true because I heard this horn myself, only a matter of weeks ago. The Last Judgment is here, the day of Allah's return is upon us, and I have made this happen! Praise be to Allah. Praise be to me."

Al Janaddi's eyebrows knitted together in confusion. How was the president responsible for this prophecy coming about?

Moshaddam continued speaking, but he was not focused on the scientist anymore. He seemed to be talking more to himself than to anyone else in the room. He closed his eyes and Al Janaddi took the opportunity to look at the others. The bodyguards looked bored, as though they had heard this before. But Mostafa Hossein was watching the president with narrowed eyes, as if he were hearing this for the first time and didn't approve of it.

The president began to recite his favourite verses of the seventy-fifth sura: "All the men and women of the world will fall down unconscious. Those who distorted or ignored the word of Allah will be judged, and if guilty will be engulfed in hellfire. Those who are truly pious will be taken to Jannah, and the rest of the world will be collapsed and destroyed. The Earth, the Sun and the Moon will turn black, and the beast shall rise; healed wounds will reopen, children will become hoary-headed and women will miscarry. Even the angels will be fearful as, on this day, it is said that God will be angrier than ever before and his wrath will be terrible." Though he continued to smile, tears were running down the president's face; he seemed almost rapturous. He tilted his head up to the ceiling, as though bathing his face in sunshine. "All will be judged, but so few will be saved, my friend. Allah has asked that from every 1000, take out 999 and cast them to Jahannam, and this is just in the lands of Islam! The West will be made barren and its unholy people tormented for eternity. Oh, Allah be praised."

The president turned his wet face to Al Janaddi and nodded slowly. "The people will beseech Abraham, Moses and Adam to intercede on their behalf, but they will turn their backs. But not I; I will not turn my back on my truly penitent people. I will beseech Allah that he saves all those who repent. But in turn we all must face the Judgment and cross the bridge over the abyss. The flames and torments of Jahannam await those who fall."

Al Janaddi remembered from his study of the Hadith in school how difficult it was to cross the bridge across the abyss to reach paradise. For sinners, the bridge appeared as a thorny path as thin as a human hair and as sharp as the edge of a sword. But those who were true would see it as a wide stone bridge covered in the softest grass. They would cross safely to Jannah, heaven, while all others would fall to an eternity of torment in Jahannam, hell.

He glanced again at Mostafa Hossein and saw that the old man's jaw worked in his jowly, bearded face, as though he were grinding his teeth. He took a sip from his own water then replaced the glass on the table so it made a loud *thunk*. "Perhaps that time is not yet here," he said. "Perhaps the signs are not being read clearly. After all, it is also written that the archangels themselves said, 'With Allah alone is the knowledge of the Hour.' We must be careful not to bear false testimony regarding the coming of the hour, for that in itself is a sin before Allah, his glorious name be praised."

President Moshaddam stood and placed both fists knuckle-down on the table. His arms were shaking, not from strain, but from his sobbing. "I am not surprised you do not recognise this day for what it is, or even recognise me, my brother. For some time now I have fought against my destiny. I refused to believe I was worthy, and I tried to ignore it—but no more. The signs are there and more will come. I have been chosen by Allah and told to reveal my true destiny; I have returned to my people to lead not just them but all the faithful peoples of the world. I will lead them to the al-Kawthar, the lake of honeyed milk, and whoever drinks from it will never thirst again. I will lead them all to the river of paradise and beyond. It is I, my brother; *I have returned.*"

Hossein's eyes were wide in disbelief and horror as he finally understood what the president was saying. Moshaddam actually believed himself to be the Twelfth Imam, the Returned Prophet whose coming heralded the end of the world.

Hossein stood slowly, shaking his head. The president's desecration of the Qur'an was clearly too much for him. "Blasphemer!" he cried. "You are not the Mahdi! Many have claimed to be He, but were not. Many have deceived and have been judged harshly, as you will be judged harshly, Mahmoud Moshaddam. The Ayatollah will remove you from power and have you locked away for your crimes against the word of Islam and its one true prophet, Allah!" The old man, head of the most powerful religious body in Iran, was visibly shaking with rage as he finished speaking.

Moshaddam lifted his left arm and drew his sleeve across his eyes to wipe away the tears. When his other hand came up it held a small black pistol. He fired point-blank into Hossein's face. The cleric stood for a few seconds as if in disbelief, his mouth forming an "O." A second hole had appeared above his right eye and he slid silently to the floor.

Al Janaddi fell back in his chair, white-faced, his mouth opening and closing like a fish gulping for air. The other scientists cried out, and some raised their hands up over their faces. The president's bodyguards didn't even flinch; they just sat motionless, watching the president.

Al Janaddi looked at them more closely. Each had a star and crescent scar on his temple—the sign of the Urakher, the warrior dead. Trained from the age of six to kill with weapons or bare hands, these soldiers had been specially selected by the president himself to provide an impenetrable and deadly barrier of protection wherever he went. They would follow him into the furnaces of hell if called to. Even the Takavaran knew to avoid any conflict with these giant, indomitable warriors.

"Someone throw a rug over that garbage," the president ordered. "If I am wrong, I will be judged harshly; but if I am right, I will have returned the peoples of this world to Allah. None may stand in the way of his word, not even the Ayatollah." He turned to Al Janaddi. "Please, continue with your briefing."

Al Janaddi tried to speak but no words would come, just a few squeaks from a throat constricted by fear. All his dreams of a Nobel Prize were disappearing as quickly as early snow on a warm Markazi road.

"Please go on, *Agha-ye*, Al Janaddi," the president prompted again. "You have already talked briefly about controlling the Judgment Event once you have created it, but please explain— how exactly is this done?"

The president glanced over his shoulder at one of his Urakher bodyguards. The man acknowledged the contact with a small nod. Al Janaddi saw the small exchange and it worried him. He licked his dry, nervous lips and finally found his voice.

"The problems we initially faced, my President, were that

the black hole was nanoscopic in size and existed for mere milliseconds before it evaporated and took its energy and immense radiation with it. We needed to find a way to contain the black hole, to hold it and grow it so we can, in effect, milk it." Al Janaddi couldn't help it, he felt that tingling of excitement again—this was his life's work after all. "Increasing its size is easily achieved—we simply feed it what it desires: pure matter, super-concentrated, and in a dosage that we can control.

"We feed the condensed matter to the black hole via an electrically charged ionised beam of pure plasma. The more concentrated the beam, the larger the black hole grows." Janaddi took a few deep breaths; he could feel his heart galloping in his chest.

"But how does one contain something with the power of a million suns? Impossible for mortals, you may think." Al Janaddi didn't wait for a response; he was too hyped up now. "We discovered we could contain the black hole between magnetic domains, using electromagnetic solenoids with a ferromagnetic core. We could slow the particle oscillations by generating Foucault eddy currents to exhibit electron braking—we can *imprison* them; chain them within super magnetic bonds.

"Once the black hole was frozen, there was one final problem to be solved. The power required here is phenomenal. Increasing the dark matter in size by even one millionth of a micron would take a quantum amount of energy—and the larger the black hole, the more energy required. If we weren't careful, we could blackout all of Tehran with our energy needs and still not satisfy the entity's hunger."

Al Janaddi felt he had finally gained the president's full attention. *Now he understands*, he thought proudly. *Now he will appreciate my talent.* Encouraged, the scientist babbled on.

"Then I realised that the solution to my problem was already available—*I* had already imagined, designed and created it. Using my thermoelectric cubes, we are able to trap the power from the black hole! Each of the cubes can contain hundreds of gigawatts of power, and we now have thousands of them built into the lead-lined casement walls of the sphere room. In fact, the energy source is self-sustaining—the larger the event, the more power is generated and the more energy is absorbed for storage. And, of course, that means more energy is available for us to use."

The president interrupted him. "Is there no limit to the size of the Judgment Event you could create here, my friend? What would happen if you gave it more . . . plasma?"

Al Janaddi grew serious. "This is all theoretical, my President. These phenomena are the most powerful entities that exist in our universe. They eat whole star systems, and we are attempting to control them. There is a danger that if we 'overfeed' the black hole it will exceed our ability to control it. Once it escapes the magnetic domain fields, it will surely absorb us—and, if it continues to grow, everything else on the planet."

Al Janaddi expected the president to display horror or at least concern, but instead he clapped his hands together. "Excellent work, my most dear friend. You are as brilliant as you are modest. Surely Allah will reward you. In fact, I will see to it personally."

The president came around the table and lifted Al Janaddi out of his seat and hugged him. "Now, I want you to show me this magical sphere of yours, and then together we will make history by creating Judgment Day on Earth."

Al Janaddi couldn't help feeling some disquiet about Moshaddam's last remark. He'd made a mistake, surely? He meant Judgment Event, not Judgment Day? Also, he still hadn't said who would be entering the lead capsule for this event initiation.

Al Janaddi felt his stomach flip greasily inside him. Something wasn't right.

# Forty-two

The creature easily traced the thermal residue from the HAWCs' footprints leading up the steps. Those images, combined with the scent of the warm fluids within their bodies, drew it onward. Its powerful segmented legs scrabbled for purchase on the smooth steps, and chips of concrete flicked away into the stairwell as it climbed. Its multiple antennae and fan-like whips waved in the air, tasting the environment for danger or further traces of the soft creatures it followed.

It slowed as it detected the footfalls of a number of the little animals approaching. It listened, judging their distance—they were closer than the prey it had originally been pursuing. It could feed now and then continue its hunt for the creatures that had set that fiery object upon it. It halted, coming upright and wavering slightly in the air, like an enormous praying mantis waiting for its prey to stumble into range.

The ten-man Takavaran squad assigned to level three had received a brief garbled message from the squad leader down on the sub-basement level that was abruptly cut off and replaced by wet, panicked screaming. They couldn't tell if the screams were their fellow Takavaran or their adversaries.

While they were deciding on their next course of action, they heard a muffled explosion in the fortified stairwell. They could only assume they were under attack by an enemy force or infiltration agents.

The Takavaran moved quickly, entering the stairwell and

fanning out up and down the steps. The enclosed space was still thick with smoke, and the unit leader ordered two men to cover their rear while the rest descended slowly, single file. All were exuberant at the prospect of combat, and it took a few seconds to decide who would have the honour of going first.

The creature sensed the men approaching long before it could see them. Though the soldiers probably believed they moved as silently as ghosts, the vibrations on the hard concrete, their breathing and the heat vapour they gave off made them an easy target for the creature. It knew how to ambush; it knew stalking and herding and how to collect the most prey from a hunt. While the men were pressed up against the wall as they slowly descended, the creature flattened its body and shot past them on the inside railing. It had no intention of escaping—its objective was simply to cut the men off from retreat.

In the smoky gloom, the men barely registered the creature's presence until it reared up behind them. The squad leader, who was descending last, felt the hairs on the back of his neck rise. He turned to settle his nerves and satisfy himself that nothing was following them. He was wrong—there was.

A spray of blood covered the three men below him on the steps, and his head bounced down the concrete staircase, making wet, smacking sounds as it struck the sharp-edged surfaces.

Gunfire rang out and bullets ricocheted from both concrete and hardened carapace. Men shouted and then screamed as their limbs were torn and their warm bodies opened. The creature injected some with its venom-like saliva, just enough to stun them. Their bodies fell with eyes open, perhaps still seeing the gruesome carnage but unable to do anything about it.

The creature's body reared up and flared open in attack, totally blocking the stairwell. Of the eight men who had

descended, only one remained. He chose to escape on his
own terms. He placed his pistol to his chin, yelled a defiant
*"Allahu Akbar"* to the approaching creature and pulled
the trigger.

The two Takavaran left to cover their team's rear heard the
commotion, their comrade's final call to Allah, and then the
silence that fell afterwards. They froze. They could smell
the mix of cordite and blood from the stairs below. It had all
been so quick, and something wasn't right—this didn't feel
like an enemy attack. It sounded more like the eight men had
fallen into a giant shredder.

The elder of the two soldiers told his fellow Takavaran to
call it in. At the very least he wanted more men here before
they proceeded down to the lower levels.

The younger man nodded and knelt while he pressed the
communication stud into his ear. The connection was made
and he turned to give his companion the thumbs up, then
froze. His mouth hung open in confusion—he couldn't understand what he was seeing.

His fellow Takavaran was a large man, but he was being
lifted in the air as if he were a toy. His face was distorted, his
tongue protruded and his eyes bulged. As the soldier watched,
the man's skin darkened, crinkled and folded; his shoes
dropped off and his legs and arms climbed back up into his
clothing—the man was shrinking before his eyes. The worst
thing was the sound he made—not a voice anymore, more the
mewling of a small, trapped animal. His bulging eyes fixed
on his fellow soldier in a silent plea.

The monster's eyestalks quivered, as if in delight at its
feast, then the black eyes fixed on the last Takavaran. There
was no mistaking its intention. The Takavaran's final message was never sent.

Al Janaddi led the president and two of his bodyguards into
the sphere room. He couldn't help it: whenever he showed
the fantastic technology to new people his self-esteem soared.

Its incredible design was only matched by its extraordinary potential.

The gleaming silver sphere suspended above the floor looked like a small planet. It dominated the senses, and even in standby mode gave off a form of static energy that made one's skin creep and one's back teeth tingle. Al Janaddi noticed that the president put his hand over his jaw, as if concerned his teeth were about to be pulled from his head. The room smelled of fresh concrete, and something else—something earthy and primitive.

The scientist stopped in front of the machine and turned to face the small group. He ran them through the basic structure of the sphere, pointing out its encircling ring and describing the molecule collision process that would occur within the miniaturised particle collider.

Then he waved his hand towards the roof. The walls and ceiling of the vast space became hidden in darkness as every light beam focused downwards onto the sphere. He showed the group how the shielding plates of lead and the panel sections were studded with thousands upon thousands of the thermoelectric power cubes—his invention.

Al Janaddi took a few steps around the sphere, continuing with his explanation, when the president spotted the coffin-shaped structure standing on the white line circling the device. "Aah," he said, and nearly walked over the top of Al Janaddi in his haste to reach it. He paced around it slowly, running his hand over the smooth outer shell, tracing the Persian calligraphy with a fingertip, patting it as if to feel its weight and structure. Then he motioned for Al Janaddi to open it. The capsule was close to seven feet tall and included all the refinements that the president had instructed: a space for standing, water bottles, food, and several different communication and location devices—some triggered automatically and some operated by finger control.

The president waved his hand in front of the open capsule and his lips moved silently. He seemed to be blessing the heavy lead casket. When he was done, he opened the small padded container attached at waist level on the inside of the capsule. From his jacket pocket he brought forth a small, exquisitely decorated silver box encrusted with rubies, sapphires and emeralds. He stroked it and then, with great reverence, lifted the lid. He spoke to the scientist without looking up. "Do you know what this is, my friend?"

Al Janaddi saw that the box held a smooth dark rock. He shook his head.

"It is a piece of the Black Stone, the al-Hajar-ul-Aswad. This holiest of objects fell to Earth in the time of Adam and Eve. It was pure white then. Over the centuries it has turned black because of the sins of man. It has been lost and found many times, and it is said that once, when it was thought to have been lost forever, the archangel Gabriel himself retrieved it from beneath a mountain and gave it to Abraham when he rebuilt the Kaaba, the sacred building in the Grand Mosque in Mecca."

The president looked up from the box and into the scientist's face with eyes like black ice. "Do you know why I have brought this piece of the holy Black Stone here, my friend?"

Al Janaddi shook his head; he guessed he wasn't supposed to answer.

"A messenger of Allah has foretold that on the Day of the Last Judgment, the stone will be given eyes to see and a mouth to speak. When it speaks, it will testify in favour of the faithful." The president paused, as if to slow down an overexcited heartbeat. He rubbed a finger over the smooth surface of the stone and then kissed it, holding his lips hard in place for a few seconds. "It will speak to me, and it will testify on my behalf when I lead our people across the bridge into Jannah. It will favour me when I alone stand before Allah."

The president lifted the stone from the box, then dropped the beautifully crafted silver relic to the floor as if it were no more than a discarded apple core. He placed the stone reverently in the capsule's padded box. Then he turned to Al Janaddi and embraced him, planting a small kiss on each of his cheeks. He stepped back, nodded to his bodyguards and, to Al Janaddi's surprise, stepped up into the lead capsule's padded interior. He clasped his hands in prayer and rocked back and forth for a few moments, before opening his eyes to fix them on the scientist. He dropped his hand to the box where the sacred black stone now resided. "It has started to speak to me already, my friend."

The president ordered one of his bodyguards to close the capsule before the heavy door slammed into place, he looked over Al Janaddi's head to the other guards. "You know what to do. *Allahu Akbar!*"

The tall man nodded.

# Forty-three

Adira whispered a brief prayer as the team waited for Alex's sign. He nodded and the HAWCs entered the level one corridor. They made their way quickly and quietly around the curve, flat against the inside wall, guns drawn. Lagudi led, followed by O'Riordan and Adira, Zachariah, and then Sam. Alex was a few paces behind, guarding against anyone or anything that decided to follow.

In less than two minutes they all stood before a fortified steel door. Alex pushed the heavy silver slab with his hand; it wasn't open like the rest. "Formidable, and solidly locked—for now." He kept his hand on the door for a moment and it seemed to Adira as if he was listening through it somehow. He removed his hand and turned to the group. "This is it, ladies and gentlemen—this is why we are here. When we go through that door, prepare to be given hell—and to release it in return."

The HAWCs nodded their readiness. Adira was ready too; she could feel the adrenalin pumping through her.

Sam smiled. "Go in fast, come out smiling."

"Uncle, give me an entrance," Alex ordered. "Irish, Rocky, plant some spiders for any uninvited guests who may be following us."

Sam headed to the code pad and pulled cords and wires from the pouches on the front of his suit. He pulled a box from his belt, licked a suction cap at the back and stuck it beside the number pad. In a few moments he had jacked the small system in and a red LED screen was displaying a rapid search of the keypad's memory for the digital code that would open it.

While Zach watched Sam work the electronic combination, Adira walked up to Alex. She stood in very close to his chest and looked up into his face. "Thank you for saving me back there. This now makes us even, I think."

"You don't have to—"

Alex never finished. With a grin, Adira reached forward to grab at his belt. "I'll take this back now. I might need it," she said, removing the gun that Alex had taken from her on the lower level and deftly slotting it into its waiting holster. She half-turned and then paused, the smile coming back onto her lips. "If I've left anything down there, I'll be back for it later."

Alex laughed softly and shook his head. Adira liked the sound of his laugh, and had to keep her back to him as her face burned and butterflies danced in her belly. *I think he's interested too*, she thought, then forced herself to clear her head for the coming assault.

Rocky and Irish had secreted spiders beside doorframes and fire extinguishers—anywhere that offered concealment of the lethal little boxes and their twenty-first century claymore technology.

"Hope these guys don't have a tea lady," Rocky said as he armed the last of the little motion-sensitive explosives.

The two men planted themselves up some distance from the group as lookouts and sighted their guns along the corridor—they were ready.

Sam's LED screen stopped and flashed. Alex and Adira immediately drew and aimed their weapons as the silver door hissed open to blast them with negative pressure air. It revealed a small, brilliant white corridor with yet another doorway at its end; just as imposing, but this time with a flat screen about waist height and angled upwards.

"Damnit, a DNA scanner," Sam said. "Great. And look at the ceiling—they're gas vents. Guess if you use the wrong finger you're going to end up with the Ayatollah's bad breath blowing down on you." Sam plucked at his bottom lip as he thought it through.

"Can you open it?" Alex asked over his shoulder as he looked up and down the corridor. "I can open it," Sam said, "but I'll need a few minutes. I think I should go in by myself first."

Alex's head whipped around to stare in one direction and again Adira thought he looked as though he was listening to something no one else could hear. His expression changed and she didn't like it. It seemed he'd picked up on whatever it was he was waiting for.

The creature entered the scientifics floor through the door left ajar by the HAWCs. The brightness of the corridor made it hesitate for a few seconds, but it could sense more of the fluid-filled creatures further inside. It dropped down onto all of its legs, flattened its low, wide body and sped down the corridor, a blur of mottled ochre and green carapace, drawn on by the tingling sensation of residual gamma particles in the air and the scent of the soft liquid sacks that had now become its food source.

It came at O'Riordan so fast that it outpaced the electronic senses of the spider explosive. Before O'Riordan had comprehended there was danger, the monster arthropod was rearing up before him. His finger wouldn't work on the trigger and his mouth hung open as the leviathan loomed above him.

The spider bombs finally caught up and exploded and the blast shook O'Riordan from his inanimate state. "Not again, you fuckin' big bug," he yelled, and leaped to the side. The creature had been knocked off its feet by the explosion and its legs made a loud clacking sound as they drummed momentarily on the hard floor.

O'Riordan ejected the magazine from his gun onto the ground and withdrew another from a pouch at his waist—this one with a red stripe banding the metal cartridge. It snapped in instantly, he swung the muzzle up and fired three times. The bullets struck the creature in the mid-section where the greasy armour plates came together like mottled green tiles. It immediately clamped down to protect the weaker area.

O'Riordan got to his feet and took a step forward. "Yeah, felt those, didn't ya? Flat-tipped tungsten—armour-piercing babies. Want some more?"

He fired another three rounds and was satisfied to see three more direct hits and a small piece of shell flick off to skid away down the corridor.

The creature slowly rose up to its full height and towered ten feet above O'Riordan; he saw its eyestalks craning down to look at him. It had planted itself in the centre of the corridor on its sharply-pointed, thick bristled legs and seemed to shiver slightly.

"I'm not running this time, ugly, and you're not getting past me to my guys." O'Riordan fired three again—another three hits. *That leaves me three and then back to standard lead jackets*, he thought.

The creature shivered again and the HAWC mistook the movement for the trembling of fear. He smiled and advanced. "That's right—and you can go straight back to hell."

He fired his last three armour-piercing bullets.

The explosion rang out from the direction Alex was facing. His face became a mixture of resignation and simmering anger.

He turned to Sam. "Uncle, get 'em all inside. Then shut the door and take it from here—you know your orders."

Sam hesitated. The explosion meant Irish was going head to head with someone. If it was a bigger force than last time, Alex would be overwhelmed, even with his unique powers. He was about to try to negotiate with his superior officer when he heard a noise that chilled his blood—the mad clacking of giant arthropod legs on a hard surface.

"Oh, shit, boss—I don't think O'Riordan's dancing with the locals back there."

Rocky joined the group, drawn back by the explosion and

gunfire. He must also have heard the scrabbling of the unearthly creature as his face was white, making the black stubble on his cheeks and chin more pronounced. He continued to point his gun down the corridor, but Sam noticed the muzzle shook slightly.

"Soldiers, this time you will follow orders," Alex said. He pointed over his shoulder towards the sounds of mortal combat down the corridor. "This is just a distraction. The main game is behind that door. You must be ready for extreme force. Believe me, it's waiting for you. I cannot allow us to be decimated before we even commence to fight."

Adira stepped forward with a deep scowl on her face, but Alex held up his hand before she could speak. "No. You must stand and fight here. You know what it will mean for your country if this facility fully develops the technology. You know what it could mean for all of us."

For a brief moment Adira looked as though she was going to argue. Then her shoulders slumped and she simply nodded.

"I'll buy you some time and catch up when I'm through," Alex said, but he didn't meet her eyes when he said it. Sam guessed he expected to be a while.

"Don't forget to duck and weave," Sam said, and winked.

Alex smiled and turned away down the corridor.

Sam took a last look as his captain disappeared around the corner. "Ah crap." He shook his head and turned to the team. "Let's go, people. We're probably all about to be gassed to death anyway."

An image of his father jumped into his head as he remembered when things started to get really bad on their drought-affected farm. Sam had helped his father plough back in several fields of tinder dry corn stalks so they could sow dry weather potatoes. Afterwards, while they shared cold drinks, his father had looked out at the fields and slapped him on the back. "Sammy, when the shit hits the fan, get outta the fan business." Sam smiled now and shook his head again: *Too late, Pop.*

# Forty-four

The Arak facility had been Al Janaddi's home for months; it had always felt like a high-tech cocoon—sterile, but comforting. Now its pristine walls made him feel claustrophobic and a little nauseous—as if it were a prison cell and he was awaiting execution.

He looked at the six nervous scientists and technicians in the sphere room with him. The president's four enormous Urakher bodyguards towered over them all.

The Urakher lifted their sports bags onto the table and removed from them dark, heavy-looking vests. They removed their jackets and strapped the vests professionally into place. *Why do they need those,* Al Janaddi thought.

The largest Urakher strode up to Al Janaddi, took him firmly by the upper arm and led him to the console. He pointed one enormous hand at the keyboards. "Begin the test, honourable Ahmad Al Janaddi, and please show me everything."

Al Janaddi blinked and swallowed. He had a feeling that the final page of his brilliant career was being turned. Whatever happened to the president would be upon his head. He had the intense feeling he had to tell someone, had to get a message out to the ruling council, or perhaps even to the intruders. The Americans surely wouldn't let this happen; they'd stop the test and rescue him.

"What does this show, and this?" The Urakher pointed to the computer screens—they were covered in graphs, dials and long columns of numbers. "Quickly!"

The man's abrupt tone made Al Janaddi jump. "Ah, this room is the command centre for the entire Jamshid II sphere program. My fellow scientists and technicians monitor each area, each part of the process. This dial here controls the flow of plasma electrons in the beam; the screen gives the calculations and displays a three-dimensional image of the theoretical event being formed—its size, energy output and also the gross energy required to hold it in stasis." Al Janaddi pointed to another graph. "These figures and the information they provide are fed across to the magnetic domains so we can calibrate the energy currents within the synthetic gravitational field."

The Urakher pressed a key; nothing happened. He looked at the scientist's face with such hostility and disdain that Al Janaddi felt bile jump into the back of his throat.

"Oh yes, I'm sorry," he said. "I need to enter my code or access to the system is locked." He began to type in some numbers—mistyping several times in his fear—until at last the screen rippled and the fields changed colour.

He pointed to another screen that was covered in hundreds of small images of batteries. "These are representations of the thermoelectric power cubes—the screens go for many pages. As each battery, then each row, is filled, the pages scroll down. The bigger the Judgment Event, the more cubes should be filled and the battery image on the screen will turn from yellow to blue. Now the lead panel—"

The Urakher grabbed the back of his collar, cutting him short. "Ready the test for commencement now, most honourable Al Janaddi, and tell me again how to control the size of the event. Tell me your password, tell me everything, and omit nothing or I will be forced to hurt you."

Al Janaddi gulped and felt the fullness of his bladder; he really needed to piss. The three other Urakher had herded his fellow scientists and technicians to the centre of the room and had taken up guard positions around the walls. His colleagues stared at him, their faces white and fearful. They seemed to be waiting for him to do something . . . but what?

The Urakher shook him and Al Janaddi did the only thing he could think of. He began to pray.

Alex pulled the KBELT laser from over his shoulder and picked up speed down the corridor. There were no more sounds coming from O'Riordan's location and Alex found that more worrying than the sounds of combat.

The curve of the corridor meant that he could only see about a dozen feet ahead. He slowed and pressed himself to the inside wall and reached out, not with his hands but with his senses. He paused for a moment as an image began to form in his mind. Alex was becoming adept at using his new skills. He knew he was still changing, growing, becoming different every day. He reached out again, this time hard. It felt like a spike was being driven through his head—from the inside out. He ground his teeth and pushed once more, regardless of the pain. The image took shape. The monster was there, just around the bend.

He could perceive that O'Riordan was still alive, but his presence was weakening, fading like a photograph left out in the sun. He sensed something else too—the raw power and crude animal intelligence he had felt out in the desert and at the mouth of the cave. The creature was not able to reason, but was capable of planning an ambush. He knew that it was watching him in the same way he watched it. It knew he was coming; it was waiting for him.

With O'Riordan still alive, Alex had no choice; he had to try to save his man, he had to engage. *Oh God, it's gonna be bad*, he thought. He sucked in a deep breath and stepped out into the centre of the corridor.

He was wrong: it was worse, much worse.

This was the first time Alex had seen the creature clearly. In the harsh artificial light of the corridor, it was magnificent in its hideousness. It had reared up on its four hind legs, each as thick as Alex's thigh at the top, but tapering to a black bristled point where it met the ground. Alex remembered a line from Mr. Haniford's long past literature class—"There are more things in heaven and earth, Horatio, than are dreamt of in your philosophy." *More like somewhere a lot lower than either of those places*, thought Alex.

The strange being's upper body was flared open like a massive insectoid cobra, and it held O'Riordan tightly to its core. Its smaller thoracic legs squeezed him softly, almost tenderly, undulating up and down as if it were milking him. The mandibles in its bullet-shaped head had opened and a sharp spike protruded into the man's neck. Though Alex could not see O'Riordan's face, he could sense he was still alive within that revolting embrace. Even as he watched, O'Riordan's body collapsed, wrinkled and shortened. He was slowly being turned into an empty bag of skin as the creature contentedly sucked out and digested his bodily fluids. Alex groaned in despair.

The creature's two long eyestalks swivelled to fix on Alex, and he could see the multiple pupils in each. He tried to imagine the vision it received from those soulless triscopic bulbs. Alex couldn't help thinking that the creature looked as though it belonged a mile deep under the ocean in some dark sunless trench, not standing in the middle of a surgically white corridor within the realm of man.

He and the creature stood only a dozen feet apart, not moving, weighing each other up. He could sense no fear from it, not even wariness, just the savage confidence of a predator over its prey. *Why shouldn't it be confident?* It had triumphed over every human it had encountered and knew their weapons had no effect. Alex was probably just another moving bag of fluid to be drained when it had finished with O'Riordan.

Alex blinked several times as he felt something he hadn't felt in a long time—fear. The creature had easily bested him in the cave—it was faster, stronger and infinitely more savage. *But this time I've got a surprise*, he thought.

The compressed packets of high energy shot out in a faster-than-light pulse from the bulbed muzzle of the laser and struck the creature in the upper body. They passed straight through its carapace, leaving several pencil-thin smoking holes. The creature, taken by surprise, dropped the shrunken husk that had been O'Riordan to the floor. Alex felt the beast's scream of rage and pain in his head as it retracted its flared thorax, flattened its body and prepared to charge.

Though he had struck it several times, there seemed to be little serious damage at all. The rifle's high-energy setting was deadly to humans, but against this creature he might as well have been trimming its nails. He changed the setting to the lower-energy wide beam and fired again. The explosive punch struck the creature and rocked it back, causing its sharp legs to dig furrows in the floor. Small bits of carapace splintered away as connective cartilage was smashed from its ten-foot frame. He fired once again and was rewarded by one of its eyestalks exploding off the top of its head.

The inhuman scream came again in his head, and then the creature charged. It came at him with a speed that almost overwhelmed him. One second it was twelve feet away and the next it was rearing up in his face. Time slowed for Alex as the creature shot out its raptorial claws, both heavily spiked blades moving so quickly that they actually created a shock wave in the air. Though Alex moved faster than a normal man could, all he had time to do was lessen the blades' impact—he dropped and rolled, but not before the KBELT in his hands was sliced in two. One massive claw continued on to slice his head and Alex felt blood trickling down over his eye.

He was thankful for the creature's slight loss of depth perception due to the missing eye. Possibly it had also underestimated his own speed and agility. Alex knew it wouldn't make that same mistake again. After his recent run-in, he knew it was smart enough to adapt its attack.

Alex got to his feet and the creature once again flared open its thorax cavity, displaying gristly flaps and tendrils. Colour rippled over its front cartilage and abdominal plates as it finally recognised Alex for what he was—not food but an adversary. Its single eye fixed on the HAWC and its claws drew back ready to strike.

Alex balanced on his toes, ready to duck or move as best he could, but he knew he couldn't stay out of the way of those sharp blades forever. Now that the laser had been destroyed, he would have to use more conventional weapons. He withdrew his pistol and the long black Ka-Bar knife—probably useless but at least he was armed. He held the twelve-inch blade out to his side. The dark folded chromium steel of the Ka-Bar made it one of the hardest knives in the US military, and it had a scalpel-sharp edge. Alex only needed two things: a lethal strike area, and an opportunity.

All living creatures had a brain or central nervous system that controlled locomotion, logic and autonomous function. This thing had a head, so Alex assumed that its controlling organ was located there. He fired twice, delivering two unerring headshots to the epicuticle plate where the eyestalks had met. The creature didn't react at all, even though Alex could see small creases where the copper-jacketed lead bullets had glanced off the exoskeletal skull.

It reared up to its full height and its giant alien form packed the corridor. Its subsonic scream filled Alex's head like a thousand needles. Bands of colour pulsed up and down its body in an obvious aggressive challenge. It used one of its hind legs to scoop up O'Riordan's lifeless body and pass it to its higher claws; then it tore the body down the middle—either to show Alex what was in store for him, or as a display of strength, the way the black mountain gorilla smashed trees and pounded branches into the earth to build its rage before it charged.

Alex's eyes widened momentarily at the desecration of his fellow HAWC's body. Anger filled him. He gritted his teeth, and his hand on the knife handle tightened so fiercely the leather squealed in protest.

Two powerful and deadly creatures from different worlds stood before each other, ready for battle. There would only be one survivor.

# Forty-five

Sam, Rocky, Adira and Zach stood together in the DNA scanner booth. Sam looked up at the ceiling towards the gas vents. None of them had brought gas masks, as they had needed to travel light. Still, it didn't really matter that they had no masks as many of the lethal or incapacitating gases today worked on the skin as well as the respiratory system. Gas masks didn't save your life; they just stopped you from vomiting up your lungs before you died—which, admittedly, did leave a prettier corpse.

"At least we have a way out," Lagudi said, jerking his head towards the steel door they had come through. A silver button the size of a coin was fixed on the wall at about waist height.

Sam slid back one of the recessed doors in the room to reveal some clothing, dust-coated shoes and a thermos. He thought they probably belonged to one of the technicians who would wear sterile overalls to protect the hi-tech equipment. He drew the thermos out into the bright light, held it at both ends and turned it around slowly, looking at the detail on its surface.

"Okay, this might work," he said. He pulled some plastic tape from a belt pouch, tore off a one-inch strip and laid it over a section of the thermos. He pressed it down, ripped it off and then held it up to the light. "Ever seen a fingerprint under a microscope? The ridges and troughs make the Grand Canyon look like a dip in the road. They're rich in dirt, bacteria and oil—and in that oil . . . DNA."

He crossed himself twice and stuck the tape on the flat screen.

There was a hissing sound. Zach covered his face.

Alex needed to stay out of reach of the creature's razor-sharp claws, but get in close enough to find some sort of vital organ. His money was still on the head, and probably his life too.

Alex leapt at the creature, feinting to the left and going right. His plan was to use the wall to bounce up and at the creature's head, which was quite a few feet above his own. His speed would have delighted the scientists back in the USSTRATCOM labs and amazed his fellow HAWCs, but in comparison to a creature that could move its attack claws fast enough to break the sound barrier, he was an easy target.

While he was still in midair, the creature turned to track him with its remaining triscopic eye. It shot out its claws, striking towards Alex's mid-section. Alex sensed the movement before he saw it and swivelled slightly, taking the blow on the remaining ceramic plates across his chest. The laboratory-hardened material shattered and his pectoral muscles were laid bare.

There was a spray of blood and he was thrown ten feet down the corridor. Small fan-like structures waved at the end of the creature's proboscis as it scooped at the air. The released blood and fluids must have excited it. It sped forward, probably intending to impale Alex on that hideous spike and suck him dry.

As he sensed the creature moving in for the killer blow, Alex rolled fast and came to his feet. Even his rapid metabolism would take some time to knit the chest wound, and the bleeding needed to be staunched artificially or he would lose energy. The strike and his impact on the floor had not dislodged the knife and gun in his hands, but these now seemed like a feeble armoury against a high-speed tank of an animal with two spring-loaded machetes.

In his mind, Alex could hear the creature's squeal of triumph as it closed in for the kill. *It has too many advantages.*

*Gotta even things up a bit*, he thought as he got to one knee and sighted along the pistol barrel. *Too many advantages, but I'm betting you hunt primarily by vision.*

Four shots came in rapid succession at a target closing faster than a human eye could follow. The remaining bulb at the top of the eyestalk exploded, but Alex only had time to move slightly to absorb the impact—he was still thrown backwards.

The scream in his head now turned to one of pain and rage. *Good*, he thought. He taunted the creature: "On Earth we say, don't skin your deer until it's caught, ugly."

A plume of wet-looking fans and tendrils was waving frantically from the front of its head as it tried to taste Alex's position from the surrounding air. Alex knew he couldn't take another impact from the creature; his energy was ebbing. *Last chance*, he thought.

He tore the shredded para-aramid suit material from his upper body and wiped as much blood off himself as he could. The creature somehow registered where Alex was and charged. Alex threw the wadded, blood-soaked material up and to the left of the oncoming monstrosity while he leapt in the other direction. As he hoped, the claws shot out and caught the clothing. It would take at least a second for the creature to relocate him and attack again—and that was all the time he needed. In midair, Alex brought his arm down in a hammer blow that combined his full weight and all the abnormal muscle strength his frame could muster. The twelve-inch Ka-Bar blade pierced the monster's chitinous skull with a crunching brittle sound and sank to the hilt. Alex used the momentum of his leap to keep sailing past and land several feet behind the giant arthropod.

When he turned, he knew from the creature's spastic movements that he had found if not its brain, then at least some sort of nerve junction. The creature collided with the wall with a cracking impact. It fell onto its back and its multiple legs scrabbled in the air for a while, before it righted itself and then reared up to spit its caustic venom along the corridor.

Alex had heard that the common household cockroach could survive for a week without its head, and even then only died from dehydration and starvation. Who knew how long this thing could live? He felt for the medkit at his waist—there was no time for a full workup, but enough for a quick field repair. He knelt and squirted wound adhesive into the gaping slash across his chest, then pinched the wound together for a few seconds until he was sure it would hold, all the time keeping his eyes on the mad skittering of the giant creature.

He stood and walked to where O'Riordan's torn body lay. The tattered uniform covered the ragged mess of dried entrails, muscle and bone beneath. Alex closed the man's eyes; there was no time for words now.

He took some of O'Riordan's ammunition and his long Ka-Bar knife, which he placed in his own empty scabbard. He was about to stand when he noticed a single explosive spider resting in a pouch at the fallen HAWC's waist. Alex pulled the small metal box free and looked at the creature. It was still making mad uncoordinated movements along the corridor. He stood slowly with the box in his hand and stared down at the mess that had been one of his men. The skittering came a little closer and the creature's claws lashed out blindly, probably in a dying reflex. Alex knew he had to get back to his team . . . but there was one more thing he needed to do first.

He tensed his body. "For Irish," he said, and leaped.

He landed on the monster's back, grabbed his knife where it was embedded in the heavily armoured skull and twisted. In his other hand he held the spider up high, battling to stay on the thing's back as it bucked beneath him. Even with a pierced brain it reacted to the attack. Alex brought more strength to the blade as he tried to turn it again—still it held. He screamed his hatred and anger and twisted with a burst of strength that caused the creature's skull to split open a few inches along a biological seam.

"We own this fucking planet," Alex said. He pressed a small button on the spider and jammed it into the crack in the skull. The small silver legs immediately sprang out of the device and grasped the edges of the break, locking it in place.

Alex jumped free and rolled twice to avoid the explosion. In the reinforced corridor, the blast was condensed and delivered up and down the passage. There was a rushing dry heat, and mix of metal and biological shrapnel peppered his back and upper arms.

Alex got to his feet and smiled grimly. Where the creature's head had been, there was just a sizzling crater, like a boiled egg with its top sliced off ready for consumption. A smell like cooked shellfish and sickly sweet vinegar filled the air. The body quivered for another moment and then lay still.

"Now we're done," Alex said.

He looked down at his own bleeding and battered body. There was a shard sticking out of his upper arm and he pulled it free—an inch-long piece of dark mottled shell, thick, extremely hard and slightly waxy. He rubbed it with his thumb and pushed it into his pocket.

Alex's wounds stopped bleeding as he jogged back down the corridor. He ached all over but pushed the pain from his mind. The solid steel door loomed before him. *Hope I'm not late for the party*, he thought.

# Forty-six

Five . . . four . . . three . . . two . . . one . . . a red light turned green. The hissing stopped. Zach dropped his hands from his face and looked embarrassed.

Sam turned to Adira and Zach and said, "Get behind us."

"Not a chance." Adira had her gun up and her eyes burned with a focused intensity.

Zach also had his gun drawn, but he stood a little behind Lagudi. He saw the HAWC cross himself once and suck in a deep breath.

The door slid open.

"*Kadima!*" Adira screamed—an ancient Hebrew battle cry that made the giant Urakher waiting for them on the other side of the door bellow in anger. She pushed past Rocky and Sam and dived to the floor, firing as she went.

Lagudi and Sam were through just as fast, fanning left and right. Zach jammed a knife into the door rail to stop it from closing, then followed Adira, wriggling on his stomach towards a hiding place under the table.

The four Urakher had obviously been expecting this, Al Janaddi thought. That was why they were wearing the protective vests. The man with Al Janaddi placed his huge hand behind the scientist's neck and hissed into his ear, "Start the Event now, little man, or you will die."

The other three Urakher came forward in a solid wall of flesh, providing cover for their companion and Al Janaddi. They fired at the intruders with a skill that told of many years of training. The gunfire was frighteningly loud in the small room, and the dull smacking of bullets impacting against the Americans' armour and the Urakhers' reinforced vests sounded like heavy rain on a canvas sail. If the Urakher felt the pain of the impacts, they gave no sign.

The HAWCs and Adira each picked a target and engaged it with a volley of bullets. They quickly found that, for large men, these soldiers moved quickly and were without fear. Adira spotted the star and crescent tattoo on the temple of one of the men and couldn't suppress a shudder of fear and revulsion. *Achhh, Urakher—the warrior dead*—she hadn't thought they still existed. They were madmen, known for their fearlessness in battle and their total disdain for their own or any other life. In all her time in Metsada, Adira had never heard of one being killed.

The technicians and scientists in the room dived to cower beneath tables or anywhere they could find refuge. One of the technicians ducked under the table next to Zach, who just looked at him with raised eyebrows and shrugged.

Lagudi had closed the gap on his man and was now in range of a pair of gigantic arms with fists the size of bricks. The Urakher seized Lagudi's gun hand and brought his elbow around towards the HAWC's chin, expecting to connect in a bone-shattering strike. Lagudi blocked the powerful thrust, recognising the martial arts strike. "Not bad, but now you're playing in my sandpit, asshole." He released his gun and brought a flat-handed strike up under his opponent's chin. The Urakher's head snapped back, but instead of the rewarding sound of cartilage and bone snapping, Lagudi saw the man's head immediately come back down. There was no pain or anger in those black eyes—just a calmness that the muscular little HAWC found unsettling.

Adira had managed to put a bullet in the thigh and upper arm of her opponent, but he kept coming forward. She didn't want to get within reach of those hands—the fanatical giant could literally tear her arms off. She fired again and rolled to keep a little distance between herself and the black-clad titan. But eventually she would be backed into a corner or would run out of ammunition—and she knew there would be no time for a reload.

She heard a booming sound coming from outside the closed entry door to the security chamber that led into the lab. Just then Sam Reid came hurtling across the room at about head height, only to smash into a wall and crumple to the ground. *This is not going well*, she thought.

The booming sound came again.

*We need more time*, Adira thought, and then 250 pounds of muscle wrapped in Kevlar landed on top of her. *Dafook! Caught,* she thought. *Time's up—make it count.*

The security door was thick and made of a condensed alloy especially toughened to resist bullets and heat. Alex could hear the sound of gunfire and mayhem through the steel, and could feel pain being registered. There was a battle going on in there—his HAWCs against an unknown number of highly trained opponents—and he needed to be part of it.

The number pad and its code were inaccessible to him, so he withdrew his two remaining spiders and placed them together in one corner of the door, setting them for five seconds. He ran a few feet around the curve of the corridor. The explosion blew tiles off the ceiling and floor above and around the door, but the security alloy held. It was burnt and abraded but not even cracked.

"Shit!" Alex yelled, and punched the door. He kicked out at it, and then punched it again and again. The booming clangs of his blows became just as loud as the explosives he had used and with each one Alex's anger built. More steroids and more adrenalin flushed into his system, natural stimulants mixing with the unique chemical compounds introduced in a laboratory on the other side of the world, until his entire body almost hummed with unnatural strength.

Alex struck the door with a two-fisted overhead blow and was rewarded by a large dent in its centre. *Too long*, he thought. His fists bled, but the pain in his hands was nothing compared to the agonised red screaming in his head. It was

becoming hard to think clearly. He withdrew O'Riordan's
Ka-Bar blade and assessed the best place to strike. It was
going to be futile, but rage was now beginning to cloud his
logic. He backed up a step, lifted the blade high and launched
himself at the door.

The Urakher standing guard over Al Janaddi watched closely
as the scientist initiated the Judgment Event. He spoke quietly
into his ear: "Turn on the microphone to the capsule."

The scientist complied, then tried to squirm out of the giant hand that was crushing his neck. The Urakher squeezed a
little harder and gazed reverently through the window at the
lead capsule. "We have begun the program, my Mahdi, O
Allah be praised," he said.

From the capsule came the response: "*Allahu Akbar*, faithful one, I will intercede for you, your family and all your an-
cestors."

Incredibly, Al Janaddi heard singing through the speaker.
It was the Adhan, the call to prayer—the first song heard
by a Muslim newborn, the first song sung in a school or new
home, the song for a new beginning. The president's voice
was as haunting as it was melodious. It was said that the more
powerful the voice, the more powerful the prayer.

In the sphere room, a low horn sounded and the lights
began to dim.

# Forty-seven

"I'm sorry, Jack. You know we can't let our enemies perfect nuclear technology," General Meir Shavit said. "They have said they wish to burn us from the map. They are only words until they have the technology to actually do it."

Major Hammerson knew what a risk his friend was taking in preparing to strike first against Iran. Such an act could set fire to the entire Middle East; but failing to act now could mean the future obliteration of his country. It was a devil of a choice.

"Meir, just give me two hours," the Hammer replied. "My team is still in there, and until I hear different, I have to assume they will succeed."

There was silence on the phone for nearly thirty seconds; Hammerson's hand tightened as he waited for a response.

"The one you call Arcadian is there, isn't he," the general said. "I think he must be very valuable. One day we will talk further on this . . . And remember, I also have a team in there. I can give you just one hour." The phone went dead.

Hammerson rubbed his forehead, disconnected the call and then immediately picked up the phone again. "Annie, get me the president."

Lagudi's forearms were heavily bruised, and one of the thick metacarpal bones in the back of his hand was broken. His training had taught him to ignore pain, but he knew he was wearing down. His opponent's face was cut and battered but he was still strong—stronger than he was.

The HAWC struck out again with a flat-handed strike followed by a roundhouse kick, and once again they were both blocked. The Urakher countered with two massive lunge punches and a vicious snap-kick. Lagudi deflected the punches, but was only partially successful in diminishing the kick's power—he felt something else splinter in his body. Lagudi was good, but he realised that his opponent was better. The oldest maxim in the fighting world kept sneaking into his head: *A good big man will always beat a good little man.*

The two-fingered snake strike flicked out at his neck so quickly he only registered it after it had been executed, and he knew immediately his larynx was crushed. It'd be a slow, suffocating death without a tracheotomy, and he doubted his opponent would give him a few minutes to cut a hole in his own throat and insert a breathing tube. Another immense blow smashed him to the ground—he had no breath left in his lungs.

The Urakher drew his leg back, preparing to deliver a massive kick to Lagudi's head. He didn't need finesse this time, just a lot of power to smash the skull.

Five gunshots rang out. Only two were on target; but as their target was the back of the Urakher's head, two were enough—the man was dead before he fell to the ground.

Rocky looked across to see Dr. Shomron sighting along his shaking pistol from under a table. The HAWC gave the scientist a bloody smile through lips that were turning a deep blue, and slowly nodded his thanks. Then he closed his eyes.

The Urakher lifted Adira as easily as if she were a child, one hand around her neck, the other on her gun. He tore it from her fingers and flung it away with disdain. He smiled; Adira could tell he was expecting to enjoy this.

She could hear the booming impacts against the door again—she needed to place a bet. If it was the Takavaran, it didn't matter—she was dead anyway. If it was Alex, they stood a chance. From her sleeves she drew a pair of throwing spikes. She stabbed the first into the forearm of the Urakher up to the hilt, inserted between the ulna and radius bones and into the meat of the brachiordial muscle, and pushed the blade hard to the side. Not totally debilitating, but she knew it would hurt like hell—and, no matter how strong the man was, would cause the hand to automatically open. It did and she fell to the floor. A few seconds was all she needed . . .

She sighted the exit button at the far end of the white entrance corridor and, with unerring aim, launched the thin black blade. It struck the button perfectly and the door slid back.

She smiled when she saw what was on the other side. She had bet correctly.

The Urakher lifted her again and punched her hard in the face. Before she lost consciousness, she had a vision of a giant red bird flying towards her. *Come the Arcadian*, she thought, as everything went dark.


The toughened blade of the Ka-Bar shattered against the dense alloy of the security door, leaving Alex with only balled fists and a volcanic rage. He screamed his fury at the obstruction and backed away to the far wall. He lowered his shoulder, every muscle tensed as he commenced his charge. At that exact moment the door slid open. He continued anyway and went through like a red-streaked missile.

Alex's body and senses were so supercharged that the world seemed to crawl around him. He took in the broken figure of Sam being pummelled by a towering man; the battered and still body of Rocky Lagudi, a dead giant next to him; another enormous man holding a small man in a lab coat at the far end of the command centre; and a fourth ogre, his foot lifted over Adira's head, about to stomp the life from her.

The giant looming over Adira turned to Alex. His eyes widened slightly as he took in the man streaking towards him faster than a desert jaguar. Alex's uniform top was shredded and singed at the edges, and blood streaked his face and his body. But it was his eyes, blazing with a murderous rage, that made the tall Urakher feel things he hadn't felt since he was a small boy—fear and doubt.

The Urakher drew his gun, but Alex had reached him before he had a chance to fire. Alex struck the man on the cheekbone with enough force to crush his head and propel his body across the room. His large shape struck one of the metal computer cabinets and embedded itself into the steel frame.

The Urakher with Al Janaddi witnessed the blow and his eyes momentarily widened in disbelief. He called to his remaining colleague to finish with Sam and deal with Alex; he needed a few more minutes with the little man.

Through the viewing panel, the sphere glowed, then seemed to shrink into a dot of nothingness inside a white halo: Al Janaddi had initiated and opened the president's Judgment Event. The plasma beam directed a purplish stream of charged electrons into the centre of the black hole and began to feed it. The screens in the viewing room registered movement—the rows of batteries began to fill and a graphic representation of the event showed as a small dot held in stasis between the encircling magnetic domains.

"You have your event," the scientist said. He knew what was coming now, and tried to half-turn to see the battle behind him. Perhaps the Americans would be victorious. They would point their guns at the ugly monster next to him and shout, *Step away.*

He reached into his pocket, withdrew the small mass storage device and tried to turn his body a little more. *If I can just show them what I have here . . .*

The Urakher felt Al Janaddi try to twist in his grip, and he applied more pressure to the little man's neck. He brought his other hand up to push once against the side of the scientist's skull—the snap was barely audible. He threw the scientist's body out of the way like a sack of rubbish and quickly turned back to the console to increase the plasma feed rate.

As the computer showed the plasma feed moving upwards,

he began to sing softly—about the Mahdi, the Day of Judgment and Reckoning, Allah and his own coming martyrdom.

The matter surrounding the black hole now began to be absorbed. The president's capsule seemed to elongate and point towards the pinprick of darkness in the centre of the room, then it lengthened, streaked, and disappeared into the nothingness.

"Oh, blessed is the Mahdi!" screamed the Urakher as he pushed the plasma stream rationing up to its maximum. Everyone in the room felt a wave of nausea pass over them as the black hole began to grow.

The Urakher at the console stared through the lead-plated glass at the pinprick of nothing that was darker and more powerful than anything that had ever existed on Earth. He felt the waves of energy wash over him and his singing became even louder.

Zachariah could feel the distortion in the atmosphere and in the very core of his own physical being. He didn't know whether the Iranians had planned this, but the black hole was beginning to break out of whatever technology they were using to contain it. In a few minutes, it would either evaporate, or would start to feed on the matter around it and continue to grow until the planet ceased to exist.

Zach knew he couldn't take down the massive Urakher at the console; besides, it may be too late to halt the black hole now. He could see it beginning to consume the laboratory behind the glass. He was scared and racked with indecision.

He shivered and felt light-headed—he thought he might be going into shock. His mouth was so dry. He wanted to get out, to run through the open door, and keep running until he was back home with Aunt Dodah. He was a little boy again, standing in a Tel Aviv street that swirled with heat and dust and shouting and madness. The charred smell of burnt flesh filled the air, and where his father had been just seconds before was now a blackened crater with red staining its edges. His mother was lying across him and she wouldn't wake up; the back of her head and shoulders smoked as if on fire.

He closed his eyes for a second, and when he opened them he no longer saw his parents, but the shattered body of Rocky Lagudi, a moaning Sam Reid and then Adira's blood-covered face. So much pain, so much sacrifice.

*When the time comes, what will you do, Zach?* Adira's words came into his head and he touched his chest. There was warmth there. More words came: *Without sacrifice, there is no freedom. Without freedom, there is no life.*

Zachariah Shomron got to his feet, whispering to himself as he steeled his nerves.

# Forty-eight

Sam lay crumpled on the floor. His arm was bent at an impossible angle, his eyes were swollen almost shut, and a vicious knife wound had parted the synthetic fibres of his combat suit to slice open his torso from collarbone to navel. It looked as if the Urakher had been indulging himself by killing the HAWC slowly. He was obviously an expert with a knife and Alex guessed he had been looking forward to inflicting all manner of torture on the fallen man before the final killing blow.

Now his blade weaved back and forth as if slowly slicing the air in front of him—perhaps he was deciding where to cut his foe next. Alex knew the blade—a Karud dagger, as old as Persia itself: fire-forged steel, thin and slightly curved. Its ancient design was intended to penetrate chainmail armour—and it had performed its job well against the HAWC suit's toughened fibres.

Alex knew Sam needed his help or he'd be dead soon. But he also felt the distortion from within the sphere room and judged that the large bodyguard at the console was initiating the black hole event. The scenarios that Adira and Zachariah had outlined in their initial briefing would be realised unless he stopped the man immediately.

The Urakher that had been torturing Sam now had his eyes fixed on Alex and started to move in his direction. He held the curved dagger out in front of him and wore a ghastly smile as he closed the distance. Alex noticed the blade was still wet with Sam's blood, and his own teeth ground together in anger.

He looked to Adira and saw that she was trying to force herself into a sitting position, still half-unconscious and very weak. Like Sam, she needed medical attention fast; but she was alive and, at least for now, not in any immediate danger. Alex was preparing to engage the large Urakher approaching him when he saw Zachariah rise to his feet from under a table; he was talking softly to himself and nodding as though receiving instructions. Alex couldn't risk the young Israeli scientist being hurt or killed just when he needed his expertise to disable the black hole generator. The urgency was increasing—Alex had to take down both of the giant guards quickly.

The Urakher at the console was fully occupied, but the one that had tortured Sam was moving in to attack—Alex's choice was made for him.

Alex still held O'Riordan's broken Ka-Bar knife in his hand. He stared hard at the approaching man and gritted his teeth as he thought of Sam's battered form and the look of enjoyment on the giant's face. Alex smiled without a trace of humour.

The Urakher slowed and his own smile dropped. Perhaps there was something in Alex's burning gaze that urged caution. He was nearly a head taller than Alex, but from his careful movements Alex could tell he was now wary. Perhaps it was the total lack of fear in Alex's eyes, or the sense of danger that he carried with him. Then Alex saw the man's eyes travel down to his wounds again and the smile returned. *That's right, I'm hurt, I'll be an easy kill. Now hurry up.* Time was running out, and Alex felt another distortion wave pass over the complex. This one didn't dissipate; it remained to create a constant sense of illness and total physical . . . wrongness.

The Urakher weaved the curved blade slowly before him, feinted to the left and then swung back like a striking snake to the right—a manoeuvre that would have caught a normal

man off guard and impaled him through the neck. Alex
ducked under the blade and gripped his own tighter. He
didn't have a lot of time left. He knew he could simply disarm
or incapacitate the large man. But he had seen the twisted
wrecks that remained of some of his comrades and the pleasure that these giant beasts had drawn from their torture. For
Alex, they had forfeited any right to mercy—there would be
no prisoners taken today.

The Urakher struck out again. This time Alex blocked
the blade and moved in close, bringing the broken Ka-Bar
up with his full force under the man's chin, up through the
oral cavity, through the palate and into the frontal lobe of
the brain. The Urakher's arms dropped to his sides and his
own curved blade fell from his fingers. He wasn't dead yet,
but soon would be.

Alex held him upright with one hand. He lifted the blade
slightly and the big man's feet left the floor. Alex looked up
into his eyes. "This is HAWC steel—you can keep it." He let
the man fall with the knife still in place.

Another wave of nausea and dizziness passed through his
body, making him grunt and stagger. The room was starting
to blur—the black hole was beginning to flex its muscles and
test its bounds. He only had a few more minutes. He turned
his attention to the giant at the console.

The last Urakher had locked the plasma beam feed rate on
maximum and then used the dead scientist's password to sign
out of the system. He looked up, as though seeing through
the ceiling and into the heavens, and yelled a final prayer
before wrenching the keyboard from the console and smashing it over his knee.

He sucked in a deep victorious breath. The air around him
felt thick and congealed; the mercury fillings in his teeth
started to tingle and his vision began to distort. He turned and
saw two men approaching—one a skinny youth, who he ignored; the other, much more formidable. It was this one he
faced with a broad smile. He opened his arms wide as to embrace the man before him. In the palm of each hand he held a

small metal box. Wires ran from the boxes down his sleeves and the outlines of large packets were visible circling his waist.

This was his final duty—his final gift to the Mahdi. There would be no interference to the Day of Judgment.

Alex took in the large man, the wires trailing down his sleeves and the explosives around his waist. He gambled on the design being a standard detonation vest. Usually that meant an immediate initiation switch in one hand and a failsafe button in the other. He should have about ten seconds on the delayed failsafe button. If he was right, he'd get one chance. And a few more seconds was all he would need.

Zachariah was walking towards the large man, his gun up and ready to fire. Alex called to the young Israeli.

"Dr. Shomron—no! Go for the glass. Zach—shoot the glass!"

Alex wasn't sure Zach had heard until the young man moved his gun a few inches to the left and fired the rest of his clip. Seven bullets hit the lead-plated glass and left snowy circles in its four-inch-thick surface. Alex would have liked a closer spread, but at least Zach had hit the window with all of his shots—it would have to do.

The Urakher laughed and said something in Farsi— probably to do with Zach's perceived bad aim.

Alex moved past the large table in the centre of the room; its surface was covered with papers, pens and overflowing ashtrays, and Mostafa Hossein's blood. Both Alex and the Urakher were playing for time. Alex guessed that his opponent wanted to wait till the last moment to detonate his explosives. Though he probably believed that the Judgment Event was irreversible, he wouldn't want to take the chance that his bomb would somehow disable it.

Alex took another step—he just needed to be a little closer. He bunched up his muscles and prepared to act. As he went past the table he opened his arms wide as if showing he had no weapons in his hands. The Urakher broadened his smile and shrugged.

Alex moved faster than the Urakher's eyes could follow—he swept up one of the glass ashtrays from the table and launched it like a spinning disc at the brutal giant's outstretched right hand. It was a calculated gamble—the fingers of the right hand were flat on the detonation trigger, whereas the left hand hovered just over the trigger.

The ashtray struck the man's wrist with a crack that could be heard across the room and the fingers of his right hand went limp. Surprise rather than pain registered on the giant's face, and his fingers immediately depressed the left-hand switch—but by then Alex had closed the distance.

The Urakher weighed around 250 pounds, but Alex easily lifted him above his head. He threw the struggling body at the glass window with every ounce of strength he could muster. As he'd hoped, the bullet strikes had weakened the glass just enough to compromise its structural integrity—the Urakher burst through just as the explosives detonated.

Alex held his arm up over his face, but there was no heat. The blast plume was a magnificent orange and red, but was soundless. No debris flew towards Zach or Alex; instead, the Urakher, the thermals from the explosion and all its lethal debris streaked into the black hole to become more energy for it to digest.

The black curtain advanced another inch towards the containment walls.

Klaxon horns screamed all over the facility and above the ground. The electronic wail bounced off mountain sides and rolled down the cliffs to the city of Arak. Hundreds of heads turned in confusion and fear.

Regular troops standing idle and squads of Takavaran stationed on the perimeter of the laboratory froze and looked at each other for mere seconds before acting. They all knew what the alarms heralded: the installation was compromised—nuclear breakout.

Some men threw meals aside, some dropped guns, others didn't even bother dressing. All headed for the trucks. They all knew the safest place was a long way away.

# Forty-nine

The Southern Israeli Desert

Thirty miles south of Dimona, the dry surface of the Negev Desert broke open. Coolant seeped into the air as a thirty-foot disc slid back to reveal a six-storey-deep silo. The rounded lump of a nose-cone could just be made out by anyone peering down into the dark hole, its top decorated with Hebrew script—a final prayer for those it was about to annihilate.

The Jericho-III missile was equipped with 100-kiloton, 1000-pound thermonuclear payload. Its arrowhead technology could penetrate up to fifty feet into the ground before nuclear fission took place. The sleek, lethal spear was designed to seek out and melt deep-ground facilities. It was a man-made earthquake.

Lights flicked on and, deep under the earth, a wailing horn sounded as the countdown began.

Zach rushed to the bank of computer terminals, grabbed a keyboard and plugged it into the command console. The screen showed the hundreds of batteries at eighty per cent full and the remaining thermal power cubes filling rapidly. Soon the capacity to absorb the black-hole energy would be surpassed, and then it would break its bounds and be free to consume Earth. Zach began to type furiously. Nothing happened.

"*Achhh!* Password protection." He pressed a combination

of keys and brought up a command line. He immediately dived into the operating-system code.

"Can you hack in?" Alex asked.

"With enough time, anything is hackable. But I guess time's something we don't have a lot of now." He lifted his arm to wipe his face with his sleeve. "Ah, I don't feel well."

Zach continued to type, but Alex saw that he was sweating and becoming pale.

In the sphere room, the power cubes were being pulled from the walls and into the centre of the black hole; they looked like a flock of tiny birds rushing back to their nests. Zach turned his head away from the keyboard and threw up. The distortion was starting to drag hard at his atomic structure. He wiped his mouth and turned to Alex, having to shout over the unearthly screaming from the sphere room.

"The black hole is growing too fast and getting too strong. It will soon exceed its boundaries, and once the plasma is gone, its magnetic chains will be thrown off and it will be free to start swallowing everything around it—the entire planet.

Zach shook his head as if to clear it. Alex knew what he was experiencing; the air seemed thicker and denser as the molecular structure of the atmosphere began to stretch, and it was getting hard to move.

Zach looked around at Alex for encouragement, or advice, anything. Alex nodded and tried to look confident, but all he could manage was a rueful half-smile. The fact was, he felt powerless. The mission wouldn't complete and his team would be totally wiped out. They would be the first and last people on Earth to witness the genesis of a true apocalyptic event, but that wasn't much consolation. He put a hand on Zach's shoulder, hoping at least to give the young scientist some kind of support.

Zach wiped his eyes and turned back to the screen. He keyed different code strings into the computer—and this time was rewarded by a long string of binary code filling the screen. He yelled to Alex, "I've found a back door, but I need more time. Even if I begin to shut it down now, the radiation levels will still build to a point that will literally melt our flesh."

Alex flinched as he felt a hand on his arm and he turned quickly. Adira stood beside him; she managed a weak smile through heavily bruised lips. One of her eyes was blackened and closing fast, and there was a trickle of blood from her ear. Alex knew she was seriously hurt.

She must have seen him examining her injuries because she straightened slightly and let go of his arm. "Sure, I'm not so pretty today, but so what? How much time have we got?"

Zach looked around and smiled at her, then whipped his head back to the console. "Next to none. All I can do is slow it and buy you some time. But you all need to get out of here—now!" He glanced at Alex, "Please." He went back to his typing, his fingers flying across the keys.

"Not without you, little brother," Adira said. She staggered towards him but Alex stopped her. She looked at him sharply and tried to pull out of his grip. He held on and shook his head.

"He's right, Addy. He stays or we all die. Zach is giving us—giving the entire planet—a chance. We mustn't waste it."

*"Achhh!"* She pulled her arm free and looked about to strike him. Alex dropped his arms, prepared to take the blow if she delivered it. Instead, she turned her back on them. Alex could tell she was struggling to discipline her emotions.

*"Yasher koach aschoti,"* Zach told her. "Have great strength, my sister." Adira didn't turn or respond. The only sign that she heard him was a slight hunching of her shoulders, as if she were preparing herself for a blow.

Alex wanted to tell Zach he was brave, valorous . . . to thank him. But he guessed the young Israeli wasn't looking for that, or about the sacrifice he was making. There were no other words, and no more time. He squeezed Zach's shoulder once and turned to Adira. She had her fists up to her temples and staggered slightly, her body leaning in towards the shattered glass of the observation window. Alex could feel it too; the gravitational drag was pulling hard at the very organic fibre of their bodies. He had to use all of his great strength just to walk over to Adira. It felt as if everything around them was tilting towards the sphere room. He grabbed her around the waist and she slumped against him, unconscious now.

Alex hoisted her over his shoulder and pushed his way to the exit. He felt like a deep-sea diver, a mile down under water pressure that could crush steel. He stepped over the body of the little scientist whose neck had been broken only minutes before. The man's face still registered the pain and anguish he had experienced in his last brutal seconds of life. Alex saw the small object clasped in his fist and recognised it as a storage device. He hesitated . . . *this is not good technology for any country to possess*—his own words rushed through his mind. He adjusted Adira on his shoulder and reached down for the device. It was small in his hand . . . he should crush it to powder . . . But he couldn't. He had his orders.

He placed it in his pocket and pushed on to where Sam Reid was sprawled on the floor, coughing blood. He lifted Sam over his other shoulder and then focused on the door— one foot after the other, like moving through viscous oil.

As he reached the exit, Alex looked back across the room. The remaining scientists and technicians were clutching onto the legs of chairs and tables as they felt the drag of the gravitational tide drawing them into the black hole. The equipment closest to the sphere room was starting to streak and stretch, and he knew it wouldn't be long before the outer gravitational corona reached them and they too would begin their voyage to somewhere . . . else. Alex tried not to think about the deformed creature he had seen in the containment room one level up.

Once the outer door was closed, the solid steel shielding gave him some insulation and he was able to speed up. Down the stairs he raced, along the tunnel and through the caverns. He planted Sam's last spider against the rockfall, and covered him and Adira with his body as the explosion opened a way back to the cave mouth through which they'd entered.

With Sam and Adira over his shoulders again, he ran. He ran at a speed faster than any living creature on Earth. He ran until he couldn't feel the gravitational pull anymore; until he couldn't feel his own legs. He ran for hours until his body simply switched off from fatigue.

A mighty horn sounded far behind him. He fell forward as the world spun and then went black.

Zach managed to keep the remaining power cubes working as he reduced the feed to the dark monster in the other room. He knew the typed codes by memory now and so was able to shut his eyes. He didn't want to look at his hands anymore; his fingers scared him—they looked longer and thinner than he remembered, the legs of some spindly deep-sea creature crawling over the keyboard.

Something wet ran down his face and he knew it was blood. Blistering sores opened on his forehead and cheeks as the severe radiation peeled back his outer layer of skin.

*"Baruch Shem Kivod Malchito LeOlam Va'ed!"* he whispered, a last prayer to God, and the words gave him strength. *Just a few seconds more*, he thought, *so they can get far away.* He tried to pray again, but this time his mouth wouldn't work. His tongue was too large and refused to bend around the shape of the words.

He felt a tingling warmth on his face and opened his eyes. The black hole was fraying around the edges. It was so large and close now that the dark curtain had reached the edge of the window. *Am I winning? Am I sending it back?*

He looked into the entity's very core—and saw something in there that no human being should have to bear. He screamed a single word as he felt himself pulled from his chair: *Gehinnom!* The ancient Hebrew word for hell.

# Fifty

The black hole had ceased to exist. It had evaporated, taking with it the entire Jamshid II facility and a large chunk of the mountain. Dr. Zach Shomron had done his job.

Hammerson was screaming at someone in Israel to be put through to General Shavit. The Hammer and most of the US military leaders had been summoned to the Mole Hole, and the president was on his way. Strategic Air Command had picked up the heat signature of the Israeli missile as it was warming to countdown. If the missile was fired, there would be retaliation. There would be war.

Hammerson tilted his coffee cup to his lips and realised he had finished it ages ago. He looked at his screen again. From space, the crater was a perfect circle—three miles wide and one and a half miles deep. He reread the underlying data: in summary, a furious vertical burst of radiation, and then nothing. The hidden laboratory had ceased to exist; it had disintegrated, been digested, or, as the young Israeli scientist had theorised, perhaps been transported elsewhere.

Another screen on Hammerson's desk showed a white bloom spewing from the hidden missile silo. A white nose-cone slowly lifted free from the billowing smoke. The Jericho was on its way.

"Shit!" Hammerson threw his cup across the room.

He was about to scream again at the calm young man on the phone when he was finally put through.

"I'm sorry, my friend. Israel has decided that we must

risk war today to avoid total destruction tomorrow," General Meir Shavit said.

The general sounded miserable. Hammerson knew that Shavit, like himself, hated war—but if he thought his country was being threatened, he would fight to the death, no quarter given.

Hammerson wasn't authorised to send secret data, even to allies, but he encrypted the Arak images and sent them high priority to the general. "Arak is already gone," he said. "Look at the images being sent, I repeat, look at the images. There is no need for a strike." He was pacing as he watched the glowing white spear catch the sunlight and pick up speed on its deadly mission. It was almost beautiful.

"I think it is too late, my friend."

"You can abort, you kno—" But the phone had gone dead.

Hammerson sat down and rubbed his face for a few minutes before typing a brief message to Alex's SFPDA. Once the failure message came up. He took the headset off and gathered some folders from his desk. Before he left, he looked one last time at the red circle on his screen. "I hope you're well away from there, son—it's about to get real hot."

Then he headed for the secure bunker, where the president and his top-level military would observe the expected blowback from the Israeli first strike.

In Tel Aviv, General Meir Shavit looked at the images Major Hammerson had sent through. He compared them to his own satellite data and field reports from the Markazi desert, then reached for his phone.

Thirty-three seconds later, a fireball erupted in the sky over western Iraq. There would be no need for a retrieval mission as nothing larger than a baseball would fall to the ground.

Instantly, the Israeli Minister for Foreign Affairs made contact with her counterpart in Iraq. It seemed there had been a misfire of an obsolete armament. Compensation for any clean-up was available on request.

# Fifty-one

Warmth, strange scents, the hum of life.

Alex opened his eyes and had to blink as brilliant sunshine flooded his senses. He was lying on soft, sandy soil, partially shaded by the branches of a large tree. Small yellow bees buzzed around sticky-looking fruit nestled in amongst the leaves. He quickly looked at his hands and feet and felt his face. No elongation; and other than some tightness across his chest where the lacerations were healing, he felt fine.

Beside him lay Adira, her chest rising and falling as if she were deep in sleep. Except for a black eye and bruising on her top lip, she was perfect. Sam, too, was laid out on the sand, groaning now as he came around.

Alex moved across and helped Sam sit up. He pulled his drink flask from his waist and lifted it to Sam's lips. The HAWC coughed, opened one eye and drank. He looked like he'd fallen in front of a cattle stampede and managed to get caught by every horn and hoof. He had open gashes on his cheeks and chin, and both of his eye sockets were purple. A huge knife wound ran from his collarbone to navel. Alex could see it had separated the skin and some of the deeper fatty tissue—horribly painful, but his innards wouldn't come tumbling out.

Sam raised a blood-crusted eyebrow at Alex and smiled. One of his front teeth was missing. "You should see the other guy," he said, and coughed some more.

Alex laughed, and quickly checked the HAWC's shoulders, arms and ribcage for breaks. Sam groaned as Alex extended one of his arms and then pressed his side.

"Broken ribs as well, big guy," Alex said.

Sam coughed again, spat red onto the sand, and winced. He noticed the damage to Alex and got serious. "Sorry, boss, I tried to hold them. I saw Rocky go down, then that big bastard caught me a good one and everything went black."

"Take it easy, Uncle. I think he caught you with about fifty good ones. We're all lucky to be alive. Those guys were bloody tough, like no one I've ever encountered."

He paused for a second and sat back on his haunches. "Sam, Rocky didn't make it. Irish neither." He pushed one hand up through his sweat-soaked hair and looked down into the sand.

Sam's brow creased. "Rocky and Irish? I never even saw Irish come back."

"No, he didn't. He took on that thing from hell. Stopped it from ambushing us outside the laboratory and gave us the time we needed to engage. I couldn't get to him in time." An image of Hex Winter burning in a chair pushed into his mind. "I never get to them in time, Sam."

Sam groaned again as he sat forward. He saw Adira lying on the sand, then quickly looked left and right. "Where's the kid?"

Alex just shook his head.

"Ah, shit. They killed him too?"

"No. No, he stayed. Look around—nothing eating the planet, no incinerated landscape. He shut it down. He knew it would kill him, but he did it anyway. We're alive because of him. He saved us all."

Alex got to his feet and brushed the sand from his hands. "Anyway, soldier, patch those wounds. We're not home yet."

"You got it, boss. Hey, by the way, where are we?"

"I've no idea. Can you take some scans? I seem to have lost some of my kit."

Sam laughed. Alex looked as though he had been shot out of a cannon and landed in some thorn bushes. His super-toughened suit with the ceramic armour plating was just a tattered rag circling his waist, and the pants were punctured and red with blood.

Adira groaned, and Alex went over to her and lifted her head. "Slowly, slowly, we're safe now. I think it's all over."

Adira sat forward and put her elbows on her knees and drew in some deep breaths. "It's over? Where's Zach?"

Alex exhaled slowly through his nose and wiped sand from her cheek before responding. "I'm sorry. He didn't make it."

Adira's eyes went a little dead for a moment, then she looked up at the sky. "No one weeps for heroes in Israel anymore, Alex. The tears would drown us all."

Alex allowed the silence to stretch, giving her time to recover. He looked around at the horizon and then back down to her. "I think we're lost." He raised his brows at Sam.

Sam shook his head. "It's all fused, nothing works." He dropped the useless scanners and communication devices to the sand. "But it still looks like Iran to me."

Adira looked up at the branches above them. "That's a wild desert fig tree—they only grow to this size near Kashan. I have people there—we'll be safe."

"Safe." Alex tested the word in his mouth. It felt strange, unnatural, and no longer relevant. He now knew there was another world hidden behind the one most people knew. A world where monsters existed, where horrific things crept in the dark, dropped from the sky or slithered up from the depths.

He lay back and closed his eyes against the sun and thought about a beach somewhere on the east coast of Australia. He inhaled salt and heard waves crashing on a breach. "Yes, safe now." *Soon*, he thought, *very soon*.

# Fifty-two

General Meir Shavit sat at his desk, the transcript of Captain Adira Senesh's debrief in his hands. After his niece's retrieval from the Iranian desert, she had spent just one hour in hospital having her wounds tended to. While there, she had agreed to a short military interview. The general gave a half-smile; he knew his niece well—there was no way anyone could make her do anything she didn't want to do.

The black hole technology she detailed in her report was astounding, and he prayed its genesis was an aberration—an invention by accident rather than by design. He also hoped that with the destruction of the laboratory, all knowledge of the technology's capability and creation had ceased to exist. *Such power is the rightful property of no country*, he thought.

The old man sat back and looked at the ceiling for a moment, his eyes tracing the plaster flowers in the ornate moulding. Humans were creative and self-destructive in equal measures, and once they had managed to imagine something, it was only a matter of time until they brought it into existence. *We have merely bought ourselves some time*, he thought.

He drew a deep breath, poured himself some more thick, dark coffee, and turned to the last page of Adira's report, headed "EWP—Enhanced Warrior Project," with a subheading: "The Arcadian Subject." His eyebrows rose slightly as he read her account of the subject's capabilities. As he had expected, the Americans had sent their secret weapon on the mission and Adira had witnessed it in action. But although she had been close enough to record its features in detail, she hadn't managed to get any new data, not even a tissue sample. He looked at the grainy photograph she had supplied of the HAWC: Francis "Irish" O'Riordan, a red-haired warrior, according to the report; an awesome soldier in combat. It was a shame he had been vaporised in the explosion.

The general blew air through his closed lips and shook his head. Without any body for the Israelis to retrieve, any samples or concrete evidence, the Americans still held all the cards—while Israel had nothing. He narrowed his eyes. Just because the primary subject was gone, the Arcadian project would not end, he was sure of that. But there was no reason for the Americans to share their results with Israel; they wouldn't even admit the project existed.

He picked up his cup but held it without drinking. As his mind worked, he looked across the room and caught sight of his aged visage staring back at him from within a long gilded mirror. He continued to stare trance-like at the image as his thoughts turned inwards. *Israel needs these new soldiers*, he mused. *We are the smallest army in the Middle East and surrounded by an ocean of hatred. It is only a matter of time before that ocean drowns us all.* He blinked, and looked down at Adira's report again. *If Israel cannot have more men, we must make more of the men we have. We need to get a little closer.*

He looked again at the transcribing officer's notation at the foot of the report. Unusually, Adira had requested immediate leave to escort the two Americans to their waiting transport plane. *Hmm, what are you up to, Addy?* Shavit thought. Perhaps there was a bond there, something he could use. He rubbed his chin with the back of his hand; they needed someone inside the Americans' tent, someone who had already been exposed to the Arcadian's capabilities . . . Someone Israel could rely on, and someone the Americans trusted.

Yes, she would be perfect. Jack Hammerson owed him, and he wouldn't be able to refuse a soldier of Captain Senesh's capabilities.

The general made a small notation in the file and closed it. "Your job isn't quite finished yet, Addy."

Parvid Davoodi, the newly elected leader of Iran, cleared away the possessions of the former president, preparing the office for his own inhabitation. He picked up a framed picture of a smiling Mahmoud Moshaddam and shook his head. "How could you not know that all false prophets go to hell? Though perhaps now you do." He dropped the picture into the waste bin beside the desk.

One of Davoodi's first acts in office had been to call the American president to assure him that the secret facilities at Natanz, Persepolis and Arak would be closed forever. During that conversation he had accepted an invitation to visit the United States—the first time in a generation that an Iranian leader had been invited by an American president onto their soil. *Perhaps this is a new beginning for Iran*, he thought.

He picked up his Qur'an, already open at his favourite page. From an open window, a warm square of sunlight lit the beautiful writing as he began to read.

At USSTRATCOM in Nebraska it was night and the weather was not so benign. Rain smashed against the dark window of Hammerson's office. He was working late, and had turned off the lights so he could enjoy the storm passing over the base. He liked just sitting and watching nature's power and raw aggression.

The secure phone beeped and he contemplated ignoring it. The mission was a success, but, he guessed, not quite over yet. *Fuck it.* He picked up the call. He squeezed the phone tight when he heard the deep voice on the other end.

"Arcadian has secured the information as instructed, sir," he said. "It's on its way to us now—potential unlimited energy for . . . Yes, sir, we believe weaponisation is possible."

He listened some more and his eyes narrowed. "I'm not sure I agree with that assessment, sir. His value in the field is undeniable. Yes, sir, I understand that, so far, we can't reproduce his result without a more invasive study, but his capabilities develop every day—there is so much more to learn while he's active. Once we retire him, that line of research will be lost forever. It is my recommendation that he stay on active duty, sir. His new capability development and this success compels it. Give me another year, sir. Science can wait at least that long."

Hammerson inhaled and held the breath for a few seconds as he waited and listened. He exhaled when he heard the response.

"Very good, sir."

He hung up the phone just as the sky outside flashed, then boomed with rolling thunder. He had managed to extend Alex Hunter's lifeline for just one more year. For the first time in his life, the Hammer felt old.

# Epilogue

Warmth, strange scents, the hum of life.

Mahmoud Moshaddam opened the capsule door a little farther and more of the thick, humid air rushed in.

He stepped out into a mist-shrouded, boggy landscape lush with ropey vines and twisted vegetation. Bulbous hair-covered leaves and plump fruit-like protuberances hung low from rampant foliage in an impenetrable tangle. He stepped forward and sank to his calves in brackish water. Already his ankles itched as if something were crawling over them.

He reached back into the capsule to open the box that held the small piece of sacred Black Stone. If he was to be judged, he wanted the sacred relic with him to show his worthiness.

He inhaled the earthy odour of rotting vegetation and caught a slight whiff of sharp vinegar and almond. He racked his brain for any references to such a place as this in the Qur'an or the Hadith—could it be Jannah and he just needed to find the bridge to paradise?

Someone was coming; he could hear footfalls in the mud—lots of them, stealthy. The smell of vinegar grew stronger, and the short hairs on the back of his neck rose as his primal instincts went into overdrive. Now he could make out giant shapes in the mist—the Almighty was coming and bringing all the prophets with him.

The president fell to his knees in the mud and started to sing loudly and strongly to show his faith. The shapes stopped just out of sight in the mist, as if waiting for something. The president's singing slowly tapered off and he held out his hand to show the Black Stone. His knees began to shake in the crawling mud. Something was wrong; this couldn't be heaven.

When the attack came, it was swift. The mist swirled violently and the creatures came through it from all sides. The largest shot out its raptorial claws and pinned the man face down on the boggy ground. The others darted forward to claim a piece of the body and insert their sharp proboscises. The largest bent its eyestalks towards the man's face, as if searching for some sign of intelligence. Then its gristly mandibles opened.

The creatures began to feed.